An Angry God

Paul D. Snyder

Published by

Wicklow Media
Weymouth, MA

This book is a publication of Wicklow Media, 67 Spring Street, Weymouth, MA 02188.

Library of Congress information:
ISBN: 978-0-9965759-0-4

First printing February 2016 ;
Cover design by:
Sean Snyder
www.seansnyderink.com
Cover photo from www.istockphoto.com, Printed in the United States of America

DEDICATION

As authors, we're supported by a number of people. I'm particularly indebted to my wife, Sheila, my children, and many friends for putting up with me and reading innumerable drafts of this novel. Kevin Walsh, my publisher, has put his heart and soul into the book, and has encouraged me in the course of reviewing and editing it. I'm indeed fortunate to collaborate with such wonderful people.

PREFACE

Combat - The Curse of An Angry God?

History is written about wars, cataclysmic events, epic social movements, and great men and women. But really, history is about the millions of daily interactions between people over the course of our lifetimes. These become stories that we pass on to our children and grandchildren. These stories focus on people like Dan Fleming, a recent high school graduate working in a local hardware store during the day, and playing basketball with his buddies at night. Dan is a young man who, after Pearl Harbor, is wondering what his life is all about and where fate will take him as the country mobilizes for war. He knows that the reality of his current life will soon be changing, that the world he knows will be ending, and that a new world will be thrust upon him.

This story is a fictional account of the history of Dan Fleming and his interactions during and after World War II. This war could be any war, though, and the Dan Fleming character could be any of the millions of men and women who have experienced the horrors of combat, and who have to deal with those horrors when the war is done and over...over for everyone but for them.

CHAPTER ONE

It All Begins Somewhere

The July temperature had been in the eighties during the day, and the evening didn't bring much relief.

"What's this all about anyway?" said the young man sitting in the dark under the far basket on the hot asphalt basketball court while sipping a bottle of warm beer.

"What are you talking about? What's 'what' all about?"

The six sweaty young men hanging around on the basketball court in the far corner of the St. Columbkille Church parking lot were talking, the chain link "netting" above them barely visible in the dark, and the bare rim at the other end of the court not visible at all. They'd played three-on-three until the encroaching darkness made it dangerous to continue, leaving them to sit around, some guzzling warm beer, and others bottles of water that they'd brought from home.

"What I mean," said the muscled young man with the blond hair, "is that beyond playing basketball every night, life's different for each of us; the way we look at life; what we each do every day - other than playing basketball together - and where we're each going with our lives. Our worlds, I think, are different. Maybe we each have a different view about life; maybe there's a different reality for each of us...maybe we each create our own reality. I don't know...I'm starting to find all this stuff confusing when it used to be so simple.

"Sully, you worry about going to Hell if you don't make it to confession at least every two weeks. O'Brien, you never go to church, and all you talk about is picking up girls. The way you each look at life and reality is totally different."

"Yeah, thanks, Fleming. So, what's your reality? How do you look at life?"

"Well...I'm not sure. Other than about a minute ago, I'd never really thought much about it. I guess right now though, my take on life is that I'd better go home, jump in the shower, and get to bed. If I'm not at work by 7:00 tomorrow morning, Johnson will dock me an hour's pay. He does that if I'm more than five minutes late."

As he was saying this, Dan Fleming pulled himself upright, chugged the remaining beer, and walked over to the pile of clothing behind the basket. He sorted through it till he found the blue work shirt with "Johnson's Hardware and Home Goods" printed on the back.

"Oh, so you don't worry about meeting girls or going to Hell, but just about keeping Johnson satisfied? Your reality stuff is all bullshit, Fleming."

"Yeah, maybe. I've got to think about it some more, O'Brien, but you and I do live different lives right now."

"Yeah...how so?"

"Well, you're a senior in high school...you're hanging around after school...you don't have to go to work every day. I've been out for a year now and have responsibilities. You'll get it at some point when you've gotta get a job and your old man tells you he wants you to pay rent. That's when you'll understand what I'm talking about."

"Pay rent in my own house...no way!"

"You'll grow up some time and find that the free ride's over...that's when your world will really start to change and you'll start thinking about some of this shit.

"But, I've gotta get outta here guys. Same time, same place tomorrow?"

"Yeah...I'm in."

"Me, too."

Five voices responded in the affirmative.

"Obie, see if you can get some air in the ball; it started to feel a little soft toward the end, like it has a slow leak or something."

"Yeah, OK. See you guys tomorrow."

As they all drifted away into the darkness, Dan Fleming threw the work shirt over his shoulder, the shirt that had lain in the pile during the games as they played "skins and shirts."

"God, do we stink," said Michael Adenezio, as he and Dan walked down Market Street towards the neighborhood where they both lived, the streetlights outlining their moving shadows with each step they took. Some of the other players headed toward the housing projects, and a couple more lived up towards

Brighton Center, the high rent district, a relative term in their working class community.

"If we were heading the other way...up Market Street to St. Col's on a Monday morning...looking like this, things would be totally different. Is that what you mean by reality?"

"Yeah, I think so...sort of. Look...this thing just struck me after sweating like a pig and throwing down a couple of beers. But, if we're heading to St. Col's on a Monday morning, we'd have jackets and ties on, and if we ever walked in looking like this, one of the nuns would have sent us over to the rectory to see the Monsignor.

"When you think about it, it seems that reality changes for each of us depending on how much power we have over our own lives. Sometimes we can create our own reality, and sometimes other people or other circumstances do that for us, and we've got no choice but to accept it.

"Imagine if we were living in France right now. We'd probably each have a rifle and be crawling around looking for some Germans to kill and worrying about one of them killing us...totally different, and the only thing separating them from us is distance. Maybe it's only a little shit-luck that we were born American and not French."

"This stuff's too heavy for me, Dan. I'm so tired, I might even skip a shower and just sleep on the porch, it's so hot. I'll see you tomorrow night."

"Yeah, good night, Mike."

Walking the remaining two blocks alone, Dan wondered how his life would be changing over the next few months. When Pearl Harbor was bombed the previous December, the country went to war and the draft started working furiously to take men into the armed services.

They were hiring at the Watertown Arsenal, and he'd like to leave his job at Johnson's Hardware and Homegoods. Mr. Johnson wasn't too bad, but from time to time he could be a bastard to work for, especially after he'd thrown down a few beers at lunch. The money wasn't great, but it had been a steady job last year after he'd graduated from St. Col's. That was a time when jobs were hard to find. Things were different now.

He was concerned about leaving Johnson's, though, because his life had settled into a routine. He could plan his days – at least after work and on weekends. He had a couple of bucks in his pocket and was living at home. His one passion was playing basketball, and he did that every chance he got. Most of his former high school teammates were still in school and felt the same way. They'd be out there every day they could, sometimes even shoveling snow off the court in the winter if there was a sunny Saturday afternoon when they could get together.

Dan Fleming didn't particularly like change, didn't go looking for it, but he seemed to be able to adapt when change was thrust upon him. He'd been out of school for a little more than a month when Johnson had hired him, and he had no trouble fitting into the routine of the store.

"Life is good," he thought, but he had a feeling that his life was on the verge of changing. The Selective Service System was in full swing and was registering all men in the country as soon as they turned eighteen. He'd just registered and was supposed to go for his physical that Wednesday at the Boston Army Base. Mr. Johnson hadn't been happy about giving him the time off, but did so reluctantly, telling Dan that he wouldn't be able to pay him for the time he was away from work. He knew he had no choice but to let Dan go, but he'd be damned if he'd pay him for his junket to downtown Boston and the waterfront.

Dan knew that if he passed his physical and was classified 1-A, he'd likely be drafted into the service. He wasn't particularly excited by that prospect, but it didn't bother him either. His philosophy was that whatever was meant to happen would happen, but it did make him wonder about how his life would be changing in the near future.

Dan had taken the MTA to South Boston many times in the past, but those trips were to go swimming at Carson Beach. The Boston Army Base, a little bit up the coast from the beach, had always seemed to be an intimidating place, perhaps because of the armed soldiers patrolling the perimeter and standing in the guard post at the entrance.

He felt a little nervous today as he approached that same guard post, expecting to be challenged. Dan was somewhat surprised when the guard waved him though after he had flashed the letter from his draft board.

Finding the correct building for his physical exam was easy because there were signs all over the place. As he entered the warehouse building, Dan saw cubicles set up all over. He noticed a series of olive drab metal desks greeting him with a bunch of soldiers in tan uniforms sitting behind them. Dan approached one of the desks that had only a couple of recruits standing in front of it.

"OK, Mac, let me see your papers. I don't have all day, ya' know."

There was nowhere to go because the line in front of him wasn't moving, but Dan kept his mouth shut and handed the clerk behind the desk the papers his draft board had given him to take to the physical exam.

"Brighton, huh?" the black-haired clerk in the tan army uniform said. "'La Campagna', that's what my uncle used to call it. I grew up in the North End, but he got a job in Brighton and was able to buy a small brick house with a small garden on Union Street.

"No matter." Now his tone changed. "All right, everyone in front of my desk, listen up. I want you to strip down to your shorts. Carry your clothes and your shoes in your arms in front of you with your papers on top. You'll move as a group from station to station. Wait until everyone in your group finishes before the corpsman at that station tells you to move to the next one. If you have any medical records with you, keep them under the papers.

"Corporal, they're all yours."

"OK, let's move it up. Stay in line and give me your papers when your turn comes. We're doing heights and weights at this station before we move you on to have your eyes and ears checked. If you have any problem, we don't want to hear about it till you get to the doctor at the last station."

Dan noticed that the guy in front of him had one leg shriveled like he'd been in an accident or something. Pale and frail, one of his calves was about as thick as Dan's forearm. He clutched a pile of papers and a folder of X-rays on top of the clothing in his arms. The group ran through about ten stations where they were checked out to see if they were fit specimens to be inducted into the military. At the last station, they were checked by the doctor for hemorrhoids and hernias. After they were told to pull up their shorts, the doctor, an Army captain, asked if anyone had a physical reason why he couldn't go into the service. The kid with the shriveled leg raised his hand. Approaching him, the doctor remarked sarcastically, "What's the matter, kid? You trying to get out of going?" as he looked with disdain at the stack of medical records the pale recruit was holding out to him.

Dan felt more than a little disgust at the way the doctor acted. It was obvious to everyone in the group that the fellow with the shriveled leg couldn't fight in a war, and in fact would be a detriment in combat, not only to himself, but to everyone around him. With a sense of relief, Dan left the Boston Army Base carrying an envelope to take back to his draft board. As he suspected, he was in excellent physical condition and was likely to be classified 1-A, or as he and his friends jokingly referred to it, as "prime draft bait" or "prime cannon fodder."

"Nice of you to make it back, Mr. Fleming." Henry Johnson sometimes acted like he was Dan's owner rather than his employer.

"Sorry, Mr. Johnson. I took the MTA to Central Square but the 1:30 Cleveland Circle bus never came."

"Well...doesn't matter...doesn't matter. I've been here by myself and the store hasn't collapsed. I can only pay you for the time you're here, but I'll give you an extra hour if you want to work till five-thirty."

"Thanks, Mr. Johnson. That'd be fine…"

"Those bags of cement in the cellar…they need to be moved to the shed in back in case we get another one of those hurricanes in the fall. And, God knows where you'll be then, probably at some army camp somewhere in the world.

"An hour should do it…you should get them all moved out there by 5:30."

"Mr. Johnson, each of those bags weighs 60 pounds, and there are a couple of pallets of them. That's a lot of work in one hour at the end of the day."

"Now Fleming, don't be a slacker. I've tried to train you about the virtue and benefits of hard work and punctuality. Those will stand you in good stead wherever you go in life. Besides, you know you'll always have a job here waiting for you wherever your life takes you in the interim."

"Yeah, well thanks, Mr. Johnson. I'd better get busy now."

"That's it, lad…be careful that you don't break any of the bags; they're expensive, you know."

After working his overtime, Dan headed down from Brighton Center to join his buddies in their evening game of basketball. Walking out onto the court, he heard it loud and clear from his friends:

"Hey guys…look at the gray ghost.

"Fuck you, O'Brien."

"Jesus, Dan, you'd better not work up any more of a sweat or that cement will harden and there'll be a statue of you frozen on the court."

"Yeah, Dan, you can be a permanent pick cemented near the basket. What the hell did Johnson have you doing anyway…rolling in that stuff?"

"I tell you, Mike…I'm getting pretty fed up with it. He gives me a shitty job to do and then tries to sweet-talk me by telling me that he'll always have a job for me wherever my life takes me in the meantime."

"You mean if you get drafted but don't get killed, he'll give you the honor of carrying more bags of cement around in his store when you get back?"

"Yeah…something like that."

"Hey, if we're not on the same team tonight, just don't cover me too closely. I don't want to get that shit all over me."

"I don't need to cover you. You couldn't make a shot if you were all alone and on a ladder. Cover you closely? Bullshit! I don't need to cover you at all."

And so it went, one night like the last, and a harbinger of the next. Dan played ball at night and worked during the day, finding it harder and harder to put up with Henry Johnson.

He'd settled into a rhythm at home as well. His dad had been working at the Dean Rubber plant in Watertown for over twenty years and things were really picking up. Dean just got a big contract from the Navy for waterproof boots and slickers to be worn on deck in foul weather. Dan's younger brother was in junior high school and really hadn't started to grow yet. Dan, when he wasn't playing basketball with the guys, would pick up the bat and glove he had used in high school and take Tommy down to Faneuil Park to hit some flies to him. The glove and bat were otherwise enshrined in the corner of Dan's bedroom, a memento to his lost youth.

His mother, though, was worried about what was happening in Europe. It seemed to her that the whole world was on the brink of madness. She'd been a child when the First World War, the "Great War," had ended, the war to end all wars. Her uncle had been caught in a gas attack and was never right till the day he died. He always had trouble breathing, fighting and gasping to fill his damaged lungs, even when he wasn't in the hospital. It had been a blessing for all of them when he finally died, relieved at long last from his struggles. Mary Fleming looked at her older son and feared that he too would get sucked into the same sort of madness that had destroyed her uncle.

"Dan...Dan, is that you?"

"Yeah, Ma, I'm just getting in. I went up to the school yard after work and was shooting some baskets with the guys."

"What do you have all over you?"

"Cement! Johnson gave me an hour's overtime today when I got back from my draft physical...after he docked me for half a day's pay. He had me moving sixty-pound bags of cement up from the cellar to the shed in back of the store. I can't wait to get out of there, Ma."

"I know, Dan...I know. That job has been a big help to us though when the plant put everyone on reduced hours. But this new contract with the Navy is a God-send, and now your father can work as much overtime as he wants.

"How did it go today at the Army Base?"

Her tone softened and her speech slowed as she asked the last question, hoping to hear that her son had some minor ailment that wouldn't interfere with his life, but which would disqualify him from the service.

She got the response that she'd feared and anticipated, though, rather than the one that she had hoped for.

"The doctor said that I'm a prime physical specimen, Ma. I knew that already though. After hauling stuff around the store all day and playing ball all night, I'd have to work at it to flunk an Army physical. Ma, the truth is that they'll take every warm body they can get. The kid next to me in line had one leg about as thick as my arm, and a pile of medical records to boot. All you had to do was to look at him to realize that he couldn't go into the service, yet the doctor who examined us at the end of the testing accused him of trying to get out of the draft.

"What a jerk! The poor kid walked with an obvious limp and he turned white as a sheet when the doctor accused him of being a draft-dodger. I thought that he was gonna pass out he looked so weak and shocked."

"Danny – will you go if they draw your number?"

"I guess I won't have much of a choice, Ma, will I now? I'll go."

"I knew you'd say that, dear. You know that I don't want you to go, and that I'd support you if you decided not to."

"I know that, Ma, but how could I not go? I've got a duty to my country, and if they call me, I'll go. I don't want to go either, but I can't spend my life living with you, Tommy, and Dad, working at the hardware store days and playing basketball every night.

"You know...I've been wondering lately about life, how one person's reality differs from another's. We talk about the war quite a bit when we're resting between games or just hanging around. Some of the guys like Obie can't wait to get into the service and are planning to enlist as soon as they graduate from St. Col's. To them, it's a chance to see the world, to fight for our country. I don't know much about war, but I don't imagine it's like a basketball game where one side wins and the other loses. You come back to play another night in basketball; I don't imagine that the losers in battle, if they survive, look forward to doing it again."

"The way Mikey O'Brien looks at it, war's a glamorous adventure. But I can't imagine that the reality of war is anything like his imagination," said Dan's mother. "Your Uncle Jim never looked like he'd been through a glamorous adventure, although I was young when he died. All I remember of him was how he'd cough and gasp when he was trying to talk to me. The bugler and the soldiers firing their rifles at his grave were impressive, but they hadn't been gassed; they could breathe without struggling, and maybe for them their service was a glorious adventure, but I don't see Uncle Jim thinking that way.

"It's different for a woman, Danny, different for a mother who brings her sons up and then sends them off to a bugle call. I don't wish any other mother's son to go off and into battle, and I don't want either of my sons to have to do that. Your father's too old to be drafted, though not by too much. He did go into the service at the end of the last war, but it was over before he could get sent overseas. And, Tommy's too young. Whatever happens will be over by the time he gets out of high school. I'm worried about you though, Danny. You're young and healthy and the right age to get drafted."

"I'll be OK, Ma – I promise. I'll keep my mouth shut and my head down, and I won't volunteer for anything. That's what Dad told me are the secrets to surviving in the Army."

It wasn't much more than a couple of weeks after his physical that the letter from the War Department arrived in the mail. Dan knew what it was and when he opened it, and saw that it started off: "Greetings from the President of the United States...." He was to report to the Boston Army Base in two weeks for assignment to Army basic training at Fort Dix in New Jersey. His orders said that after he reported, he'd have two hours before boarding buses for South Station, where he and the other draftees who were reporting that day would board a special train that'd take them directly to their training base.

He played ball that night and told the others that soon they'd be playing one man down because he'd received his induction notice and orders to report to the Army.

"You lucky bastard, Dan. The fucking war will probably be over before I graduate from St. Col's. Some guys have all the luck. You'll show up here in uniform and all the girls'll be crazy about you."

"Don't be an asshole, Obie. Do you think of anything else besides sex and war? Oh yeah, and basketball?"

"No. Think of it, Dan. You come home from basic training with a rock hard body all tanned and muscled in a pressed and starched uniform and Linda Santucci will be all over you."

"Yeah, that'll do me a lot of good if I go and get my nuts shot off somewhere. Thanks pal; you can take my place in line anytime.

"OK, who's got the ball, skins or shirts? I didn't come down to screw around with you all night, O'Brien; I came to play my last two weeks of night basketball."

CHAPTER TWO

Leaving For Basic Training
Was Different From the Movies

It hadn't been like he'd seen in the newsreels where bands and crowds saw inductees off as they boarded trains for the Army. They boarded buses at the Army base as a sergeant with a clipboard called their names. When they got to South Station, they went through the same drill all over, with another sergeant assigning them to different railroad cars.

Dan had never been west of Worcester, and saw the whole train ride as a big adventure. He was a little nervous because this was his first time away from home, but he didn't want to let the others around him know he was scared. He tried to look out the window to see the places the train was passing through. But, after a couple of hours it was getting dark outside, and they had dimmed the lights in his car. He fell asleep to the rhythmic clacking of the train's wheels on the iron track, waking only briefly to the sound of soft crying coming from the boy sitting next to him.

The train had stopped about three or four times to pick up inductees from other towns along the way. Dan fell deeper into sleep as the train moved on headed through the night.

"All right, you sorry sacks of shit, get up! Get up! Get up!"

A half dozen men came running through the train, pounding with heavy wooden sticks on the overhead chrome luggage racks and screaming at the sleeping recruits and draftees.

"Get out! Get out! Move it! Now! Now! Faster! Faster!"

Another group of screaming men was waiting for them as they poured out of the train into the night and onto the platform.

"Line up along this line! Hurry up! Hurry up! We don't have all night! You're in the fucking Army now! And your sorry asses belong to me! Move it! Move it!"

Woken out of a deep sleep, Dan and the other men on the train grabbed their bags and ran in a blind panic to comply with the madmen who were screaming at them.

"Sir, I have to go to the bathroom, Sir?" The voice belonged to Dan's seatmate, who had been sobbing quietly in his sleep.

"I ain't no fucking 'Sir,' boy. You can stand there and piss in your pants until you call me Sergeant!"

"Yes, Sir...I mean, Sergeant...I've got to go real bad."

"You get your sorry ass behind that caboose and get back here on the double! You hear me, boy?"

"Yes, Sir..."

"I told you, boy, I ain't no fucking 'Sir'! You understand, boy?"

"Yes, Sergeant."

"Sound off like you got a pair, boy! I want to hear it!"

"Yes, Sergeant!"

"That's better! Get out of here, boy! Get out of here!"

And so it went. Dan's introduction to the Army was sudden and intense. They hadn't eaten since ten that morning, so they were all marched to the chow hall for a late meal at 2:00 A.M. and then marched to their temporary barracks at the reception station, where each of them collapsed out of exhaustion.

The lights went on at 4:00 A.M. as another sergeant walked briskly down the squad bay pounding the end of each metal bunk bed, shaking a couple of them, and screaming for them to wake up, get dressed, and fall out in fifteen minutes in front of the barracks. And they had better be clean-shaven. This precipitated a mad rush into the latrine, with the men in the bunks closest to it racing to be the first in line. One draftee was vomiting into the closest of the five porcelain commodes lined up, one beside another with no separation between them. Dan's seatmate from the night before was quivering in the back of one of the lines in front of the sinks, knowing that he wouldn't be dressed and clean-shaven in time to fall out. Dan, second in line behind a recruit who was frantically shaving his face, turned to his former seat-mate and said, "Here, take my place. My hair's pretty light, and if I don't get to shave, they probably won't notice it."

The grateful recruit muttered "Thank you" and moved up as Dan went back into the squad bay to get dressed. Pulling on his clothes, he chuckled to himself at the thought of Obie moving through boot camp, with his dreams of glory, war, and women. He got dressed, gathered his belongings together, and went back into the latrine, where one of the sinks was now vacant. Dan shaved quickly, and though he was among the last three or four recruits to leave the barracks, he didn't call any particular attention to himself, as he remembered his father's advice: "Keep your mouth shut, your head down, and don't volunteer."

In fact, the shock of his first night in the Army wasn't as bad on Dan as it had been on some of the others because his father had prepared him for it, telling him how the drill instructors abused and debased the recruits to break them down as individuals so they could mold them into a functioning disciplined unit.

Dan knew that what they were going through wasn't real, but that understanding didn't make the situation any more pleasant; it seemed real enough for him now as he was living it.

They initially went to the base barbershop to get haircuts. The first draftee in line stepped into the chair and the barber asked him how he'd like his hair cut. The surprised recruit asked if he could take a little off the side. The barber said, "Sho 'nuff," and proceeded to run the clippers along the top middle of the recruit's head from front to back as close to the skin on his scalp as he could.

The other barbers chuckled at what must have been a common joke with each new group.

"Gratuitous, sadistic bastards," Dan thought to himself, seeing no reason for the barbers to do this.

With shaved heads, they all lost a good deal of their individual identities. Next they went to the clothing checkpoint, where they were issued all of the clothing and uniforms they'd be wearing for the next two or three months.

More medical examinations and forms to be filled out, and they were issued their dog tags, a set of two steel identity disks that they wore around their necks with their name, serial number, blood type, and religion impressed on them.

"Why do they give us two of them?" one of the inductees asked.

"One of them goes with the graves registration guys and the other gets jammed between your front teeth after you're killed so they know who you were and where to send your body."

There were no follow-up questions.

They didn't get a lot more harassment at the reception station over the week it took to get them processed into the Army. At one point, they were marched to the headquarters building to stand by for work details around the base. Dan and three of the other recruits had been assigned to be trainee staff, to lead the

13

makeshift platoon before they all got separated and sent to their different training companies. Dan was told to march the platoon to the grassy lawn behind the headquarters where they were allowed to fall out along with three other platoons, two in front of them, and a fourth behind them.

About every ten minutes while they were sitting around talking, a corporal would lean out of the door of the building and shout something like, "I want the next ten men to fall in over here; get rakes, and go with Private Smith to police the area around the officers' club."

This happened from time to time over half an hour as different work details were filled out of the First Platoon. After Dan had figured out what was going on, he talked it over with the men in his platoon and suggested that by twos and threes they should periodically drift away out of the area to avoid being called.

By the time the corporal had worked his way through most of each platoon, Dan and one of the other trainee leaders were the last two left of their platoon. They both stood up and casually walked over into a tree line next to the road, following it into the woods till they were out of sight. They then walked very business-like down the road to where they had spotted the post exchange building during their in-processing.

It felt good to "beat the system" and to order a soda at the PX, almost like being back on the streets in Brighton. Even if it was illusory and temporary, it buoyed their spirits for however brief a period.

The next day was their last day in the reception station, and they'd now be assigned to their basic training companies. So far, it had gone pretty much like Dan's father had told him. He knew that things would get tougher when they got to their permanent training assignment, but he'd just take it one day at a time, as he took everything in life.

A sergeant approached Dan's group and yelled at one of them, "You looking me in the eye, boy?"

"No, Sergeant!"

"You want to fuck me, boy? You one of them there queers, boy?"

"What a dumb fuck. How did we ever get him for a DI?" Dan thought to himself, as the sergeant terrorized his former seatmate from the train ride.

"No, Sergeant! No, Sergeant! I ain't no queer! No, Sergeant!"

"That's better, boy! I don't want to see you looking me in the eye again, boy! You understand?"

"Yes, Sergeant!"

"Good! We'll make a man out of you yet, boy!"

Dan's father had told him that they pick on the weakest member of the platoon to break him first because the unit is only as strong as its weakest link.

Now they were trying to humiliate and break the recruit they'd identified as the weakest link.

"Oh shit, that bastard's marching us to the low crawl pit again."

"I don't wanna hear no fucking chatter in the ranks or I'll drop you all for 200 push-ups! You hear me, Third Platoon?"

"Yes, Sergeant!" they all answered in unison.

"I can't hear you, Third Platoon!"

"Yes, Sergeant!" they answered, even louder than before.

As they approached the low crawl pit behind their barracks they could see the dry dust blowing with even the faintest breeze.

"Plaatoon hallt!" the drill instructor commanded, and the unit came to an orderly halt.

"Lefft Faace!" As with his other commands, the sergeant dragged out each of his words.

"All right, Third Platoon. On the whistle, I want the first order down on the deck crawling your asses off. Asses and elbows; keep moving."

Before he could blow the whistle, Dan jumped in at the end of the first order. He knew that the way to survive this was to be in the first order and to run up about three yards when the whistle blew so as to be in the front of the rest of the group. That way he'd be ahead of the dust that the front line of men would kick up as they low-crawled across the barren field.

The whistle blew; Dan ran up about four yards and finished the low-crawl for the thirty yards to the other side of the pit in front of the others. As they got up, the slower crawlers were hacking and coughing from all the dust they'd inhaled.

The second order or line got into position, and the whistle blew. They all scrambled across the dust, but one man stopped half way across and lay in the dirt while the others went ahead, kicking up plumes of dirt in his face.

Dan recognized what was happening and he and one of his friends ran out to the middle of the field, grabbed the soldier, and pulled him to the side, out of the dust. The recruit was choking and gasping for air. The DI noticed what was happening and ran over to the three soldiers.

"What are you doing?" he screamed. "Put this man down!" he ordered.

"Sergeant, he can't breathe."

"Let him go! Do you hear me, Fleming? He's faking it!"

"I…I've got asthma…" the weak voice was barely able to force through and out of his lungs.

"You're faking it, Wilburn! I said let him go! I won't say it again!" The drill instructor, his face turning red, was nearly apoplectic by now.

Fleming and the other man stepped back, and Private Wilburn slumped to the ground and started turning from pale white to blue, his labored breathing now on the verge of stopping altogether.

The sergeant turned pale himself. Turning to Dan, he said, almost in a panic, "Fleming, run to the squad room and have the duty sergeant call an ambulance here on the double. Move, man! Move!"

Dan did as he was told and it took the ambulance fifteen minutes to arrive while the platoon stood huddled at the end of the low crawl pit. Standing over him, the drill instructor implored Private Wilburn not to die. "You can make this, Wilburn! You're a tough American soldier, a member of the United States Army. You can do this, Wilburn!"

Finally, the ambulance did arrive, and Private Wilburn was driven away to the hospital, never to be seen again by any of the Third Platoon.

"All right, men, fall in here on the edge of the tarmac!"

Grudgingly, and with defiant glares in their eyes, the members of the Third Platoon fell in, looking at the drill instructor in front of them with the kind of contempt that can only come from deep within a man.

"You all saw what happened. Wilburn just fell over. There was nothing I could do...There was nothing anyone could do..." his voice trailed off. "OK, OK, fall out. Make sure the squad bay is clean for tomorrow's inspection."

"That asshole almost killed Wilburn...if he didn't actually kill him." "He's more dangerous than the Krauts!"

Two weeks later at their afternoon formation, the company commander held the Third Platoon after he had dismissed the other three platoons.

Moving up in front of the platoon, the captain said, "Men, I want to introduce your new platoon sergeant, Sergeant Banks. Sergeant Banks will take Sergeant Killibrew's place for the remainder of basic.

"Sergeant." The captain turned to the headquarters building as he spoke, and the new drill instructor came out as the captain called his name.

Saluting the captain smartly, the new DI said, "Sir!" "Sergeant, take command of your platoon."

"Yes, Sir." The new DI again saluted smartly.

The captain returned the salute, executed an about face, and went back to the company headquarters.

"Men...I'll be with you for the remainder of your basic training. I know you're wondering what happened to Sergeant Killibrew...I don't know. I'll do my best to prepare you to go into battle. I want each of you to feel free to talk with me if you have any questions or problems."

Then reverting to his command voice, the new DI said, "Platoon Disss-missed!"

The remainder of basic went much smoother for the men of the Third Platoon under the leadership and tutelage of Sergeant Banks.

As part of their final testing before graduating from basic training, the company had to qualify on the rifle range with the M-1 rifle. At the evening formation before their day at the range, the captain spoke to them about the forthcoming testing. "Men...tomorrow you'll be firing for effect. Now, Captain Hanlon of Dog Company and I have a little wager about which company will score higher at the range. I know I can count on you to make me proud, and I'm authorizing a weekend pass to every soldier who shoots expert."

"Hey, Jocko," Dan Fleming collared one of his squad mates after the formation was dismissed, "What was that all about: 'make me proud'?"

"I think it looks good on his record if his company has a very high score at the range; makes him look like an effective company commander when they're wondering whether to promote him to Major.

"'Make me proud' my ass! I heard the skinny cook at the mess hall complaining that he wasn't going to be one of the scorers on the firing line tomorrow. I guess the scorers are all on the take and if you grease them with some cash, you make expert, the captain looks good to his review board, and you get a weekend pass for your investment."

"You're shitting me? We're going off to war and the guys who're supposed to teach us to shoot straight want us to pay off the scorers so they look good to their superiors and the scorers make a shit-load of money. You're right, everyone makes out on this. The captain looks good to the colonel. Guys like us, who haven't seen the outside of this training area in six weeks, get a weekend pass, and the scorers make a killing.

"My dad was right, they <u>are</u> incompetent and corrupt." "What are you gonna do?"

"Whaddya mean?"

"Are you gonna' grease them a couple of bucks to score expert?"

"Well, shit...I could never score it on my own. I can barely see the target without my glasses."

Fleming thought a moment. "Well...I don't know what I'm gonna' do. Somebody probably has to flunk so it doesn't look funny, and it sure won't be one of the guys who pays them off. That means they'll flunk some guys who shoot OK, just so the brass don't get suspicious about what's going on. It's immoral and probably illegal, but what can we do? How much are they looking for?"

"I heard the cook say that for two bucks they'll score you as an expert, and for ten bucks, they'll give you a perfect score."

"Ten bucks! That's a whole week's pay...those bastards!" Dan was upset. He hated the thought of bribing anyone; on the other hand, he hated the thought of sticking around in the company area all weekend while the other guys in his platoon were on liberty.

The following morning, Sergeant Banks switched the lights on in the squad bay at 04:00.

"OK, men, time to roll out of those racks and get ready. Today's a big day at the range and I want to see a lot of experts out of this platoon. Make the captain and me proud." Then lowering his voice to almost a stage whisper he said, "I've heard that a couple of those scorers have sick kids and are in tough shape for money...you might want to talk with them when you're on the range...you know, to see if there's anything they could do to help you a little bit to get one of those weekend passes, and maybe out of gratitude you might want to help them with their sick kids. Just a suggestion, but something you might want to think about. It might be good to have a couple of bucks with you when we fall out this morning. You never know when it'll come in handy..."

Dan thought to himself that some of his platoon mates were so dumb that even this heavy handed admonishment to bribe the scorers would go right over their heads.

They fell out on the company street at 05:00 and marched to chow. After chow, they double-timed it to the range, where they arrived at about 06:30.

"All right, men...fall out!" the sergeant leading the forced march ordered. "Smoke 'em if you've got 'em."

"Jesus Christ! All we do is hurry up and wait. A nice leisurely march to morning chow, a filling breakfast of shit on a shingle, and then with full bellies, they run us over to the range where now we have to hang around and wait for the range staff to show up. These guys are all fucking idiots!"

Finally, about half an hour later, the range staff came driving up in two Jeeps and three deuce and a halfs (two and a half-ton trucks with canvas tops over the back and with benches running along each side.) The company fell in, and a group of forty men was marched onto the range in single file, each of them stopping eventually at a firing position that was manned by a PFC or a corporal. This went on all morning, and it wasn't till after field chow was over in the afternoon that Dan's platoon got to fire.

After three or four groups had fired, Dan came up in the fifth firing order and marched out onto the range with his group. The soldier at Dan's position actually looked hostile, Dan thought...beyond being merely anti-social. Dan handed him the clipboard with his scorecard on it.

"Get in the prone position, Fleming! Come on, move it, move it!"

"Great," Dan thought to himself, "I probably couldn't bribe this guy if I wanted to."

Lying on his stomach and with a full clip in his M-1 rifle, Dan could barely see the target, let alone the tiny ring in the center.

"Ready on the left?" the range officer yelled.

The sergeant in charge of the twenty firing positions on the left side of the range looked at all of the scorers on his side. They all had their hands in the air.

"The left is ready, Sir!"

"Ready on the right?"

"The right is ready, Sir!"

"Commence firing!"

At that command, the range exploded in the staccato sound of forty rifles firing at random.

When he had finished his clip, Dan waited for the order closing the range and ending the firing. While he was waiting, the sullen scorer standing behind him said under his breath nervously, "I heard that if you score expert, you'll get a weekend pass."

"Yeah...I'd really like to do that," Dan replied, knowing full well what was going on.

"Two bucks under the sand bag," came the reply.

Dan picked up the sandbag and saw what looked to be more cash than he'd ever seen in one place before. He couldn't believe his eyes. There must have been more than three hundred dollars in cash all stuffed in.

"I wonder if he'd take a personal check," Dan mused silently to himself.

Dan stuffed a couple of bucks under the sandbag and started firing from the prone position a couple of more times. Then the range officer ordered the men to switch positions and go to a different scorer, probably designed, Dan thought, to prevent someone from bribing a scorer.

Dan was taken aback by this. He was thinking that he may have blown his chance to shoot expert because he had just given away the last two dollars in his wallet.

His worries were groundless. Before he moved to the next position, the scorer took Dan's scorecard off the clipboard and placed it back on, upside down so that the bottom of the sheet was at the top of the clipboard.

Moving over to the next firing position, Dan handed the clipboard to his new scorer who, upon seeing that the score sheet was upside down, turned it right side up and remarked, "Ah...I see that we have another potential expert."

"They're all fucking corrupt," Dan thought to himself, but then he realized that he was the one offering the bribe, and didn't feel quite so self-righteous after that.

Dan jumped into the foxhole, not very deep he thought, and began firing on command. He could hardly help but notice that the sandbag by his right elbow was barely able to conceal the mound of cash it was resting on, with dollar bills bulging out beneath and beside it.

The firing stopped and the range was again cleared. The scorer handed Fleming his clipboard and scorecard. "Congratulations, Fleming. You shot expert. Hope you enjoy the weekend pass. It's been a pleasure doing business with you. Come again some time."

Dan didn't say anything. He just filed off of the range and turned his score sheet over to the company clerk, who sat at a portable field desk off to the side.

"Nice job, Fleming," the company clerk said. "The captain will be proud of you."

The weekend pass was a welcome relief from all the shit Dan and the others had been taking so far over basic, almost worth the hangover he had returning to the company area on Sunday afternoon.

Gradually, the training cadre lightened up on the platoon, and eventually the group graduated from basic training. They felt cocky and invincible. Dan was in the best shape of his life, even better than when he was throwing around 60 pound bags of cement for Mr. Johnson.

The rumor was that the company was going to ship out as a unit for some place in England. That's all they heard. They were given two weeks leave and told to order their affairs because they were going to be in combat at some point. They were instructed to report back to the base no later than 17:00 hours two weeks from the following Sunday. Lawyers from the Judge Advocate's Office would help them make out their wills.

The two weeks flew by, and his mother's tears at their goodbye were something that Dan wished he could forget. His father had looked at him as if it'd be the last time ever that he'd be seeing his son. "Keep your head down, Danny, and don't try to be a hero."

The train pulled into Fort Dix. This time their exit was more orderly than his first arrival six or so months ago. To Dan, the time between then and now seemed at once to have been an eternity yet, at the same time, to have passed in the blink of an eye. His two week leave seemed surreal; he didn't feel that he belonged on the streets of Brighton any more. He met the guys for an afternoon of basketball but was so aggressive that everyone backed off from covering him. Even his teammates seemed to give him a wide berth. They asked him about basic training and where he'd be going. He couldn't answer all of their questions because they'd specifically been ordered not to reveal anything about their potential destination.

Dan felt removed from his old friends. In a sense, they were still children, playing children's games and dreaming children's dreams. The previous three months had moved them apart. He was trained to kill and was steeling himself to do that; he was concentrated on how to kill and how to stay alive, a different reality, a whole different focus from the world that they continued to live in.

From time to time, he imagined what his wake and funeral would be like if he came home in a casket; his family and friends standing around talking about him and remembering the good times they'd shared over the years. Obie would be telling his mother how much ribbing there was when Dan showed up to play ball, covered with cement. There'd be stories and more stories, a Catholic funeral with the priest in black, and the church filled with incense as they carried him out to the dirge called "Dies Ire." Then there would be a military burial at the gravesite, with taps and a final rifle salute. Everyone would go back to the Knights of Columbus Hall afterwards to eat a catered lunch. When it broke up three or so hours later, Dan's mother would go home clutching the American flag she'd been given at the grave, as well as his medals and the letter from his commanding officer. She'd cry with the grief that only a woman can know...a woman who had carried a child in her womb for nine months...suckled it and brought it up, only to have it cut down before the prime of life, cut down by an insanity that men create...an insanity that they call "war."

Well, he was back on the base now; no need to wallow in depressing thoughts. He'd survive to see his grandchildren and tell them about his time during the war.

"Hey, Smitty, how was your leave?" Dan had arrived back a couple of hours before the 5:00 P.M. formation, which was when they were all supposed to report in for roll-call. He was unpacking things into his wall locker when his bunkmate, Michael Smith, showed up, back from his home in New Jersey. Dan had the top bunk and Smitty the bottom. They had both grown up Catholic and had graduated from Catholic high schools. Smitty's experience at St. Peter's was very similar to Dan's at St. Col's, as they had learned over many a whispered conversation after "lights-out."

Smitty was the kind of guy who had no guile, no "filters", as the slang would later come to be used, that allowed him to hold back what he was thinking when he was talking with you. If he liked you, he told you so, and if he didn't – well, he let you know that as well. Today he wore his heart on his sleeve. Dan didn't have to hear a word from him before knowing that. Smitty's face was forlorn; he reminded Dan of a bloodhound with sad eyes and a hangdog expression. Smitty was in love with his high school girlfriend, Gwendolyn, and Dan knew that his best friend in the Army was hurting.

"Dan...I almost didn't come back. I miss Gwen so much. I was thinking about deserting, running off with her someplace where we could be married and forget this crazy war, go live in some town where no one knows us and get a job in a defense plant, maybe buy a house after a couple of years and raise a family. It sounded so good, Dan, but I couldn't do it; it couldn't happen."

"I know, Smitty...I know how much you love her, and how you want to be together again, but this war won't last forever. You'll come home a hero and create a life together, just like you both dream of.

"But, it's almost Sunday night and we have a formation at 17:00. We're back in the Army now; that's our world for the duration. I wonder how many guys will be AWOL. I bet we have at least two or three missing from formation."

"Dan...I miss her. I don't want to be here. I want to be with her."

Smitty seemed almost on the verge of crying, and Dan was at a loss about how he could distract his friend from pining for Gwen as they both went out to the company area for the formation.

"Ericson!"

"Here!"

"Fleming!"

"Here!"

"Frisoli!"

No answer came from the empty space next to Dan's right shoulder. "Frisoli! ...Does anyone know where Frisoli is? Corporal, mark Frisoli as AWOL."

"Yes, Sergeant."

"...Gephart!"...and so the roll call continued. Almost as Dan had predicted, there were five men who hadn't made it back for the formation.

After completing the roll call, Sergeant Banks addressed his platoon. "I'm glad that most of you made it back. I know that we've all been anxious about where they'd be sending us after training. I had sealed orders waiting for me when I got back yesterday. We're packing up and preparing the company area for the next training rotation and will embark by ship for England. We'll be leaving

Fort Dix this Friday, transiting to the Brooklyn Navy Yard, and then we sail a week from tomorrow.

"There'll be a lot of work ahead of us this week, and I've asked the captain if he could schedule one more day at the range. We can do that if we can manage to get the company area pretty much secured by Wednesday.

"This time we'll be shooting for real," he said in not too thin a veiled reference to their previous trip to the range.

"I don't need to tell you that this information's top secret. I don't want any of you telling your family, friends, or sweethearts about where you're going. If you're talking to them and they ask, just tell them that you'll be moving to an undisclosed location. Don't mention the unit or tell them whether you've been individually assigned or are moving with the company. The Nazis have spies everywhere in this country, and we don't want to tip them off about any troop movements.

"Do I make myself clear about that?"

Hearing a few mumbled "yeahs", a couple of mumbles and grunts, Sergeant Banks reverted to his command voice: "Platoon...do I make myself clear about that?"

"Yes, Sergeant!"

"Good, now are there any questions?"

"Cuneo."

"Sergeant, I don't have any money left; are we gonna' have to pay off the scorers again?"

At this, the whole platoon broke out laughing. Even Sergeant Banks fought to keep from chuckling, though he couldn't withhold a smile.

"Private Cuneo, there won't be anyone to score you. We'll be firing to perfect your shooting skills. The final score will come when you kill some poor German bastard before he kills you because you have better shooting skills than he does."

There was no laughter from the platoon at that remark, just the realization that their military training had been ratcheted up a notch or two.

They worked hard for the remainder of the week, cleaning and painting the barracks, inside and out. They did manage an afternoon at the firing range on Wednesday and this time there was no chatter, laughing, or joking like before. This time they all realized that their own survival might well depend on how proficient they were in firing their M-1 rifles.

The move was a lot of work, but otherwise uneventful. They turned in their company gear on Thursday morning, packed all of their personal issue in duffel bags, and were ready to move out. Friday morning they fell out in formation at

04:00 hours, standing behind their packed duffels. They were instructed to return to the barracks one last time to strip their bedding, fold the mattresses in half, and leave them and their blankets at the foot end of the bunks. Then they proceeded to the armorer and drew the weapon that they'd be carrying into combat. Dan laughed as he remembered the first time they'd been issued their weapons and one of the more naïve recruits referred to his as a "gun." Sergeant Killibrew had made him stand in front of the platoon, alternatively holding his rifle out in front of him and grabbing his crotch as he repeated over and over till Killibrew's amusement had been sated. "This is my rifle," holding up the rifle. "This is my gun," grabbing his crotch. "This is for shooting"...again holding the rifle in front of him. "This is for fun."

Killibrew had seemed to get pleasure out of humiliating the men under his charge. Sergeant Banks wasn't like that at all. He was a tough professional soldier and drill sergeant. He demanded hard work from his men and commanded respect from them by the way he carried himself.

Fleming was snapped back to the present when the armorer told him he'd better run a cloth through his barrel because there was going to be a bore inspection before they left, and that this was the weapon he'd be carrying for his full tour in the Army.

A rifle bore or barrel must be almost surgically clean and lightly oiled for the weapon to work effectively. Dirt in the barrel could even cause the weapon to explode in its user's face. Sergeant Banks had a passion about cleaning rifles and he instilled that in every member of the Third Platoon. Dan knew this and he realized that his life in the service would depend on how clean he was able to keep his rifle.

Once the rifles were issued, the men fell back in formation. It was about 05:30, and before they were marched over to the mess hall for morning chow, they once again had to stand for a bore inspection.

As the soldiers would stand at attention with their rifles by their sides, Sergeant Banks would walk down the ranks, and as he stopped in front of each soldier, he'd execute a sharp left face or right face directly in front of the soldier. The soldier would then bring his weapon up for inspection, holding it out in front of himself and opening the chamber. Banks would look down into the chamber, then take the weapon from the soldier, grabbing it out of his hands with a sharp motion, and hold it up so that sunlight peeking over the horizon would shine down the inside of the weapon's barrel. He'd then look through the muzzle end of the rifle to make sure the bore was clean. Normally he did this for every member of the platoon, but today, because they were in a hurry to leave, he skipped over the men who he knew always cared for their weapon "as if it were your lover." This was a phrase he used over and over as he had them break down and clean their rifles to the point where they could do it blindfolded. He had a stop-watch, and when they didn't have a company training event, he'd have them bring blankets out onto the grass in front of their barracks and time them as they field stripped their weapons. The quickest time got its holder to skip KP when his name next came up in the rotation.

CHAPTER THREE

Trained and Combat Ready,
They Leave for England

At 06:00, they marched off for chow, leaving two members of Dog Company to stand guard over their equipment and belongings. When they returned, they saw a line of deuce and a halfs waiting to transport them to the Brooklyn Navy Yard. There they would meet the ship that would take them to the jumping-off place for their war. As they stood in formation they were randomly assigned to trucks, probably to confuse some poor German spy who managed to get a copy of the truck rosters. Dan, worried about his heart-broken, homesick friend, had already spoken with the company clerk, who for a two dollar "tip" had arranged for him and Smitty to share the same truck for the ride into New York City. There was a sense of foreboding as well as they pulled out of the company area, their home for the past six months, and headed off on the road leading to battle. Looking back over the tailgate, Dan felt a certain nostalgia for the sparkling painted barracks that in all likelihood he'd never see again in his lifetime, however short or long that might be.

It was a beautiful day as the sun rose and the men in the trucks began to come to life. "Fingers" O'Shaughnessy, sitting across from Dan, began to kid around with the soldier seated next to him. The other guy didn't like it, and the two of them began pushing and wrestling. As the truck lurched through a pothole in the road, Fingers lost his balance and fell back over the tailgate.

Traveling in close formation, the truck behind theirs couldn't stop or swerve in time to avoid hitting the figure that suddenly ejected from the leading truck and bounced on the road in front of it.

The whole convoy stopped and the medics in the ambulance that followed the last truck came up to the front of the column, accompanied by the M.P. jeep that was the last vehicle in line.

One look at Fingers and the medics realized that he was beyond their skill level to save, or anyone's skill level for that matter. The two trucks involved in the accident were ordered to stay at the scene. Fingers was covered with a blanket from the ambulance, and the rest of the convoy, minus the M.P.s and their jeep, proceeded on its way to the waiting ship.

Eventually, the local coroner showed up and got into an argument with the M.P.s about who had jurisdiction over Fingers' body. A group of sheriff's deputies armed with shot guns arrived in two squad cars, and the logic of their arrival settled the jurisdictional issue nicely. Two Army M.P.s with pistols, facing six men, most of whom were armed with shotguns; that fact helped the M.P.s realize that the acceptable procedure would be to get the remaining two trucks to rejoin their convoy as soon as possible in order to help with the war effort. Fingers would be shipped home to his family with a nice note from the commanding officer, telling his mother what a good soldier he had been and how much he would be missed by his fellow servicemen. It was a shame he hadn't been killed in combat because then she would have received a Purple Heart, and probably a Bronze Star, in return for her son's life.

The sheriff and one of his deputies, accompanied by the two M.P.s, took statements from each of the men in the two trucks. By the end of that process, and after two hours had passed, sheriffs and M.P.s were chatting and joking together like old buddies. The coroner's men packed Fingers into their black hearse, which left before the deputies would abandon their newfound friends. When the hearse had about a fifteen-minute head start, the deputies said good-bye, piled into their squad cars, and went off in the same direction.

"Well, I think we'd better move out," said the M.P. corporal, the senior person in the group. The men climbed back aboard the two trucks, and led by the M.P. jeep, proceeded to catch up with the rest of the group about five hours later at the Brooklyn Navy Yard.

The crossing to England was fairly uneventful, though they did get called to their lifeboats about half a dozen times on the ten day journey, usually in the middle of the night when there was a U-boat alert. About four days out, they ran into a bad storm and they were all confined to their bunks, throwing up all over the place. All in all, they were relieved when they saw their first flock of gulls, and shortly after that made landfall.

Dan had started going to daily Mass on ship. They had all been packed in below decks, and aside from regular calisthenics on deck and cleaning their

27

weapons, there was little to occupy their time. Dan figured that it would be a good time for him to make peace with his God, not knowing what might lie ahead for him. He frequently found himself standing next to the platoon leader for the Second Platoon, and usually followed him to receive Communion. Edward Henry Miller, a first lieutenant from South Bend, Indiana, was married with one child. Dan learned from talking with him after Mass that he had entered the Army and gone to OCS shortly after graduating from the University of Notre Dame. Dan knew of Notre Dame; his parish priest at Saint Columbkille's spoke of the place often in glowing terms. At first, Dan and Lieutenant Miller didn't have much to say to each other after Mass beyond exchanging pleasantries. Miller was an officer with an entire platoon to look out for, and Fleming was a grunt in another platoon. But after a week or so, they found that in spite of a five year age difference, they had a lot in common. Unbeknown to both men, their fates would become inextricably intertwined in the weeks and months ahead.

When they landed in England, another convoy of trucks took them to their new quarters at an abandoned World War I training base with a grass airstrip. The grass field that had been used for a runway during the Great War was much too short to handle the higher speed aircraft of this conflict, and the Quartermaster Corps had used it to set up large tan colored tents, enough to house the battalion over the length of the field.

His stay in England, the calm before the storm, was one of the most pleasant times of Dan's young life. Climbing ropes, running and training all day, the men had most evenings off and could go into the small English town about three kilometers from their camp. The English girls were free spirits and enjoyed the company of the young American soldiers. But, some of the British troops stationed nearby weren't so enthusiastic about the Yanks' presence, and it was not an uncommon occurrence to see a dozen or more men wearing allied uniforms of both countries battling it out in town. The usual time for these melees was shortly after the pubs had closed. Back home these would be called riots, but here it was just a blood sport for the locals who seemed to enjoy watching the late evening contests that erupted every so often. The combats usually lasted for about fifteen minutes, enough time for the entire drunken lot to wear itself out. When that happened, the British and American M.P.s showed up, usually together, and used their truncheons to beat on any of the combatants still looking to engage in hostilities. When everyone's blood lust had been sated, the M.P.s hauled the now beaten horde off to the stockade, where they were routinely court-martialed and then sent back to their units.

The engineers had set up a mock landing craft in a pond on the base with cargo nets thrown over its sides. A bunch of small boats were tied up under the cargo nets. It was actually a mock-up of only half a landing craft. Someone must have gotten their orders screwed up because it was welded together in the form of a landing craft, but it was half again as tall as a troop ship, somewhat of a hybrid. When it was used as a landing craft, the men would crouch in its bottom, waiting to storm out into the pond and capture the beach after the front gate had been cranked down. The engineers had set up a bunch of floating rafts with sandbags and pyrotechnics to make the rehearsed landings seem real. With full combat gear, the platoon would crouch in position ready to attack, and on cue would run out screaming and yelling through the explosions on the rafts. After they had secured a beachhead – again – they would have to march back to their company area to wash and dry their clothing. Pond scum was the major hazard of these training exercises.

The better exercise, though, was embarking from the mock troop carrier by climbing down the cargo nets and entering the assault landing craft that would actually deliver troops to the beach. This was a little tricky and required more skill than screaming and splashing through the pond scum. The complexity of the issue was driven home when one soldier from the Second Platoon missed his footing on the net near the top and hurtled past his descending comrades to land on top of his pack in the bottom of one of the smaller boats. The medics took him to the base hospital with a broken spine. There he was placed in a full-body cast and denied the days of glory that lie ahead for his "luckier" comrades.

A couple of the more fortunate troopers who had missed their footing on the nets managed to land in the pond and merely had to worry about slipping out of their full combat packs and keeping above water without drowning.

CHAPTER FOUR

They Receive a New Company Commander

They'd been spending a good deal of time training to fight with rifles, hand grenades, bayonets, and hand to hand. They could only train so much, and so they ended up after about a month or so in England with a good deal of time on their hands. Some company commanders let their troops use the time during the day when they were not training as free time where they could go into town or take a jeep out of the company motor pool and drive around the English countryside. Captain Stadholm, their new company commander, wasn't like that. He kept his men in the company area when they weren't in training and went out of his way to let them know that he was in charge. He took great pleasure knowing that he could control their lives. The great chess master, he could move his pawns and rooks all over the board at his whim and pleasure. His men were there to do as he pleased, to kill for him and to die for him, and now it was his pleasure that they entertain him.

The Army loved contests. Pitting one man against the other, one group against the other, instilled competitiveness and developed spirit and camaraderie. Captain Stadholm was more competitive than most. Their previous company commander had been promoted to major – no doubt due to the leadership qualities he had displayed in developing such great marksmen during the company's basic training – and moved to a state-side billet with the War Department. Stadholm had succeeded him, and it wasn't long till the entire company realized that the fates had placed their futures in the hands of a mean, vicious, ruthless, and ambitious man.

They had plenty of downtime during their training, often entire days when nothing had been scheduled. Stadholm had developed a regular boxing program for the company to take up their time when they had a day or a large block of time unscheduled. He told his platoon leaders that he wanted to instill competitiveness in the men. He had members of each platoon fight members from the other platoons in a makeshift ring. Each man had to participate, and the platoon with the most victories was given a weekend pass, while the others had to go out to the "General Lee" (the nick-name they had given to their amphibious hybrid) to jump in the water and climb down cargo nets.

It was a chilly March day and Stadholm had called for the all-day tournament to begin at 10:00 hours. He sat at ringside for all the matches, just leaving long enough to take a piss or grab a drink of water and a shot of whiskey. He was usually shit-faced by the time the matches ended at 17:00 hours.

Dan had fought early against a member of the First Platoon who was smaller than he, and scared. Dan knocked him down in the first round, and his opponent was afraid to leave his stool for the start of the second round...notch up one victory for the Third Platoon. Stadholm screamed at the losing fighter and threatened to court-martial him for cowardice.

No one had any kind thoughts for their new company commander, especially Dan Fleming. It seems that on the day of one of his sporting events, Stadholm was in a particularly bad mood, and more abusive than usual. Smitty was scheduled to fight a much larger opponent from the Second Platoon and wasn't about to enter the ring against him.

"Look, Dan, they pay me to go out and maybe get killed by the Germans; I understand that, but they don't pay me to get my face rearranged by this big son-of-a-bitch. That asshole Stadholm can court-martial me, send me to the stockade if he wants, but I'm not gonna fight Grabowski. He'll fucken kill me."

Dan thought a bit and finally said to Smitty, "You know, Mike...I think I've got a plan. Sit tight for a few minutes; you won't be going into the ring for at least another half-hour. I'll get back to you before then. Just don't do anything that'll get Stadholm on your ass; he's a vindictive bastard."

"I'm not gonna to do it, Dan; I won't go into the ring with Grabowski."

"Yeah...yeah, Mike. OK...OK."

Now it was not unknown for members of the company to place occasional wagers on some of these contests. It was even rumored that the first sergeant had been laying down bets for the captain. Dan walked over to where the Second Platoon was warming up, waiting for their chances to get into the ring.

"Hey Grabowski, Lieutenant Miller wants to see you." Now everyone in the Second Platoon had noticed the warm relationship between their platoon leader and this grunt from the Third Platoon, and Grabowski willingly followed Fleming to where he thought Miller would be waiting.

When they got alone outside of the platoon area, Dan turned to Grabowski and said, "I think there's going to be heavy betting on you to take Smitty out. I'm proposing that you take a dive in the first round, and I'll place heavy bucks on Smitty with the bloods from the First Platoon. I'll either put your money on Smitty, or give you ten percent of what we make on the fight...what do you think?"

"Jesus, Fleming, they'll kill both of us if they ever find out what we're doing. How about I put up a hundred bucks and you give me 10 percent of your winnings?"

"We've got a deal, my friend."

Going their separate ways, Dan worked his way back to the Third Platoon area, where he found Smitty in a high state of agitation.

"OK, Smitty, it's all arranged. Grabowski will take it easy on you; just hit you enough times so he wins the fight. You go out there and fight with all you've got so it doesn't look phony. Believe me, Mike, this is the best way out. You don't get chewed up by either Grabowski or Stadholm...capish?"

"Yeah, yeah. I hear you, Dan. You're sure that Grabowski will follow through on his end?"

"Hey, leave it to me. I told you, it's a deal. But, I've got to run; I've got some business over with the First Platoon. Good luck, Smitty. Everything will be OK"

"Look at what the cat dragged in, Private Fleming from the Third Platoon. Looking to hang around with some real men, sonny?"

"Kiss my ass, Leinhard. I just came by to see your guys get their asses whipped today."

"You got a big mouth, boy...why don't you put your money where your mouth is."

"I would, fuck-face, but I'm saving it to put down on my bunkmate against the Second Platoon."

"You're putting money on that match? Smith versus Grabowski?"

"Well, pretty boy, you finally got something straight; first time in your life probably."

"Hey...I'll take some of that money."

"Me too...wait a minute...."

"Hold on, boys; Smitty's my bunk mate, but I'm no fool. I've seen them both in the ring too, and I may have been born at night, but it wasn't last night. I'm doing this out of loyalty to my bunk-mate, but I want odds. I've got three hundred bucks that I want to lay off on the fight, my entire winnings from the last three weeks...who wants a piece of me? Let's hear it."

With that, a bidding war ensued, with Dan making side bets with a number of soldiers from the First Platoon.

"Hey, Cuneo...you're Italian; you know how the Mafia works. Take twenty bucks out of the pot and hold the stakes for Grabowski versus Smith."

"My pleasure."

Dan handed him a slip of paper with a series of names, odds, and amounts of money written on them. If all went as planned, Dan would walk away with more than $1,000 after giving Grabowski his cut. One of the names on the slip belonged to the first sergeant, who had given Dan four to one odds that Grabowski would win. That worried Dan because he figured that it was probably Stadholm's cash he was playing with, but he figured, "Oh, what the hell; the captain has the same right to get screwed as anyone else in the company."

The time had come for the fight to begin. There seemed to be an unusual interest among the troops in the outcome of this battle, because they all crowded around the ring. The referee gave the instructions, and then the timer rang the bell to start the match.

Smitty, with his head down, came charging out after Grabowski. Grabowski stepped out of his way, with Smitty running headlong into one of Grabowski's seconds who'd been a little slow getting out of the ring. The second turned and slugged Smitty, knocking him down, but also enraging him. Smitty got up and started fighting with the second. Dan jumped into the ring and pulled the second off while Grabowski stood there not knowing what to do. Smitty continued punching at the second as Dan was trying to pull him out of the ring. Stadholm, who by now was very drunk, stood up and started screaming, and then climbed into the ring, running up to Smitty while trying to slug him in the back of his head. He missed his head, but hit him in the shoulder. This further enraged Smitty, who turned and cold-cocked Stadholm with one punch. The entire crowd started laughing at this spectacle, except for Grabowski, who was waiting for his fight with Smitty to begin. In the meantime, the timekeeper kept pounding on the bell with his hammer, trying to get some control of the melee. The referee jumped on Smitty's back and pulled him back towards his corner. Dan had never seen Smitty so infuriated.

"I'm going to forfeit this fucking fight to your opponent, you crazy shit!"

The referee wasn't kidding around, and Dan could see a lot of his hard-earned money going down the drain. So could Grabowski, who leaped off of Smitty's stool where he'd been waiting, once he saw what the referee was about to do. Grabowski charged across the ring, pushing the ref out of the way while trying to get to Smitty.

"Don't you take away my chance to kill this little fucker for what he did to my trainer. I'll murder the little bastard."

"Get the fuck back to your corner!"

Smitty was on his feet by now.

"Fuck you, Grabowski!"

They finally dragged Stadholm out and cleared the ring. Instead of forfeiting the fight, the ref thought it might be fitting justice to see Grabowski pound the shit out of Smitty.

"When the bell rings, come out fighting for round two – everyone else, keep the hell out of the ring!"

The timer hit the bell and Smitty came charging out of his corner, meeting Grabowski at center ring and connecting with a flurry of punches, which were more of an annoyance than a threat to the larger man.

"The face, you idiot, hit me in the fucking face."

Instinctively, Smitty did what the other man said, and as Grabowski began falling back in his dive, Smitty wondered what the hell was going on.

Half of the Third Platoon poured into the ring to congratulate Smitty and even the fallen Grabowski, who had by now pulled himself up on the ropes, and after shaking his head a couple of times (an obligatory gesture from a boxer who's been knocked out), went over to congratulate Smitty.

"Nice punch, kid…when are we gonna have a rematch?"

Cuneo sought Dan out at ringside, and after taking out his twenty bucks, gave the remainder over to the brains behind the whole scheme. Dan, of course, happened to run into Grabowski later in the day and handed him a sealed, stamped envelope with his name on it and his mother's home address on the upper left hand corner.

"This was left over from yesterday's mail call. It got stuck in the bottom of the bag and the clerk didn't see it."

Stadholm, when he regained consciousness alone in his tent, couldn't remember anything about the day, except that the fights were boring and he had a bad headache.

And so their lives went over the winter and spring. Day by day, more troops were moving into the English countryside. The old RAF base looked like downtown Chicago, with all of the new units crammed in to take up residence. They all knew it would be a temporary residence, but none of them looked forward to ending it. They shipped the soldier who had broken his back falling from the General Lee back to the States. As March turned to April and the English countryside began to warm up, their training increased. There was less time now to hang around in town at the British pubs; night maneuvers and night firing exercises consumed much of their energy. Smitty and Dan continued to develop their close friendship.

One Friday night after they'd returned from ambushing and shooting up an abandoned French motor car in what they thought was a senseless training exercise, Dan and Smitty were sitting on the ends of their bunks talking. Dan turned to Smitty and handed him an envelope with five-hundred dollars in it.

"What's this, Dan? What's in the envelope?"

"Open it, Smitty...it's for you."

"What is it, Dan? It seems bulky, like it's stuffed with paper."

"So open it already!"

"Oh my god, Dan...I've never seen this much money in one place before in my life. Where did it come from, and why are you giving it to me?"

"Well, you earned it. You see, I had a couple of side bets on your match with Grabowski the other day, and these are half of the winnings. You're the guy who did the heavy lifting, so I thought you should be entitled to half the winnings."

"Wait a minute, Dan...wait a minute. Are you telling me that Grabowski threw the fight? That's not right, Dan! That's not right! Here, take the money...I don't want it."

"Smitty! Hey! Look at me. We're not at home. This isn't polite society where everyone treats each other decently. We're in with a bunch of animals here, and in a couple of months, half of us are probably gonna' be dead. This is a different world, Smitty, different from anything that either of us has ever seen. These guys are a bunch of animals, Smitty. They were howling for your blood and fighting with each other to give me greater odds that Grabowski would pulverize you. If we manage to live through the war, you and I will probably keep in touch over the years, but most of these guys will go off into the blue somewhere. We were thrown together by the War Department, and as soon as the war's over, they'll stop paying those of us lucky enough to have lived through it all and then throw us out.

"Mike, this is a different reality. This isn't the world we came from...this is an unreal world. If we survive, maybe we'll be able to go back to that other world and live like humans and not animals.

"Take the money, Smitty...it'll be a nice down payment on a house for you and Gwen when all of this shit's over and done with. Take it down to the battalion post office in the morning; they're open till 10:00 hours on Saturdays. They'll give you a money order to send home. It's pretty good. I did it this morning when I was supposed to be on K.P. They give you a receipt and something that looks like a bank check with the amount filled out on it. You fill in the name of the recipient and then mail it home. I made it out to my mother.

She can use the money, and if I get killed, part of it will be used for a big party after the wake. I sent my dad a separate note telling him that. I couldn't say that to my mother."

"It's not right, Dan, but it would be a nice down-payment on a home for Gwen and me. You know, Dan, it's still not right, but it's true that nothing's right here. This is a world that's different from anything I've ever heard of....paying scorers on the firing range, non-coms stealing food. I remember wondering why we got so little to eat at basic when all of the other companies were throwing tons of leftover food out. I didn't wonder after the mess sergeant had me carry a bunch of canned goods and three sacks of flour out to his car one night when I was on K.P. The bastard must have been selling the stuff outside the base, probably feeding half his neighborhood on what he should have been serving to us.

"I don't want to take the money, Dan, but I will. You are right; it's a different world here, Dan. I'll send it home to Gwen tomorrow."

"None of my business, Smitty, but why don't you keep out a hundred or so for yourself and send the rest to your father or mother to hold for you. It might be hard for Gwen to explain where she got all that money when she goes to the bank to deposit the money order....you know how people talk."

"That's right, Dan. That's a good idea."

"And besides, Smitty, if things don't work out between the two of you, you're not out five hundred bucks."

"That'd never happen, Dan...never! We're deeply in love with each other."

CHAPTER FIVE

They Land In Normandy

Finally, as they knew it had to, the training stopped and they were ordered to prepare combat packs, draw ammunition and hand grenades from the armorer, and be ready to board another troop ship, this time on the Channel side of the island, facing towards France.

Crammed together in the dark hold of the ship with only red lights on in the hatchways, faces covered with black grease, they were tense and scared. A couple of them cracked nervous jokes, while others prayed.

"Dan...I'm scared."

"Me, too, Smitty."

"I don't want to do this, Dan; I don't want to die."

"It's too late for that now, Smitty. I think it's out of our hands now."

"Dan...did you pay Grabowski to throw that fight?"

"For Chris' sake, Smitty, you went to confession before we left. You weren't part of the scheme. If anyone'll be going to hell for that, it'll be me. Forget it, Smitty! Forget it!

Is your rifle bore clean? "

"I ran a patch through it just before we boarded."

Their discussion was broken up by Captain Stadholm, who had just entered the company area in the hold.

"OK...listen up! I want us to go topside and over the rail into the landing craft, platoon by platoon, starting with the First Platoon. No lights; you don't want to ruin your night vision and we don't want the Krauts to see us till we're ready to land. Let's move out now."

37

"That asshole Stadholm sounds like he loves this shit, ordering his men into battle. I hope the little shit doesn't do something to get us killed?"

"You think he'll be in the first landing craft, Dan?"

"No way! The little shit's gonna go in last so he can position HIS troops, like the grand chess-master he'd like to be."

"Third Platoon up! Come on! Move it! Move it! Move it!"

They ran up the stairs and over to the ship's railing where one of the crew was waiting to help them onto the nets.

"OK, lads, over you go now. God be with you!"

They climbed over the railing and onto the cargo nets, but any similarity to the General Lee ended there. The ship was rocking in the tide and the landing craft kept moving back and forth as their skippers struggled to try to keep them in contact with the ship. A couple of the troops fell off into the water. They never surfaced like they did in the pond in England. Dan was more afraid than he'd ever been before in his life. But, his fear for that day was nowhere near peaking.

They were packed together in the landing craft so tightly that there was no room to turn around. As they raced towards the beach, a voice came up out of the packed mass, "Where's the latrine? I've got to go to the bathroom." They all laughed, even the ones who were more scared than Dan.

Soon they came within range of the German shore artillery, and waterspouts and explosions started erupting all around them. They were being bracketed, and the landing craft started zigzagging to keep the spotters from targeting them. They missed the boat next to them by barely ten feet as they both tried to evade the German barrage. Two boats over took a direct hit, and they could hear the screaming of the wounded and the dying. There'd be no survivors; there was no rescue boat to pick up the wounded and they'd all be left to drown. There'd be no stopping of the successive waves of landing craft as the Americans raced to shore to establish a beachhead on the continent.

"We're coming in hard, guys, thirty seconds to go." The boatswain never got to give another update because he was cut down by the machine gun fire that otherwise bounced helplessly off the front ramp of the landing craft. The German gunner firing from a pillbox somewhere on the beach continued to pound the ramp with regular staccato bursts of fire.

"Jesus, Smitty...we're all going to die!"

"I know, Dan...I know."

And then Smitty started praying:

"Oh, my God, I'm heartily sorry for having offended Thee..."

There was a grinding noise as the craft scraped along the beach. Before it had stopped, one of the crewmen who had replaced the dead bosun dropped the ramp at the same time the German gunner started firing again. It wasn't like the General Lee and the explosions on the rafts. This was for real, and after the explosions, there were dead bodies floating in the water which was now turning pink, stained with the blood of the first two ranks who had already exited the landing craft. Dan and Smitty were screaming now, fully expecting to run off to their deaths, but another landing craft had beached, and the German gunner turned his fire to greet those troops as they ran into hell. Racing out into the chest deep water and wading to the beach, Smitty saw the face of Grabowski as the dead man's corpse floated peacefully by.

They raced for cover on the beach and huddled behind a sand dune that an earlier tide had thrown up. There were mines everywhere, and the German bunkers and pillboxes had overlapping fields of fire where they could cover every square inch of the beach. The second wave had hit the beach now, and another bunch of scared soldiers ran up to crouch behind the sand dune. Captain Stadholm was huddled in that group right behind Dan. Shortly after Stadholm arrived, Dan noticed a foul smell behind him, a smell like when one of the toilets in the latrine at basic had been clogged and everyone kept using it regardless.

"We've got to do something," Dan yelled, "or they'll pick us off like flies!" While he was saying this, little sprays of sand would kick up as the German gunners tried to kill the trapped Americans.

Shortly after that, the pillbox on his right stopped firing.

"They must be changing ammunition belts," Dan thought. He broke out of the cover of the dune and ran directly at the pillbox. He was met by sporadic small arms fire that didn't come close to hitting him. Reaching the pillbox, he could see the frightened faces of the German gunners as they tried to clear a jammed cartridge out of the gun. He could see the soldier who was firing at him frantically trying to shove another clip into his Luger. Dan ran beside the concrete pillbox, which had been dug into the sand, and rolled onto its roof. Pulling a grenade, he counted to three, stuffed it into one of the firing ports, and then rolled back onto the roof.

The explosion in the confines of the reinforced concrete box echoed loudly. Dan looked up as a bloody human hand sailed out of the gun port and came to rest on the part of the beach where he had just been standing.

Jumping off the pillbox, Dan stuck his M-1 rifle into one of the ports and quickly dispatched the dying German soldiers who had been manning the machine gun.

Dan stood on top of the concrete box and waved to his comrades trapped behind the dune to come running. About twenty men advanced quickly up to Dan's position.

"Spread out!" he ordered, and they then started moving up the beach in some semblance of a skirmish line.

As they moved up the beach they encountered the German's second line of defenses, but this time they had some cover and a toehold on the continent.

"I think we should dig in here and prepare to defend this position," Dan shouted out to the twenty soldiers strung out along the woods at the top of the dunes. Stadholm was numb and useless. He was holding a Garand carbine, a nice light officer's weapon, but he hadn't fired it, and it seemed like a useless appendage in his hands.

Hearing firing coming from behind him and off to one side, Dan then said, "Let's get a squad to move back toward the beach and take out that bunker firing over on the left. They're gonna kill a lot of our guys unless we get them before that next wave of LSTs hits the beach."

Three men, including Smitty, moved out with Dan toward the bunker. This was larger than the pillbox Dan had captured, and he estimated that it was probably manned by about eight or ten soldiers. He'd been lucky with the pillbox, but a grenade through the firing port of the bunker probably wouldn't get all of them, he thought, though the element of surprise was on their side because the Germans didn't know they were surrounded.

"Casey, you and Smitty cover the door to the bunker. Hannaford, come with me and we'll try to stick a couple of grenades through those two firing ports." Moving lightly through the beach vegetation, the two men climbed up on the bunker, crawling out over the front overhang of its concrete roof.

The occupants heard them though, and suddenly the back door to the bunker opened, and a German soldier leaped out and started firing. He killed Hannaford, but Smitty shot him before he could get Dan. Dan raced to the door and threw two grenades in succession into the open hatch. One of them was thrown back, so Dan rolled off the top of the bunker in front of the faces of the startled gunners before the other grenades went off, the first explosion in back of the bunker, and the second inside it.

Casey and Smitty were at the ready as about five or six half-blinded, wounded German soldiers came out of the hatch with their hands over their heads.

"What do we do with them, Casey...they killed Dan and Hannaford?"

It wasn't clear who fired first, but it was clear to both men that they were in no position to take prisoners. They just started firing, executing the surrendering Germans.

"That's for Dan Fleming, you Nazi son-of-a-bitch"

"Smitty! Smitty! I'm alive. They didn't get me. Hold your fire!"

"Dan...you're alive. Oh Jesus! Oh Jesus!"

They rested now, ignoring the bleeding corpses beside them as the next wave hit the beach and the troops disembarked in front of the two smoldering battle-stations. It was as if they were running out of the General Lee. As the rest of the beach exploded in front of the landing troops, the sector in front of the remnants of the Third Platoon was a cakewalk for the disembarking G.I.s. For all intents and purposes, their landing could be a stroll on the beach at Coney Island – except that the water was pink instead of blue.

The flies started buzzing around the dead as the living stopped to rest before moving on.

Rejoining the others who were spread out behind the first line of beach defenses, Dan asked no one in particular, "Wadda we do now?"

Smitty was quick to answer. "I think we should move laterally behind the other bunkers in the first ring before we try to break through their next line. Maybe we can take some pressure off the others who are landing down the beach. We don't have any sappers with us. The frogmen went in last night to blow up the obstacles in the water, but no one thought to send the engineers in with the first wave to take out the pillboxes and bunkers."

As he said that, there was an explosion about a half-mile down the beach. The night before D-day, the allies had landed paratroopers behind the German defenses, and those who had survived the jump were working their way back to the beach after blowing up bridges and dropping trees across the roads. After sealing off access to the shoreline so the Germans couldn't rush reinforcements to the battle area, the paratroopers fought their way back down toward the beach to support the landing. After the explosion, Dan and his comrades saw a figure climb up on the bunker and plant a small American flag.

"I guess the engineers came in the back door."

They were still talking, and Dan was quickly running an oily patch through the bore of his smoking rifle before inserting a fresh clip. While he was doing this, a German soldier wandered in confusion out of the woods, probably someone who had gone to the latrine before the action had started, and was trying to make his way back to his position in the darkness. He was as shocked to stumble into the huddled group of Americans as they were to see him suddenly appear.

"Take him, Captain, take him!"

Stadholm stood motionless, numbed by fear. Quickly dropping his now-useless weapon, Dan grabbed the carbine out of Stadholm's hands. The German pulled the safety back on his machine pistol, leveled it at the group of Americans, and started cursing as the weapon jammed. Dan was luckier: he got off two shots before Stadholm's carbine jammed. The German was down, writhing on the ground in pain. Stadholm pulled his .45 caliber pistol out of its holster and slowly walked over to the severely wounded soldier.

"You know something, you Nazi bastard? You're gonna die and I'm gonna be your executioner. I'm your god and I can decide whether you live or die, and I've decided to kill you."

The German didn't understand Stadholm's words, but he knew what was going to happen to him. The look of terror in his eyes fed Stadholm and invigorated him with the soon-to-be-dead soldier's acknowledgement of Stadholm's power over him.

Flushed with power, Stadholm continued toward the wounded man, bent over him to look him in the face, and pointed the pistol at his head, about two inches from the man's temple. As his last living act, the German soldier spat into Stadholm's face, deflating the other man's triumph by this final defiant act.

"What a sick bastard," Smitty whispered to Dan.

"Yeah, but we always knew that.

"We better move out of here though; there are probably a shit load of Germans wandering through the bushes, either looking for us or trying to get away from us."

Dan looked at the other soldiers. "Anyone wounded? Whadda we have? No one?

"OK..how about ammo? I'm pretty light...anyone spare a couple of clips?"

"Crawford...can you get Hannaford's ammo belt? He's not gonna be needing it."

They moved up into the woods. The fighting continued to be ferocious, as they were the first to land and logically the first to confront opposition as they moved inland.

At one point they were on the verge of firing at a figure who had stepped out of the bushes in front of them when they heard, "Don't shoot, Yanks...I'm one of you!"

Approaching cautiously, wary of a German ruse, one by one they emerged out of the darkness to come face to face with what appeared to be one of the British commandos who had landed in a glider the night before.

"I got separated from my mates and I'm just trying to make my way down to the beach."

Dan thought there was something funny about the man's British accent. They had spent a lot of time in the English pubs before the invasion, and though the voice sounded as though it could be English, it wasn't perfect.

Dan demanded, "Show me your dog tags!"

The blank and scared expression on the Brit's face alerted Dan that all may not be as it appeared to be.

"Your identity disks!" Dan demanded, suspicious that the ostensible British commando didn't know the American slang for the steel identity tags that all allied troops wore around their necks.

The man started opening his shirt, fumbling with his top button, and then turned and bolted back towards the underbrush. Instinctively, the closest three Americans fired on him, killing him before he could make it back to cover.

"It must take a lot of balls for a German intelligence agent to try to get through us to find out what's happening down on the beach," one of them said.

With the beachhead secured, they held their position as reinforcements poured onto the beach and up into the woods.

An officer approached Dan and asked, "Who's in charge here, soldier?"

"Captain Stadholm, Sir."

"What's your organization?"

"Huh?"

"Your unit, soldier, what unit is this?"

"Uh...Third Platoon, Sir...Charlie Company, Third Brigade."

"Good, good...Where's your CO? Stadholm...that's his name?"

"Yes, Sir. He's about a hundred yards back down towards the beach, off the road in a fox hole."

"What the hell's he doing there? This is the forward edge of the battle area, isn't it?"

"I think so, Sir. At least that's where the shooting comes from, that direction in front of us, Sir."

"Thank you, soldier." At that, the major, his radio operator, and the brigade executive officer turned to head back to get Stadholm, not hesitating as a couple of rifle shots flew around them and imbedded into a tree beside where they were walking. Nor were they distracted when the soldier they had just been talking to started firing back in the direction the shots had come from.

About 100 yards down the road, the entourage stopped.

"Where's Captain Stadholm?" the major shouted.

Hearing no response, he shouted even louder, "Where the fuck is Stadholm? Get your ass out here right now!"

Not one to ignore a direct order, no matter how inexpertly it's phrased, Stadholm crawled out of the hole he had dug beside the road.

Lying on the ground in front of the major, Stadholm said, "It's not safe to be standing here sir. The battle's raging all around us."

"Stadholm, girls are probably gonna be selling coffee here within the next fifteen minutes. The battle zone's that way," he said, pointing up the road in the direction from which he had just come.

Hearing more firing in the distance, the major turned to his aid and radio operator and said, "Billy, why don't you and Ryan go back up where we just came from and find out what's going on. I'll stay here and get debriefed by Captain Stadholm."

"Yes, Sir!"

After the two men left, the major turned and faced Stadholm. "Get hold of yourself, Man! Your troops are forward and you're back here cringing in a hole!

"Stadholm, is that bourbon that I smell on your breath?"

"No! No, Sir! I'm no coward, Sir! This is where I can best exercise command and control of my company."

"Command and control – my ass! Stadholm, your fucking company's about a quarter mile down the road by now, engaging the German Army while you're cowering here in a hole. I'm relieving you of your command and I'm going to have you court-martialed for cowardice."

"Sir, quick, behind you!"

The major turned, and with the same demonical look on his face as when he killed the wounded soldier, Stadholm quickly unsheathed his pistol and killed for the second time within a couple of days, placing his pistol about two inches from the other man's left scapular before firing.

The noise of the pistol shot was lost in the sporadic bursts of fire coming from down the road.

"You're gonna relieve my command, asshole; well, I just relieved you of yours."

Saying this, Stadholm removed a hand grenade from its canvas container on his pistol belt, rolled the dead major onto his stomach, pulled the pin on the grenade, and placed it under his body, right under the spot where the bullet had exited. Loosening his grip on the safety handle, Stadholm sprinted down the road as fast as he could and was safely out of range when he heard the muffled explosion and thump as the grenade lifted the dead major's body off the ground.

Returning, he looked contemptuously at the body and said sarcastically, "Thanks for diving on that grenade and saving my life, Major. I hope they give you a medal."

In the meantime, the battle in front of them had grown hotter, and it seemed that the Germans were amassing enough firepower to turn Charlie Company's advance. The radio officer had called for reinforcements, and Stadholm could hear the sound of men running up the trail from behind him. A young lieutenant

44

at the front of a column of about fifty men stopped his group when he came across the dead major and the living captain.

Before the lieutenant could ask what was happening, Stadholm spoke first. "The major threw himself on a grenade! He saved my life. Tell your men to be careful, the battle's going on all around us, especially up the road.

"Have your men advance forward, lieutenant, but be careful because the Jerries are all around us."

"Yes, Sir," the lieutenant said, as he turned to start running toward the direction of the firing.

"Lieutenant!"

Surprised by the intensity of Stadholm's call, the other man stopped, turned, and said, "What?"

"That's no way to address a superior officer, Lieutenant! And, when you take leave of a superior officer, even in battle, you salute him."

Looking at Stadholm's glazed eyes, the younger officer simply said, "Fuck you...Fuck you, sir!" before leading his troops away and towards the fight.

And so it went, hour by hour, turning into day by day, eventually becoming a routine of total and utter boredom, punctuated by episodes of sheer panic. Sometimes it was a sporadic sniper, who seemed to kill at random. Other times it was a mine or a booby trap that would claim the unwary. But it was now all turning into a routine. Brigade had sent up reinforcements, so the company was at full strength, and as men were killed or seriously wounded, there was steady traffic up from the replacement depot, usually no more than a three or four-day turnaround after the body or the wounded man had been evacuated.

Patrols went out to probe the strength and location of the enemy forces, made contact and engaged them, and then called for reinforcements. The Americans usually won these skirmishes and battles.

CHAPTER SIX

Dan's Big Mistake

One day, as the war had settled into a routine of sheer boredom, punctuated by sheer terror, a messenger from the command tent was sent to have Fleming report to Captain Stadholm.

"What does that asshole want now?" Dan asked no one in particular.

Smitty, who was sitting closest to Dan while they both were cleaning their rifles, piped up, "He probably wants to give you a medal for your prowess in the boxing ring."

"Yeah, maybe he'll give me a special award. At least it won't be posthumously...not yet, anyway."

Entering the command post tent, Dan came to attention and saluted smartly. "Sir! Corporal Fleming reporting as ordered!" During the recent battles, a battlefield promotion had resulted in Dan's promotion to corporal.

"At ease, Fleming. Nice report...very professional."

"Thank you, Sir."

"Fleming, I want to congratulate you for your performance on D-day. We both saw a lot of action then, and we both performed admirably while under fire. I intend to put you in for a Silver Star because of that."

Dan was both shocked and disgusted that Stadholm was doing this. Dan and his comrades were effectively leaderless as far as Stadholm was concerned. He almost got them killed by freezing when the German soldier had leveled his machine pistol on them. If the thing didn't jam, they'd all be dead by now. Dan bit his tongue and didn't say anything...at least not yet. Stadholm proceeded to read him the citation that he'd prepared:

"…and Corporal Fleming, while under my command and with me throughout this engagement, was able to destroy the gun crew in one pillbox and a subsequent bunker after we had frontally assaulted it…."

"Sir," Fleming interrupted. "Meaning no disrespect, Sir, but that's a load of bullshit. You were nowhere near me when I took out those two emplacements. We didn't see you till the action was nearly completed on the beachhead, and then you disappeared while we were moving inland. Sir, you can take your Silver Star recommendation and shove it up your ass. And, Sir, if you court-martial me for insubordination, I'll finish up this war in the stockade at Leavenworth and come out alive. If there's nothing else, Sir, I'll get back to my squad."

Stadholm was dumbfounded. He sat there glaring at Fleming, unable to utter a word. Fleming again saluted smartly, executed an about-face, and left the red-faced captain seething in his command tent. After Fleming left, Stadholm tore the Silver Star recommendation into shreds and the two men never had a face-to-face conversation after that.

"Whadde want?" Smitty saw that Dan had an ashen look on his face.

"You were right, Smitty. The asshole wanted to put me in for a Silver Star."

"No shit? Wow…what did he say?"

"He read the citation that made it sound like he and I took on the entire German Army and that he was with me when we took the pillbox and bunker on D-day. The write-up was for his own self-glorification so the brass at brigade could see what a fucking hero he was. I was only mentioned because he couldn't put himself in for the medal."

"What a shit-head. What did you say to him?"

"I told him to shove his Silver Star recommendation up his ass and that if he had me court-martialed for insubordination, I'd probably sit out the war fat, dumb, and happy in the stockade at Fort Leavenworth."

Standing up to Stadholm was one mistake that nearly cost Dan his life. Fuming after Dan had left his tent, Stadholm sent for Lieutenant Collingsworth, the most recent leader of the Third Platoon. Collingsworth was made the platoon sergeant after Banks had been killed on D-day, but received a battlefield commission and had become the third, but not the last, platoon leader for the Third Platoon in the European Campaign, courtesy of some very accurate German sniper fire.

"Sir, you wanted to see me?"

"Nice report, Collingsworth. Military courtesy is very important, especially in battle."

Collingsworth didn't reply. He'd seen enough of Stadholm to know what he was like, and like all of the other men in the company, he had no respect for, nor any use for, the man the War Department had placed in control of their destinies.

"Lieutenant, whenever you patrol in either platoon strength or squad strength, I want Corporal Fleming to walk point."

The point position is where the first man in the patrol walked. It was the soldier walking point who first showed his face to enemy ambushes or triggered enemy mines. It was an unwritten rule that everyone rotated through walking point on patrol. That spread the greater risk of getting killed around more or less evenly.

"Do I understand you correctly, Sir? You want Fleming to always walk in the point position?"

"You heard me, Lieutenant! What is it that you don't understand about my order?"

"Sir...the point position, as the Captain knows, is the most dangerous position in a patrol. More men have been killed so far while walking point than any other position during combat patrols."

"Lieutenant, you heard and understood my order and I don't want to hear any shit from you. Fleming has just been assigned to be the permanent point whenever your platoon or his squad goes out on patrol. Now get out of here before I decide to break you back down to sergeant again."

Disgusted, Collingsworth turned to leave the tent.

"Collingsworth!" Stadholm called him up short.

"Did you forget how to take leave of a superior officer once you got promoted?"

Collingsworth turned, saluted, and asked Stadholm in disgust, "Permission to leave, Sir?"

"Permission granted."

Once outside the tent, Collingsworth turned back and gave Stadholm the finger.

"That salute's for you, Sir." he mumbled softly under his breath.

Returning to the position that the Third Platoon was holding, Lieutenant Collingsworth walked over to Dan Fleming's squad.

"Dan, could I see you for a moment...privately?"

"Sure, Lieutenant...what's up?"

"I just got called up to the Company Command Post. Stadholm has a hair across his ass against you for some reason and ordered me to place you in the point position for every patrol that your squad or the platoon makes till the war ends or the Jerries kill you. What did you ever do to him to get him so pissed off at you?"

"I told him to shove his Silver Star recommendation for me up his ass."

"What, are you crazy? One, you deserve a Silver Star for what you did on D-Day alone, and two, it's sheer stupidity to go out of your way to set him off. He's a nut, and if we're not careful, he'll get us all fucking killed. Now he's on your case and I don't know what to do. If I disobey his order he'll bust me, and the two of us will be sharing the point. I hate to do this, Dan, but you're our new permanent point. Keep your bayonet sharpened and tread lightly over those German anti-personnel mines."

Dan felt pretty stupid and didn't know how to answer the lieutenant, his third lieutenant who had also become his friend from all that they'd been through together.

"Look, don't worry about it. It was my own stupid mouth that fucked me. You're right, I should have kept my mouth shut, but that asshole was writing me up to make it look like he and I did all that stuff together. I almost puked when he started reading the citation to me. He wanted the staff at brigade to think that he was a hero rather than the scared rat in a hole that he actually was. 'Out of communication with his company in the fog of war' means that he had dug himself in and was hiding in a hole in the rear while we faced the German gunners. That lieutenant who led the platoon up to pull our nuts out of the fire said that he was close to a quarter mile behind the front. I guess some major who had been with him was killed. I can't understand how that could have happened though because we'd done a pretty good job of clearing that site, and the battle was clearly moving down the road from where that little shit was holed up. I don't understand how someone got close enough to take him out with a grenade. The only Germans in that area had been dead for at least two and a half hours."

"Yeah...well anyway, congratulations on your new job. Anything you want me to tell your mother if they end up sending you home in a box?"

"You know, Collingsworth, you didn't have to say that! I did what I did to Stadholm and I'll have to pay for it, but you don't have to make it worse. Point, medics, and officers...that's what those snipers like to focus on. I think we've lost almost as many officers as we have points, so please don't give me any more shit than I've already got."

The war moved forward and Dan got used to walking the point position on patrol. All of his senses became incredibly sharpened, especially his powers of observation. He developed both a wide and deep peripheral vision as well as a sharply focused vision. Over the time that he walked point he spotted two trip-wires for anti-personnel mines, as well as a pressure plate mine that would have killed him and half the squad if any of them had stepped on it.

He spotted and avoided three ambushes, one because he noticed a faint movement in the distance beside the road that his squad was patrolling, and the other two because he saw that someone had recently cut brush beside the road they were on, cut brush to camouflage their ambush position further up the road.

It was his last patrol at point, though, that brought him closer to his death than any time before or after that.

CHAPTER SEVEN

The Combat Patrol – War on a Retail Level

The war wasn't going well for the Germans. Dan's company was patrolling a sector about 150 kilometers from the French border with Germany. Their advance had been halted as they waited for their supply lines to catch up with them. They were low on ammunition and would be sitting targets if they ran out. They were in a defensive position around a small town. A few of the men had discovered a brothel in the town and word spread quickly among the troops. Smitty, pining for Gwen, his intended, took some comfort there, and over the three days they were waiting for their supply line to reach them, had managed to blow the $100 he had kept out of his winnings from the Grabowski fight on a French prostitute.

As they were moving forward out of town, Smitty confided to his best friend, "Dan, you won't believe this, but I'm in love."

"I know, I know, Smitty. If you spent as much time cleaning your rifle as you do looking at that picture of Gwen, you'd have a better chance of getting out of here alive and back to her."

"No...no, Dan. I realize now that I was infatuated with Gwen. You were right, and I'm glad that I took your advice and sent the money from the fight to my mother. No, Dan, this time I'm really in love with Yvette, the woman I just met when we were holed up for three days. I love her and she loves me. She said that she'd wait for me and marry me after the war.

"Dan...I mean it. This is real. This time I know that I'm really in love and that she loves me...."

"Smitty, you don't mean that whore that you've been spending time with?"

"She's no whore, Dan, and you have no right to talk about her that way! She was working at that brothel, cooking and doing stuff like that. She told me that it was different when she saw me, that it was love at first sight.

"She loves me, Dan, and she wants to marry me and have my babies. You don't have any right to talk about her that way, Dan!"

"OK..OK..Smitty. I'm sorry...I didn't mean to hurt your feelings. You did pay her to have her sleep with you, didn't you?"

"I gave her money! She never charged me anything. Dan, she loves me."

"Yeah...yeah...I'm sorry, Smitty. I didn't mean anything. I just misunderstood the situation. I didn't mean to hurt you or anything like that."

"Look, Dan...I want to ask you a favor. I love Yvette and I've written a letter that I'd like you to give to her if...if ...you know, if I get killed or something. She works in a brothel that's called "The House of the Lone Ranger."

"OK, Smitty, I'll do that. You know I didn't mean anything. You're the best friend I have in the world and I'd never say anything to hurt you."

"I know, Dan...I know. I'm just a little sensitive about it. Leinhard has been giving me a lot of shit about it and it's starting to get to me."

"Ignore Leinhard. He's pissed at you because he lost $300 on your fight with Grabowski. He's a shit-head."

After smoothing over his relationship with Smitty, Dan continued cleaning his rifle. He placed the letter in the bottom of his combat pack, hoping that he'd never have to deliver it.

Dan was starting to feel a little cocky about his prowess walking point. In fact, he had become somewhat of a legend in the company because of that, as well as his insubordination to Stadholm. Picking up the mines and the potential ambushes made him a hero to most of the men in his squad...the ones who were still alive anyway, but after hearing what he had said to Stadholm, Dan had become a hero to all of his comrades.

The new first sergeant came into the Third Platoon's area, walked over to Dan's squad, and said, "I need two volunteers from each platoon for a dangerous mission...Fleming and Smith, come with me to HQ."

"Volunteer ...my ass!"

"Come on; come on; come on...stop bitching. I'm just giving you guys a chance to become the war's latest heroes. You'll both be on the cover of Stars and Stripes.

The ten "volunteers" assembled and were briefed by Lieutenant Miller, Dan's friend from the troop ship ride across the Atlantic. Dan thought that Miller looked ashen and upset.

"We know that there's a concentration of German forces somewhere in the valley ahead of us. Intelligence tells us that there may be some Panzer elements attached to the troop concentration as well. We want you to probe the enemy position and try to get an idea of where they are and how large the concentration is. I don't want you to make contact if you can avoid it. Any questions?

"Remember...the war's going the right way for us. I don't want to see anyone get killed. No heroes...just let us know where they are and how many of them are there ...if you can find that out. OK, Sergeant, they're yours...good luck."

Miller looked nervous and upset and intuitively Dan knew that there was something wrong with his friend.

Sergeant Crawford was tough and had been involved in a lot of action. "Before we move out, make sure everything's secured. Check the man in front of you. No unnecessary noise and make sure that anything that's shiny is either removed or covered.

"OK, let's go. Keep fifteen yards apart and be ready to get into the bushes as soon as the point signals. You heard the lieutenant...no heroes. If Jerry drives by without seeing us ...I don't want any ambush. Let him go and we'll just move along and mind our own business."

Sergeant Crawford and the eight men he was leading knew the routine by now. They had confidence with Fleming in the lead and they understood that their mission was to look and see rather than to stop and fight.

They had also become expert in the art of camouflage. You could walk to within two feet of them before realizing that you were standing in front of a human being instead of a bush. Dan had perfected the art better than any of his squad mates. Crawford was in the middle of the group, and after they started out, Smitty said to Dan, "Look – this isn't right. You've saved our asses enough times. I'm walking point on this one. Get behind me!"

Dan wasn't interested in fighting with his closest friend in the Army, but he refused to let Smitty pass him as they moved out along the shoulders of the wooded dirt road.

They were about an hour and a half into the patrol and fifteen minutes after their first break, during which Smitty had taped his canteen cover shut. They moved slowly, one at a time out of the bushes and ahead for ten yards or so, with the men in the bush covering the person who was moving. The dirt road was about sixteen feet wide with heavy forest and brush on each side. It was Dan's turn to move, and from his point position, he could see that the road turned to the right about 150 yards ahead of him. He was a little nervous because there was a waterfall somewhere in the woods around the corner that was making a lot of noise. He couldn't hear very well and he wouldn't be able to hear anything coming from around the corner.

Dan had a funny feeling, a sixth sense if you will, that this wasn't a good situation. He was more concerned, though, with the possibility of mines in the road rather than with something coming around the corner. The last man in the patrol had moved into cover, and now Dan stepped cautiously out of the bushes on the left side of the road and moved toward the center. The mines he had come across in the past had been placed along the sides of the road where they'd be triggered by the tires of a vehicle or the treads of a tank. From Dan's experience, he thought it safer to advance along the center of the road to his next place of cover.

Moving in a crouch, slowly and with his rifle at the ready, Dan had gone only about two yards when he heard a loud clanking noise in front of him over the sound of the waterfall and was stunned to see a tracked German Panther tank turn the corner, traveling at about thirty miles per hour.

The turret gunner saw Dan almost instantly and started firing at him, but the speed of the tank made anything like accurate marksmanship, even with a machine gun, near impossible.

Dan turned and raced back in the direction from which they had just come, away from the tank and towards a large rock off to his left on the side of the road. Diving behind the rock, Dan could hear the bullets cutting off small branches on the trees all around him.

Smitty held his position in the woods on the same side of the road as Dan raced past him toward the cover of the rock. And the tank, now moving slowly and more deliberately, passed him by and stopped about fifteen feet from the rock so the turret gunner could take better aim at Dan's position.

Stepping quickly from his cover, Smitty moved around behind the tank and carefully mounted it, moving up behind the turret. His canteen, which he had secured with black friction tape, somehow worked itself loose out of its broken carrier, and just as Smitty noiselessly dropped a grenade into the tank hatch behind the turret gunner, the canteen fell and clattered loudly down the outside of the tank to the ground.

The turret gunner, hearing the canteen, turned as he pulled a Luger pistol out of his shoulder holster and shot Smitty in the head at point blank range just as the grenade exploded. The explosion badly wounded the turret gunner, and the next man in the patrol behind Smitty shot and killed the wounded tanker just before the ammunition stored in the bowels of the tank, triggered by the grenade explosion, began to explode.

Smitty had fallen off the tank and was crying out loudly in pain. Dan bolted from his cover and raced to his dying friend.

"Dan...Dan...the letter to Yvette...promise me you'll deliver that to her...promise me, Dan...promise me, Dan...tell her I love her."

Dan could barely make out the words coming from Smitty's mouth now because he was gurgling with blood in his throat and spitting large volumes of blood as he spoke.

"I will, Smitty...I will."

And as he said those words, the best friend that Dan Fleming had in the world died in his arms.

By now, the fire in the tank was raging, and Dan could hear the screams of the dying tank crew, trapped in their iron coffin. The dead turret gunner hung with the top half of his body resting over the open hatch on his machine gun, enveloped in flames and smoke, appearing to jump every time another shell exploded beneath him.

Dan could hear their screams of agony and smell their burning flesh. It was a smell that he'd carry with him for the rest of his life.

Crawford came running up and said, "We've gotta move. There's bound to be more of them around the corner and the explosions will bring them all here. Let's get Smitty on a poncho and get the hell out of here before half the German Army shows up to reclaim their tank."

One of the men took the Army-issue poncho off his pistol belt and spread it out beside Smitty. A couple of them picked him up gently and placed him on the olive drab rubber sheet. Then four of them each took a corner of the poncho, lifted Smitty off the ground, and started running back down the road in front of the others in the patrol who were covering the rear.

By now, there were no more screams coming from the burning hulk of the German vehicle, but the stench of burning flesh was overwhelming, as flames and smoke poured out of the turret.

Thoughts of Smitty and the German tank crew branded themselves on Dan's mind as he turned to follow the others. Their screams, the smell of their burning flesh...these young German tankers; they were probably much like himself, Dan thought...probably draftees who'd been put in the tank corps instead of the infantry. Would their mothers ever know that they'd died towards the end of a war, consumed in pain and agony by the fires of Hell? In all likelihood, he thought, they'd all died anonymously, ignominious and anonymous, known only to their god, and in an abstract way, to the men who had killed them. Dan was behind the others as they raced away from the area. He glanced back just as they turned another corner of the road. His final view of the tragic scene behind him included about half a dozen German soldiers standing in awe while looking at the body of the turret gunner. The dead gunner was still hanging half on his machine gun and half way in the tank and was being consumed by the hellfires, still jumping with each explosion.

The patrol now raced back from the charnel house in the road, carrying the body of their dead comrade.

As they approached their position, the forward sentry challenged them.

"Halt! Who goes there?"

"Friend!"

"Show yourself, friend. Advance and be recognized." And the patrol came into view of the sentry.

"What color's the White House today, friend?"

"Green," came the reply.

"Oh, shit...who got it now?" the sentry said, as he spotted the four men carrying a body on the poncho.

"Smitty...he took out a German tank and saved us all. It was unbelievable, the most courageous thing I've ever seen, and we're alive because of it."

Crawford wasn't that close to Smitty, but he'd witnessed the heroism of the other man's final sacrifice.

"Shit...I'm sorry to hear that...you missed all the action back here."

"Oh, yeah...what happened?" Crawford asked.

"A sniper took out Stadholm."

"What a shame...what a shame it didn't happen before now. Hey, Fleming!" Crawford turned to the morose soldier who had taken over from one of the soldiers carrying Smitty back. Dan was attached to one corner of the poncho holding Smitty's body. "Your time in hell's over...Stadholm's dead...you'll never have to walk point again."

Dan didn't say anything. He was overwhelmed by the death of one of the only two men in the company he'd become close to. Crawford understood that and turning to the sentry asked, "Who's the company commander now?"

"Lieutenant Miller, from the Second Platoon."

"Good...Miller's a decent guy. How'd Stadholm get it?"

"All I know is that it was a sniper. The graves registration guys are coming up to take him back...ship him back to whatever hole he had crawled out of before he went in the Army. They'll probably pack Smitty up and take him with them.

"Miller was given a battlefield promotion to captain and it doesn't look like battalion's going to replace him...at least till he gets killed. "

Dan was still in shock over Smitty's death and walked back to his squad to break the news. He just wanted to crawl away himself and die somewhere. His friend died saving his life and Dan couldn't do anything to save him. The gurgling sound of Smitty's voice and the smell of the tank crew's burning flesh wouldn't leave Dan's mind. The other guys in the squad knew enough to leave Dan alone in his grief. He appreciated that and went off away from the others, alone in his thoughts and sorrow.

The day was moving on and they were preparing for night. New sentry posts had been set out in the woods surrounding their position and they all dug in for the night. Dan was exhausted and soon fell asleep, with the pain of the earlier encounter still searing and burning in his mind.

The morning came too quickly, and one of the company clerks came up to Dan's foxhole, shaking him awake.

"Dan...sorry to bother you, but Lieutenant...I mean, Captain Miller wants to see you at the command tent."

"Yeah...yeah, I'm coming."

Pulling himself out of his hole, Dan walked the 200 yards or so over to the command post. Entering, he saw his other friend, a disheveled looking Captain Miller talking on the field phone, looking as if he hadn't slept in a week.

"Dan, come in."

"Captain...what happened? You look more exhausted than usual?"

"The nightmare gets worse, Dan. Stadholm got killed and I'm trying to figure out how to run the company. I've just been fighting with battalion to get more supplies up here. They want us to continue to advance, but they don't understand that we can't fight the Wehrmacht by throwing stones at them.

"Look, I've not been in the Army that long, but the colonel wants me to take command of the company. I wanted to ask you about Smitty's death because I want to send a letter home to his mother when things slow down, and from what I hear from Crawford, I want to put Smitty in for the Congressional Medal of Honor, posthumously. I'd like you to fill me in on the details of the action."

Dan spent twenty minutes with Ed Miller, both making an after-action report, as well as crying on his friend's shoulder about the death of Smitty. Again, Dan thought that there was something wrong with his friend, but attributed it to the stress of taking command of the entire company.

CHAPTER EIGHT

Michael Smith and
The Congressional Medal of Honor

They concluded their discussion, with Miller telling Dan that he'd like him to take the company jeep and drive back to battalion with the recommendation for Smitty to be awarded the Medal of Honor. He said that he'd need a day to prepare it, but that he wanted to get it there as soon as possible before another crisis intervened. He told Dan that he'd like him to report back at 0:730 the next morning, and that he'd have it prepared by then.

Reporting back with the jeep the next morning, Dan found Miller. Miller handed Dan the envelope with the recommendation.

"Here, Dan. Open it and see if it's accurate. I tried to make it as factual as I could, and at the same time emphasize Smitty's heroics."

Dan took a couple of minutes to read the citation and Captain Miller could see the tears forming as Dan turned to the second page.

"It's fine, Lieu...Captain."

"Good, thanks Dan. When you get back to battalion – I think they're located in that last town we were holed up in – give this to Corporal Lancilotti, the colonel's aide. Lancilotti will be expecting it. Then get back as soon as you can. We're not likely to remain here very long because they're supposed to get a convoy with ammo and supplies up here sometime this afternoon. If we do move forward, just be careful that you don't outrun us and drive into the retreating German Army."

"Yes, Sir...I'll get back ASAP."

"Good...be careful, Dan. There are still plenty of detached German troops wandering around in the woods, and I'd hate to see you run into one or more of them."

"Thank you, Sir. I'll be careful, and I'll get the battalion motor pool to change the oil and transmission fluid on this chariot."

"Better yet," said Miller, "maybe you can trade it in on a newer model, maybe a green Studebaker with a sun visor in front? Or at least dump it and steal another one that will always work when we want to use it."

His drive through the woods to the rear was uneventful, and Dan soon found himself in the town they'd left a couple of days ago. The motor pool had been set up in a bombed out stone building that had once been the first floor of a factory. The front wall of the building had been demolished in an artillery barrage, leaving a gaping hole that trucks and jeeps could drive through, perfect for garaging any vehicles that needed work.

Sergeant Henry Kasienski was in charge of the motor pool and he greeted Dan as he drove through the hole in the wall. Someone had piled the rubble from the blown out wall in two piles beside the opening, and Dan thought that it looked like a nice architectural feature, an entryway to the bay of the building.

"Hey, kid – what can I do for you?"

Kasienski was chewing on a cigar that looked like it had been in his mouth from birth.

"Sarge, Captain Miller from Charlie Company told me to bring this in to get it checked over and worked on. Sometimes it won't start, and the brakes don't work a lot. Do you think we could trade it in for a new one?"

"Not likely, kid, but we'll have it good as new in no time. How soon do you need it?"

"I'd like to get back to my unit by tomorrow. Do you think you can have it ready by then?"

"No sweat, kid. Show up after 0:930 and I'll have it ready to roll."

"Thanks Sarge. One other thing...Do you know where I can find the House of the Lone Ranger?"

"You want to get laid? Sure, kid. When you go out front here, take a right and walk down three blocks. You'll see a church in front of you on a corner. When you turn the corner, you'll see the Lone Ranger next to the church...big sign out front."

"Thanks again, Sarge. See you in the morning."

Walking down the street, Dan saw that the town was starting to come back to life now that the battle zone had moved ten miles or so east. The town was fast becoming a staging area for the American Army, with truck after truck rolling in towards the end of the supply chain. That chain originated in places all over America, crossed the Atlantic by ship, and ended up in convoys of two and a half ton trucks fanning out all over Europe, moving eastward toward the front.

There was an MP jeep parked in front of the building next to the church. The structure looked like it could have been a rectory or a convent in an earlier life. As the motor pool sergeant had told him, there was a large hand-lettered sign in front of it that read: "Welcome to the House of the Lone Ranger American Soldiers."

Dan decided that it might be better to explore the town, try to rustle up some chow, and return later when the house was not being guarded by the MPs.

Dan wanted to find Battalion HQ, so he asked one of the MPs standing in front of the brothel for directions. The MP responded, "You know where the motor pool is? Three or four blocks beyond that is the town hall. The colonel has set up shop there."

"Thanks...what's going on here?"

"The place doesn't open till 19:00 hours, and the proprietor wants us to keep her eager customers away till then so her employees can get some sleep."

"Oh."

Dan walked away from the House of the Lone Ranger. He headed back past the motor pool towards the town hall, the new battalion command center. Entering the building, he was surprised to run into a soldier wearing a clean, pressed, and starched uniform.

"Excuse me. Is Corporal Lancilotti around?"

"Yeah, down the hall, just inside the mayor's outer office."

Heading down the hall, Dan noticed that the ornate detail of the building got richer and richer as he got closer to the seat of power, now the American Army rather than the civilian mayor.

"Excuse me, Corporal...I'm Corporal Fleming from Charlie Company. Captain Miller said you'd be expecting me."

"Yeah, come in Corporal. You're Fleming?"

"Yeah."

"Before the field phone went dead, Captain Miller told me that you were on the patrol with the dead man and close to him when he got killed, and that he'd died in your arms. Tell me what happened and I'll try to work on Miller's recommendation a little before sending it on to brigade. From what the captain told me, this is one we want to push hard."

Dan told him the story of the patrol, the tank, and Smitty's death. Lancilotti listened in awed respect as Dan, with tears in his eyes, went through every detail of the combat, and how Smitty had died in his arms.

"This blood on my uniform is his."

"Look, Fleming, I'm really sorry about your friend. I have a buddy of mine who works at brigade...for the general...and I'll make sure this gets to him, and I'll ask him what, if anything, he can do to move it along."

"Thanks...I appreciate it. He was a good friend and he died a hero. It'd be good to see him recognized for that."

Dan hung around the city hall for a while, at one point finding an out-of-the-way place in the cellar where he fell asleep for about four or five hours. It was dark when he awoke, but when he went upstairs, the place was still buzzing. If anything, it was busier than when he was there in the afternoon. Going outside into the early evening air, Dan was surprised at how refreshed he felt. This was the longest uninterrupted sleep he'd been able to grab since before they'd landed on D-Day.

Chapter Nine

Dan's Visit to the House of the Lone Ranger

Retracing his steps, Dan passed the church and, feeling very uncomfortable, entered the House of the Lone Ranger. He was right; it had been a convent at some point. Off to the left, just inside the door, was the convent chapel, intact and well maintained, as if the whores were expecting to be called to Mass or the Angelus at any minute.

"Welcome, soldier" the Madam said in accented English as she approached Dan. "Would you like a nice girl?"

"I'm looking for Yvette."

"Yes, she's a lovely young girl, one of our favorites...she's been away from us for over a month, but has just returned."

"Yvette."

"Oui, Mama."

"The girls call me mother because I take such good care of them."

"Yvette, my name is Dan..."

"Voulez vous coucher avec moi, monsieur?"

"Yvette, I'm a friend of Michael Smith. He had asked me to give you something if he got killed. He died in combat two days ago...in my arms...and with his dying breath he asked me to give you this letter."

Dan's eyes were welling up with tears as he spoke.

"This Michael Smith," Yvette said in flawless English, "do I know him? Was he one of my customers?"

At those words, Dan Fleming felt a sharp pain, the hurt of his dead friend's naiveté was his own hurt now, and Smitty's betrayal by this woman seemed to him to be the betrayal of Smitty and Dan by all women. It'd be a couple of years before he'd realize how wrong he was.

"He was one of your customers. He was here about six weeks ago before our unit moved on, and he was in love with you."

"All of my customers are in love with me, and I love them too. I love you too, John, and I'll go back to America with you and have your babies. But that will be then and this is now; you can sleep with me now, if you have my price in dollars...no scrip.

"Tell me about this Michael Smith. How many times did he have me?"

"He loved you, Yvette, naïve bastard that he was, and he did want to marry you and take you home to America. But, he's dead, and his dying words were for you. He was killed saving my life, and he asked me to give you this letter he had written to you before we were ambushed."

Yvette was slowly unbuttoning her blouse while Dan was talking and now pulled it back off her breasts.

"Here, Yvette, take the letter."

"I don't want to see it, John. He's dead. You're here with me now, John, and you're alive. Sleep with me, John. Pay me now, but take me back to America. Marry me and I'll have your babies."

"What kind of fucking animal are you?" Dan exploded, the irony in his question escaping him. "You fucking whore...you take all his money for sex and the poor bastard goes out and dies to liberate your piss-ant country. You don't give a shit one way or another, you fucking, heartless whore!"

"John – you arrogant bastard – you all die! Germans, Americans, it makes no difference to me. You're all like praying mantises; you have sex with me for money, then after your orgasms, you go off to die."

Dan's anger had overcome him, but the sight of this lithe, naked woman aroused him like he'd never been aroused before. The combined passions of his lust and his hatred consumed Dan. He wanted her as badly as he wanted to strike her for the way she had treated his dead friend.

"John....come to me," she said, as she started to unbutton his uniform shirt, and in the end he couldn't resist her, and followed her meekly to her room.

"This was your first time, wasn't it, Corporal Fleming?" she said as she played with the dog tags around Dan's neck.

Dan didn't answer her. He was angry with himself for what he had just done. He felt that he'd just violated the trust of the man who had died for him.

"Daniel Fleming….take me back to America, marry me, and I will have your babies! I know you hate me for what I do, but I do this to survive. I can't get involved with my customers. It's business to me, a way for me to survive, and so many of them like your friend go off to be killed. Like lambs to the slaughter they all go, and I'm their last comfort before they die. How many hundreds of dead men have slept with me on the way to their graves? I don't know, and I could never know. If I thought about them as individuals rather than as a collective 'John', I'd go insane.

"You're different, Daniel. I don't want to see you go; I won't let you die. I don't know why I say this, but there's something between us that I don't feel with my customers. Here, take your money back. I don't want it. I want you! You're different, and you have to understand me and how I came to be in this place…in this business.

"I had lived in this building for three years as a postulate in an order of nuns that has been in this village for hundreds of years.

When the Germans came, an SS unit was the first to enter the town. After forcing the door and entering the convent, the soldiers called all of the sisters together in the front hall. We were terrified. Then each of them took one of us and forced us to lead them to our rooms, where they raped us. It was the first time ever for me. I was terrified. My rapist, a young soldier, felt terribly guilty after what he had done. When he was on top of me, I saw that he was wearing a scapular around his neck.

"Someone blew a whistle, and the soldiers started pushing the sisters out of their rooms, forcing them downstairs. My soldier put his index finger to his lips and motioned for me to get under the bed. There was a pounding on my door, and one of my soldier's superiors came in yelling, asking where I was. I know enough German to understand that my soldier said he had killed me for resisting him and stuffed my body into the closet. Then they both ran out into the hall, firing pistols into the ceiling as they pushed the older and slower nuns down the stairs.

"The next thing I heard was when they were forcing all of the sisters out into the snow on the steps in front, where they murdered every last one of them. Trucks came by the next morning, and I saw some of the Jewish men from town being forced to throw their bodies onto the trucks. I've never seen those men again. I heard later that the Nazis had dug through the earth at one part of the cemetery with bulldozers and had their Jewish captives unload the bodies of the sisters into that hole. Then they killed the Jewish men, threw them into the hole, and covered over the whole thing.

"I was in shock after they left, still terrified. The temperature was dropping, so I went to my closet and the closets of some of the dead sisters to get warm clothing, and then returned under my bed.

"I snuck a look out of the corner of the window at one point and saw the blood red snow on the steps, slowly turning pink as new snow was falling, turning the massacre scene into one of peace and tranquility.

"Daniel...I've been to America. I lived there for three years before entering the convent. My father was a French foreign diplomat, and when the Vichy government came into power, they recalled him. This was before the diplomats were interred. Though my mother wanted him to stay in America and defect, they returned to France, where the Nazis murdered my entire family. I'm the only one left, and if it hadn't been for the young S.S. corporal, I would have joined them in death.

"I didn't know what to do after all of the sisters were murdered, so I stayed under the bed for two days till Jurgen...that was his name...returned with food and water. He fed me. I ate ravenously, and then he raped me again. This continued over a two-week period till one day he was leaving, and a partisan sniper killed him with one shot through his forehead. I saw him lying face up in the snow on the steps where my sisters had been murdered. His eyes were open and he looked very much at peace.

"One of the sentries spotted the sniper and called out. They surrounded the building he was in and exchanged gunfire with him till one of them set the building on fire. He kept shooting at them till the end, when the flames reached the top floor. There was a lull in the firing while the entire building was consumed with flames. Then I heard one more shot from the top of the building, and after that, just the noise of the fire, as the whole thing was consumed.

"I didn't know what to do, but a week later two Wehrmacht trucks pulled up in front of the convent and twenty women were sent inside. They were all speaking in French, and when I heard that, I went to the balcony over the foyer and called out to them. Most of them were from Marseilles and had been rounded up by the SS to service their troops in a field brothel. They gave me the name Yvette, and I joined them. So, from Sister Mary Magdalene the nun, I became Yvette, the prostitute.

"Marry me, Daniel. Take me to America and let me have your babies. I mean it. You're different! I sense that, and I want you."

"Yvette...I'm sorry. I had no idea. But...no....I won't marry you and take you to America. I've been lucky so far...God, you don't know how lucky I've been, but I'm like all of the other Johns you've slept with. I could be dead in a very

PAUL D. SNYDER

short time. You don't know where it might come from. Like your young SS corporal, a sniper could take me out tomorrow.

"I'll give you my address in America, Yvette, and if we both survive this war, I'll do what I can to help you, and I'll pray for you and for all of us who are consumed by this madness, this unreal madness.

"I have to go, Yvette; I'm going back to the front soon. Pray for me and for my dead friend.

"Michael Smith loved you, and his dying words were for you...now I see why."

Dan wrote his name and Boston address on a piece of paper and then handed it to the young prostitute.

"Dan Fleming," she said, reading the paper closely, "and is this your real address?" she asked quizzically. "I've been to Boston, Dan, once with Papa. We went by train from Union Station in Washington to your South Station. He went to address a French-American friendship group on Bastille Day. They had a rally at your Faneuil Hall. That was another lifetime, Dan, another world; another place all together. I was Marie LeMay then. They called me Mary la Fleur, Mary the flower, because people said I was beautiful. I don't feel beautiful, Dan. Dan, please take me with you to America. I mean it. I do want to marry you and have your babies...please, Dan."

"I'm going, Yvette. Write me after the war if you survive, and if I'm not dead, I'll see what I can do to help you."

"Don't say good-bye, Dan, say au revoir...till later."

"Yeah....bye Yvette," Dan said, as he walked through the door of her convent room onto the upstairs balcony of the House of the Lone Ranger.

Dan headed back to the battalion motor pool to get his Jeep to take him back to the company.

"Good morning, Sergeant."

"Hey, kid...did you find the whore house OK last night?"

"Yeah, I did, Sarge. Your directions were perfect."

"Good! What can I do for you today?"

"I'd like to sign out my Jeep to take me back to Charlie Company."

"I think your jeep has gone to a better place. It was worse than I thought. The transmission was shot and the front bearings were almost stripped. I'm using it for parts now, but I've got one coming in, in about fifteen minutes. The night duty officer signed it out at about 4:00 A.M. I think you might have bumped into him over at the Lone Ranger. He's kind of a crazy fuck. None of the grunts in the command can stand him. Truth is that most of them hate his guts. I'm surprised that no one has tried to kill him, he's such an asshole. When he's OD, he routinely has the duty NCO wake everyone in the middle of the night to fall in on the street. Then he keeps them in formation for about fifteen minutes, counting off over and over. A lot of people have complained to the C.O., but the Major hasn't done anything about him. They're both a couple of assholes, if you ask me."

The motor pool sergeant's discourse was interrupted by the ringing of the field phone.

"Wait a minute...wait a minute. Hold on. I'm coming as fast as I can."

The sergeant moved as quickly as he could across the motor pool.

"I got it! I got it! Hang on!!

342nd Motor Pool. Sergeant Kasienski speaking, Sir."

...

"Yes, Sir; Yes, Colonel!"

...

"Holy shit...we were just talking about him. Do they know who did it? Friendly fire...no shit?"

...

"No, sir. I'm sorry, Sir."

...

"No, Sir, I don't usually address an officer like that. It's just such a shock, Sir.

"Yes, Sir. I'll send someone right over to pick up the Jeep. Will the M.P.s release it, Sir?"

...

"Yes, Sir. Thank you, Sir."

Turning to Fleming, the motor pool sergeant's voice had an incredulous ring to it.

"Unbelievable, Fleming...simply un-fucking believable. Ulrich, the guy I was just telling you about, was killed a couple of hours ago, not too far from the Lone Ranger...shot in the head by a sniper. The only question is whether he was killed by a German, a civilian, or one of his own men. The MPs are investigating, but the colonel said that they'd released his Jeep. They'll probably pack him up and ship him home a hero. We'll all be heroes, Fleming, if we travel home in a box. They'll give the asshole a couple of medals and tell his family that he made the ultimate sacrifice for his country and died a hero. His citation won't mention that he was probably killed by one of the men under his command, and that he died around the corner from a French whorehouse in a town that no one'll remember. O'Brien will have to do a lot of fancy writing to tell Mrs. Ulrich how her husband died a hero protecting his men from the scourge of VD.

"Look....his Jeep's back around the corner from the Lone Ranger. Go over and get it. It should have plenty of gas, but bring it back here if there's less than three-quarters of a tank. You leave a vehicle for more than twenty minutes here and one of these Frog bastards will try to siphon all of the gas out of it.

"The front has been moving forward at rapid speed. You'll probably be surprised at how far you'll have to go to catch up with Charlie Company. They're probably well inside Germany by now. The Krauts are in full retreat and our guys, from what I hear, are mopping up rather than fighting tactical battles with them. On to Berlin...and then home. I just hope that they don't have another Bulge up their sleeves...regrouping for a massive counterattack.

"But, at any rate, battalion got orders to move forward another 50 Kilometers, and that's a lot of real estate to cover. I've got to get all of this crap, tools, spare parts, oil and the tankers out of here by twelve hundred hours this Thursday.

"Take good care of Ulrich's Jeep. I hope it brings you better luck than it did him."

"Thanks, Sarge...we couldn't have moved that far in a couple of days. Charlie Company was only fifteen miles from battalion the other day when I came in."

"You don't understand, Fleming, either the sneaky bastards are regrouping for another attack, sucking us into their trap, or this is a full-scale rout. Charlie Company's probably outrunning its supply line in chasing them down."

Dan was skeptical about Kasinski's view of things. The screams of the German soldiers, trapped in their burning tank, were too recent in his mind for him to believe that the rest of the war would be a motor tour across Germany.

Smitty's heroism and death were vivid in his mind too...no, they were burned into his soul, and the thought that the ferocious skirmish he'd been in a few days earlier was for naught, the dying embers from a conflagration; this was difficult to accept. "No," he thought, "the European campaign wouldn't turn into a walk in the park."

"You might be right, Sarge. They might be regrouping, and we may have another Battle of the Bulge before this thing's over."

"OK, Fleming, the Jeep's signed out to Charlie Company in your name. Go get it and get out of my hair. I've got to pack all of this shit and move on."

Retracing his steps, Fleming passed in front of the House of the Lone Ranger in search of the Jeep. His movements were followed from an upstairs bedroom by the eyes of a lithe young woman who was gently holding her stomach.

CHAPTER TEN

Dan Attempts to Rejoin His Company

The lieutenant's body was covered with a blanket, and a couple of MPs were standing around guarding it, chatting like a couple of neighbors talking over the backyard hedge on an early spring morning. As Dan approached them, their casual conversation changed, and they became all business...hard-assed, like all MPs were to enlisted men beneath their rank.

"Don't come any further, soldier!" one of the MPs said, turning to challenge Fleming. "This is a murder scene and we don't want you screwing up any of the evidence!"

"Look, I've come for the Jeep. Sergeant Kasienski at the motor pool told me that the investigators had released it, and I signed it out to Charlie Company."

"Sorry, soldier....that Jeep's going nowhere till the colonel himself releases it and tells me personally that it's OK for you to take it."

"Look, I've got to get back to my unit. I used another Jeep as a messenger and was supposed to take this one back to my company. This guy in the mud had taken it when someone killed him. I'm gonna be friggin AWOL and get myself court martialed if I don't get my ass back there."

"Sorry pal, that's your tough shit. Orders are orders. Why don't you hitch a ride with some of the guys in the transportation unit? They're moving Battalion HQ closer to the front, and they'll at least get you closer to your unit."

"I guess I don't have much choice...where's the best place to catch a lift?"

"They're assembling a couple of blocks over in the center of town, by the bandstand, and I think they'll be pulling out within the hour."

"Thanks for nothing! I'll get over there....take good care of that guy under the blanket, and thank him for fucking up my Jeep ride through the countryside."

"Yeah....fuck you, too. You'd better get out of here before we throw your ass in the stockade."

"Hey, Corporal, can you tell me who's in charge of marshalling this convoy?"

"Talk with Major James; he's down around the fifth truck behind the water buffalo. Don't even think about smoking though. Half the trucks are loaded with ammo, and it would hardly do for you to blow yourself up just as the war's ending."

"Yeah...bad habit. I should give it up," Dan said, scuffing a half smoked cigarette out in the mud.

A cigarette ad jingle suddenly came to his mind. How odd that after listening to that jingle and smoking all through high school, it had just come to Dan's mind for the first time since he had landed on D-day. The words resonated in his mind, bringing him back to other times, worlds ago, worlds impossible to conceive; worlds that never could have happened; fantasy worlds. Those were worlds where you didn't sit down to lunch after passing a pile of immolated corpses and only being concerned because you were eating canned meat for your third consecutive meal. A pile of burned corpses. Just another day in the battle against fascism.

How could he have ever lived in a world where his biggest concern was whether he'd have a date on a Saturday night, or pass French for the semester? "Voulez vous coucher avec moi?" He remembered saying that to his French teacher in the first week of class, not knowing what the words meant, but having been put up to it by one of his classmates who claimed a superior knowledge of the language. He'd wondered why she'd turned beet red and told him to report to the principal's office while the class roared in laughter.

Now he knew what those words meant.

That world must be living in his imagination, because it couldn't be living in his memory. Smoking a butt on the way home from football practice with the guys, talking about all of the girls in their class, which were the prettiest, and which were easy...that must have been a fantasy. Now, nothing was as important as the next meal or bowel movement. A blanket-covered body in the mud guarded by a couple of MPs...nothing to get excited about, just part of the routine.

Close relationships shattered as, one after another, his friends were killed or maimed..."Would Tracy Higgins go to the senior prom with me if I asked her, or would she rather go with Mike Harrington, the captain of the basketball team?"

"Another world...a whole different reality," he thought. "How could I have been so shallow?"

Dan Fleming didn't realize it on that raw cold day in early spring, but his world would never...could never...be the same again. The world he'd known before the war was gone now, changed and gone forever, and he'd never be able to go back. Once you've entered the gates of hell there's no turning back.

Fleming's world had become a never-ending battle for survival that totally consumed him. He had honed his self-preservation instinct to a razor fine edge. The smallest detail, from not carrying loose change in his pocket because it could make noise, to not wearing a watch on his wrist because the reflection might give his position away; Dan thought of everything and anything that might possibly slant the odds of staying alive in his favor. The other members of his squad used to ride him about how often he cleaned his rifle, how often he sharpened his bayonet, and how much effort he put into digging and camouflaging his fox hole when the platoon would dig in for a night or a couple of days.

Once, a couple of weeks before he got killed, Smitty joked that they should preserve Dan's foxholes after the unit moved through an area.

"Danno, your excavations should remain as a tribute and a monument to the American fighting man," Smitty used to say. "They should put a sign saying, 'Fleming slept here' instead of all that 'Kilroy was here' shit that's painted everywhere...at least in the rear."

Dan thought that digging a deep foxhole and concealing it well would increase his chances for survival. Sometimes he thought it'd be nice if he could just stay in one of his holes till the end of the war. Then he could come out, drink champagne, and go home to his family. He knew, though, that he couldn't stop the random wheel of fate. When it landed on your number, all your precautions were for naught. But, in spite of that, he still thought that you should do whatever you could to shave the odds a little in your favor.

His months of leading the squad from the point position had sharpened Dan's instincts and his senses. He was sensitive to what he heard, saw, and smelled, and those instincts never let him down. He was alert even when he was joking with his buddies in the squad. This intense focus on the things around him had cheated fate and saved his life on at least five occasions during his walk from the English Channel. Perhaps it was his relaxed focus that had resulted in Smitty's death. That thought kept occurring to him, especially in the night when he was sleeping. "If only I'd been more alert and gotten into the bushes, that tank would've driven right past us, and Smitty and the tank crew would still be alive today." Dan's obsessiveness and overly-scrupulous conscience would trouble him over the course of his life, and now both of these traits were in high gear.

"What if I had gotten into those bushes? Would the tank have passed harmlessly down the road, and would Smitty and I be sitting in the back of a deuce and a half today racing for Berlin? Would Smitty be pining for Yvette and sharing his post-war wedding plans with me? 'Dan, we'll buy a small house and have a whole bunch of kids.' 'You'd better buy a big house if you're gonna have all those kids,' I would have said, laughing and punching him on the shoulder. Instead, I fucked his lover after he died, a whore who didn't even know Smitty's name."

"Hey soldier....you looking for me?"

Saluting, Dan said, "Yes, Sir...Major. I just delivered a message to battalion and I'm trying to catch a ride back to Charlie Company. Can you fit me in anywhere?"

"We're not going as far as the battle area, but we'll move up a lot closer than we normally would because the front's moving forward so fast. Hop in the back of this deuce and a half, but don't smoke. It's loaded with howitzer shells, and if one of them goes off, the whole thing will go up and they'll be picking you up with a tweezers."

"What a comforting thought," Dan thought to himself.

"Yes, Sir! Thank you, Sir!"

"Hey, the major said that you're coming with us and riding in my truck. I'm Mike Fitzgerald," the driver said, extending his hand, and speaking with more than a hint of an Irish brogue, an accent that Dan was familiar with from having grown up in Boston.

"Hi, Mike...Dan Fleming. I'm heading up to Charlie Company, if I can ever catch them. From what I hear, they seem determined to keep running away from me."

"I'm sorry that you've gotta ride in back, Dan. Just squeeze yourself in between those boxes of shells. They even piled the crap up to the ceiling on the passenger side of my cab.

"Things might get a little bumpy because the guys from the motor pool just welded a piece of iron to reinforce one of the springs that had been splitting from all of the weight we've been packing on this poor old truck. The ride in front's pretty stiff, and in back, I'm sure that you'll feel every bump and pothole in the road, not that you can call these ruts through the woods a road.

"At least we're not the lead truck...that's no fun, knowing that you'll be the first to hit any mines that Jerry has placed in the road.

"Keep your M-1 handy too. There may be a lot of German stragglers along the way to take pot shots at us. You may want to find a spot on the floor rather than on the bench.

"You're from Boston?"

"Yeah, how'd you know that?"

"Can you say 'Pawk youah cah in the Havahd Yahd?'"

"You've got to be shitting me, Fitzgerald. Pawk youah cah in the Havahd Yahd."

"A friend of my parents came from Boston...he talks like you. I'm from Indianapolis, and I'd like to get up to Boston someday. The closest I ever got was when we embarked for England from New York City."

"Did you like New York?"

"Yeah, but it was too big...not like Indianapolis at all."

"Boston's not like that. We've got everything New York has, but not as much. The good thing about Boston, though, is that you can be in the country, the ocean, or the mountains very quickly. Boston is a wonderful place! What's Indianapolis like?"

"It's like any other city, I guess. When the Legislature's in session, it can be pretty busy downtown, but most of us are either farmers or guys selling stuff to farmers and their families. My family runs a grain and feed business that my uncle and father had started when they came over from Ireland. People tell me that I talk with a brogue, like I just got off the boat from Ireland, but that's how my mother and father taught me to talk.

"I got a lot of shit from the other kids when I started going to school. They called me 'Bog-Trotter'. I had no idea what it meant, and I couldn't understand why my dad got so angry when I told him about that. He told me that if anyone called me 'Bog-Trotter,' I should immediately punch him in the face and keep punching him till either he went down, I went down, or somebody broke it up. He said to me that no one likes getting hit in the face, and that even if I got beat up, the other kids would stop picking on me because they wouldn't want to get in a fight with me and get hit in the face.

"I was in the third grade and going to school one day when a group of fourth graders stopped me. One of them pushed me and called me 'Bog-Trotter'. I didn't want to do it, but I remembered what my father had told me. I started crying and punching him in the face as hard and fast as I could. He fell to the ground and the other kids took off. I kept punching him and bloodied his nose, but he got up and ran away too.

"I got called into the principal's office when I got to school, and they called my mother to come down and take me home for the rest of the day. She scolded me terribly. But, when my father got home from work that night, he said, 'Son...I'm proud of you. You're a man now, and never let anyone push you around.'

"You know what...he was right. No one ever tried to push me around after that. I heard that behind my back they called me 'The Crazy Irishman', but none of them dared say it to my face. And none of them ever called me 'Bog-Trotter' after that.

"You're not Irish, are you Dan? But, there are a lot of Irish in Boston, or so I've heard."

"Yeah, my grandfather was from Ireland. I'm from Brighton, the western part of the city. Brighton's mostly Irish and Italian. The gangs of kids are always fighting with each other, fistfights...they seem so stupid now. Some Irish kid will call one of the Italians a "guinea," and all of a sudden there'll be fifteen or so kids punching and kicking each other until one of the neighbors calls the cops.

"The cops usually arrest a couple of the Italian kids and take them to the station."

"What do they do to the Irish kids?"

"Nothing ...the cops in Boston are all Irish.

"They let the Irish kids go with a boot in the ass and a warning. The Italians, though, they book them and have their parents come to the station house to pick them up. Usually, they have to appear in juvenile court in a week or so."

"What happens to them then?"

"Well, usually nothing. All the judges are Yankees, with a few Irish, but the Yankees must figure that this is how the peasants amuse themselves, so they usually don't send them away unless one of them has used a knife. Then it's a different story."

Mike had a similar experience. "Yeah, it's kind of like that in Indianapolis too, except there are no Italians. It's the Irish kids, though, who always get into trouble. My senior year in high school, we played South Bend Central in March for the state basketball championship. There aren't a lot of Catholics in Indiana, and when we beat them by one point, the place went wild. The South Bend guys started punching and hitting anyone wearing our colors, not the team, but the fans.

"The cops had a riot themselves, just wading into the crowd with billy clubs. A lot of people got beaten up pretty badly that night.

"But, you're right. That seems like child's play compared to what's going on here."

"Yeah, it's like someone pulled a cork out of a bottle and let out an evil genie who won't go back into the bottle until he's caused enough carnage and destruction to satisfy himself."

"Wow, that's a good way to describe the hell we live in now. Did you come up with that yourself?"

"No, there's a priest at battalion, the new chaplain, who mentioned it to me once when we were talking after Mass."

Mike figured that his new passenger had seen some heavy combat. "I'm sure that you've seen a lot more action than me."

"I've seen more than I ever wanted to see, and from what I've heard around headquarters, I hope that I've seen the last of it, and that someone puts that son-of-a-bitch of a genie back in his bottle."

"I've come under fire a couple of times, but nothing serious. For the most part, I'm a glorified teamster, driving a truck instead of a team of horses. Mostly, we've been packing and moving battalion headquarters all over France, and now it looks like we'll be heading into Germany. I've hauled ammunition before, but I don't like it. It wouldn't take much to set this lot off."

"If we come under fire and the convoy stops, get as far away from this truck as you can, as quickly as you can. Head toward the fire-fight and remember that if a stray round hits the truck, they'll see the explosion from here to Paris."

"Don't worry about me, Mike. I'm out of here as soon as I hear shots and you stop.

"Look, if you ever make it to Boston, look me up. We have a spare bedroom that my parents use to put up company. I'm sure they'd love to have a visitor from Indiana. My aunt Mary-Ann, my mother's sister, sleeps there every Christmas when she comes down from Maine to stay with us for about a week. We open presents early Christmas morning after we come back from Midnight Mass."

"Yeah, well don't hold your breath till I get there, but I would like to do that sometime." Handing Dan a small notebook, Fitzgerald said, "Here, why don't you write your name and address in this? Do you have a sister, by any chance?"

"If I did, I sure as hell wouldn't let you get near her. I've got more sense than that."

Dan liked Mike Fitzgerald. You know how it is when you meet someone, and you instantly like each other? You know you seem to have a lot in common, and you both feel that you'd like to get to know each other better. At the same time, though, Dan was afraid to make a new friend because so many of his friends had been maimed or killed. He hoped, though, that they'd meet again.

Leaning back out of the driver's side window, Mike called, "Hey, Dan, at the briefing, they told us that there was one stretch of the road that's paved concrete, about ten miles worth. It'll be like driving at home when we hit that stretch."

"Yeah, just watch the speed limit. I'd hate to see the MPs haul you into traffic court and take your license away from you."

"If I lost my license, maybe they'd send me home and I could finish the war doing KP at Fort Benjamin Harrison. I like that idea. I wonder what the speed limit is around here. Maybe I should drop a nickel to the MPs to keep a watch on that stretch of road...Oh, shit, we're moving. Hop in and hang on!"

Again, Dan thought that this Fitzgerald fellow was someone he could become friendly with. Honesty and openness were two traits that had been drummed into him since childhood. He was a pretty good intuitive judge of character, and he figured that Fitzgerald had been brought up the same way.

Dan found a semi-comfortable spot on a case of artillery shells and settled in for the ride. The jostling and bouncing made his back sore, but there wasn't a lot he could do about it. The ride did get considerably worse, though, after the welded spring reinforcement broke when they went over a particularly rough stretch of road. Finally, they came to the paved section, and Dan hoped the reprieve would last as the ride smoothed out. And except for the high pitched scratching sound as the broken spring dragged along the concrete, they could have been driving down Commonwealth Avenue in Newton, out to the Norumbega Amusement Park.

Suddenly, Dan smelled something burning and leaned over the side of the truck to see a loose piece of canvas on fire, ignited by sparks from the steel reinforcement dragging along the pavement. He leaned over the side of the truck and tried to cut it off with his bayonet, but he couldn't reach it. Fanned by the speed of the truck, the wind fed the flames, and they raced up the side of the canvas, quickly engulfing the canvas top on the deuce and a half.

"Mike! Fire!" Mike! Fire! Fire! Fire!" Dan screamed at the top of his lungs. By now the fire had engulfed the entire canvas canopy. Whipped by the wind into an inferno, the wood slat benches had ignited now, and some of the wooden boxes housing the artillery shells were starting to catch.

The driver of the next truck in line, knowing what was inevitable, slowed to a crawl, and Dan, seeing the distance between them grow, knew what he had to do.

Unknowingly, Mike Fitzgerald downshifted to slow down as he reached a corner.

Dan, as best as he could, looked for a soft landing place and leaped from the truck as it slowed going around the curve. Landing in an overgrown hedgerow, Dan was punctured, bleeding, and stunned from the shock of his landing. The giant explosion and fireball about 500 yards down the road was deafening, and the searing heat gave him the look of a sunburn on one side of his face and on the back of his hand as he tried to protect his eyes.

Falling out of the hedgerow, Dan lay on the ground in shock and in a pool of his own blood. Looking skyward, Dan noticed the formations of puffy white clouds against the field of bright blue. It was his last vision before losing consciousness.

CHAPTER ELEVEN

Dan Meets Mary O' Daugherty

"Well...it's about time you decided to wake up."

When he opened his eyes, there was a face looking down on him; not a man's face, well at least it was well shaven if it was a man. Blinking a little, he focused on a very Irish looking face, a woman's face for sure. Groggy and fuzzy, Dan looked around and saw that he was in a hospital ward and the face belonged to First Lieutenant Mary O'Daugherty, an Army nurse.

"Where am I? How'd I get here?" Dan asked in rapid order.

"You leaped from a truck just before it exploded, according to the medics who brought you in."

The blurring haze on Dan's brain slowly began to lift. He raised his head to the nurse and asked, "What happened to the driver?"

"The medic described the scene to the charge nurse the night they brought you in. He said that there wasn't enough of him left to send home."

Seeing the pained look on Dan's face, she paused, "I'm sorry. Were you friends?"

"No...actually I'd just met him, but he was the type of person you liked instantly when you met him, and you would've wanted to get to know him better.

"He was from Indianapolis and was a couple of years out of high school, wondering what to do with his life. Well, I guess he doesn't have that worry anymore.

"What's your name?"

"Mary...Mary O'Daugherty."

"Mary, I'm always getting in trouble for violating military protocol...should I salute and call you Lieutenant?"

"Mary's fine."

"Why does this happen, Mary?"

"Why does what happen?"

"You know, people are getting killed and maimed, deliberately and by chance. Fitzy got his by chance, a broken spring on his truck that dragged along the road, causing sparks that set his truck on fire.

"You and one of the guys in your unit become friends, and then he's dead...just like that, and it's like he never existed. No grieving like at home; he's just not there anymore, and they send someone else to take his place, and you're always wondering whether you or the new guy will get it first.

"The first time I saw combat was when we landed in Normandy. I was scared shitless, and I knew that we were in trouble when the guy crawling up the beach next to me had his leg blown off. Then I lost a friend who died saving my life by blowing up a tank full of German soldiers. I heard their screams as they burned to death, trapped in their flaming tank.

"Why, Mary, why? You're a nurse. You spend your life helping people. I'm a dogface, not that I had any choice. I live in mud, in holes in the ground, and I spend my time killing people who are trying to kill me, and who've killed a lot of the people I started out with.

"I don't know them. They speak a different language, but I have nothing against them. They probably got drafted like I did, and their mothers are worried about them as much as our mothers are worried about us, and their officers must send brief notes back to their families when we kill one of them. 'Fritz was a good soldier, and died fighting for the fatherland'...they probably say, and Fritz's mother probably collapses in tears when she reads that letter. She knows what it is when the post-man delivers it to the door, and she hates us because we killed her son, and we're waiting to be killed by one of her other sons, or one of their cousins or uncles or someone like that.

"They told Fritz to go out and kill me, and my country told me to go out and kill him. Why? Are there mad men running this world? Is this a sadistic plot by an angry god, an evil god who enjoys stomping on ant hills and watching all of us flee in panic and terror, leaving our dead behind?

"We're fighting for glory, Mary!" Dan was screaming now.

"We fight for democracy, for the American way, for bullshit, Mary! It's all bullshit, and they're all fucking madmen! They're crazy, fucking lunatics, Mary!"

Then he started crying and his voice softened, "Mary...Mary..." he sobbed, "why is this happening to us?"

As he was raving though, Mary had taken a syringe that she'd been holding behind her back and injected it carefully into her patient's IV line. Dan's eyes began to blur over again as the medication started to take its effect.

"Mary...Mary..." His voice trailed off, as the morphine started to dull his central nervous system.

The next day, Dan awoke to the sound of a new voice. "Come on soldier, rise and shine. Time to move out."

"Where's Mary? What time is it?"

"It's almost 13:00 hours, and we're not holding chow for you any longer. Time to get out of here. We've got massive casualties coming in pretty soon and we need your bed. Let's get you out of bed and dressed. The government got you a new uniform because you ruined yours on the way in here."

"Where's Mary?"

"Lieutenant O'Daugherty? She's been assigned to another ward today. They just brought in a load of burn victims and she's had a lot of experience with them at Fort Sam, so she's over there. I'm Lieutenant Deignan, and it's up to me to get you back to the front, and back in action.

Colonel Coughlin was in this morning awarding the Purple Heart and Bronze Star to the men who earned them. You were sedated, so he left yours next to the bed. Fill your name in on the citations and give them to your company clerk. The colonel already signed them."

"The last time I was put in for a medal, I ended up walking point for six months till my company commander was killed."

"Yeah...that's real tough, soldier, but you've got to get out of here pretty quick because we really need your bed, and you're OK to go back to your unit. You may be a little fuzzy, but as soon as the anesthetic wears off, you'll be sharp as a tack. You may be feeling some pain then from the punctures and scrapes, but here, take some aspirin with you and use it as soon as you first feel pain. Try to stay ahead of the pain with the medicine. If any of your wounds get infected, go on sick call back in your unit.

"Come on now, I want you out of here by 14:00 hours. Eat your chow, get dressed, and get a move on. Don't forget to take your medals with you."

Dan felt a growing urge to take the nurse by the throat and slowly choke the life out of her.

"Yes, Ma'am," Dan said crisply...as crisply as he could through the fog of his pounding head and the anger welling up from deep inside of him.

Quickly, he ate the food she'd left, and dressed in the torn and filthy uniform that had been thrown in a heap behind the bed, leaving the new clean uniform behind him. His head started to clear now, and he left the hospital ward, pausing only to drop the medals and citations in the rubbish barrel just inside the door to the corridor.

Dan went to the central desk in the hospital and asked the clerk which ward Mary O'Daugherty was working on.

"Why do you want to know?"

"We're friends from the same home town and I thought that I'd drop in to say hello before I go back to the front. By the way, where's supply? I'd like to pick up a sewing kit to repair some of the tears in my uniform."

"Lieutenant O'Daugherty's in the burn unit on the third floor. Take the elevator off that corridor. Central supply's in the basement. Take that same elevator down one floor, and you'll see the signs, although I think they are still in German."

The former German military hospital was well laid out, organized and efficient by design, with signs in the corridors in German, directing people around the building. Getting on the elevator, he noticed that in the European custom, the ground floor was marked with a zero, and the second floor, the one above the ground floor, would be marked as the "first floor." On a hunch, Dan pressed "two," figuring the clerk had meant the third floor using American standards.

As the elevator door was opening at its destination, Dan could hear the soft moans of men in pain...men in pain, with large doses of morphine running through their systems. Their pain could be dulled by massive amounts of the drug, but it was a pain that couldn't totally be denied. Dan would soon experience a similar type of pain, not a physical pain, but a psychological pain that couldn't be denied, and which would live beneath the surface of his mind.

"Is Lieutenant O'Daugherty available?" Dan asked one of the corpsmen on the floor.

"Take a left at the end of the ward...she's in the triage wing." The orderly gave Dan a skeptical look, as if he were debating whether to call the MPs to have him thrown out, but then he hurried on to respond to a muffled groan from one of the rooms off the central ward.

Walking down between the two rows of beds occupied by unconscious or semi-conscious men, Dan heard the sobbing and groans growing louder as he approached the triage unit. Turning the corner at the end of the ward, Dan entered the unit, not a lot bigger than a private room, or a large storage closet, he thought. Lying on canvas cots, and some still on gurneys, there were seven badly burned men in this section of the dead end room, alone at the end of the ward and out of the way. This was unlike the other wards. These men didn't seem like they'd be in this ward for long. They were crammed in with little space, and the place had a feeling of being a temporary holding area, as if they were waiting to be moved to somewhere else.

Mary was bending over one of the burned men, carefully adjusting his morphine drip.

"Mary?"

"Oh, my God!" Mary jumped, an intense, startled look in her eyes. Her eyes were raw, as if from crying, and she had a primal savage look on her face. She looked like a frightened animal more than a human being.

"Mary, I'm Dan Fleming. You took care of me the other night. They just discharged me this morning and I wanted to thank you and say good-bye."

Taking him by the arm, she pulled him around the corner out of the sight of the wounded men and into a small open supply closet off the main ward.

"Hold me. Hold me, please!" she pleaded, as she pulled Dan near to her.

"I don't know if I can keep doing this...if I can go back in there. Those seven are so badly burned or injured that they're all going to die. I'm to medicate them as best I can so they die with as little pain as possible.

"I'm sorry...I'm sorry," she blurted, blotting at her eyes with a facecloth.

"Nurse...Nurse!" It was a plaintiff cry from one of the seven.

"I have to go. His nervous system's destroyed so he feels no pain...he'll be dead by nightfall."

Pushing away from Fleming, First Lieutenant Mary O'Daugherty composed herself and moved stridently back into the room of seven, followed by Fleming, who hung back a little.

"Nurse...Nurse...I'm gonna be all right, aren't I?" the patient asked. Dan saw the frightened look in the wounded man's eyes as he looked into Mary's face for support.

"You'll be all right, soldier," she said, looking at him while trying to comfort him. "You'll be going home soon," she said, turning her face away from his and looking down, a tear forming in her eye.

Dan left the room without a word, leaving Nurse O'Daugherty to watch over the soon to be dead men under her care, never expecting to see her again. Back down the elevator, and out of the hospital, forgetting about his sewing kit, Fleming headed for the replacement depot to look for an official ride back to his unit.

Chapter Twelve

There Are Warriors and There Are Bureaucrats

"Let me see your papers, soldier!"

The clerk at the desk in the replacement depot struck Dan as an officious little shit in a clean uniform, freshly shaven, and smelling of after shave lotion, someone who enjoyed wielding the modicum of authority vested in his position by the United States government.

"Mr. Johnson could be like that," Dan thought to himself. Whenever Johnson had a couple of beers at lunch, he'd come back to the store and start ordering Dan around. Most of the time, though, he was pretty good to work for, and Dan could tolerate his occasional abuse, especially because in pre-war Boston, jobs were hard to come by. This clerk, though, was too much.

"Where are your orders? All you have here are your hospital discharge papers. We can't send you anywhere, soldier, unless you have a set of orders. You should know that!"

Dan chuckled inwardly. It was ironic that not only did he have to fight the Germans, but he also had to fight with the American Army for the pleasure of doing that.

"I'm sorry, I wasn't traveling under orders. I was a messenger sent to the rear by my C.O. and I was injured in a truck accident."

"Well, the regulations say that we need travel orders before we can provide you with transportation."

Dan reached over the desk, lifting the clerk by his necktie and collar out of his chair. "Listen, you little shit, I've killed men I didn't know and for no reason at all. I'm getting to know you and I don't like you. Don't give me a fucking reason to want to kill you. Get me on the next fucking truck to Charlie Company before I get pissed off and do something that we'll both regret. You understand?" Dan dropped the clerk unceremoniously back into his chair.

Visibly shaken, the clerk cowered down into his seat, thinking, perhaps correctly, that he was dealing with a mad man.

"You don't have to get physical you know...I'll get you something right away. I can make space for you in a truck that's leaving for Charlie Company within the hour."

The clerk thought about calling the MPs, but the crazed look in Dan's eyes convinced him that the best thing to do would be to get this wild man out of there as quickly as he could.

Shuffling his papers till he found the roster for the truck to Charlie Company, he called out a name. "Torgeson! Is Torgeson in the area?"

Dan watched as the officious son-of-a-bitch exerted his authority over someone else.

"Private...there's been a change. You're going to lay over till tomorrow. You'll go to Baker Company in the morning at 0900. Here's a chit for a billet, and the mess tent's down the block on the right."

"But...but why am I being bumped? I want to stay with my buddies. They're going to Charlie Company."

"Listen, soldier," said the officious clerk, who swelled with the chance to assert his authority, "in this man's army, you do what you're told. Now get out of here. I don't want to see you till tomorrow morning. Any more shit from you and you'll end up in the stockade!"

Dan watched the whole scene, barely able to conceal his contempt for the clerk, pathetic shit that he was. People were fighting and dying about thirty miles from where they were, but this whole apparatus was different from the world he inhabited on the front. In the forward area, he lived in a netherworld populated by humans acting like animals, and they were moved around like pawns on a chess board by an apparatus populated by shop clerks. Like Mr. Johnson after a couple of pops telling him to move plumbing material, these glorified clerks were moving men to their deaths.

"Fleming, today I want you to move plumbing supplies from aisle three to aisle two. The new winter supplies, snow shovels, rock salt, scrapers, and all of that stuff should be coming in next week, and I want it in aisle three."

"Small matter that he wanted it in aisle two last year, but it's his store, and as long as he pays me, I'll put it wherever he wants it..."

"Fleming, I want you and twenty-three other men on those two deuce and a halfs to move thirty miles forward. I want you to kill a bunch of Germans, and then you'll probably die, but that's the way it goes. It really doesn't matter, but I want it done now."

"It really doesn't matter," Dan thought. "Old men and clerks are sending young men like me off to kill and die. The old men were clerks once themselves, or lucky enough to have survived other killing grounds. They collect the medals that they award to each other like kids collect bottle caps or baseball cards.

"They send enough of us out to kill and die till both sides have satisfied their blood lust, then they have a parade, award each other more medals, and march away till the next time someone rubs the lamp and lets the evil genie out. They march away all right, leaving the shattered hulks of the men in their command who managed by some act of fate to not get killed. Then they write romantic books about battles and campaigns to make themselves look important to their wives and families."

"Fleming! Where the hell is Fleming?" The noncommissioned officer with the clipboard was red in the face, very flustered and very aggravated.

"Here, Sergeant. What's the matter?"

"The fucking truck's fifteen minutes late and you're the last name on the roster. Get your sorry ass up there!"

Bringing his M-1 rifle up to his shoulder, Dan Fleming aimed it directly at the Sergeant's left temple.

"You know what, mother-fucker? I could kill you right now. One little squeeze on this trigger and they'll send you home to your momma in a box with a medal. What truck am I on, asshole? Tell me, then start walking backwards out of the field. Keep walking till you can't see me anymore."

Fleming's voice had become evil now. He had to get away from these clerks and back to the killing. He wasn't fit for Army life. They'd made him into a killer, a vicious killing animal, and he was disgusted with himself and with them for what he had become. Still, the thought of blowing the brains out of this cowering non-com, though appealing in an obsessive way, was at the same time repulsive to him.

"Keep walking, you sorry asshole, and if I get any shit because of this, I'll come looking for you. Remember, you can't win a combat with a dead man, and I'm a walking dead man, fucker. If you don't get out of here quick, you're gonna be dead yourself, dead before me, and you won't be walking, just lying in a box with your medal on your way home to momma."

Without a word, the sergeant with the clipboard began walking backwards. Dan, keeping his rifle trained on the non-com glorified clerk's forehead, hopped up ass-first on the floor of the truck, then got on the bench that ran along the right side, taking the last seat in that row.

A corporal came by, closed the tailgate, and cautiously backed away as the truck took off, leaving the back-pedaling sergeant on the far edge of the field.

The other eleven men in the truck looked at Fleming with both a sense of awe and a sense of fear. They had all crowded away from him, sliding forward on the two parallel bench seats on each side of the truck. After the trucks had left the marshalling area, Dan turned to his eleven new companions with a wild look in his eyes and shouted at the top of his lungs, "BOO!" Dan then laughed uproariously at the spectacle he had become.

"My name's Fleming. I'm from Boston, and I'm fucking crazy...you understand? And let me tell you, if any of you manage to stay alive, you'll be crazy too.

"When you kill little children who you thought were German soldiers, you'll go crazy too. When your closest friend dies in your arms, you will absolutely go crazy.

"If you're lucky, you'll get wounded...not bad enough to fuck you up for life, but enough to get you sent home.

"There are two kinds of people in life- clerks and killers.

"We're leaving the world of asshole non-coms and going straight to hell. I've been with Charlie Company since D-day, probably when most of you were still in high school. Only about twenty percent of us are still alive and in one piece. We're all fucking crazy though, and like I said, if you live, you'll be crazy too."

In the front of the truck, on the bench sitting across from Dan, one of the soldiers began laughing almost as hard as Dan had been.

"Did you see the look on that asshole change after you trained your weapon on him? I was wishing that you were going to tell him to drop trou and start quacking like a duck."

At that, the whole truckload of young soldiers started laughing, and Dan transitioned from crazy man to folk hero, soon to be the Den-Mother of the eleven replacements going up to the front with Charlie Company, to bring it up to strength because of the casualties it had suffered.

"You guys could do OK, and a couple of you might even make it out alive. Let me give you a couple of tips. When you're on patrol...like they tell you in basic...don't bunch up. Keep at least ten yards behind the guy in front of you and cover him like he was your lover. Don't pick up souvenirs; leave them for the rear echelon heroes to blow themselves up with. The Germans booby-trap things like cameras, Lugers, swords, things like that, things you'd like to smuggle home to show around the neighborhood.

"When you're on patrol, unless you're in a hurry, keep off the road, and walk in the brush, about five yards from the road's edge. The Germans mine the roads, and you'll be better off in an ambush if you have some cover handy.

"Don't make noise. Move as quietly as you can. No smoking, no fancy perfumed after-shave lotion, and keep your gear from clanking. Don't all move at once; move one at a time, slowly, cautiously, and look all around before you move.

"Don't worry about the officers in Charlie Company, they're all good shits. They're good guys who want us all to come out of this alive. The asshole officers were either killed in battle or killed by their own men a long time ago. That sounds terrible, to kill your own officers, but they would have gotten us all killed eventually. So, one or two guys took them out. Those guys had balls. Everyone knows who did it, and no one would say anything because we're all grateful. Those guys saved our lives from our own officers – for however long. One guy rolled a hand grenade into one of the asshole's tents when he was sleeping, and a few months later his replacement was killed in battle, shot in the back of the head under his helmet line. Both of them were sent home in a box, each with a medal and a note from the captain saying how they had died heroes.

"The K-rations suck, and there's no earthly way to disinfect yourself with all of the filth you're gonna be living in, so look on your lice and fleas as your personal pets and learn to live with them. And don't even think about taking a shit within twenty yards of my foxhole!

"In about twenty minutes, sit on the floor because as we get closer to the front, we could run into German snipers. I've heard that things are moving so fast that the hunter/killer guys haven't been deployed yet to mop up behind the lines.

"If you see a corpse and it's not bloated, that means that there was recent action in the area, and you'd better keep on your toes, even more than normal.

"One last thing and I'll shut up. When you dig in a position, dig deep and camouflage like you were an artist creating a natural painting of the country. Especially at night, don't make it easy for them when they come looking for you in the dark. More than once we've found our perimeter guards in shallow holes in the morning with slit throats.

"Oh...and clean your rifle every day if you can. Keep it cocked with one round in the chamber, and with the bayonet fixed when you're in your hole for the night. Better to have it ready, even though it's a pain in the ass, because when trouble comes to you, all you can do is react. You won't have time then to prepare."

"I guess you've seen a lot of shit, huh?" The soldier in the front of the truck who had first laughed when Dan faced down the transportation sergeant wasn't joking now, but asked his question with a tone of respect.

"Yeah, I have, but don't be jealous, because there's still enough war left for each of you to get your own little piece of hell."

The rest of the ride was uneventful, except for a sniper round that tore through the canvas side on the truck just above the steel plating on the left side. The soldier who was sitting on the floor below the bench turned ashen when he realized what had just happened and turned toward Dan. "You saved my life. That round had my name on it, and if you hadn't told us to get down off the benches, I'd be a dead man right now."

"Well, don't get discouraged now, you'll still have plenty of other opportunities to die. Just remember that we're all walking dead men, but if it misses you by an inch, it misses you by a mile. You're as safe and alive as old clipboard back there counting his sheep, or his trucks, or whatever it is that he does. But, if it doesn't miss you, well that's the way things go in hell.

"We'll file a report on this, an after-action report, and the hunter/killer guys will get it in about a week and fan out in the area till they kill the son-of-a-bitch. Ambushes, firefights, those are random and purposeless; both sides happen to be in the wrong place at the wrong time; but snipers, that's another story. If we capture their guys in a skirmish, we turn them over as POW's and take them to a stockade somewhere in the rear. They're the lucky ones...the war's over for them. They get three squares a day and wait till the end of hostilities, when they get repatriated and go back home to their families.

"But, snipers, though, that's a different matter. That's personal, when someone picks you out and tries to kill you. Snipers don't get captured. The hunter/killer guys don't usually bring snipers back alive. And they're pretty good at what they do. Most of them are hillbilly coon hunters who can trail a raccoon for two days before treeing and killing it. That guy who took a pot shot at us will be dead by a week from Friday, unless the hunter/killer guys have a hot card game going. I've seen these poker games go on for weeks at a time as one squad comes in off patrol, and some of their members replace guys who have to leave. Some guys in that outfit have won thousands of dollars playing cards, and most of them, good old boys from Kentucky and places like that, are pretty good with a rifle, and have the patience to sit in a tree for seven hours waiting for our German sniper friend to come walking by in the woods. That's what they do back home when they hunt coons or deer to feed their families.

"When there's a sniper active in an area, they just fan out and sit...that's if they're not playing cards. At some point, the sniper leaves his position to get food or water, and then he's dead. They have plenty of water and rations, and they're like fucking camels, so they can outwait him. Those guys have a lot of notches on their rifle stocks, considering the fact that they're looked on by the brass as rear-echelon troops. They've been following us across Europe, and it's good to know that they're cleaning up behind us, covering our asses, so to speak."

They sat quietly for the rest of the ride, each of them pondering his own potential fate, and glancing from time to time at the torn canvas where the bullet had gone through. The canvas was flapping a little in the wind as the two trucks drove relentlessly toward the front.

Dan continued to wrestle with his own demons as they each continued to ponder their individual fates.

CHAPTER THIRTEEN

Dan Returns to Charlie Company

"OK….OK...fall out...come on, let's go. The Army has a lot of use for these two trucks."

"Holy shit….hey guys, look who's come back from his vacation on the Riviera...Dan Fleming. Look, he was in the sun too long, and one side of his face is burned. You should have turned over Danno, you dumb shit. You'll look good at your court martial. The captain kept carrying you as MIA, but brigade was giving him shit and wanted you listed as a deserter, or at least as AWOL. You must have some friends in high places who would like to see your ass swinging in the breeze. Where the hell have you been anyway?"

"O'Neill, you asshole, you wouldn't believe me if I told you, but I got frozen out of a Jeep because a dead lieutenant had been using it to get laid and the MPs wouldn't release it to me. I got a ride on an ammo truck that got blown up, and I ended up in the hospital for a week. And then I nearly had to kill a couple of clerks who didn't want to send me back to you.

"Now that you mention it though, I could use some R&R. Do you think the captain would approve some leave for me...a week or two to tan the other side of my face in the Mediterranean sun?

"Forget I asked. That was a rhetorical question...you know what that means, you dumb bastard, don't you?"

Ignoring Fleming, O'Neill addressed the troops who were gathered loosely in two ranks in front of him.

"Welcome to Charlie Company, gentlemen. I'm Top Sergeant O'Neill. You can call me 'Top' or 'O'Neill, just don't call me 'Sarge.' I ain't no fuckin'

'Sarge'! Everyone understand? I'm your mother, your father, and your best friend while you're here and still alive. My job's to keep you alive and to kill Krauts, not necessarily in that order. So far we've killed a lot of Krauts, but I've still got a lot of work to do on the other part. Only twenty percent of us who arrived on this sorry continent on D-day are still alive and fully functioning human beings...well, sort of fully functioning, excluding Fleming, who you've already met. But, the Army has been giving me on-the-job-training, and I'm going to try to do better than twenty percent with you guys on the second part of my job.

"I was a corporal when I got off the LST at Omaha Beach, and since the non-coms above me couldn't keep themselves alive, I gradually moved up the ranks as they got carried out with one of their dog tags jammed between their upper front teeth. That's right; give the Krauts close to a perfect kill record for non-coms in this company. I'm next on the list, but if my luck holds out, I may make it through at least till the end of the week.

"They tell us from battalion that the Jerries are licked. I don't believe them. The guys in front of us are smart bastards. I have a lot more respect for them than I do for those shit heads in the rear who're telling us what to do. If the Jerries are retreating, they're probably trying to suck us into another trap like they did at the Bulge. I'm more afraid of our leaders in the rear, though, than I am of the Germans. They order us to do stupid things that get men killed. We know what we're doing, how to kill people, but they're like a bunch of kids playing with toy soldiers. Remember to trust your gut rather than what some rear-echelon type tells you.

"Captain Miller's a good shit, and we're all the same out here. Officers and non-coms die as readily as enlisted men. Forget the military protocol, unless a major or colonel comes up to write a report about what he did on his summer vacation.

"Enlisted men always eat first before non-coms and officers. We've been moving so fast lately that there's been some delay in getting food up to us. But, we recently sent out a foraging party that managed to liberate a couple of hundred pounds of K-rations from one of the battalion supply depots with the help of some very good bolt cutters we bought from one of the guys in the motor pool for fifty bucks.

"As far as the war goes, don't take it personal with these bastards who are trying to kill you. They're professionals, and they're good at what they do, considering that they're running out of ammunition and supplies. Just be quicker and smarter than them and kill them first...that's the professional way to do it. It's a lot cleaner that way, and the captain doesn't have to write any more letters home to your mothers and widows to send with your casket, telling them what heroes you were when you died stepping on one of their land mines on the way to the latrine.

"Any questions? None?

"OK, Paulie, would you take these guys around and introduce them to their squads?

"Oh...one other thing. They gave you a lot of shit when you were going through basic. It's different up here. Like I said, our mission at Charlie Company is to keep each other alive and to kill Krauts. I'll do everything I can to keep each of you alive, and I'd appreciate the same in return.

"Welcome to Charlie Company."

Dan listened to this welcoming speech to the new replacements and walked up to O'Neill after they were heading off to their respective platoons. Slapping his first sergeant on the shoulder, Dan said, "For Chris' sake, O'Neill, you sound like a football coach giving a half-time pep talk."

"Yeah, well I hope they listened. We're alive, at least for now."

"I talked with the kids on my truck and tried to give them some advice about how to stay alive. I told them to get off the benches and onto the floor. A few miles after that, a sniper put a round through the canvas where one of them had been sitting. They think I'm Jesus Christ and that I walk on water. The guy who'd been sitting on the bench where the bullet had passed through turned white as a sheet and almost shit his pants."

"You did good, Fleming, and saved me a lot of work. If the sniper had taken him out, I would have had to write another report, and then requisition another body for the company. We haven't lost anyone for about three weeks now since Smitty got it, and it's been like a vacation for me. All I have to worry about lately is where we can steal enough gas to keep our drive to Berlin alive."

"You look at them, Top. You know that we're only a couple of years older than they are, but it could easily be a couple of centuries, when you think of what they've experienced in their lives, and what we've been through. How do you explain this to them? How can you explain it to anyone who hasn't been through it? I had a couple of tough times when I was trying to get back to the unit. I lost it twice and was ready to kill a couple of clerk types who were giving me shit. I don't know if I could ever live in a normal world again."

"What's normal?" asked Top. "Did you ever think that this might be normal, and the way we used to live is abnormal? You can't explain this to the replacements though. You're right, they're going to have to experience it for themselves...and I hope they get to understand it before it kills them. It's one thing for them to stick a bayonet into a rubber tire during basic training, and another thing to run it through the chest of another human being."

Those words would again come to Dan Fleming before he was finished with this killing business.

"Well, Top, maybe we're lucky. That's one thing that you and I haven't experienced. We've done our killing the civilized way, with bullets and high explosives. I wouldn't be upset, though, if I ended my military career without adding the bayonet merit badge to my killing sash."

"You know...battalion has been pushing Miller to write you up as a deserter. I wonder if some of your new found friends back there remember who you are and where you live?"

"You know, Top, I could take a court-martial. A couple of years in the stockade till the war is over, and a dishonorable discharge, but at least I'd be alive and out of this shit. Why don't you turn me in, and I'll give you that Luger I liberated before my last trip to the rear. They can't expect me to fight if I'm handcuffed, and I'll probably have two MPs to protect me on my ride back. Maybe they'll hold my court-martial in England."

'Will the clerk read the charge before this court?'

'Yes, Sir. Corporal Daniel G. Fleming of Charlie Company, of the 82nd Infantry, on March 15, 1944, did knowingly point his M-1 rifle at Sergeant Idon'tgiveashit, and told Sergeant Idon'tgiveashit to drop his uniform trousers and to start quacking like a duck, whereupon Sergeant Idon'tgiveashit did as he was instructed, thereby ruining a perfectly good pair of military issue trousers. Corporal Fleming is charged herein with causing the wanton and malicious destruction of government issued property.'

"Top, I can see it now. I'll be in the stockade in England, and visitors will come by with candy and books for us to read. Then, when I plead guilty, they'll sentence me and ship me stateside to someplace like Kansas or Iowa to serve out my time, and I'll sit there till they get tired of having you guys kill Krauts."

"You know, Fleming, you're fucking nuts.

"Look...stop the bullshit. We just got orders to stop advancing and to set up a perimeter defense around the top of this hill outside of that town down the valley in front of us. The mayor and a delegation of his council came walking up the hill toward our forward positions. We blindfolded them and brought them back here. Herb Hohmann is fluent in German...his father grew up in the country...and he interpreted for us.

"They say that there are no organized German forces in the town, and only a few stragglers and wounded in the fields and countryside. They want to surrender

93

the town and the wounded soldiers to us, but the captain doesn't trust them, after a group surrendering over at D Company last week pulled grenades out of their jackets and killed three of our guys before they were mowed down by one of the guards with an automatic rifle."

CHAPTER FOURTEEN

Dan Meets Heinrich Richter

"At any rate, now that you're back and semi-healthy, I'd like to send you out as a forward observer in front of your squad, and have you dig in facing the village...about 300 yards in front of our position. We're in a perimeter defense around the top of the hill above the village. You'll have a field phone, and have the artillery zero in on you before nightfall. If the sneaky bastards try to infiltrate, give three clicks on the phone and they'll bracket your position with fire."

"Top, I knew you'd give me a warm welcome when I got back. I do like the court-martial option better, but I guess I don't have much of a choice though. Before I move out, I'd like to stop by the armorer and get some more ammo and about half a dozen grenades. I like a hand grenade in that situation. Nothing in it, like in a rifle, to get jammed or misfire when you need it most. Nice and simple; pull pin, throw, and duck."

"Yeah, he's set up in the bunker under those trees, where the sandbags are. Welcome back, Dan. The snow has melted and it's muddy enough now for you to dig one of your trademark foxholes. Here's a map with an overlay of grid coordinates. If Jerry comes creeping up the hill, give a few clicks on the field phone and cover up. The howitzers will take care of the rest of it.

"Remember, I'd rather kill a few innocent cattle wandering around at night than let a battalion of German infantry surprise us, so don't be shy about calling in the heavy stuff. I told these kids I'd do everything I could to get them home alive, and I meant that. No surprises. Cover up the wire from the field phone...hell, I don't have to tell you that."

Dan smiled, turned, and headed over to the ammo bunker. In one way, it was good to be back. It seemed like he belonged in this place with these men. As much as they all hated it, he wondered if they'd be fit for any other life if they survived.

"Hey, Rabelski, how about a little service here!"

Looking up from the sandbag reinforced hole in the ground, the company armorer had a smile on his face.

"Jeeze, I thought the MPs would be hauling you back here in cuffs from what I've been hearing. I hope at least that she was good looking."

"Sorry, no such luck. A truck accident, and a little time in the hospital, and I'm pronounced fit for duty as soon as they needed my bed for someone else. Can you give me a half dozen grenades and ten clips for my M-1? I'm gonna set up a forward OP, and I want to be prepared for any night visitors."

"You've got 'em. Welcome back, and don't fall asleep out there. They always go for the ammo bunker first when they infiltrate. Look at what happened over at Baker Company last year when they got overrun without even knowing it. The first thing people knew about it was when the ammo went up."

Dan carefully strung the wire for the field phone through the mud and dried grass. Here and there a bud of something green poked through the muck, getting ready to welcome the spring. He was aware that not only was this wire his lifeline to the company, but also that it would lead any wandering Germans straight to his hole. It had happened more than once that a unit had been attacked at night, only to find the sentry in the forward observation post the next day with his throat slit from ear to ear, as Dan had mentioned to the replacements on the truck. Death was so casual, a part of life, like the next cigarette break, or the next chow call. You didn't get close to too many people so you wouldn't be destroyed when they were killed. Yet, you were close with all of them at a very deep and intimate, and at the same time, very impersonal, level. It was a relationship that you couldn't understand unless you'd been in the situation yourself.

Dan picked a place on the hill overlooking the town. It was on the edge of a beautiful wood, a good vantage point to view the meadow and the road that ran down into the valley. The woods ran up the hill to where Charlie Company was bivouacked in a perimeter defense around the crest.

True to form, Dan's foxhole was a work of art, deeper than he was tall, with a firing step and a camouflaged cover of fresh spruce. You could walk right by his position without knowing that in it there was a rifleman with a poised bayonet ready to do combat.

"Red Eagle, this is Fox Trot One. Do you read me?"

"Roger, Fox Trot One. This is Red Eagle. What's your position?"

"Red Eagle, I'm located at grid coordinates one - five on the X axis and three - two on the Y axis."

"Roger, Fox Trot One. That's one - five on the X axis and three - two on the Y axis."

"Red Eagle, this is Fox Trot One. That's affirmative."

"Red Eagle, this is Fox Trot One. Could you send a spotting round to coordinate two - one on the X axis and four - zero on the Y axis?"

"Affirmative, Fox Trot One. Two – one on the X axis, and four – zero on the Y axis. Tuck your head in, Fox Trot One; we'll be coming over in a bit."

In about thirty seconds, Dan heard the explosion as the artillery company, code named Red Eagle, fired a round to the coordinates he had given them on his map. He heard the shell sailing over him, and heard and felt it explode about thirty yards in front of his foxhole. There was more back and forth on the field phone and a few more spotting rounds, until Red Eagle had bracketed the area from about thirty yards in front of Dan's position back to the company lines and forward to the bottom of the hill.

After sending those three or four spotting rounds, Red Eagle could now obliterate the entire area between just forward of Dan's position back to Charlie Company in pitch black darkness by relying on the grid coordinates they had just set up. The spotting rounds allowed them to work their barrage around Dan's position. Once the barrage started, he'd be safe if he stayed in his hole.

Dan was now dug in with his sharpened bayonet fixed on the rifle mount. His rifle bore was clean and oiled, and the hand grenades were laid out in a row on a little shelf he had dug in the earth, about waist deep when he was standing on the firing step. He had one round chambered in his rifle, and it was time for him to have his usual gourmet dinner of canned meat and chocolate. It'd be a long night and it was still pretty chilly. He was covered by his government-issue poncho with a heavy wool blanket underneath. He had been doing this for so long that he felt naturally part of the earth. Like an enlarged earthworm, Dan was as comfortable as he could be in his subterranean place of repose, standing in the earth up to his neck and looking for anything that might approach him. He was ready to report any movement toward Charlie Company.

Three clicks on his radio's "transmit" key would bring the wrath of the artillery gods down on this peaceful and lovely place, raining hellfire all around him.

"Stay home, Jerry, stay home!" he thought to himself. "It'd be a shame to destroy the beauty and tranquility of this place by calling Red Eagle in on it."

"Three clicks," Dan thought to himself, "and I become the avenging angel, calling down death and destruction on all that's around me. It's a terrible power that I've been given. Three clicks and I can destroy everything within a mile in each direction."

As the sun set and darkness began to grow, Dan became even more vigilant, scanning the village below him, looking for any sign of an enemy presence. Part of a helmet showing over the top course of bricks in a wall, the glint of the fading sunlight reflecting off a rifle barrel, perhaps trained on the American position. Were they real or phantoms? Dan saw nothing other than what his imagination conjured up for him. A creeping Nazi turned out to be an alley cat that knocked over the top of a garbage pail; the mortar being set up next to a building was the bottom half of a broken roof drain pointing skyward.

And so it went as dusk yielded to pitch darkness, and Dan was left alone in the night in a hole in the woods of a strange country. Alone with his ammo clips, his bayonet, and his hand grenades, as well as the power to destroy everything within his reach, Dan reflected on the current state of his life and the craziness that surrounded him.

Dead comrades spoke to him, followed by the screams of young men in German Army uniforms being burned alive in their tank, the smell of their burning flesh now as much a part of Dan Fleming as his own fingerprints. These memories will follow him all of his life, however brief or long that might be.

Dan remembered the battles during last winter's freezing cold, battles that numbed their souls even more than the weather had numbed their bodies.

Stacked like cordwood waiting to be fed into a fire, frozen and stiff, legs sticking out from under a grimy canvas tarp, ten pairs of shoes were smeared with blood and mud. Twenty shoes were laced and tied that morning as their owners awoke from a cold restless sleep, preparing to resume the combat that would end them up together that evening. It was a rag-tag collection of footwear in varying states of condition. A couple of pairs of military issue combat boots, laced tightly and double knotted around the ankle, one set of shoes torn in random patterns by the shrapnel that had shredded its owners legs, strips of brown leather dyed a deeper darker shade by the dried blood of its owner.

Dan remembered those shoes, waiting for their ultimate disposition as the battle ebbed and flowed, to be disposed of by whoever ended up controlling the ground on which they rested. As the cold deepened and the howling wind intensified, Dan thought that those shoes stood as silent sentinels to the madness. The deviance in human nature that set their owners against each other in battle; opponents in life, their owners were united in death, united as in a pile of cordwood.

Dan thought of the randomness of it all, and how seemingly unconnected events mean life or death. If Stadholm had been killed by a sniper earlier, Dan probably wouldn't have been leading that patrol when they ran into the Panzer, and Smitty might be alive now.

A random shot in the night and your life becomes a part of history, a sad memory for your parents, family, and friends. Your life to them was a gleaming, flickering light, sharpened by their pain when they first hear the news of your death, but gradually diminishing over time to a dull and sporadic glow, the glow of your memory and a potential that was never to be lived.

How will the families of those young German tankers learn that their sons, brothers, and husbands are dead? Will not knowing how they died haunt the surviving families for the rest of their own lives? What monumental forces of evil had set these two small groups of strangers against each other on that muddy road late in the winter, late in a war that Germany seemed destined to lose? Could Smitty's death and the deaths of that German tank crew ever be justified by cries to nationalism or appeals to some greater good?

"This Hell proves that evil exists in the world," Dan thought, as he scanned the darkness in front of him, though he couldn't penetrate it enough to see the hand in front of his face.

Life was simple when he was a child; school, play, chores, and homework. Sunday school after the 9:00 A.M. Mass taught him about a loving, caring God, a father who loved the smallest of his creatures.

"Who made you?"

"God made me."

"Why did God make you?"

"God made me to know, love, and serve Him in this world, and to be happy with Him in the next."

"Funny words...kind of a vain guy, is this God fellow, who wants us to love him and serve him. Are we serving him by killing German soldiers? Are they serving him by killing us? I wonder..." Dan thought to himself.

"Did God make me to sit in a hole outside of some forsaken town in Germany, ready to call down Armageddon on a bunch of fellow human beings who happen to be wearing different uniforms from mine? Those poor bastards don't want to be here anymore than I do. But, maybe they have artillery too, waiting for the moment of their counter attack to rain Armageddon down on me and my buddies.

"Maybe he's an angry god? [1]

---

[1] "The wrath of God is like great waters that are dammed for the present; they increase more and more, and rise higher and higher, till an outlet is given; and the longer the stream is stopped, the more rapid and mighty is its course, when once it is let loose. It is true, that judgment against your evil works has not been executed hitherto; the floods of God's vengeance have been withheld; but

"So who's the smug bastard now? I kill them; they kill me; maybe another Panzer comes rolling out of the village, up the hill, and over this miserable hole in the ground, burying me for eternity, alone and in a grave that I dug for myself.

"Maybe, in a thousand years, some German farmer will see my bayonet poking through the soil, and a whole team of archeologists will excavate me, study me, and put me on display in a museum somewhere. 'He was in a crouching position when he died, ready to fight.' Why did he have the bayonet on his rifle?' they'll ask.

'Was he a volunteer eager for combat, or a hapless victim, forced by his government to fight and die for some cause or another that was important to them at the time?'"

Dan does have a morose side to his personality, and he easily becomes despondent when thoughts like these enter his mind. There are no adjectives to describe the horror that he and his comrades face every day. There's no way to describe how a man feels when he knows that there are other men somewhere out there who are thinking about ways to kill him. He and his companions live like this day after day, never knowing when their purported killers will be successful, or where they might come from. And the sheer randomness of it all heightens the terror they live in. Yet, in some ways, the terror becomes mundane, as one by one they get picked off; a mine here, a fire-fight there, a sniper somewhere else; regular occurrences around Charlie Company.

Walking through mud and snow, sleeping in the ground, fighting with lice and vermin, monotony and boredom, punctuated by moments of sheer terror where nothing matters but staying alive, killing other men so they won't kill you. And then...and then suddenly, it's all over. The enemy escapes, or they all die in place. Then you pick up your dead and wounded, and you bury theirs, if you're able to,

---

your guilt in the meantime is constantly increasing, and you are every day treasuring up more wrath; the waters are constantly rising, and waxing more and more mighty; and there is nothing but the mere pleasure of God, that holds the waters back, that are unwilling to be stopped, and press hard to go forward. If God should only withdraw his hand from the flood-gate, it would immediately fly open, and the fiery floods of the fierceness and wrath of God, would rush forth with inconceivable fury, and would come upon you with omnipotent power; and if your strength were ten thousand times greater than it is, yea, ten thousand times greater than the strength of the stoutest, sturdiest devil in hell, it would be nothing to withstand or endure it." _Sinners in the Hands of an Angry God_, Jonathan Edwards, Enfield, Connecticut July 8, 1741

and gradually you settle down into the monotony again till next time. Fighting a war is like that.

Life happens and death happens. We try to control what goes on around us, but sometimes we only have the control of a pine branch, being swept in the torrent of a raging mountain river in the spring. Hopefully we're swept out of the torrent into a calm pool, a peaceful backwater randomly chosen by the uncontrollable surge of raw power that had enveloped us, and which just as easily and randomly could have broken us into a million match sticks. War is like that.

"I can camouflage my foxhole, clean my rifle, and sharpen my bayonet, but when that Panzer comes surging out of the village toward me, then I'm a fossil in the making for some archeologist some day in the future."

As the night grew darker, Dan forced himself to become more alert, causing him to worry, "Was that snapping of a branch down the hill a squad of Germans, or just a fox prowling for food on a moonless night?"

Alone in a hole in the ground on a dark and raw night in March, your mind plays tricks on you. Dan had made it a practice all during the war to protect his night vision, but tonight, with no moon or stars, he had no eyes to rely on to protect his comrades.

Dan had stood a night watch many times in the course of the war, and he knew how his mind and his nerves played tricks on him. Typically, the minutes passed like hours, and the light of dawn would find him nervous, hungry, and exhausted.

This night he did see ghosts. Smitty came to him, asking, "Did you see Yvette, Dan? Was she heart-broken knowing that I'm dead? Dan...Dan...why do you keep looking away from me? Why are you crying?"

"Look, you asshole soldier..." Smitty's image faded as the dead company commander came through one of the dirt walls of Dan's' hole "...nobody tells me to shove a Silver Star recommendation up my ass. You little shit...you'll be sorry that you ever laid eyes on me..."

Another snap ..."Maybe that's not a fox or my nerves." Dan felt for the radio with one hand and pulled his rifle with the bayonet closer to him.

Sweat began to bead up on Dan's forehead as he tried to do with his ears what he couldn't do with his eyes. He was sweating profusely now as another breaking twig was followed by a scuffing heel, then the swish of a small branch snapping back into place, then a faint whisper, barely audible, but in a language that wasn't English.

Just as Dan clicked his radio three times, there was the sound of breaking brush in front of his foxhole. Clutching his rifle and charged by adrenaline, Dan screamed "Arrrgh!" as the form in front of him leaped, tripped, or fell into him

Dan thrust his bayonet upwards with all of the strength in his body. The scream of the soon-to-be-dying German soldier seemed to be echoing somewhere in the distance, as if Dan were in a dream. Then gravity brought this lump of a dying human being down into the hole, with Dan's rifle still protruding from his chest cavity, twisted out of Dan's hands.

This was horrifying, plunging your bayonet into another man's chest...not even a little bit like sticking tires during basic training.

Surging on adrenaline, Dan grabbed the falling German by the throat, ready to choke him to death with his bare hands, but there was no combat left in this soon-to-be-dead soldier. Dan relaxed his death grip on the other man's throat when he realized that this other occupant of his hole could no longer cause him any harm.

Then his victim began to speak. The words came softly and in German. Dan didn't know what the other man was saying, but the cadence of the words was very familiar to Dan, a part of him since the age of seven. Dan spoke the English words in cadence with the other's German. "Oh, my God, I am heartily sorry for having offended Thee....."

"Jesus Christ...the fucking German's Catholic and he's making an act of contrition as he prepares to die!" Dan thought to himself in a panic. "Oh, Jesus Christ! Oh, Jesus Christ! What have I done! What can I do to help this poor bastard? What have I done? Oh, God, what have I done?"

Dan was now screaming and crying at the top of his lungs, oblivious to the possibility that the man's companions would harm him. His words were soon lost in the cacophony of Armageddon, as the howitzers turned the forest around Dan into toothpicks. The noise of the explosions was punctuated by the screams of other dying Germans, breaking the night's silence as the gunners reloaded.

Dan couldn't remove the bayonet with the rifle on it. There was no room in the foxhole, so he unfixed the rifle from the bayonet, allowing him to cradle his adversary in his arms. They both huddled in the cold, dark, and wet hole, with Armageddon raging around him, and the screams of the dying man's comrades penetrating the night. Dan covered the dying German with his own body as spent shrapnel from exploded shells sporadically rained into their shelter.

The German's breathing became more labored as he reached into his pocket and pulled out a rosary, his pay book, and a small pocket light. Realizing that Dan could do nothing more to harm him, he held out the book to him. Inside the book was a letter with a velvet ribbon and the picture of a young blond woman, very pretty, and holding a newborn child. Pointing at the picture, the dying man said in a voice tinged both with sorrow and fondness, "Mein frau; Mein kinder", and then he died...he died in the arms of Dan Fleming, looking at the picture of his wife and new child. He died in the arms of Dan Fleming, killed at the hands of Dan Fleming.

As the shelling continued around them, Dan sheltered the dead man, fingering the rosary beads that he had pried from the German's hands. Dan went through the night saying the sorrowful mysteries over and over, sobbing for himself, and for the man whose life he had just taken.

Dan had killed men in combat before, but it was always at a distance with a rifle shot or a hand grenade, never close in with hand-to-hand fighting. This was very personal. There was now a bond between Fleming and the dead German, a bond that neither of them would have wanted, but a bond that would join them for the rest of Fleming's life.

How do two lovers find each other, marry, and spend a lifetime together? The random twist of fate, the rolling of dice, and the improbability of that linkage occurring. It's the same as meeting the man who'll kill you or the man that you'll kill, a random trip up a dark hill, falling into the hole of someone paid to kill you, and your young wife becomes a widow, and your newly-born child an orphan.

"So, who's the smug bastard now?"

"Heinrich Richter, I'd like you to meet Herr Fleming, the son of a factory worker in America, a store-clerk in civilian life, and the man who will send you to an early grave."

"Herr Fleming, I'd like to introduce you to Heinrich Richter, he was a university student before the war. He wanted to go to medical school, but he was drafted and sent to fight in France. He and Anka were married before he had to report for duty. She conceived during their two weeks of married life together and gave birth to their daughter while he was at war. He's never seen his daughter, and because you'll kill him very shortly, he'll never have that opportunity. He'll never hold her or hear her call him 'Daddy'. He and Anka will not grow old together, and this because of you, Herr Fleming."

The voice of fate had spoken. The will of the god of the toy soldiers must be fulfilled. An angry god, he had cast his dice so that Heinrich Richter must die, and Daniel Fleming must kill him, two men joined for eternity in the strange fellowship of the murdered and the murderer. One of these two strangers would go to his reward in the other world, while the tortured hulk of his tormented survivor lives the life that was so randomly and so cruelly taken from the other.

The light of dawn began to break through the darkness, barely a glimmer, when Dan heard voices in English. "Fleming...are you out there? Dan, can you hear us?"

Poking through the camouflage of his foxhole and the broken pine boughs from the shattered tree next to him, Dan shouted out, "Jones! I'm over here! I need some help!"

The six-man squad rushed over to Dan's position, surrounding him, kneeling or crouching in a defensive posture, weapons pointing outward, like the points on a Christmas tree star. Having secured the immediate area and being satisfied that there were no living German soldiers nearby, the squad leader started pulling pine branches off the place that Dan had imagined would be his grave.

"Oh, Jesus!" The smell of excrement and the sight of the two men huddled together in that hole and covered with blood shocked Corporal Jones.

"Dan, are you wounded anywhere?"

"No, Jonesy, that's his blood. He's dead. I murdered him."

"Hey, let's get you out of here. I don't know what's going on, but there are parts of dead Krauts all over here. The artillery got them last night while they were trying to infiltrate our position.

"You saved a lot of our lives by calling in the strike. The howitzer guys will probably all get medals because of you. Funny thing though, none of them were wearing helmets, and I haven't seen any weapons yet. I've been looking for a Luger to bring home as a souvenir, but the only thing I see here are body parts and pieces of German uniforms.

"Hurry out of there though. The captain is worried about another attack like the Bulge, and we'd be better off inside the perimeter at the top of the hill."

"Hang on, Jonesy, there's one thing I have to do."

Bending over the dead German, Dan removed the man's identity discs from around his neck, kissed him gently on the forehead, and said, "I'm sorry, my friend, that fate had us meet this way. I'll look after your frau and your kinder. Rest in peace, my friend, till we meet again in some other place."

Fighting to hold back tears, Dan pulled himself out of the hole, taking his rifle but leaving his grenades and the bloody bayonet protruding from the chest of the dead German soldier.

Once out of the other man's tomb, Dan took his entrenching tool off his belt and began filling in the hole.

"Dan...no time for that; Jerry may be all around us."

"You go back, Jonesy. I have to finish this thing that I never meant to start. I killed him, Jonesy. I never meant to, but I had no choice. It's not like I could avoid it. The least thing I can do is to bury his corpse so the animals don't eat it."

"Fleming, get a hold of yourself! It was you or him. You did what you had to do. Stop shaking and crying, for Christ's sake, and let's finish burying the poor bastard as quick as we can and get out of here."

When Fleming and Jones had finished burying Heinrich Richter, protected by the now five pointed star of shooters, Dan threw one last shovel-full of dirt on the man's grave and thrust his entrenching tool into the mound of soft earth, handle end first, with the shovel end pointing up. After removing one of the discs from the chain he had taken from the dead man's neck, Dan wrapped the chain with the remaining disk around the top of the shovel before leaving that place.

Besides his bayonet and hand grenades, Dan Fleming left a piece of his soul in that hole outside a small nondescript village somewhere in Germany.

When the small group of soldiers returned to the platoon, Dan's captain asked, "How you doing, Dan?"

"I'll be OK, Captain."

"You had a rough night out there."

"Yeah."

"Dan, we sent a couple of squads out to reconnoiter the area, looking to make contact with the enemy, but I don't think there's a German soldier within twenty miles of here, except for those poor, dead bastards who got caught in the 105 fire last night.

"We do have a little problem though. We've found body parts from fifteen German soldiers, no helmets, no weapons, and the shattered remains of a broom handle with half a white bed sheet attached to it.

"These poor, dumb bastards were trying to surrender, and we blew them to pieces.

"Before you go, Dan...there's something else. I'm not supposed to say anything; battalion said to keep it quiet till it happens, but the war is over at eleven hundred hours. Germany has signed an unconditional surrender.

"Those guys were probably the last German soldiers to be killed in World War II. But we've got a problem. They were trying to surrender, and we killed them. Of course, we had no way of knowing what their intentions were, and when they came through your position, you followed orders and called in artillery fire on the sector.

"You know that, I know that, and every American soldier in this unit knows that. But, the villagers are bound to be upset, and I don't want them to trigger an investigation by some starched shirt staff officer about whether we violated the Geneva Convention and murdered troops who were attempting to surrender.

"Dan...I know you won't like this, but I'm putting you in again for a Silver Star. I want to document what happened last night for the record, but knowing what I know now, I don't want to file a false after-action report with battalion; I'd get court-martialed for that. But, describing the situation from your perspective as you saw it unfolding last night, I could cover all of our asses without perjuring myself."

"Look...I...um...I...um..."

"I don't want to hear it, Dan. You and I and the others have been through a lot together, especially after my asshole predecessor was killed. This is the best way to do it, and if you don't want to wear it, throw your medal in a drawer for your kids to find after you die.

"Now, get out of here and get some sleep! We're about to switch from being combat troops to becoming an occupying force. Haircuts, shined boots, and buttoned buttons. The MPs will be all over you if they spot you with an unbuttoned button on your jacket or shirt.

"Get some chow, Dan, and some rest. The war is over, Dan, and we'll be going home soon."

"Yes, Sir," Dan sighed, as he saluted wearily, tormented by what he'd just heard and by what he'd done the previous evening. The death of Private Heinrich Richter still burned deeply in Dan's soul, and now the deaths of the fifteen other men would be charged to him as well, and he'd receive a medal for that.

For not the first time in his military career, Dan fell asleep exhausted, while sobbing uncontrollably and oblivious to the cold and raw rain that ran off the rubber poncho covering him as lay curled up on the hard ground.

CHAPTER FIFTEEN

Corporal Hohmann Saves the Day and the Mayor's Ceiling Gets Cleaned

While Dan was sleeping, something unusual began to take place. Forming inside the gate on the dirt road leading out of the town was a group of men in civilian clothes. One of them was dressed in formal clothing with a top hat and a sash running over one shoulder and across his chest. He also wore a large gold-colored amulet on a chain around his neck. Another was holding a broomstick with a large, white piece of cloth tied to it.

Slowly, the group...there were seven of them, all men, and all seemingly too old for military service...began making their way up the hill toward the Americans' position.

"Shit, it's the mayor and council again. Nungesser, would you run and get Hohmann for me. I think he's serving Mass now for Father Porcelli, but this can't wait. If they're at the Consecration, wait till that's over, but before or after that, get him up here on the double. Apologize to the chaplain for me."

Captain Miller straightened his uniform and looked in the cracked mirror hanging on the center pole in the headquarters tent. For the first time since he had left England an eternity ago, he noticed the droopy eyes that looked back at him and the wrinkles on his dirty unshaven face.

"The war has aged me," he thought, as he looked in partial disbelief at the reflected figure in the glass. "None of us will ever be the same as we were before this, but Fleming will need more help than the others. I must see that he gets help. Since the chaplain's around, I should have him talk with Fleming in the next day or two."

107

Now that peace was at hand, the thought occurred to him that more mirrors would be cropping up around the place, more staff people popping in, and more bureaucratic Army bullshit.

"Get someone to fire a burst over their heads. I don't want to give them a cheap view of our set-up here. Hohmann and I will go out to meet them, and I want an escort of two men with Tommy guns, just like a gangster has, only in uniforms."

The reverberation of the automatic rifle brought the men to an abrupt halt as the volley of bullets flew harmlessly over their heads. The volley was clearly meant as a warning for them to stop and not advance any further.

"Whaddya see, Top?" the captain asked, as the first sergeant scanned the delegation with a set of high powered binoculars, looking for signs of anything suspicious, perhaps a bulge concealing a weapon, or some sort of signaling device, anything that might put his men in danger.

"Nothing, Sir. They look clean, but be careful anyway. We'll keep you covered from here and we have enough snipers to take the group out before they know what hit them."

In short order, Captain Miller, Corporal Hohmann, and their two-man escort started down the hill.

"Good morning, Mister Mayor," said Hohmann, as he translated the captain's greeting into flawless German.

"What do you assholes want?" Miller asked.

Hohmann translated into German, "Your Excellency, to what do we owe the pleasure of your visit?"

Speaking in rapid German, the mayor said, "You American pigs! You killed fifteen innocent men who were just trying to surrender to you." The German went on and became more agitated as he spoke, challenging Miller and his escort to gun them down as they had the group of fifteen the previous day.

"Hohmann, what did he say; what was he saying about swine, and why's he so worked up?"

"He's welcoming the Americans to his town and assures us of their cooperation. They even have some pigs that survived the war and he said they'd slaughter them for the Americans to show us that we're welcome."

"I don't want any shit from him! Tell him we want all German soldiers in town to surrender as a unit tomorrow in front of the town hall at twelve hundred hours."

Turning toward the mayor, the interpreter spoke in German, "Captain Miller reiterates that what happened last night was a tragic mistake. He suggests that you give any soldiers remaining in town civilian clothing and have them leave at once to return to their own homes and families. He said that you should tell them to leave all of their military uniforms and weapons with you, and we will send a patrol into town tomorrow at noontime to pick them up. We will also take into custody at that time any soldiers who need medical attention. They will be treated as prisoners of war, of course, and cared for as we would care for our own troops."

"Hohmann, why is this fucking guy so agitated? Tell him to calm down or we'll throw him and his entire government into the stockade."

"He's just nervous, Captain. He's excited that the war's almost over and he's eager to please us so that we'll help his people."

"The captain says that he appreciates your cooperation and understanding, and that he looks forward to working with you and your people."

"I'm glad that your captain's so sensitive. We've been through a lot. The deaths of those fifteen young men were tragic. Tell your captain that we'll have the weapons and uniforms in my office in the town hall by noon tomorrow, and will send the other young men back to their homes and villages, as he suggested.

"You will treat the wounded?"

"Yes, have them with you when you surrender the weapons and uniforms and we'll see that their injuries are treated."

Reaching across to the interpreter, the mayor smiled and extended his hand. Hohmann smiled and extended his.

Captain Miller managed a confused smile as he too shook hands with the German mayor. "Hohmann, what the hell's going on here?" the captain asked, as the delegation lined up to shake first the interpreter's hand, and then the captain's hand, before turning and heading back toward their village.

The two guards with the guns eyed the German delegation nervously, and did nothing to lock the safety switches on their weapons.

"He appreciates your understanding, Sir. He'll surrender the remaining troops in town, as well as weapons and uniforms of the ones who have left to return to their homes tomorrow at noon in his office in the town hall."

The delegation finished shaking hands with the two GIs, and under the watchful eyes of the guards, turned to walk back down the road into the village.

Turning toward the mayor, one of the village council members said, "You really told those bastards off."

"Yes, I guess we told them what was on our minds, and I'm glad they backed down. Maybe we can work with the ignorant sons of bitches."

After the German delegation was half way down the hill, the four Americans turned to walk back to their position. One of the gunners turned to Captain Miller and said, "You really told those Kraut bastards off."

"Yeah, I guess I did, and I'm glad that Hohmann's so proficient in German. You could tell from looking at the expressions on the mayor's face that they understood everything we were telling them. I think we can work with these dumb sons of bitches."

Corporal Hohmann breathed a silent sigh of relief and a brief prayer of thanksgiving.

When they got back to the command post, Captain Miller turned to the interpreter and said, "Herb, before you go back to your post, would you go to the chaplain and ask him to stop by when he gets a chance. I'd like to have a few words with him."

"Yes, Sir," Hohmann said, saluting sharply.

"Oh, and Herb...you did a nice job interpreting out there. Being able to communicate with these guys will make all of our lives easier."

"Thank you, Sir."

Meanwhile, as Fleming slept, and Hohmann sought out the chaplain, there was a drama being enacted down the hill in the center of town.

The mayor, after returning from his meeting with the Americans, was sitting behind his desk in the town hall with three members of the town's police force lounging around his office. They weren't showing any arms, but there was a double-barreled shotgun under the couch across from the mayor's desk, and four handguns in the ornate credenza next to it. It would be clear to any onlooker that these men were there to protect the mayor, whether they were armed or not.

The mayor was busy drafting a proclamation announcing Germany's surrender, with instructions for all civilians and military personnel under his jurisdiction. With his head down and pencil in hand, he was engrossed in what he was doing when the door to his office burst open. The commander of the decimated SS detachment in the town stormed in and confronted him about the rumored surrender that was rapidly spreading among the troops and civilians in town.

"Mr. Mayor, my men will never surrender! We'll fight to the end and die here as brave and honorable German soldiers. We'll not run or surrender like those traitors who tried to sneak away under cover of darkness last night. Those Wehrmacht cowards got what they deserved; they were murdered in cold blood like pigs at the slaughter."

The death's head tattoo on the back of the German officer's hand throbbed as blood pulsated through his arteries and veins.

Slowly, noiselessly, the sofa yielded its hidden treasure to the hands of one of the mayor's guards.

"We'll die in glory and we'll take many of the American bastards with us in death!"

"Look, Lieutenant, the war's over. Germany has surrendered. This town's now under civilian control, and I don't want any more death or destruction. We're running out of food and soon it'll be time for spring planting. My people will find it difficult enough to survive without you pursuing your own private war to the end. I suggest that you surrender your weapons to me, change to civilian clothes, and get your ass back to Bavaria or wherever it is that you come from. And you might want to get that tattoo removed from the back of your hand."

Pulling his pistol from his holster in a rage, the SS lieutenant halted in mid-draw by the feel on the back of his head just above his neck of something cold...very cold and very hard, like two steel pipes.

"Your instincts are very good, Lieutenant. That is indeed a double-barreled shot gun pressed into your head. Slowly take your pistol by its barrel and place it on the floor in front of you. Good, now kick it across the floor toward me. It would have been a shame for both of us if you had resisted. You would have had no future if you were dead, and I would have had one hell of a time cleaning your brains off my ceiling."

"Well done," the mayor said, as he picked up the weapon. "Now, take your clothes off."

"Never! I'll die in this uniform!" the SS man screamed, as he reached for the back-up pistol he had concealed in his waist, and started to turn to confront the man behind him. There was a very loud retort, and it took the rest of the day and all night to clean and repaint the ceiling in the mayor's office.

The messenger under a white flag walked toward the American lines half way up the hill and stopped.

"Top, send someone to get Hohmann up here on the double. It looks like the Krauts want to talk again."

"Sir, the mayor isn't with them this time. Do you want me or one of the platoon leaders to meet with the messenger?"

"Nah, I'll go. I want to hear what they have to say while they're saying it, and Hohmann's a crackerjack interpreter. Just have someone get him up here pretty quick."

"Yes, Sir."

"I wonder what they want, Herb." The company commander and his interpreter walked down the road to meet the messenger half way. No armed escort this time, but the rifles of four snipers were trained on the messenger's heart.

"I don't know, Sir, but we'll find out pretty soon."

"Herb, just make sure that we position ourselves so that we can draw on him if there's any funny stuff without shooting at each other."

"Yes, Sir."

"You wanted to speak with us?" Hohmann said in German.

"Yes. The mayor would like an additional twenty-four hours to get all of the troops into the city to surrender. Some of the wounded have to be carried in, and they have to be moved gently."

"What did he say?"

"They need another day to round up all of their wounded to surrender."

"I don't like this. They could be preparing something. I don't want to walk into an ambush, although it makes sense that it could take some time to collect all of their wounded.

"Tell him that's OK, but if there's any funny stuff, we'll turn his town into a pile of match-sticks."

"The captain says that he agrees to another twenty-four hours. You'll surrender the remaining soldiers the day after tomorrow at noontime. The captain also wants you to tell the mayor that if any of our troops are ambushed, there will be severe retaliation, including the total destruction of your town."

"I understand, and will tell our mayor what your captain has said."

"The mayor also told me to ask if we can keep some weapons for our police and for hunting. Our food stocks are dangerously low, and we'll soon have to plant for this year's harvest. The mayor's afraid that people will eat the seed grain and roots in order to survive. If people could hunt, they could feed themselves till this year's crops come in."

"Captain, they're asking about keeping weapons for their police and for hunting. They're running out of food, and the mayor's afraid that they'll eat their seed crops to avoid starvation."

"Damn it....I don't know whether I'm supposed to kill these bastards or keep them alive. We're supposed to feed them under the Geneva Convention, but there's no way that's going to happen with their whole country collapsing into chaos.

"Tell him we want all of the weapons turned in, and we'll issue a limited number of side arms and hunting rifles...no military weapons...directly to him. It'll be a capital offense for anyone to have a weapon other than the ones we issue. Anyone with an unauthorized weapon will face death by firing squad."

After passing the information on to the messenger, the two GIs started walking back to their encampment.

"Captain, what did you do before the war?"

"I was an insurance adjuster. I got out of Notre Dame in 1941 with a degree in History. My father had an insurance business in Elkhart, Indiana, but at the time, the business wasn't big enough to support me, so he got me a job working for one of the companies he wrote for.

"It's funny, looking back from this perspective, on what we did before the war. Every spring in Indiana, we have a bunch of tornadoes. I'd go out to adjust a casualty loss and see a house with kids' toys on the lawn where they had left them before the storm. The house next door, the one that I'd be adjusting the claim for, would just be a pile of splinters, like over there," gesturing to the forest that'd been destroyed by the artillery barrage of the previous evening, "only worse.

"Boy, I could make a fortune adjusting casualty losses in this country.

"How about you, Herb, what did you do before the war?"

"Well, I was in the seminary for a couple of years, but left in my second year. I'm not sure the priesthood's for me, especially after what we've all been through. I think we'll all need some time...assuming we get back home alive...to sort all of this out in our minds. For me, I keep asking the question: What kind of god lets all of this horror happen?"

"That reminds me," said the captain, "did you ever get to talk with the chaplain?"

"I did, Sir. He said that he'd drop by this afternoon, if you were gonna be in the area. He seemed to be pretty down in the dumps when I saw him."

"Good...thanks, Herb. I'm a little concerned about Fleming and what he went through the other night. I thought that maybe the chaplain might be able to help him. I know that Fleming's Catholic, and I thought that'd be worth a try. Frankly though, after what we've been through, I don't know if anyone or anything could blot this out of our minds. I don't know that religion can answer any of these questions for Fleming especially, but it's worth a try."

"You're right, Captain. It's hard to conceive how an all-just, all-loving god could let all of this happen. It'll take some time for each of us to sort this out."

The two men remained silent over the two hundred yard walk back to Charlie Company, each caught up in his own review of the war to date and wondering what life would have in store for them now that it was officially over.

The olive drab headquarters tent was continually staffed by a radio operator and a company clerk, as well as an officer of the day and a duty non-commissioned officer. During daylight hours, the first sergeant and Captain Miller also worked out of the HQ tent.

113

Crossing back into the position, Miller went directly for the HQ tent, and Hohmann reported back to his platoon.

"Hey, Top, did I miss anything while I was out on my little walk?"

"Not a lot, Captain, just the usual stuff. Brigade's sending a truckload of replacements and battalion has signed off on the Medal of Honor for Smith. Now, they send it up to division and then to theater HQ.

It sounds pretty good that it sailed through brigade and battalion so quickly."

"Yeah, that's good news; that is fast, which reminds me, I'd better get a letter out to Smitty's parents. I'd like the letter to get there before his body.

"Will you take this group of replacements around and introduce them to their squads? Emphasize to them that this thing's winding down, but they should still be operating at a high level of combat readiness. There'll be a whole bunch of fully armed German soldiers running around the country. Don't assume that they've gotten word that the war's over, or that they have good intentions. We have to maintain combat readiness and the integrity of our position at all times. I don't want any of the new guys to think they can wander around outside the perimeter of our position to pick daisies."

"Yes, Sir, I'll take care of the replacements. Will you put a personal word from me in that letter? I'd like you to tell Mrs. Smith that I think her son was the bravest and most heroic person that I've ever met."

"I'll do that, Top. It's a humbling thing to try to encapsulate her son's life on a couple of pieces of paper, knowing that she'll have that letter close to her for the rest of her life. When she's overcome by thinking about his death, she'll open it, reread it, cry over it, and gently fold it before putting it away, tear-stained into a bureau drawer.

"Would you see that I'm not disturbed for at least half an hour, unless Father Porcelli comes by?"

"Yes, Sir," came the response from the first sergeant, saluting before he turned to leave.

"It's funny," Miller thought to himself, "the clearest evidence that the war's coming to an end is that O'Neill saluted. He hasn't saluted me since before D-day."

"Dear Mrs. Smith," the letter began, "It saddens me to have to tell you that your son, Michael, was killed in combat. I got to know Michael well over the time that we both served together in Charlie Company. He was always telling us stories about his family and the good times that you all had together, about giving his sister, Mary, her first driving lesson when they almost ended up in the brook near your house. He told me about his love for Gwen, and how he hoped to marry her after he returned home and got a job. He spoke frequently of Gwen.

"I have recommended Michael for the Congressional Medal of Honor because of his actions on the day of his death. A German tank had surprised the patrol Michael was with. It looked like all of the members of his patrol would be killed by the turret gunner. With total disregard for his own safety, and in order to save his comrades, Michael leaped onto the tank and threw a hand grenade into the open turret behind the gunner, who was firing on the other members of the patrol. Sadly, the gunner killed Michael before being killed himself by one of your son's friends.

"Michael's heroic and selfless action undoubtedly saved the lives of the other men in the patrol. I am told that Michael died instantly and didn't suffer.

"On a personal note, I always found Michael to be deeply religious, and a very popular member of Charlie Company. His friends in the Third Platoon thought highly of him, and we will remember him and pray for him.

"Sergeant O'Neill, our first sergeant, asked me to express his sorrow to you and to tell you that Michael was the bravest and most heroic person he has ever met.

"Please express our condolences to the other members of your family, and to Gwen and Michael's friends.

Sincerely,

H. Edward

Miller, Captain,

United States Army."

Miller read the letter over a couple of times, made a couple of changes, and finally was satisfied with it. He hadn't mentioned that the graves registration people would be sending her son's personal effects, because he wasn't sure what, if anything, they found on his body and whether it'd be suitable to send home to a dead soldier's mother. A wallet, perhaps shredded and stained with her son's blood, for example, would not be something that would likely make its way into Mrs. Smith's hands.

Chapter Sixteen

Dan Talks With the Chaplain
and Ends Up In the Hospital Again

In the course of reading the letter for the third time, the captain was interrupted by the chaplain's voice.

"Hello, Ed, how are you doing today?"

"Hi, Father, come in and sit down. Take a load off your feet."

"I understand that you just got back from another meeting with people in the town."

"Yeah, nothing major...they just wanted another day to round up the German casualties and surrender them and any remaining forces. No big deal. I suspect that any remaining German soldiers are well on their way out of here, heading for home, and wanting to put the war behind them...like us. Good luck to them, as long as they're not wearing uniforms and firing on us.

"Father, thanks for coming by. I wanted to ask if you'd check in with Dan Fleming. He's been through a lot lately, and I'm afraid that he could snap at any minute. I've been with him almost every day since D-day. There are fewer than a quarter of us left out of the company that landed on the beach that day. If there's a hell, we've been living it for the last couple of years, and I'm concerned that it's taking a toll on Fleming."

"Ed, I've only been with the battalion for three months, but I've seen more than I can handle. I can't imagine what your men feel when they're out on patrol. I see the results of their skirmishes when the front moves forward. I give last rites to the men before they die, and I've anointed German soldiers and civilians as

I've come across their bodies. I don't know how much more of this I can take myself...but I'll talk with Fleming."

"Father, one other thing. You know that before this insanity began, I had graduated from Notre Dame. I've been working on Fleming to go there after the war, and I'd appreciate it if you'd mention that to him...get his mind off of all this shit and get him focused on a world beyond the killing and suffering. You belong to the same congregation that runs Notre Dame, so I think he'd listen to you."

"You've mentioned that to me before. I think he'd be a good fit. He often serves Mass for me when I say it in this company. The thought has occurred to me that he might have a vocation. I think he'd make a good priest."

"I think you're right, Father. The other men go to him with their problems. I think he'd make a good priest."

"Sometimes I wonder what kind of priest I've become. I went to the seminary to bring the grace of the sacraments to men and women. Never did I ever think that I'd be witnessing the evil and carnage that this war has wrought. Never did I think that my ministry would have me dealing with this constant unfolding horror. How can I counsel men who kill and expect to be killed at any instant?"

"Father, I know that. I lead those men that you anoint, and I send them off to their deaths. I've killed men myself, looking them in the eye, both of us panicked and desperate. I've come close to death so many times and randomly escaped it, one time when a shell exploded near me. Another ten yards and I would have been dead. When the company commander, my predecessor, died, I was closer to him than I am to you. It could as easily have been me instead of him. Why him and not me? I'm always asking myself, why me? Why have I been allowed to live this long? Is this some cruel joke, where I'll end up being the last man to die in World War II? Why have I been allowed to live when so many of the men I've served with are dead?

"Father, I don't know what the answer is. When I graduated from Notre Dame, I thought that I had all the answers, and when I got out of OCS, I was a cocky second lieutenant. Now I'm a captain because the guys above me in the chain of command have all been killed. I realize now that I don't have any of the answers...hell, I don't even know the questions. I just go on, one day after the other, trying to survive and protect the men under my command. I want all of them to go home and have lives after this war, and more and more I feel that I'm failing in this.

"Why me, Father? Why have I been allowed to live, and will I make it home? Is God like a little kid playing with armies of tin soldiers who knocks them off at whim, one at a time...an angry god...a petulant god?

"One careless step and a land mine could end my existence. They'd send me home in a box, at least as much of me as they could find, and the colonel would write a letter home to my wife like I just did to Smitty's parents....like I've done to too many parents. Chaplain, if you don't have the answers, I don't know who does.

"Anyway, you'll find the Third Platoon at a new position, just inside the town gates, down the hill over there. I've just moved them there to secure the entrance to the town and to let the locals get acclimated to us. There's a blown-up barbershop just to the left as you enter the town. That's where Fleming's squad should be.

"Stay on the road though. The engineers swept it yesterday and removed some anti-personnel mines. They didn't get a chance to check the fields off to the sides of the road though.

"Father, I'm sorry for bending your ear. I know that you're feeling this the same as all of us, and it's unfair for me to unburden myself at your expense."

"Ed, I'm a priest, I'm supposed to help people with their troubles, even if I'm struggling with those same troubles myself. I'll go talk with Fleming. I don't know how I can help him, but I'll listen to him and pray that God gives me the strength and wisdom I need to do that.

"You know, Ed, my father was an auto mechanic. He taught me everything about cars when I was a kid, but he was so proud when I told him I wanted to be a priest. I never imagined that this is how it would all work out."

Leaving the command tent, Father Porcelli headed through the company area and down the hill towards the Third Platoon. Walking down the road through the middle of the area that the artillery had destroyed two nights ago, Porcelli was overwhelmed by the scope of the devastation and destruction. Where there had once been a thick forest of evergreens, there was now a collage of shattered and twisted stumps and branches, charred and formed into a grotesque sculpture, evidence of evil incarnate in the world. Deeply despondent and disillusioned, the young priest made his way through this garden of horror.

As he drew near to the village, Porcelli noticed what appeared to be a piece of cloth or clothing on the path. Bending over, he saw that it was a German enlisted man's field cap. Picking it up, he saw the name of its owner written on the headband- "Schmidt."

"Poor Schmidt," he thought. "He must have been one of the men I anointed yesterday after the barrage." He thought to himself that more accurately, Schmidt must have been one of the deformed hunks of charred flesh that he had given the last rites to. After which, the young priest, himself on the verge of a nervous breakdown, had returned to the company area and cried and vomited until he collapsed in exhaustion.

"Where are you headed, Father?"

The voice of the young sentry woke Father Porcelli out of his morose wanderings.

"I'm looking for the Third Platoon, Dan Fleming's squad."

"Down into the town, Father, past the gates over by the barber shop. Just be careful to stay out of that field to the left of the town gates. The engineers marked it as a minefield a couple of days ago, and early in my watch I saw a cow trigger a land mine...not a pretty picture. It shook me up thinking that it could as easily have been a human being, and maybe me. Just be careful, Father."

"Thank you, soldier. I'll be careful."

Half walking, half wandering, the young priest moved toward the town gates, apprehensive about meeting this soldier who he was expected to counsel, a man not much younger than himself, who has experienced more evil than any human being should be expected to endure in a lifetime. Father Porcelli wanted to find refuge in prayer, but no prayer would come to him. His mouth was dry and he'd developed an intense headache. But, he knew that he had to pull himself together to counsel this young soldier who had seen too much and who, like himself, was ready to snap.

Entering the gates of the town, he could see the squad dug in, positioned in a defensive posture in and around the rubble of the burned-out buildings.

"Father, can I help you?"

The voice of the squad leader seemed to come from nowhere, partially a challenge and partially an offer of assistance, and that was followed by a figure with a rifle stepping out of the shadows from behind the masonry façade of a pile of rubble that used to be a barber shop.

"Yes, I'm looking for Corporal Fleming."

"Hold on, Sir, I'll get Fleming and bring him back here. Just be careful because there's a mine field just outside the gates."

"Thank you, Sergeant, I'll be careful."

Porcelli could hear the squad leader's voice as the later trotted down the main street to where Dan Fleming was placing the finishing touches on another of his foxhole creations.

"Fleming, you should get a patent on your foxhole design."

"Thanks, Sarge; what's up?"

"The chaplain's here...said he wants to talk with you."

"I wonder why he wants me, Sarge. I really don't want to talk with him right now. Between Smitty getting it, and my killing that fellow the other night, I've got a lot to sort out before I talk with a priest.

"I'm not sure that even a priest can help me. How can someone help who's not been through this shit? How can you describe to someone what it feels like to drive a bayonet into another human's chest, and how you feel holding him in your arms while he dies, knowing all the time that it was you who killed him?"

"Dan, get a hold of yourself. The war's almost over and we'll have a lifetime to work this shit out. Right now, just focus. All of us need to focus on keeping each other alive till we get out of here, get home, and put all of this shit behind us."

"Sarge, I killed him! I'll never forget his face; I'll never be able to put that behind me. He almost had a child's face, blond hair, blue eyes, lying in my arms. We prayed together, him in German, me in English. The words sounded different, but they had the same meaning. He was making an Act of Contrition in German. The cadence was the same, and I joined him in English. Then he pulled out a rosary, but died before he could say it. I took his beads and started saying Hail Marys for him. I still have his rosary.

"He had that distant, blank look that all dead men have, at least all of the dead men that I've seen. I cried then, Sarge; I broke down and cried like a baby, but no one heard me because the barrage started then, and all those poor bastards who wanted to surrender got annihilated, blown to pieces because of my three clicks on the field phone.

"I took my thumb and moved each of his eyelids down. We stayed together till morning. The hole wasn't too wide and he started stiffening up. Then his bowels let go and he shit in his pants. I'll never get the stench of his death out of my nostrils or my mind...."

Fleming was staring into space while he was speaking, as if he were alone and disembodied, at some other place within himself, and oblivious to all that was around him.

"Dan!" The sergeant's word was sharp, commanding attention, and it brought Fleming back to the reality of his situation.

"Dan," the other man said again, now more softly, "I know how you feel, but the chaplain wants to talk with you. Maybe you should tell him all of this; maybe he can help you."

Fighting to hold back tears, Fleming, almost screaming, said, "He can't help me! No one can help me! I'm a murderer! Don't you understand? I killed that poor, frightened bastard who just wanted to surrender and go home to his wife and baby...."

"Dan, I do understand, but head back to the barber shop. The major's waiting there for you. I'll watch your position till you return. I'm sorry, Dan, I'm sor…"

"You wanted to see me, Father?"

"Well, uh…yes, Dan…I've uh….not seen you at Mass for a couple of weeks and I uh…was wondering…you know…if things were OK. Is there anything I can ….you know….do….; you know….I…uh, was wondering if ….if…anything's going on?"

Porcelli couldn't hide his discomfort. He was babbling awkwardly, trying to develop some bond with this other very fragile person. Two fragile human beings, plucked out of civilian life. One sent to commit atrocity after atrocity in the name of his country and his country's honor; the other to comfort the first, and say things to him that would allow him; rather, encourage him, to commit those atrocities because he was acting in the name of his god.

One of them was the instrument of evil, and the other the facilitator of evil. One killed, and the other rationalized the killing in the name of a loving and merciful god. Or, was it a ruthless, angry, and vengeful god? Was it fate that brought them together in the rubble of this German town on this day in the history of the world?

Was this just another cruel move by their god on the chessboard, where both men were pawns? "My Queen to your Rook." Is this what was happening? Were these two pathetic figures merely pawns in some demented Grand Masters' game of chess? Was that their reality? Perhaps a game where the pieces were killed and maimed instead of being captured, a game played between a good god and a bad god, but really a game that felt to the participants like it was being played between two very bad gods…very bad and very angry.

Maybe the little boy god with his tin soldiers had placed Fleming and Porcelli together in the rubble of that bombed out barber shop, two tin soldiers, actors carrying out the little boy god's wicked fantasy. He did this to them in a place where men used to congregate to talk and to get their hair cut. The wicked fantasy of this little boy god had thrown these two fragile human beings together in this place, maybe to see what they would do to each other, these two tin soldiers, these two pawns, pawns of at least one angry god.

Fleming, never at a loss for words, stood silent and motionless as the other man babbled uncomfortably. When the priest stopped, both men stood in silence, amid the rubble of that barbershop. The setting sun silhouetted them standing there in the rubble of that place, in the rubble of their worlds.

Finally, Fleming spoke, "Aw shit, Father, I don't know what to say. I don't know what this is all about. I don't…I don't know what to do…"

Fleming spoke, and then stopped abruptly, as he felt the tears welling up inside of him. Porcelli sensed rather than saw the other man's great disturbance. He could hear it in his voice; he could see it in the way that Fleming carried himself.

"I must be strong," Porcelli thought to himself, "I'm a priest....it's my duty to help this man. Christ, give me the strength to help him...and myself."

"Do you want to talk about it? Do you want me to hear your confession?" The priest took a purple stole out of his pocket as he spoke and placed it over his shoulders. One inch wide, and three feet long, it was his badge of authority, the symbol of his power to act in the name of God and to forgive men's sins.

"Father....my sins are beyond forgiveness...by God...by you....by anyone. Father, I'm a murderer. I killed the father of a young child, bringing her half way to becoming an orphan, denying her a father's love, a father's presence, and his support for the rest of her life. She'll never have a father because I killed her father at the end of my bayonet. I killed him when he was trying to surrender.

"Confession, Father? There's no confession for me...my sin's too great, unforgivable. Nothing can absolve me of the terrible pain and guilt I feel! I made this beautiful, young child fatherless and her mother a widow. I'm beyond salvation, Father. It'd be better if one of their sharpshooters would take me out."

Looking squarely at the priest, Fleming went on, "Father, I don't deserve to live, but I don't have the courage to die, to kill myself the way I killed that innocent man. I'm sorry, Father, you wanted to know...I guess, and I told you. I'm sorry, Father, I'm sorry….." Again, Dan's words trailed off into tears. The young soldier was coming apart physically and emotionally. The things he'd seen; the things he had done as an instrument of untold horror, an instrument in a world consumed by unimaginable evil...these things tortured him, and he knew that they'd torture him for as long as he lived.

Not able to hold his own tears back, the young priest wrapped his arms around the younger soldier and they stood unashamedly in the rubble of that place, holding each other, and crying and crying until the tears came no more.

At last, stepping back, almost as a lover breaking an embrace with his loved one, Porcelli looked Fleming in the eye and counselled, "Dan, no sin's unforgivable...none, and killing a man in the course of a war's not a sin."

"No, Father, you're wrong...you're wrong! I've sinned against this man and his family, and against mankind, and against my God! I'm not a human being, Father. No one who's done what I did would be fit to call himself a human being!"

As clouds came in, the sunny day turned into a cloudy mist that yielded to a gentle spring rain, as both men stood in silence.

The priest moved to the white, ornate porcelain barber chair with a red leather seat that had strangely survived the devastation of its building. "Dan," he said gently, "I can forgive your sins through our Lord, Jesus Christ. Come to me, Dan."

Kneeling in the rubble beside the porcelain barber chair and under the spring rain, Dan began, "Bless me, Father, for I have sinned. It's been three months since my last confession. I've killed an innocent man, Father...in cold blood, Father...more brutally than any of the others I've killed. I called in an artillery strike on another group of Germans trying to surrender, and they were all killed, every last man. And I've slept with a woman."

"When men are away from home and faced with death, the comfort of a woman is often a temptation that they succumb to," the priest responded. "Try not to put yourself in a situation where this is likely to recur. Avoid the occasion of sin, and the temptation that goes with it.

"As for the death of that German soldier, the evil of these killing fields bothers me as much as it does you. It's as if an evil genie were let out of a bottle, and he won't return till people are sickened by the horror that they've unleashed. After the unremitting horror has sated itself, the genie will go back into its bottle, content for twenty years or so until the next war. But this is not a war of your causing. Dan, neither of us is here by choice. They told us to go, and we went. We're instruments, victims of this madness, not its cause.

"I've heard about the episode the other night. You're in combat, Dan. He was an enemy soldier. It was your right to kill him...it was your duty to kill him! You didn't choose to attack the German. You were ordered into the Army, and you've done your duty loyally. It's a cruel fate that put the two of you together the other night, but under the circumstances, you acted prudently in your own self-defense. As far as the artillery strike, again, you were just doing your duty as a soldier, a sentry who was charged with protecting the troops who slept that night.

"It was your duty to kill him...." The words rang in Porcelli's ears in disbelief. The thought of Schmidt entered Porcelli's mind, the dead German whose field cap Porcelli had just picked up. Porcelli understood Fleming's revulsion, though his own was worse. He wanted to curse the god who'd placed the two of them....all of them...into that situation.

"For your penance, I want you to say twelve 'Our Fathers' and twelve 'Hail Marys'; now make a good act of contrition."

"I can't, Father. I can't make an act of contrition. I can't say those words again, the words I said with him as he lay there dying. Father....Father, I'm sorry."

"I understand; I understand your sorrow, and why the words won't come to you now."

The priest raised his right arm and made a large sign of the cross over Fleming while speaking in Latin, "Absolve te in nomine Patris et Filius, et Spiritus Sanctus. Amen."

Folding the purple stole and replacing it in the breast pocket of his field jacket, the chaplain said, "I have to go, Dan. The Lord be with you."

"And with you, Father."

At that, the priest again made a sign of the cross in the direction of Fleming, muttered a blessing in Latin, and then turned and headed slowly toward the city gate, in what had become a more serious rainfall.

As he walked, he slowly began to realize...for the first time...why he was where he was. "It was your duty to kill him..." The man of God, comforting a young soldier who has killed...who has destroyed another man and his family.

"What kind of monster have I become?" he thought to himself. "I'm not here to bring the sacraments to these men. I'm here to help them kill and to rationalize the horrible and immoral acts of an army at war.

"They sent me here, and the others like me, to encourage young men to die bravely for their cause, with the comfort that their god will welcome them after their deaths because in dying, they were doing their duty.

"The German chaplains are doing the same thing for their soldiers. We are...I am ....an instrument of evil. I'm facilitating and lubricating the minds of these men so that they can risk their lives, kill, and die for their cause. Oh, my God, what have I done? What have I done?"

Turning right as he left the city gate and on to the road heading uphill to the company area, Porcelli paused at the minefield sign, blessed himself, and said, "Father, forgive me." He then turned past the minefield sign and walked straight into the field, slowly and deliberately toward the scattered remains of the dead cow that the sentry had pointed out earlier.

The sentry on the road had been watching the chaplain from the time he stepped outside the town's gate. "Hey!" he yelled. "You're in a minefield! Back out slowly in the footprints you made on the way in!"

But, the priest continued on.

Raising his rifle, the sentry fired a warning shot in the direction of the priest, but to no avail. He realized now what the chaplain's intent was and began firing at the dirt in front of the priest's path, kicking up debris in front of him. There was the roar of an explosion, almost simultaneous with, and muffling the sound of, the sentry's third shot, as the bullet detonated the mine that was ten feet in front of the priest.

Hearing the firing and the explosion, Dan ran toward the gate of the town and turned in time to see the sentry racing downhill toward the prostrate man in the field.

"Don't go in there!" the sentry screamed as he ran down the road. "It's loaded with mines!"

Ignoring the other's command, Fleming ran into the field in the footsteps of the chaplain. Porcelli lay in a heap in the mud and the straw, covered with blood and barely breathing. Fleming lifted him in a fireman's carry and began lugging him slowly and deliberately back to the road. He was almost out of the field when the weight of the other man caused him to slip in the mud. The next thing that Fleming remembered was waking in a hospital bed in England, his leg in a cast, and bandages on his head.

CHAPTER SEVENTEEN

Dan Musters Out and Returns Home

Dan Fleming was surprised at how much the lilac bushes in front of his house had grown while he was away in Europe. He hesitated to turn down the path to his front door. He had been discharged from the hospital after three months, and returned to his company, now stationed back in the States. Most of the men he had served with had already been discharged. He was at Fort Polk for only two weeks when the Army demobilized the entire unit so quickly that he barely had time to make train reservations out of Lake Charles, Louisiana.

After switching trains in Chicago, Dan had decided to surprise his parents by just showing up unannounced. The truth is that he was afraid to tell them he was coming home. He had written to them from England, and once from Fort Polk, so they knew that he was in the country. He didn't want to talk about his time in hell though, because he didn't want to inflict his pain on them. He knew they'd be curious and question him about where he'd been and what he'd done. He decided to make up a story that he'd been a cook stationed at battalion headquarters as the war moved across Europe. "I just hope they don't ask me for any recipes," he thought to himself, as he concocted the story in his own mind.

South Station had changed since he'd left for basic training three years ago, but not as much as he had. The cab ride from downtown to Brighton was a first for him, and he was surprised at how quick it was compared to the trolleys and buses.

His misgivings about not telling his family that he was coming home got stronger as he stood on the walk in front of the lilacs.

"But...there's no turning back now," he thought to himself as he turned onto the gray cement walkway that led to the front door of the large, green rented house.

He half wanted to run down the path and half wanted to turn around and run away. He didn't know if he could re-enter this world that he had left three years ago.

Slowly approaching the house, his hesitation vanished when he was spotted by his younger brother, who cried out so loudly that everyone within half a mile knew that "Danny's home! Everyone...Danny's home! He's home now! He's here now!"

Tommy Fleming raced out the front door to his older brother and half hugged and half tackled him. He was followed in short order by their mother, who was crying.

"Danny! Danny! My Baby! My Baby! You're home! You're safe! Oh, thank God! Thank the Blessed Virgin! She listened to my novenas! Thank God! Thank God!"

The tears of joy and happiness poured down his mother's cheeks, and Dan just closed his eyes and let them hold him, as tears formed in his own eyes.

"This is the happiest day of my life!" his mother said. "Why didn't you tell us you were coming? Tommy, call the plant and let your father know the good news. Tommy, first bring your brother's bag into the house."

"I've got it, Ma; I can still carry it. It's so good to be back, to be with you."

By now, half of the neighborhood was heading toward the Fleming house. "He's home; did you hear that Dan Fleming just came home? He's in front of his house. Yes....right now....this instant!"

He walked into the living room surrounded by people, and all the while his mother wouldn't loosen her grip on him, as if she were afraid that he'd leave her again if she let go.

"Why didn't you call us?" she asked.

"Ma, I got a chance to catch a train to Chicago from Louisiana, and I literally made it five minutes before it left. My orders came through, and if I didn't catch that train, there wouldn't have been another one for three days. So, I just grabbed my stuff, hopped into a base taxi, and told the driver that it'd be worth his while if I made the train. Well, we must have gone through every stop light in Lake Charles, and when we got there, I was so pleased that I paid his fare with a five-dollar bill and told him to keep the change. That was probably as much money as he took home from two day's work, but I didn't care. I knew that'd get me home sooner. It was worth every penny of it. Then, when I got to Chicago, I had to switch trains, and I had a tough time finding the train to Boston because there was another train on the track where the Boston train was supposed to be. I went back into the station to find out what was happening and had to race back out to another section of the terminal to another track, and barely made that one. I was going to call you from South Station, but by then I figured that I'd surprise you and save a nickel. Oh boy, what a trip. I'm so very excited to be home with you, Ma...with all of you. I'm very tired and very excited."

"Dan, how was it?"

Mr. Santoro lived across the street from the Flemings, and he'd been a close family friend all of Dan's life. Though he didn't want to talk about it, and he had dreaded this moment, Dan knew it was inevitable. "I was a cook, Mr. Santoro, and I didn't get to see much action. We got shot at a couple of times, but nothing serious. I read about most of it in the Army Times or the Stars and Stripes."

"Oh," the other man said, sounding slightly disappointed. "Well, I'm glad you're home."

"I'm sorry, Mr. Santoro, but the Army censors wouldn't let us write anything about where we were or what we were doing."

Dan's father came home early from the factory and was overcome with emotion, much as his wife had been earlier. Eventually the neighbors left, and Dan was alone with his family.

"Dan, you're no goddamn cook," said his father. "You could never boil a pot of water without screwing it up."

Dan thought, "Well, I never could bullshit the old man."

"Yeah, Dad, you're right, but I've seen and done so much bad stuff that I don't want to talk about it. I'll tell you and Tommy eventually, but Ma, I really don't want to share any of this with her. It's too horrible for my mother to hear. The things I've seen, the things I've done...the things I had to do....these are things that I could never tell her about, not because I don't want her to know, but because she couldn't understand. I'm not sure that I understand them, but I'll try to explain them to you, Dad, and to Tommy." At that, Dan broke down sobbing, crying like a baby.

"It's all right, Danny; it's all right," his mother said as she re-entered the room after hearing Dan's sobbing. "What's important is that you're home with us now and that you're safe. It's all over, all the bad things are over, and you're here with us now, Danny, and everything will be all right. I don't need to know what happened, but you can tell your father and brother. They're men, they'd understand. I'm your mother, and I'm here to love you and to thank God for bringing you back to us. You're exhausted, Danny. You need sleep and rest. Go take a nap, and if you're up, I'll make supper for you, your favorite, roast beef. But, if you sleep through the night, you can have it for breakfast. I love you,

Danny, and it's wonderful that you're back with us. I know that it won't be easy, Danny, but you can forget the war now. It's over, and it'll never happen again."

Tommy carried Dan's duffel bag up to his old room. Dan was surprised at how little things had changed in the three years that he'd been gone. It was almost like he could pick up his glove and call a couple of the guys for a pick-up baseball game at Faneuil Park. The glove was still sitting on his old baseball bat in the corner of the room, just where he had left them after the last time that he had hit flies to Tommy. His brother had changed though. The skinny kid he'd left to go into the Army was now a strapping fullback on the high school football team.

Dan and Tommy sat on the bed, and as soon as they were seated, their father appeared in the doorway.

"Dan, I didn't see combat in World War I, but I was stationed at a base that processed out the guys who had returned from France. A lot of them had shell shock. I guess they call it 'battle fatigue' now, but I know that Tommy and I can't begin to imagine what you've been through. Take your time. Try to get adjusted at your own pace to being home and a civilian. If and when you feel like talking about what happened, Tommy and I will give you a good ear. There's no hurry for you to do anything...and as far as everyone else is concerned, you were a cook. Christ, just don't share any recipes with any of the neighbors or you might end up poisoning half the town.

"Look....you're exhausted; you've been through a lot. Why don't you try to rest, and if you wake up later we can have supper, but don't worry about it if you sleep through.

"Come on, Tommy; let's leave your brother alone so he can get some shut-eye."

Tommy gave his brother a hug and left with his father, closing the bedroom door behind them.

CHAPTER EIGHTEEN

Dan's Demons

Dan's head was swimming. He was exhausted by his journey and totally disoriented by his rapid change from infantryman, to casualty, to garrison soldier, and then to civilian, all within a month's time. He was confused, disoriented, and discouraged. He couldn't get thoughts of Smitty, Yvette, Mike Fitzgerald, Mary O'Daugherty, Heinrich, the dead German, and Father Porcelli out of his mind. Though he was exhausted and fell into a deep sleep as soon as he got into bed, they all paraded through his mind over and over as the afternoon turned into night, and the night gave way to morning. Porcelli sat in his barber chair and the whole thing exploded in his dreams. Smitty crawled off of the burning tank and said, "Don't worry, Dan, they can't hurt us now; they're all turning crispy brown, like roasted chestnuts," followed by Mary O'Daugherty, "They'll be OK, Dan; they'll all be going home soon." Mike Fitzgerald drove up to the house in his deuce and a half and offered to take them all out to a drive-in movie in the back of the truck. Dan also kept hearing the screams of the burning men in the tank, and when the dead German soldier helped his wife and daughter into the back of the deuce and a half, Dan woke up in a cold sweat, screaming, and crying, "He's dead, for Christ's sake, can't you leave him alone; he's dead! He's dead!

"Oh God, he's dead, and I killed him!"

The door opened and the light switched on. Dan bolted upright and grabbed the first man through the door by the throat. "I killed him, you son of a bitch. I killed him, and I'm gonna kill you!"

From somewhere, he heard his mother's voice yelling, "Dan, let him go! Dan! Dan!" And he felt pounding on his back as he choked the man lying on the floor beneath him. Suddenly, he was hit, like getting blocked on the football

130

field, and was knocked backwards. Looking up, he saw Tommy's face focused and fixed on him. It was Tommy who threw the block that had knocked Dan off the German soldier who'd tried to kill him. What was he doing there and why was his mother in the room? Why were they protecting this Kraut bastard?

The figure on the floor was coughing, and began to stand up. Dan scrambled to his feet ready to attack again, but was confronted by his younger brother, who stood between him and the intruder.

"Tommy...let me kill him. Get out of the way; he'll kill us all!" Dan said, throwing his brother aside with the strength of the crazed and trapped animal that he'd become. And then he looked into the face of his attacker, smelled his breath, and was ready to engage him in a battle to the death. That's when he saw the frightened face of his father looking back at him.

"Dad, what are you doing here? Where's the German who attacked us? Did he get away?"

On the other side of the door, Dan's mother was crying again, but this time they weren't tears of joy, and his father continued gasping for breath.

"Are you all right, Dad, and where is he? Dad, talk to me! What did the bastard do to you? Dad...Dad?"

That was the last thing Dan remembered before again waking up in a hospital bed, with a powerful headache, and a lump on the back of his head, where his brother had hit him with his own baseball bat. This time was different though. His legs and hands were tied to the four corners of the bed, and he was in a private room.

"Why am I here, Doctor?"

"You were hallucinating and tried to kill your father."

"No, I'd never do that...I couldn't have done that!"

"You thought your father was a German soldier and that he was trying to kill you. He's OK, but you came close to killing him."

"Oh, God! Oh, God...what did I do? What can I do, Doctor?"

"You're suffering from a condition that we don't know a lot about; they refer to it as 'combat fatigue'. After World War I, some people called it 'shell shock'. Essentially what happens is that your nervous system's overwhelmed by the intense combat experiences that you've had, and it expresses its overload through flashbacks where you relive some of those very painful experiences.

"Apparently, you were having a nightmare and screaming in your sleep. When your father came into the room, you thought he was an attacking German soldier, and you tried to strangle him. Your brother, Tommy, separated you, but you pushed Tommy back out of the way and attacked your father again. Tommy clocked you in the back of the head with a baseball bat, and you ended up in four point restraints here in the Psych unit at Saint Edith's."

"I'm at St. E's in Brighton?"

"You got it."

"What's gonna' happen to me?"

"Well, we can't have you running around trying to kill your family members because you think they're enemy soldiers. We can't hold you here indefinitely because you've not been accused of any crime. Your father won't press charges against you, and we have to release you.

"We can give you medication and offer you psychoanalysis through the Veterans Administration, but you've got to find some way to battle with your demons. If you can't make them go away, you've just got to accept them, tie them up in a package with a knot and let them go. They belong to your past...not the present, and not your future. You don't have to relive them when something triggers their memory in your subconscious.

"If we can't help you deal with this, it's just a matter of time till you're back here, in jail, or worse. You must have been one hell of a cook to bring all of this shit back with you."

"Yeah, I was no cook. My father tells me that I can't even boil water without burning the pan. But, I've just survived a trip through hell. I don't know why I survived, and I see faces all around me...faces of all the guys who didn't survive, the friends who've been killed, the men that I killed, and the innocents who died for no reason at all.

"Did you ever kill a man, Doctor...one on one...face to face....stab him with a bayonet, and watch him die in your arms, and pray with him while he died...and see the pictures of his young wife and little girl, two women, one of whom you've just made a widow, and the other an orphan?

"No, Doctor, you save lives; you don't take them. You and I are two faces on the same coin of life. One of us gives life, and the other takes life. You're proud of what you do; I can't escape from what I've done and who I've become.

"You know, I could talk with you and a team of psychiatrists till I'm blue in the face, and none of you could understand the horror of war, and the horror of what I've been through...not unless you've been through it yourself.

"I'll be honest with you, I don't know how I'll be able to sort this all out. It's so overwhelming to me, my own little house of horrors, where I smell burning flesh and hear the screams of dying men...Germans, Americans, innocents....none of them want to be in a uniform fighting each other. I'm killing the same man over and over in my dreams, and after I kill him, I hold him in my arms while he dies. I'm surrounded by nuns who've been raped and murdered by the SS; I can't get away from them....they follow me everywhere, a parade of horribles. When one leaves my mind, another enters. I feel tremendous guilt about all the killing I've done, the evil I've seen and been a part of.

"You know...I didn't volunteer for this....my country told me to go and I went....I didn't ask for this. A priest I used to know said that to me once, and I know at some level that's true, but it doesn't help with the pain that's deep inside me.

"Doctor, you can tie me to this bed for the rest of my life; you can psychoanalyze me morning and night and medicate me into a stupor, but neither of us will ever be able to dull the pain from this parade of horrors that's always running through my mind."

The psychiatrist removed his glasses and placed them slowly and deliberately in his lap. "Dan, you're right about one thing, a psychiatrist can only help you find ways for you to help yourself...help you find the pathways through your mind, out of that wicked place where you've been, and where you're still at. You have to work this out and find the relatively peaceful and tranquil place where you'll be living for the rest of your life.

"We can try to understand your behavior and try to help you understand it, but as a society, we can't tolerate your trying to kill people when you're acting out your delusions. You've become a warrior now, whether you wanted to or not, and you're a warrior without a war. Through no fault of your own they've made you into a killer, and you have to accept that reality and somehow put it behind you. Let it go, Dan. You don't have to carry it around for the rest of your life. They made you do it. The guilt and shame of what you've done belongs to others than yourself; you only did what you had to do so you could survive.

"You've got to adjust to civilian life, a life with conflict, but a life without war, a life where conflict's resolved through civil means that don't involve killing. As part of this adjustment, you have to learn how to deal with the ghosts and demons left over from your military life.

"The alternatives aren't nice or comforting for either you or the society. If you keep acting out your delusions, eventually you'll either end up back in a place like this, or in a prison.

"I understand from your chart that you're a Catholic. If you want to deal with your guilt, why don't you go to confession and be absolved of it? That'd be good for you, both spiritually and psychologically."

"I did go to confession, Doctor, but then the priest I confessed to tried to commit suicide after he absolved me. He stepped on a mine that must have only partially detonated. I tried to pull him out of the minefield, and I must have set off another mine. The next thing I remember was waking up in another hospital.

For most of the last couple of months, it seems that I'm in the middle of something, I lose consciousness, and the next thing I know, I'm waking up in a hospital with a pounding headache. I don't know what happened to the priest...I assume he's dead. He didn't look very much alive when I was hauling him out of there.

"I know I've got to deal with my demons. I don't think that drugs or psychotherapy will do it for me though. I've got to do it on my own; I've got to deal with it myself."

The spring turned into summer, and Dan was released from St. Edith's. He continued to have nightmares and flashbacks while he slept, but with no further intervention by his family. He thought about suicide more than once, but something held him back from taking his own life. As tormented as he was, there was something that was making him hold on while he struggled and looked for a way out of the tangled morass that his life had become.

Johnson's Hardware store had given his old job to a younger man after Dan had left for the service, a younger man who "was doing nicely, thank you," according to Mr. Johnson, when Dan had approached him looking for work.

Shortly after he left the hospital, Dan received a call from his former commanding officer, Captain Miller.

CHAPTER NINETEEN

Captain Miller Calls Dan

"Hi Dan; it's Ed Miller. Yeah, that's right, Captain, or rather, former Captain Miller. Now I'm back in the insurance business in Elkhart, Indiana and I thought I'd call to see how you're doing. This whole demobilization happened so quickly. We got shipped out, and then most of us were discharged almost overnight when we got back to the States. Then, from what I understand, they went and filled the company with new trainees and new officers.

"I had heard that you were recovering fine and that they were going to discharge you directly from the hospital. How are you doing?"

"I guess I'm doing OK, Captain. It's really a pleasant surprise to hear from you. I'm glad you called. They did ship me back to the unit, but you and most of the others had already been discharged. I go to the VA Hospital in Jamaica Plain...that's in another part of Boston...once a week and they work on my leg. I still limp a little, but it seems to be coming along."

"How are you doing, Cap....Ed?"

"I'm having a little trouble adjusting to civilian life, to be honest with you. I keep looking for snipers when I'm outside, and sit with my back to the wall when I'm in the house or my office...."

"Hey, Ed, sorry to interrupt, but whatever became of the chaplain, Father Porcelli?"

"You know, I really don't have any idea. The medics pulled the two of you out of the minefield unconscious and took you to the aid station, and then to the hospital. Charlie McHenry, the Bravo Company medic, was in the area and was

135

the first to treat you. He told me afterward that Father Porcelli had lost a lot of blood and that he didn't think the situation looked good for him.

"What the hell was the priest doing in the minefield anyway? The engineers had it clearly marked, and one of the sentries on the road had warned him about it."

"I think he was trying to commit suicide."

"The priest? You've got to be shitting me!"

"No, he was pretty beaten down when he was hearing my confession. Of course, I wasn't exactly upbeat myself. In fact, I'm still having trouble with all of the shit that we went through. I wake up in the middle of the night hearing Germans in my room. I'm either screaming or sweating like a pig, or both, but it's really getting to me. People keep away from me because I scare them. The first time I had a flashback, my family came into my room and I tried to kill my father because I thought he was a Nazi soldier."

"Yeah, I'm going through the same thing, but it's not Germans I see, it's Captain Stadholm."

"That asshole; I hope he's burning in hell. The son of a bitch wanted me to get killed because I told him to shove his recommendation for a Silver Star."

"Well, you weren't the only one he wanted to get killed. Dan, you and Top are the only people alive who know this, but a sniper didn't kill Stadholm while you guys were on patrol….I did. I killed him with his own pistol, and every night as I fall asleep, he comes to me with his .45, cocks it, and empties the clip into me. I wake up screaming too. It happens so frequently that my wife has started sleeping in the guest room."

"Jeez, Ed, I'm sorry. I had no idea, but why did you kill the bastard?"

"He'd been telling me from the time that we arrived in England prior to D-day that he wanted to make the Army a career, and that he wanted battlefield promotions to full bird colonel before the campaign was over. He was more of an asshole than most people realize. He used to have me report to his tent, then dress me down for some bullshit thing, something totally insignificant that had happened in my platoon. And then, once he'd established who was boss, he'd get buddy-buddy with me. 'Here Ed, have a drink,' he'd say, and I'd have to sit there with him, listening to him tell me what a great leader he was, and that he and I were different from the dogfaces under our command. He often said that war was like a game of chess, and the enlisted troops were the pawns, that they were disposable if they could be used to achieve a tactical or strategic objective. The major tactical objective he wanted to achieve was to look good to the brass back at battalion and above so that he'd get to be a colonel by the end of the war."

"God, he was even worse than I thought," said Dan. "I thought it was just me that he wanted to get killed, but he would have had us all wiped out to get his promotion."

"Yeah, you were on the top of his shit list though. He was pissed off at you for telling him to shove his Silver Star recommendation because it damaged his ego. You were supposed to be grateful for his largesse. But, more important, he was going to use his write-up of your citation to document what a great leader he was for the desk soldiers at battalion. If he was anything, he was arrogant and sneaky.

"I suppose that I shouldn't criticize him though, because I had done the same thing to cover my own ass when the artillery wiped out those fifteen Germans who were trying to surrender.

"When he'd get really loaded, which was often, he'd bring your name up and say that he was waiting to hear that you'd stepped on a mine or had walked into an ambush."

"Why did you kill him?"

"Well, he had called me to his tent the day he died and told me that he wanted my entire platoon to reconnoiter down that long valley we had stopped at. Your squad was out at the time probing the mouth of it when Smitty got killed. I told him that it was suicide to go there in force, and that I'd rather ask for volunteers to send another squad in to scout the place after your patrol returned. He was quite drunk and started swearing at me, calling me a coward, and insubordinate. He took his .45 out of its holster, pointed it at my head, and told me that he ought to kill me for mutiny and insubordination. He actually cocked the damn thing, and with a round in the chamber; I thought he was crazy enough to do it. He was very drunk and I tackled him. We rolled around on the ground and I got the pistol out of his hand, but he still struggled, trying to get it away from me. He must have pulled the trigger. The next thing I knew was that the gun had discharged, and he was very still, with blood all over the place. Top had just come back from supply and heard the whole argument from outside the tent. When the gun discharged, Top came in and saw Stadholm on the ground in a pool of blood. A couple of guys came running over when they heard the discharge, and Top told them that it was OK, that the Captain had accidentally discharged his sidearm while cleaning it. I was in a state of shock. I had killed before, but never one of my own troops.

"Top was cool. He picked up the pistol, wiped it all over with his handkerchief, and then placed it in the dead man's hand. He squeezed it tight to get Stadholm's fingerprints all over it, and then placed it on the ground beside the Captain. He told me that we'd be interviewed by the MPs, to say that we were both talking about battalion staffing outside the HQ tent, that we heard the weapon discharge, and that when we entered the tent, me first, we saw Stadholm dead on the ground.

"He cranked up the field phone, and asked to speak with the MP captain at battalion. He told the whole story to the captain, who agreed to send someone up to investigate. The MP captain said that it wouldn't be good for morale to let out that Stadholm had committed suicide, so that we should say he was killed by a sniper. A couple of hours later, the colonel called up and told me that he was giving me a field promotion to captain, that I should take command of the company, and that he'd follow this up with orders when his clerks got on top of their typing backlog."

"That's quite a story, Captain. By killing him, you probably saved my life. If he hadn't died, I would have been leading your entire platoon into the valley and into the rest of those panzers after our squad had returned. We could never have gotten the whole platoon out of there as quickly as the squad, and we would have been wiped out in a set battle. Battalion was worried about our morale; that's funny. If you announced that you'd killed Stadholm, the company's morale would've taken off like a rocket."

"Dan, the main reason that I called was to ask if you've thought at all about college. I know that we had talked a little about Notre Dame, and that at the time you'd expressed some interest. Well, I was in South Bend last week on business, and I had lunch with my old rector at Zahm Hall. He's now the director of admissions at Notre Dame, and I told him about you. He said that if you applied for this fall, he'd see that you were accepted. I know the timing's short, but they're all screwed up with their normal admissions. They had a contract with the government during the war, where the Navy used the campus to train its officers, but they expect the Navy to cancel that contract any time now 'at the convenience of the government.' That's a clause all of the government contracts have so they can take a hike when they don't need your services any more. Whaddya think?"

"Oh shit, Ed, we're into the end of July now, and school starts when...sometime in September? To be honest with you, I've been drinking more than I should. Sometimes I get so plastered that I forget about the ghosts for a little while. I've been hanging around the American Legion Post in Brighton Center most nights. I have my own stool at the bar, in the corner, and I usually close the place up. Sometimes I don't make it home and wake up with a dog licking my face on somebody's lawn. Last week, I woke up in a grave yard and was really scared."

"If you went to school, it might take your mind off the war, and the GI Bill would cover your costs and give you a couple of bucks spending money. If I wasn't married with a kid and one on the way, I'd go back myself."

"I don't know, Ed. I'm scared, and I'm tired of being scared, running scared. Everywhere I go, everyplace I turn, I'm scared. For years I've been scared, scared of dying, scared of making friends because it hurts so bad when you see them die, one by one, sometime in groups, but mostly one by one. I've been scared about entering civilian life, scared of who I've become, scared that I might go crazy and hurt or kill someone I love. Ed...I don't know; sometimes I think I'm going nuts. What's even scarier is that I'm not afraid of dying any more. Sometimes I think it'd be better if I died so I'd be at peace with the ghosts, instead of running from them all the time. That thought scares me too. Books, college, studying; that scares me too. Ed, everything scares me."

"Dan, we both have the same type of ghosts. They may have different faces, but they're doing the same thing to us. Why don't you think about Notre Dame, and I'll give you a call next week. I know it's a lot, and I know it's short notice, but knowing you and knowing Notre Dame, I think the two of you would be a good fit. It might help you deal with some of those ghosts. Talk about it with your family and your friends and let me know next week. They'll help you with the GI Bill paperwork at Notre Dame, so all you have to do is pack up a duffel bag and get a train out here."

"Let me think about it, Ed. One of the things, though, is that I've been sending a couple of bucks for the past few months to the widow of that German soldier I killed. Maybe it's conscience money, but I wouldn't want to stop that to go to school."

"Let me get this straight, you kill an enemy soldier in combat, and now you feel responsible for supporting his family? You are nuts, Fleming, and you're just the kind of nut that belongs at Notre Dame. I'll call you next week. Good-bye."

"Thanks, Ed...thanks for calling and for thinking of me. Let me think about it and I'll let you know next week when you call."

CHAPTER TWENTY

Dan Thinks About Going to Notre Dame

"Daniel?" His mother's voice called into the hall where Dan had been sitting, talking with Ed Miller on the hall phone. "Dan, who were you talking with?"

"That was Ed Miller, Ma, the captain of our company, the guy who got me home alive."

"That's good, dear; what did he want?"

"Well, we were just catching up. I got wounded, and everything happened so fast that we never got a chance to say good-bye or anything. I got carted off to the aid station and hospital, and he got shipped home and mustered out.

"He lives in Indiana now and wants me to go to Notre Dame. He says the GI bill will pay for it all and give me a couple of bucks extra to spend every month."

"Dan, that's exciting, but do you think you could get in? Your high school marks were pretty good, but Notre Dame....that'd really be something."

"You think so, Ma? You know I'm still trying to figure out what to do with the rest of my life, and I know that you and Dad are worried about my drinking, and my nightmares; Tommy too, for that matter. I told Captain Miller that I'd talk with you about it and let him know next week when he calls back. He spoke with the admissions director, a friend of his, and he told me that they'd let me in if I want to go."

"We are worried about you, Dan, but I pray to the Blessed Virgin every night thanking her for sending you home to us, and asking her to help you get over your memories from the war."

"Ma, I know you, Dad, and Tommy love me, and that's what's keeping me going. I never appreciated how important all of you are till I was taken away from you, and sent to live that nightmare. Ed Miller is living his problems too, and he's having trouble adjusting to civilian life. I guess I'm not alone in that regard.

"You know, Ma, when I go to the Legion, I sit in a corner and have a few beers. I don't talk about the war; I'm afraid that I drink to try to forget the war. But, there are a couple of guys who have a few drinks and start telling war stories. I know they're lying because if they'd done all things they claim, they'd be sitting in a corner with me, trying to get away from their own ghosts. They call me 'Cookie' and are always asking me to share a recipe with them. I usually just smile and raise my glass to them. We all drink, then they forget about me and continue bragging about how they won the war. They're starting to get to me, but there's another fellow who sits at the other end of the bar, who's there almost every night. He's even quieter than I am and keeps to himself all night. I suspect that he's seen some heavy combat and is having the same kind of struggle as me.

"I don't know, Ma, I'm so confused. I know that I should be happy to be home with you, Dad, and Tommy, but I'm scared Ma; I'm like a powder keg with a lit fuse, waiting for something to happen."

"Dan, I do worry about you, in some ways more now than when you were overseas. Your father and I spend a lot of time talking about you, wondering if there's anything we can do to help you. I'm worried about you, Dan. Maybe Notre Dame would be good for you...help focus your mind on things other than what you've been through. I don't know; Indiana's a long way from here, but so was Europe. Would you have time off for Christmas?"

"I'll ask Ed Miller when he calls next week. It would be different, but I can't stay here for the rest of my life, working for chump change, and drinking myself to death. Ma, more than anything, I don't want to worry you and Dad. I can sort this stuff out...I know I can....I've got to."

It wasn't long after he spoke with Ed Miller that a large envelope came for Dan.

"Hey, Dan," yelled his Dad. "The mail just came. You got a big envelope from the University of Notre Dame. What are they sending you?"

"I dunno, Dad. I just got a call from my old CO and he told me that he'd spoken to the Notre Dame director of admissions, and that if I want to go, I'm in. What do you think?" I don't know much about the place, other than it's a Catholic school run by a French order of priests, and they usually have a good football team. Ma really likes the place."

"Well, it's in Indiana. That's a long way from here, but not as far as Europe. Would you be able to come home for Christmas? I'd hate to have another Christmas without you around. I dunno. Do you wanna' go there?"

"You know, you and Ma have been together for a long time. The first question she asked me when I told her about Notre Dame is whether I'd be home for Christmas. I haven't really thought too much about Notre Dame. I think the only person I know from around here who went to college was Grady Frothington. I think he was going to be a chemist or something like that. I want to think about it a little before I just jump into it."

Thinking about Notre Dame helped move some of Dan's demons out of mind for a bit. Early that evening, he was at his familiar stool at the end of the bar at the Legion Post, looking through the Notre Dame course listing that the school had mailed out to him.

"What are you looking at, Danno?" Mikey Cedrone, the bartender, asked. Mikey was leaning on the bar in Dan's corner but left briefly to pull a beer, when Dan's bookend arrived at the other end of the bar.

When he returned, Dan opened up the Notre Dame course catalogue. "I've been thinking about going to college."

"No kidding? That's great! Where are you thinking about going?"

"Well a friend of mine, my old CO, can get me into Notre Dame."

"You gonna go?"

"I think it makes sense. I'd have the GI Bill, and how many of us ever got the chance to go to college before now. Besides, what am I gonna do with the rest of my life? Hang around here till I drink myself into oblivion? Yeah, I think I probably will..."

"Hey, Cookie, whacha got cooking tonight? Any good recipes to share with a combat vet?"

"Schultzie, you were such a fucking hero, we all know that, but please don't tell us again how you took out a Japanese pillbox on Guadalcanal and killed sixteen Japs single-handed."

"You should have been there, Cookie, instead of on your baker's tour through Europe. We were surrounded by Japs, and the only way we could go was towards their pillbox. Well...I got around out of their field of fire..."

Dan's bookend, sitting at the other end of the bar, slowly got up and began walking towards Schultz. No one knew his name, but he was there every night, drinking himself into oblivion, along with Fleming. Dan looked into his face and saw the haunted, haggard look that he frequently saw staring back when he looked into a mirror. The Man with No Name moved purposefully toward Schultz, looking very intense.

"Hey, get the fuck away from me! Who the fuck do you think you ...." were Schultzie's final words before the Man with No-Name grabbed him by the throat and began strangling him.

"I was on Guadalcanal," were the only words he said as he clenched Schultzie's throat in a death grip.

Mikey Cedrone vaulted over the bar and ran to pull No-Name off Schultz, who couldn't breathe, and who was turning blue. Dan ran over as well, and the two of them finally managed to break the death-grip on Schultz' throat. Schultz lay silent on the floor with no visible signs of life. Mikey ran to call an ambulance and Dan sat next to Schultz, unfazed by the motionless man on the floor in front of him, but keeping an eye on No-Name in the event he decided to finish the business that he'd begun.

"He's a lying bastard," No Name said, breaking the silence. "If he did all the shit he says he did, he wouldn't say anything. He'd be like you and me, alone with our ghosts. You were no cook, were you?"

"No, and you saw the same kind of shit as me, didn't you?" "I did, and I can't get away from it."

"Have you talked with anyone about it?"

"No, I come down here every night and drink, trying to escape from it."

"I've been talking with a psychiatrist at the VA, and he's been good for me."

"Can you sleep without it all coming back to you?"

"Not yet, but I don't try to kill my family members at night any more. I used to think they were Nazi soldiers."

"I don't know how much more of this I can deal with. Now I've probably killed this guy, and I'll either fry, or spend the rest of my life in the state pen at Charlestown."

"He's still breathing," noted Dan. "I don't know what happened. Maybe he had too much to drink, fell off a barstool, and conked his head.

"Hey, Mikey, were you able to get an ambulance?"

"Yeah, they're on their way."

"Mikey, help me drag Schultzie over to the bar. It looks like he may have been drinking somewhere else before he got here, fell off the bar stool, and whacked the back of the head. I was in the men's room and didn't see anything."

"I getcha; I was turned away from the bar polishing glasses when he fell. I didn't see anything either. I just heard a thud, and he was lying on the floor when I turned around. That's when you came out of the men's room, and the three of us rushed over to pick him up."

An ambulance and a police car came to the lounge and took Schultz to the hospital, where he recovered and was discharged. He never returned to the Legion Hall. The Man with No Name finished his beer after the commotion ended and walked out of the lounge. It was a number of months till Dan saw him again.

After the police, the ambulance, and No Name had left, Dan and the bartender were once again the only two people in the lounge.

"Let me pull a couple of beers and I'll join you for a long one on the house."

"Thanks, Mikey...quite a day so far. Do you think Schultzie will come back OK?"

"He may come back to consciousness, but I don't want the asshole coming back here. That mouth of his probably costs the post ten times the amount of money he spends on beer. I've been waiting for you to flatten him for all the shit he gives you about being a cook. I know that it's none of my business, and I know that you don't like to talk about it, but I don't believe that you spent the war making breakfast, lunch, and dinner for a bunch of guys in pressed and starched uniforms."

"You're right, Mikey, I wasn't a cook, and I don't want to talk about the war. I do find it hard to feel bad about what happened to Schultzie though. He's a cruel bastard, isn't he? I wonder what it is about his personality that makes him puff himself up at the same time he's putting others down. I feel bad for No Name. I can understand what he's going through; I wish I could understand what I'm going through."

"Danno, if you don't mind my saying so, you drink too much."

"No shit...words of wisdom, Mikey. You can be my fucking psychiatrist."

"You could do worse, Dan. You know, there are two types of people who come in here. Some are vets who come to drink and talk with the guys; you know, sports, babes, politics. And then there are others who come here to get away from something. I've been watching you, Dan. When you get here you're in the first group, shooting the shit, and kidding with everyone good-naturedly. But then, as the night gets later and you've been drinking more, you get into the second group and become quiet and morose. I've wanted to shut you off, and I don't know why I've not done that."

"Mikey, if you shut me of, I'll just go drink somewhere else. You know that, and that's why you keep serving me. I don't make any trouble, and mind my own business. I've got some shit left over from the war that I've got to deal with. I know that. Maybe if I go away to Notre Dame, things might change for me. I really don't know what to do, but I think Notre Dame makes sense."

"Again, Danno, more unsolicited advice, but I think it would be good for you to go to college. I don't think you can run away from whatever it is that you're carrying around, but you need to get outta here. Get away from the post, and get away from a bunch of guys who'll be telling each other the same war stories and lousy jokes for the next fifty years, or till they die of cirrhosis of the liver."

"You know, Mikey, you might be right. Let me take this course catalogue and get outta here. I'll complete the application and get it in the mail in the morning."

"Dan, you're home early. It's good to see you home at this hour."

"Ma, I've been spending too much time at the Legion. I know I drink too much, and I know that it's best for me to go to Notre Dame. I'm going to complete the application tonight and get it in the mail tomorrow. It'll take at least a week to get to South Bend. I think it has to go through the central post office in Chicago and then back to South Bend. I'll also call Captain Miller in the morning to let him know that I'll be going. Ma, I love you, and I know things are going to be OK. I know it."

Dan did complete the application that evening, falling asleep with the course listing in his hands, and instead of dead Germans, his dreams that evening centered around English and Philosophy classes, as well as throwing a football around on campus. Not only his first release from the pain of combat, this was Dan's foreshadowing of a life to come, and the road away from the dark horse of hell that he'd been riding. For the first time, he realized that his life could move on, and that he didn't have to remain stuck indefinitely on the horrors of his war.

He made his decision and packed his duffel bag one more time.

Chapter Twenty-One

Dan Meets Janet Miller
and Enters Notre Dame

"Would you like a cup of tea?"

Janet Miller, pregnant with their second child, carried the hope of a new life, of the new world that Dan and her husband had recently been fighting for.

Dan had called Ed Miller on the day he had sent the application back. It was during the call that his former CO had invited him to come out for a visit a week or so before school began. The ride on the express train to Chicago and then back on the local to South Bend seemed funny to Dan because just a few months earlier, he'd been traveling on those same tracks going back to his old life. Now he was heading west to an entirely new life. He was scared, but not in a panic, as he had been earlier. Now he was more excited than scared, and the thought of seeing his former commanding officer again just sweetened the whole picture in his mind.

"Ed has told me so much about you," said Janet, "so I've been looking forward to meeting you. He told me that you were a real hero, but that you probably wouldn't want to talk too much about it. He doesn't talk about it either, and I do worry about him. He works awfully hard, and I think he told you that he has horrid nightmares about the war."

"Thanks for the offer of tea, Mrs. Miller, I'd love a cup. Where do you want me to throw my things?"

"There's a guest room at the top of the stairs on the right. The first thing Ed did when he got home was to paint all of the rooms in the house. Soon it's going to be the baby's room, and you'll probably be the last person to use it as a guest.

When I have the baby, Ed will take some time away from the office to paint it again and paper it.

"Is that all you have with you? Don't you have a steamer trunk or other bags?"

"No, Ma'am. We learned to pack light in the Army; only take what you can carry on your shoulder. I've got everything that I think I'll need in my duffel bag.

"I'll be right down for that tea. Is the bathroom upstairs? I'd like to wash my face and comb my hair after that long train ride."

"It's right across from your room."

Dan carried his bag up to the bright and cheerful room that would be his for the next week before he moved into the dormitory. He noticed how fresh and cheery the paint was, and how orderly and uncluttered things were.

Bouncing down the stairs, he noticed how pretty Janet Miller was, with her smooth complexion, and a bump where she was carrying her baby. He thought for the first time that there's something very beautiful about a pregnant woman. He had seen some women who were carrying babies when he was in Germany; they were refugees, displaced persons, and they all seemed miserable, but this was different.

This home was warm and welcoming; everything was orderly and in place. It seemed so peaceful, like Captain Miller had made his own refuge, his own retreat from the misery of the world, a picture place for him and his family. And his pregnant wife completed the picture and made it glow. Dan knew that this life would be a ways off for him, but that this is the way he wanted his world to be. For an instant, the thought of Yvette crossed his mind. He could, but wouldn't dare to, fall in love with this woman. But, he could see her in a home like this, cooking supper for him when he came back at the end of the day from whatever it was that he would end up doing with his life. It was a pleasing, though fleeting, thought. She was probably with millions of other people in Europe, displaced by the war. He could never find her even if he had wanted to try.

"There's a plate of chocolate chip cookies on the table. I just baked them and the chocolate's still hot and melted. Sit here and let me pour your tea."

"Thank you, Ma'am, you're being too kind to me, and I don't know what to say. I'm really looking forward to seeing your husband again. We were all very close. We all relied on him and he never let us down."

"Dan, call me Janet. I know you're very close to Ed, close in a way that I can never understand. He speaks of you as if you were his younger brother."

"Yes, Ma'am...err...Janet; I understand what you're saying, and it's true that there's a bond between us. You mentioned Captain Miller's nightmares. I have those nightmares too, though they've been getting slightly better lately. I went to see a psychiatrist at the VA about my nightmares, and he told me that I was suffering from what they call 'battle fatigue'. You know, your husband and I have seen so much and been through so much together that we have a bond, and with that bond comes the pain of reliving the horrors that we've been a part of. Our minds find it difficult to let go of the terror we'd been living. But, you know, that was then and this is now, a different world away both in time and space, a whole different reality, and we just have to erase it from our minds.

"This is a world with neat and tidy houses, pretty wives, and loving relatives, a world at peace where people don't end up lying dead by nightfall after they got up that morning and laced their boots or shoes to start their day. None of us want to talk about it, but let me tell you, what fascinated me more than the horrors of war; it was the randomness of it all. Every morning when I woke up and laced my boots, I would always wonder 'Will today be the day? Will some graves registration person unlace my boots at the end of the day as he prepares my body to be sent home?'

"I'm sorry, Janet, that's a brief glimpse of the world that your husband and I shared for so long, for what seemed like an eternity. But this is now, and this is your world, a world of fresh paint, little children, and new babies. This is the world the way it was meant to be, a world of peace, a world of hope for you and your children.

"This is the kind of world that I want to create for myself and my family...if I ever have a family."

"Eat those cookies and drink your tea. There are more in the cookie jar on the counter top. I want to get to know you, Dan. You and Ed have been through so much. He's not the same man he was before he went into the Army and overseas. Maybe you can help me find him. I thought that we could just pick up where we'd been when he left, but I was wrong. He's tense most of the time, not relaxed and carefree like he was before he went off to war. Now it seems like he's carrying the weight of the world on his shoulders. He works too hard. Before I got pregnant, we would have drinks together before supper. I've stopped drinking alcohol because I don't think it's good for the baby, but Ed just drinks without me. He starts when he gets home from work, and he usually doesn't stop till he falls asleep around ten at night. He becomes incoherent, his speech is slurred, and he doesn't make any sense at all. But, the next morning he's up bright and early and off to the agency."

Dan heard the front door open and heard a familiar voice as his old CO bounded into the room and gave him a big bear hug. Ed Miller then walked over to kiss his pregnant wife, put his arm around her, and started talking.

"Dan, it's great to see you again. I think we've both put on a little weight, and we both look better when we're not wearing olive drab. Can I get you a drink, a beer or something stronger?"

"No, thanks, Ed. I've been taking too much of that stuff, probably the reason I've put on so much weight, and I'm trying to start over without beer or booze in my life."

"Well, God bless you. You're certainly in the right part of the country to be a tea-totaler. We have Baptist churches within a stone's throw of wherever you happen to be in Indiana, and they'd outlaw alcohol altogether if they had their way. They were the guys that brought us the Volstead Act years ago, and they'd love to bring prohibition back."

"Ed, I admit that drinking a lot of beer has beefed me up a little, but after eating Janet's chocolate chip cookies, I can see why you've been gaining weight since you've been back. Janet, you should put this guy on a diet."

"Actually, I'm the one who has the biggest weight gain. I just hope that it's all baby."

"Honey, can I help you with the supper?"

"It's almost done. Why don't you and Dan get out of my hair and go into the living room. You can catch up, and I'll finish getting the food together."

Before moving into the living room, Ed stopped to prepare himself a drink. Mixing a scotch and water, he turned to Dan, "Are you sure you don't want one?"

"Well, maybe just one."

Sitting on the sofa across from his friend's easy chair, Dan settled in and started the conversation. "Ed, you have a wonderful setup here. This is what I want my life to be like, a wife and kids, a home to come back to at the end of the day, a job that I love working at. You've got it all. Where's little Eddie, by the way?"

"He's with Janet's parents for the week. They have a camp up on Lake Michigan, not too far from Benton Harbor, and he's with them for the last week of his summer vacation. It'll be busy here in a week, with all of the schools going back, and Notre Dame starting classes. I was talking with Father Moore the other day, and he said that they're filling their classes with a lot of vets like you. They're going to have all of you live together on one part of campus they'll call "Vetville". They'll slack up on the rules a little bit. It'd be a little tough to tell a combat vet that he has to be in his dorm by ten o'clock during the week and with his lights out by eleven."

"Yeah, I guess that we don't have a lot in common with a bunch of kids who just graduated from high school, do we?"

"No, you don't, and you know, you said I have the perfect life, and it's true; this is what I've always wanted, but part of me feels like I don't belong here, that I don't want to settle down. In some ways I miss the camaraderie and the feeling of being footloose that we had in the Army. I don't miss the killing, but there everything was in flux; nothing remained the same. You slept in a different place every few weeks; you were always struggling for a common purpose, against a common enemy. Here, everything's static. I just do the same thing day after day. From one day to the next, it's always the same. There's no thrill, no excitement to life anymore, and though at one level, intellectually I guess, I know that's not the way to live, in some ways I do miss it."

"Yeah, Captain, but the ghosts...we both can do without the ghosts. I'm tired of bayoneting that poor German soldier over and over. Maybe a little boredom and monotony isn't the worst thing in life, and I'd gladly put up with it in return for a good night's sleep."

"You're right, Dan, and now you're on the brink of another adventure. Being an undergraduate in college is a lot like being in the Army, except no one's trying to kill you, and you don't have to try to kill anyone else. I've got a good deal in life, I know that, but in some ways, I envy your freedom and the four years you have ahead of you. Are you going to play any sports on campus? They have some great athletic programs, you know?"

"I hadn't thought much about that. Maybe I should go out for the football team to try to get rid of some of this gut."

"They do give you a good workout, but it would be tough to make the team. You ready for another one?"

"Well, I really shouldn't, but maybe one more before dinner."

"Guys, the food's on the table. Come and get it while it's hot."

"Phew...saved by the bell. I know you had a pretty good command presence when you needed one, but Janet makes you look like a new recruit. We'd better get out there. And Ed...I don't think I should have any more to drink. You know that I have a problem I'm trying to lick."

"Both of us, Dan, both of us."

The meal was excellent, and the conversation light and snappy, none of the dark stuff, just the SNAFUs and stories about the funny things that happen to men in uniform.

"Do you remember that time, before we started on that twelve mile hike, when we first were sent to England? You got an ass-chewing from the colonel because a couple of your troops got into the general's latrine at headquarters while we were standing around waiting to fall in for the march. I never told you this, but Smitty and I were the ones who got you into trouble. We'd been up for a long time that morning, cleaning the squad bay and pulling together a full combat load to carry on the march. We were milling around in front of headquarters waiting for a Brit liaison to lead us through the Aberdeen woods. I had to go to the bathroom awfully bad, and the only place available seemed to be in the headquarters' building. Well, Smitty had to go too, so the two of us walked briskly into the building like we belonged there and kept walking the halls till we found a men's room on the first floor. We didn't know that it was reserved for the general, so we both went in and locked the door. I had to go worse than Smitty, so I used the can first. Smitty was using it when the general started pounding on the door and yelling at us to come out and identify ourselves, and that he was going to court-martial us for the unauthorized use of his, pardon the expression, Ma'am, "shitter."

"You know, neither Smitty nor I were the brightest guys in the world, but we were far from being stupid. We just left the general yelling and screaming in front of his locked latrine, climbed out the window, and walked around to fall in with the platoon. You had just read our orders and we were ready to take off when the colonel came up and did a number on you in front of all of us. I remember that Stadholm looked at the platoon like he could kill all of us. He probably was thinking of his military career going up in smoke because a couple of his troops had locked the general out of his latrine."

"You bastard! I would have court-martialed you, put you on KP, and had you leading every night patrol till the end of the war if I'd known that. Stadholm was ripped after the forced march. He had sprained an ankle when he fell off the trail and down into a gully, so he was walking with a cane."

Then, suddenly and without warning, Ed's mood changed.

"He came into my quarters, drunk, and started waving the cane around like it was a sword, saying he wanted me to find the men who had violated the general's latrine, or he would personally see to it that I was court-martialed. All in all, a very unpleasant time. I'm glad he's dead, though, because the thought of him being alive, running around with a bunch of armed men under his command, is frightening."

"Ed! Stop it! You aren't really glad that man's dead."

"Janet, again meaning no offense, but if he were still alive, I probably wouldn't be sitting here, and your husband would probably have sent another of his obituary letters to my mother back in Boston. Stadholm was mean and vindictive, and worse than that, he wanted to see me dead."

"I don't understand....."

"You know something, I don't either, but that's the kind of person he was; cruel, vindictive, and as Ed explained to me later, ambitious."

151

"Don't you have any purely funny stories? You guys have been through so much that even your funny stories have a dark side to them."

"Honey...I don't think we need to..."

"You don't think we need to what? I'm tired of walking on eggshells around you, Ed. I'm sorry that you had to go off to war and that now you're walking around with a big chip on your shoulder.

"Well, you know what? It was no fun being here alone with a newborn baby, trying to get by on your allotment, and wondering if you were ever going to come back to help me. Ed, I think we need to ....we need to sit down and talk about us and where we're going....where we're going as a family, and what our lives are going to be like. I don't want to spend the rest of our lives with me feeding and washing children while you go off to work and then come home and drink all night till you fall asleep in that chair. No, Sir, Captain Miller, Sir...I didn't sign on for that..... no way at all!"

"Look, maybe I should go upstairs and let the two of you work this out. I'm sorry to have raised the..."

"No, Dan, don't go. I'm sorry, that was rude and selfish of me. I didn't mean to explode. You're our guest and I'm sorry for bringing this up in front of you. I don't know what's happened...what that war did to you men, but you're all different."

Turning to her husband, Janet Miller said, unable to hold herself back from breaking into tears, "and you...you...you...I wish I'd never met you!" and she rushed out of the room in tears, pounding up the stairs, gulping for breath, swallowing air between her sobs.

"Welcome to my world, Dan. Sometimes I think it would've been better if Stadholm had killed me instead of the other way around. Janet would've grieved for me and would be on the way to re-establishing her life with someone else by now. I'm not a good husband, I'm not a good father, and now I'm going to have another kid to screw up. She doesn't understand what we've been through. How could she? "

"Ed, you can't do this to yourself. Someone told me something once when I was sober that made sense to me, and it makes sense for you. You didn't volunteer to go...they were gonna draft your ass and you went through ROTC to get a commission. You didn't pick the war....they told you to go, and you went. You did what your country told you to do, and the responsibility for all the bad shit that you did and that you saw isn't yours, Ed, it's theirs. They're to blame Ed, not us. We just did what they told us to do.

"You can't explain this to Janet. You're right, Ed, she wouldn't...she couldn't understand. Like I told you, I started seeing a psychiatrist at the VA. I don't know if all his mumbo jumbo helped me, but I think just talking with him made me feel a little better. I just want to stop the nightmares, Ed, and I know you want that too."

"Dan, I just feel so worthless, worthless and helpless. I'm in a ditch somewhere in my mind and I'm in way over my head. I can't see out of that ditch, and I don't know how I'll be able to get out of it. I feel trapped in it, Dan, and I know I need help, but I don't know how to get it. I can't take time away from the business because if I do, the customers might not be there. I need them to support my family, and Janet needs me to support her and the kids, and I'm trapped in the middle with Janet and the kids, the business, and my goddamn ghosts.

"Janet says that I treat her with casual indifference; that I'm obsessed with the business, and I don't see that she and our son need me too. She doesn't understand that if the business isn't there, we could end up losing everything. At one level, I can understand how she feels. I love her. I think she knows that, and I know she loves me. I try to be consciously sensitive to what she needs from me, but I don't feel it. On some deeper level, I can't understand how she feels. I'm so wrapped up in providing a financially secure home and future for them, I don't understand what it is that she needs from me.

"When Janet starts in on me, she hits me over the head with the war and how I neglect her. I can see her frustration when we fight, but it doesn't stay with me after it's over and I'm back at trying to make a living. Then we end up in this pattern where it builds up in her until it explodes again. I'm fighting my ghosts, I'm fighting to survive in my business, and I'm fighting to keep my marriage from falling apart.

"Fucking Stadholm...this is all your fault. You're dead, you miserable son of a bitch, and you're still fucking up my life!"

"Ed, it's about this time that I'd sit down and start drinking beer till I couldn't remember how I got to wherever I happened to be when I woke up. We don't want to do that. We can beat this thing, both of us, or we can at least learn how to live with it so it doesn't infect everyone we meet. Janet's right, you know, everything about our war experience does have a dark side to it. Maybe that kid on the truck was right, maybe I should have had that sergeant at the marshalling depot, the guy with the clip board, drop trou and start quacking like a duck."

"What are you talking about?"

"Come to think of it, I guess I never told you the story, but it's not the kind of thing an enlisted man would tell his commanding officer. When I was trying to get a ride back to the company that time in Germany, when everyone thought I was AWOL, I ran into some officious barracks sergeant who started ordering me around in an extremely disrespectful manner. I was a little crazy then, so I leveled my rifle on him and told him to keep walking backwards till he was out of sight or I'd blow his head off, and they'd send him and a medal home to his momma in the same box.

"Well, all the replacements in the truck thought that I was absolutely crazy, except one guy who thought it was funny and told me I should have had the guy with the clipboard drop trou and waddle around quacking like a duck."

"Humph...that explains a lot. I got a message in the pouch about a week after you got back. Some major in battalion had written you up and wanted me to begin a court-martial proceeding against you. I wrote him back and said that you were missing in action, and probably dead. I guess that satisfied them because I never heard from him again about it.

"Who was the guy who thought it was funny?"

"You know, I never got his name, but he went up to the First Platoon."

"You know, Dan, maybe we are crazy, maybe there's a corollary to what Janet was saying. Maybe there's a funny side to all of the dark things that happened to us."

"Let's call it a night. I don't know whether to go upstairs to Janet, or spend another night here on the couch."

"Go to her, Ed. She needs you. She needs you, ghosts and all. We'll get through this, Ed; we just need time...more time...and it'll get better every day."

"Yeah, Dan, I'll try that; good night. I'll see you in the morning."

"Good night, Ed."

The rest of his visit with the Millers went well, with no further conflict between Ed and Janet. Janet had apologized to Dan the next morning and went out of her way to be cordial and hospitable for the rest of his visit. Their time together was good for the two former comrades at arms, but it did highlight a nasty problem between Ed and Janet.

Leaving their house at the end of his visit, Dan took a cab to campus because Ed had an early morning meeting in Goshen.

Chapter Twenty-Two

Notre Dame, Charlie Costanza, Yvonne Chrysler, and Father Malachai Francis Fitzgibbon

Dan Fleming sensed the juxtaposition as he drove down the tree-lined entrance to the campus. He could feel the energy, a festive mood, not only because of the start of his college experience, but also the return to normalcy, a different reality, people walking around in seemingly random kinetic motion, moving trunks, suitcases, and more than the occasional duffel bag.

The admissions letter told him that he'd be living in Cavanaugh Hall, located on the north side of the Notre Dame campus. Dan later learned that because of the heavy enrollment from veterans, the "Veterans Village" housing was filled, and he'd be in a dormitory that was mixed with recent high school graduates as well as a few other vets.

Leaving the cab at the Circle entrance to campus, Dan came to a long table staffed by upperclassmen, his first official contact on campus.

"Hi, can I help you?"

"Yeah, I'm a freshman, and I don't have the slightest idea of where to go or what to do."

"Well, you're at the right place. I'm Ed Burke. Welcome to Notre Dame. Do you have a letter from the Admissions Office?"

"It's somewhere in this stuff. Ah, here it is."

"Thanks...let's see...you're in Cavanaugh Hall. Let me tell you how the campus is set up. The buildings on your left are on the South Quad. Straight ahead is Sacred Heart Church, and to the right of that and sort of behind it is the North Quad. When you enter the North Quad, Cavanaugh's the first building on your left. Father Fitzgibbon's the rector and he runs a tight ship. You have to be in the dorm by ten on weekdays and eleven on weekends, and you have to be at the seven o'clock Mass in the hall chapel every morning."

"Wow, I just got out of the Army; it almost sounds like I've re-enlisted."

"Yeah, this stuff may seem a little silly. They set up a sort of compound off campus to the north for guys like you. They call it "Vetville" and it's for all of the returning veterans; well, most of the returning veterans. The rumor is that they won't have parietals, and that the vets will be able to drink in their rooms, and they won't have a curfew. I heard that there was a flood of veterans applying, what with the GI Bill and all of that, and they filled all of the slots in Vetville pretty early. I heard there are a whole bunch of fellows like you who'll be living in the regular freshmen dorms.

Say, are you from Boston?"

"I am...you can tell from the way I talk, right? Actually, you sound like you could be from my neck of the woods."

"Newton, West Newton."

"Isn't that something? We're practically neighbors; I'm from Brighton."

"No kidding....where?"

Saint Columbkille's Parish. You know where Market Street is?"

"Yeah."

"Well, heading down Market Street, off to the right...Cushman Road."

"Cushman Road....near Glencoe Street?"

"Hey, you're right on the money!"

"I used to date a girl who lived on Morrow Road, but she dumped me and started going with a sailor."

"Maria Santucci?"

"Oh shit, now you know all my secrets; you must know her brother, Anthony?"

"Anthony and I were classmates at St. Cols. We both graduated together and got drafted together. The last I heard about him was that he was somewhere in the South Pacific on a destroyer.

"Maria was a foxy little girl...you were lucky. All the guys at St. Cols wanted to date her."

"Yeah, it was great while it lasted, but I guess that's life. I'm dating a Saint Mary's girl now and things seem to be working out pretty well. Maybe when you get settled I can fix you up with one of Susan's friends. She has some really cute girlfriends; some of them are really loaded too."

"Loaded?"

"They come from families with lots of money...big Catholic industrialists, a lot of them from Michigan, who send their daughters to St. Mary's so they'll marry a Notre Dame man."

"I'm not sure what any of them would see in an ex-dogface like me, but that would be great."

"Why don't you get your stuff settled at Cavanaugh and I'll be over sometime tonight. You'll probably have an orientation meeting for your hall at about seven, but it should be over by eight. I'll swing by around then and show you the campus. Maybe, if you're not too tired, we can take a walk over to St. Mary's."

"That'd be great, Ed. Say, is there any place on campus where you can get a drink?"

"Not on campus....they'll throw you out if they find you drinking or catch you with booze or beer in your room. But, there's a bar about half a mile down Notre Dame Avenue that some of us go to. Not a bad place; it's half neighborhood guys, and half Notre Dame students. It's a nice mix, and everyone's friendly. A lot of the locals work at one of the automobile factories across town."

"OK, Ed, I'm off to Cavanaugh Hall. I'll see you at eight."

Dan was starting to feel the excitement of the place. "It is infectious. Maybe this'd be the right place," he thought to himself as he walked through the front door into Cavanaugh Hall.

"And who might you be?" the voice from the other side of the table asked.

"Fleming, Dan Fleming."

"Let's see: Farley, Foley, Frawley, Fitzgerald...Ah hah, here you are, "Fleming"...Room 151. Sorry about that, Fleming, it's a forced triple...about half way down the hall on the right. You're our first customer of the day so you should be able to grab the single bed.

"Welcome to Cavanaugh Hall."

"It's like being back in the service," Dan thought to himself as he surveyed the room that was going to be his home for the next nine months. The room had olive drab beds, metal wall lockers, and a highly polished tile floor. The only difference, aside from its size, was that there were three desks with built-in bookshelves and three wooden chairs. There was also a sink with a mirror over it in one corner.

"All in all though, I'm only sharing it with two other guys instead of a whole platoon," Dan mumbled, as he started unpacking his duffel bag and hanging the wrinkled clothes in his new wall locker. Of the three lockers in the room, Dan grabbed the best one and slid it over by the end of his bed so that it gave him a little privacy when the door to the room was open. He made his own little cubbyhole, with the sink three feet from his bed and facing him at one end, and the back of his wall locker at right angles to the door way at the other end. The wall locker was like the ones he'd used at the various Army bases he'd spent time at. There were a couple of drawers on the bottom where he could store some stuff, a rod in the middle on which to hang clothes, and a couple of hooks on the side that someone had added, and which could be used to hang jackets on.

It was a beautiful morning as he looked out the windows across the quad toward what he was later to learn was Breen-Philips Hall. Now it was almost ten A.M. and the activity on the quad was working itself into a frenzy. Dan was all unpacked, settled in, and happy that he was not out there moving furniture and trunks back and forth. He was wondering about Ed's girlfriend fixing him up with a rich Saint Mary's girl. Saint Mary's was a women's college about a mile from the Notre Dame campus. It was true that many Saint Mary's students and Notre Dame students did get married, but Dan had no expectations that a well-off family would want their daughter marrying an ex-GI from Boston.

As he sat at what he had now claimed as his desk, with his feet up looking out the window, Dan wondered what it would be like sitting there, night after night, studying. Did he have the right stuff to make it through four years of this place? Could he escape from the horrors of his recent past by burying himself in the books? Dan had been through a lot in his life, but this would be different. He'd fought and survived, but this was entirely different. Here he'd be fighting with himself, struggling to learn. It had been a long time since he'd read a book or written a paper, and he wondered if he could still do that. Did he have the self-discipline to grunt through his studies night after night for the next nine months? It was, he hoped, the same type of intensity and focus that he had brought to his combat operations, but digging a perfect foxhole was not like studying Aquinas. He sat there deep in thought until he was jarred back to reality by the sound of his door being kicked open. Looking up, he saw a massive form moving through the doorway, followed by a large steamer trunk that he was dragging behind him.

"Hello, I'm Charlie Costanza."

Moving easily to where Dan was sitting, Charlie stuck out a massive paw to shake his hand.

"I guess we're roomies for the year."

"Hi. I'm Dan Fleming. Where you from?"

"Chicago, how about you?"

"Boston."

"Boston, you're a long way from home. You a vet?"

"Yeah, how do you know that?"

"You're older and you look tougher than the rest of the freshman I've seen walking around."

"I may be older, Charlie, but tougher...I don't know, but I'm probably more scared than you about what I'm doing here. It's been a long time since I've been in school, and I don't know if I can still...you know, study and pull it all together."

"You'll do fine, Dan. I was valedictorian in my high school class, and I'm pretty nervous about it myself. It's new for all of us. Maybe we should agree to have a quiet period from seven to ten every night to study and not disturb each other. My older brother's an engineering student at Purdue, and he said the first semester freshman year was crazy in the dorms."

"Yeah, that sounds like a good idea, Charlie. Let's hope that our third roommate agrees.

"You know, sometimes I have nightmares, and I can make a lot of noise at night. I don't mean to, but I'm still trying to work some stuff out from the war."

"I'm sorry that it got over before I had a chance to enlist. My father and grandfather were both in the Army, and I was looking forward to it."

"Let me tell you, you haven't missed anything. All in all, I'm lucky to be alive, and I'm trying to forget the whole thing. If I don't talk about it, it's not because I'm rude, but it's a part of my life that I don't know how to deal with yet, and I think I want to forget it if I can. But, don't buy the glamour crap about uniforms, marching bands, and all that stuff. There's nothing glorious about watching one of your buddies disintegrate in an explosion, or killing another human being who's trying to kill you.

"I tell you, Charlie, the military, ours, theirs, and everyone's, is an evil institution...keep away from it. I don't really know you, but I want us to be friends, and if I ever hear that you're thinking of joining ROTC, I'll slap you silly, even though you're twice as big and twice as strong as me."

"You have a nice way with words, Dan. You don't beat around the bush, do you?"

"Hey, I'd rather that you know how I really feel instead of waking up every morning with me boxing your ears, and you wondering why I was doing it.

"Seriously, though, the military isn't something you want to get involved with. You listen to your father and grandfather, and they probably didn't see combat, and they remember their days in the service because they were young and single. That's how you'll probably look back on Notre Dame when you're old enough to have kids of your own. Ask some twenty year old guy who's had his nuts blown off and who has only part of a leg left because he stepped on a land mine what he thinks of the military. Charlie, you're lucky you got me as a roommate. Your children and grandchildren will thank me some day, even though you're probably thinking I'm an asshole right now."

"OK, OK, you've convinced me."

"You know, I think this wall locker would look better behind the door – wanna help me move it?"

"Yeah, sure, why don't we just pick it up and carry it over there so we don't scratch the floor?"

"OK – hang on – let me find a place to grab it....I've got a spot. Drop it back and I'll grab the bottom.

There, what do you think? I think it looks better here, and it opens up the space between the windows."

"It looks good, Dan. You've got a good sense of organization. When I finish unpacking, do you want to take a walk across campus? You can show me the ROTC Building and let me know how close you'll let me get to it."

"That sounds good. Maybe we can get a frappe or something."

"A frappe, what the hell's a frappe?"

"You know...ice-cream, chocolate syrup, and milk, all whipped together."

"You mean a 'shake'."

"No, a shake's just syrup and milk."

"You guys from Boston are all screwed up. Not only do you talk funny, but you use different words than the rest of the country."

"Well, whatever you call it out here in the provinces, it's almost eleven-thirty, and I have a craving for vanilla ice cream, chocolate syrup, and milk. Hey, at least I'm not craving beer or booze, and for me, that's a good sign."

"Lemme throw the rest of this crap under the bed and I'm with you. You're making me hungry too."

It had really become a beautiful day, typical late summer, warm but not oppressive, and just a little cool at night. They chatted about themselves and their families as they walked over to the campus snack shop. Dan told Charlie about his brother, Tommy, and what a good football player he was. Charlie told Dan how a Notre Dame alumnus had come up to him after one of his own high school games and asked him if he'd like to play football for Notre Dame. When Charlie had expressed some interest, the alum had given him a couple of tickets for a Notre Dame home game. Charlie had been floored, but went to the game with his father. They both took the South Shore – South Bend Street Railway to South Bend, and when they got to their seats, the same alumnus was sitting beside them. After the game, which Notre Dame won, he took Charlie and his father to the locker room to meet the coach, who'd pulled out clippings from Charlie's high school games, and told him how he'd like to see him play at Notre Dame next year. Charlie and his dad were enthusiastic, but wary. But, the clincher came a couple of weeks later when an assistant coach came by the house to meet Charlie's mother and told her that her son would be going to Mass every morning for four years if he went to Notre Dame. She immediately told her son to call the nice man from the University of Southern California who wanted to take a trip to Chicago to meet him and let him know that he was going to Notre Dame.

"Hi guys, what can I get you?"

"I'd like some vanilla ice cream, with chocolate sauce and milk, all mixed together – what do you call that?"

"Sounds like a chocolate shake with vanilla ice cream to me."

"Son-of-a-gun, Charlie, you were right!"

"Why, what do you call it?"

"A frappe."

"Ah, you're from Boston. We have a lot of guys from Boston who go to school here. In Rhode Island, they call it a cabinet. Welcome to Indiana."

"Everybody I meet welcomes me here....you guys aren't bad."

"Look, roomie, you're paying the bills, or I should say that in your case, the government's paying the bills."

"Yeah, I suppose people should welcome us."

"Here you go. Of course we welcome you. That'll be twenty-five cents."

"Here you go yourself, and worth every penny of it.

"I have to admit this could be the best frappe or milkshake or cabinet that I've ever had. Thanks."

"Charlie, why don't we sit over there next to those two girls?

"Ladies, can we join you?"

"Well, I don't know. Are you freshmen?"

"Freshmen? We're both juniors."

Dan was nothing if not quick on his feet. His mother always said that he'd have a quick answer to Saint Peter on judgment day if he needed one.

"Now, you ladies look pretty mature. You must be upperclassmen yourselves."

"Well, we're both sophomores at St. Mary's. I'm Patti-Jo, and this is Yvonne."

Patti-Jo didn't sound very convincing, but both girls were very pretty, and they seemed to be pretty friendly.

"Nice to meet you, ladies. I'm Dan, and this is my bodyguard, Charlie."

"Not that he has a body that needs guarding," said Charlie, who was no slouch either when it came to a quick comeback.

"Yvonne, you're French?" Dan asked.

"I'm Yvonne Chrysler, and you are?"

"Fleming, from the Brighton, Massachusetts Flemings."

"You're cute."

"I'm cute? Yvonne, no woman or girl ever told me that I was cute before."

"Well, you are, and I thought I'd say so."

"Gee, after that, I don't know what to say."

"I travel ninety miles from home to play football at Notre Dame, a place where men are men, and I get a 'cute' roommate. What's the world coming to?"

"You're just jealous, Charlie, because no one ever called you cute, except maybe for your mother."

"Come to think of it, I never remember her calling me cute. You might be right, Dan. Patti-Jo, where are you from?"

"Well, I'm from Texas, and Yvonne's from Michigan, not too far from Detroit; Grosse Point, Michigan.

"Actually, we're both freshmen at St. Mary's. We just thought that you guys, being upperclassmen, wouldn't be interested in two freshmen.

"Why are you both laughing?"

"Well, we're laughing, Patti-Jo, because we're both freshmen, and we figured that you were upperclassmen and wouldn't want anything to do with a couple of lowly frosh."

The four of them laughed and giggled at Dan's admission. "We're just out exploring the campus; would you like to join us?"

Yvonne replied, "I think that'd be fun. You're both Notre Dame men of high moral character, so there'd certainly be no scandal in that."

"God, you must have gone to parochial school." "I did, but how did you figure that out?"

"That's something the nuns would say. I had nuns at St. Columbkille's High School just outside of Boston, and they were like that. They used to tell us not to dance too close to each other at the school dances, to leave enough room for the Holy Ghost."

"I knew you were from Boston by the way you talk, even before you told us."

As they were bantering, they paired off into couples. Dan went with Yvonne, and Patti-Jo fell behind with Charlie as they continued to wander over the Notre Dame campus.

"Dan, you do look a little old for a freshman; were you in the service?"

"I was, Yvonne, the Army. Vetville was all booked up, so they put me in Cavanaugh Hall, into a forced triple. Charlie and I just met. We're roommates, but we've not met the third person in our room yet."

"Were you overseas?"

"Yeah."

"Europe?
Asia?"

"Europe."

"I don't mean to pry. It's none of my business, it's just that you look, how do I say this, more serious, more mature, than some of the students we've already met."

The expression on her face showed that she was concerned, that she was looking to see if Dan was hurt by what she had said.

"She's perceptive," Dan thought to himself. He saw her concern and he found that attractive. He was starting to find himself attracted to her in the same way that he'd been attracted to Yvette the morning after he'd slept with her, and she'd explained how she had come to be where she was. Yvonne, though, was like a porcelain goddess to him, innocent and pure, naïve and sensitive. She was so much like Yvette, he thought, but in another sense she and Yvette were also different sides of the same coin. One was sweet, innocent, and protected, while the other was hardened and callused by life.

"I'm sorry, I….didn't mean to pry, Dan. I just meant...I...I..."

"Well, I guess that going off to war does have an effect on you. For one thing, you're older and have seen a lot more of life. Yvonne, I'm probably four or five years older than the average freshman, and sometimes I wonder what I'm doing here. It's been so long since I had to study, and that scares me a little; actually, it scares me a lot."

"I'm older too, Dan. I considered being a nun when I got out of high school. I stayed in the Order for two years, but when it came time to take my final vows, I realized that though I wanted to serve God, I did want to be a wife and a mother more. Dan, why are you all red? Are you getting a fever? Are you all right?"

"I'm sorry, Yvonne. I'm familiar with the order of nuns you were in. I met a nun at one of their convents when I was in France. She was the only survivor when the SS raped and murdered the other sisters."

Placing her hands to her face in shock, Yvonne blurted out, "Oh, Dan, that's horrible!"

Moving close to him, she threw her arms around him and buried her face in his chest.

"It was pretty bad."

"I was cloistered for two years, and I never heard of anything like that. I'm hearing things about the war now for the first time, and they're terrifying. Those poor women."

"The nun I met had been raped by a young German soldier who then hid her while all of the others were being murdered. He continued to rape her till he was killed by a partisan sniper a couple of weeks later."

Dan didn't want to share any more with Yvonne. He'd gone to that place deep within himself, the place he was trying to seal off from his life, but a place to which he was invariably drawn, even when he was trying to have a normal relationship, a normal conversation. Though he tried to avoid this place and tried to bury it by drinking, and then by running away to college, it was still a part of him, like a brand on a steer, one he couldn't erase.

"You had a relationship with this nun?"

"She had been involved with a close friend of mine who was killed in combat. Before he died, he had asked me to return to her and tell him that his dying thoughts were of her."

Yvonne sensed that Dan didn't want to go any further with this.

"Dan, we just met, and I don't want to cause you any pain. I'm sorry. I'm really sorry."

"Don't be sorry, Yvonne. This is something I have to work out for myself. I really like you, and I'm the one who's sorry that I opened my world of horrors for you to see. I fought to protect the purity and innocence in the world. I fought so that people like you and Patti-Jo could go to school, marry, and bring up children without worrying about some thug oppressing you and taking your freedom away from you.

"I don't mean to be melodramatic, Yvonne. I'd rather be bantering with you about mixers, football games, and classes. But I've spent a lot of time in another world, a world of pain and evil, and I sometimes have trouble getting away from it. It's not your burden, and I don't mean to unload it on you. It was probably your prayers as a nun that ended this thing and brought me home alive."

"Dan, I don't know what to say. I want you...."

Suddenly, feeling awkward, Yvonne stepped back out of Dan's arms. "I want you to know how I feel about you."

Watching her friend throw herself into Fleming's arms and then push away, Patti-Jo came rushing up to help her.

"Yvonne, are you all right? What's he doing to you?"

Seeing the tears in Yvonne's eyes and Dan's reddened face, she turned to him, her eyes flashing in anger, and yelled, "What did you do to her, you beast?"

Yvonne interrupted, "No, no, it's OK, Patti-Jo. Dan told me something that saddened me and he was upset for me, that's all. Don't be angry. It's OK. He's taking me out Saturday night, and we're friends. It's OK. Everything's all right."

Dan didn't know what to say. At the same time he was hurt, confused, upset, and very, very attracted to Yvonne Chrysler.

"Dan, we should get back to Saint Mary's. Why don't you call me and let me know what time you'll pick me up on Saturday. I'm in 235 LeMans' Hall. I don't know the telephone number for that floor, but the Saint Mary's operator will connect you to the hall phone."

At that, she turned and, with her friend, began walking quickly away from the two Notre Dame freshmen. Dan followed her with his eyes as she moved further and further away. He could see that she was crying, and that Patti-Jo was trying to comfort her.

"You screwed that one up pretty good, Roomie," Charlie said. "Things were just starting to work out between Patti-Jo and me when she noticed Yvonne crying. Now she'll probably never want to see me again. What happened between you two anyway? And if she's so upset with you, why's she going out with you on Saturday?"

"Charlie, it's like I told you earlier; I'm carrying some shit around with me, and I don't know why I told her about something that happened to me in the war. Maybe it was because I'm so attracted to her and trust her that I shared some of my baggage, not a lot, mind you, just a little, and it was too much for her to handle. I didn't know anything about a date until she mentioned it. I don't know what to do or what to say. I don't know whether I should ever call her, or ever plan on going out with her on Saturday night. She's lovely though; I like her very much, but I don't ever want to hurt her again."

CHAPTER TWENTY-THREE

Somewhere in the Mountains of Bavaria

Meanwhile, another world away, a German war widow is surprised by a visit from her village postman.

"Good morning, Frau Richter."

"Good morning, Postman Schultz. Do you have any message from my Heinrich yet?"

"None, Frau Richter. I'm sorry. But, there is a bunch of letters for you from the United States, about six of them. Most of them are postmarked from the city of Boston, but there's one from some place in Louisiana, and another from Indiana. I think those are American states, but I'm not sure where they're located."

"I'm not sure; do you think they may be from Heinrich?"

"No, I don't know who they're from, but they weren't addressed by a German. They came in with a large bag of mail just before I started my route. I sorted that mail but it was too heavy for me to carry, so I'm having people come down to pick up their letters and packages.

"The central post office in Berlin is just now starting to forward mail, and these look like they've been backed up for a while. I'll be in the office after lunch. Why don't you come down then and pick them up. They looked unusual, so I thought it'd be better if you picked them up rather than my bringing them up to you. If you have any question about how they got here or where they came from, we could ring up Berlin after you've opened them and had a chance to read them."

166

"Thank you, Herr Schultz. I'll be there at one o'clock, as soon as you return from lunch."

"Have a nice morning then, and I'll see you after lunch. Anka, one other thing, why don't you bring your father with you when you come down to pick the letters up?"

A few moments later, Anka approached her father and said, "Father, Herr Schultz, the postmaster, just came by. He said that I have a bunch of letters from the United States waiting for me at the post office. He wants me to come by after his lunch to pick them up. Father, do you think they're from Heinrich? Do you think he might be in a prisoner of war camp in America?"

"Anka, I know you don't want to accept it. I'm your father; I love you and don't want to diminish your hopes, but I think you have to accept the fact that Heinrich is dead. The Mueller boy made it home last month and said that a whole bunch of the troops from the village were killed during a barrage, and that Heinrich was with them. Mueller was wounded, and wasn't able to go with the group that was killed.

"Anka, I think you have to recognize that your life with Heinrich is over. You're a war widow, and you may never learn the fate of your husband. You must get on with your life, if for no other reason than the future of my granddaughter. You must bring Katherine up to honor the memory of her father, but you have to focus on your own survival. We're running out of food, and Katherine needs more protein if she's to develop properly. It'll be another month till we'll be able to harvest anything. We'll have enough milk for her if we don't slaughter the cow, but we've got to get food for the rest of us. We've sold just about anything we have of value on the black market, and I don't know what else we can do.

"But, Anka, you have to accept that Heinrich's dead."

"I can never do that, Father; not as long as there's the slimmest of hope."

"Let me walk with you to Herr Schultz's office after lunch. I have a feeling that a series of letters from the United States can't be a good omen." The morning sun moved across the sky till it was overhead.

Walking out of the family cottage, Hans Schneider walked over to where his daughter was rocking and singing to her own child.

"Shall we go, Anka? You can leave Katherine with your mother."

"She's beautiful, Daddy, isn't she? Do you see Heinrich's blue eyes in her?"

"She does have his eyes."

"I can't wait for him to see her." "Oh child...child...."

"Father, I know he's alive; I just know it!"

It was a short walk down the hill along the winding dirt road, and the village postmaster was open for business after lunch.

"Herr Schneider, it's good to see you today. I missed you when I was by the farm this morning."

"I was out in the fields replacing a rotted fence post, Herr Schultz. How are you doing, Jurgen?"

"I'm very busy, Hans. The central post office in Berlin just started forwarding mail, and I should be getting a three month backlog over the next couple of weeks. I've been telling people to drop by every day or two rather than wait for me to take their mail around on bicycle. They'll get it quicker that way, and I'll be able to spend my time sorting out the mountain of mail that's starting to arrive.

"Hold on and I'll get the letters from America for Anka.

"Ah, here they are, Anka."

"Thank you, Herr Schultz."

"Father, I have no idea what these are and why anyone would be writing to me from the United States. I'm afraid to open them."

"Here, child, let me see them and we'll put them in chronological order. None of this looks like Heinrich's handwriting.

"Now, open the earliest one first."

Anka took the letter from her father with trembling hand, fearing what she'd read once she opened it. She held it for what seemed to all of them like an eternity, as if she could keep her husband alive as long as she didn't break the seal on the envelope.

Finally opening the letter, Anka collapsed in tears, sobbing uncontrollably as she lay on the floor. Her father, suspecting the contents of the letter, bent, picked her up, and held her closely to him as she sobbed and sobbed, until she could cry no more.

Picking the letter off the floor, the postmaster handed the letter to Anka's father.

"Can I read it, Anka?"

"Yes," she said, and began crying again.

Unfolding the letter that was written in English, her father translated it aloud into German:

"Dear Mrs. Richter, I regret to inform you that your husband Heinrich has been killed in the line of duty. Before he died, I promised him that I would do whatever I could to support you and baby Katherine. I prefer to remain anonymous, but hope to send you money from time to time to help you recover from the war and your loss. Enclosed is a United States Postal Money Order. In order to cash it, please take it to any United States military base and show it and this letter at the gate. They'll show you how to get to the base post office. Hand the money order to the clerk, and he should give you the face amount of the order in American dollars. The loss that you and Katherine suffered is deeply felt by me.

"Please do not try to contact me."

"Father! Father! Heinrich is dead...he's dead, father...he's dead!"

"I know, child. I've been certain of his death for some time now, especially since the Mueller boy returned wounded with the story of the barrage. But why's this American writing to you and sending you money? How did he come to know Heinrich, and promise him that he'd look after you and Katherine after Heinrich's death? This is very strange. Why don't you open the other five envelopes."

Each of the envelopes contained a postal money order for $25.00, for a total of $150. There were no notes in any of the other envelopes.

"Father, why is this man sending us money?"

"Child, I have no idea, but the money comes at a good time. Now we can buy food on the black market to help us survive till things return somewhat to normal. Tomorrow we can walk over to the American base on the other side of the mountain and see if they'll honor these money orders. "

Walking back up the winding path to the ancestral home that they shared, the father and daughter each maintained silence, she out of grief and her sense of loss, he out of respect for his daughter's grief, as well as his puzzlement over these unexpected letters containing both bad news and good fortune.

"Hans, is that you and Anka? Please be quiet. Katherine's napping, and I don't want you to wake her. Did you get the letters, and what were they about?"

"This is very strange, Martha. The first letter, postmarked from the state of Louisiana, says that Heinrich's dead, and contains some sort of monetary draft for twenty-five American dollars. Four of the letters come from the City of Boston and have no message, but each of them contains the same type of draft for twenty-five American dollars. And the last one came from some town in Indiana that I never heard of."

"Hans, why would an American be doing this? And what contact would Heinrich have had with an American who moves all over their country? You're right, this is strange; it just doesn't make sense."

"Well, for whatever reason, this friend of Heinrich's, if he keeps this up, will be a tremendous benefactor to our family. Heinrich was such a kind and gentle man that it wouldn't be unusual for him to make friends, even with an American."

"Maybe Heinrich was wounded and captured and met the American in a hospital before he died."

"Why don't you stay with Anka and the baby and I'll head through the village to break the bad news to Heinrich's father. Poor bastard loses his wife and then his son. I don't know how I'd go on if we lost Anka. This war has been horrible for so many of us. Look at our poor daughter, a widow at twenty-one with a young child, and barely enough food to eat. Thank God we have the farm and we'll be able to get back to production this season. Last year was such a disaster, with all of the crops taken by the government, and paid for with paper money that was worthless. Hopefully, our new American government won't confiscate our crop this year."

Tracing his footsteps back down the winding road and through the village, Hans Schneider walked up the hill to the Richter farmstead to tell his daughter's father-in-law that his only child was dead.

"Niklas!" Hans saw his neighbor walking away from him around the barn. "Nik!"

Turning, the other man greeted his neighbor from across the valley.

"Hello, Hans, has Anka heard anything yet?" he asked in anticipation.

"I'm sorry, Nik." These two old friends had grown up together, gone to school together, raised their families together, and the happiest day of their lives was when their children had told them that they were engaged to be married.

"Anka got a letter today from America saying that Heinrich is dead. I'm sorry; I'm so sorry."

"Oh, my God...from America? Why would she get a letter from America telling her that Heinrich's dead? I don't understand...Oh, my God....Oh, my God..."

The dead man's father sat on the rough-hewn wood bench in front of the door step to his house and dissolved into tears, burying his head in his hands and sobbing uncontrollably, as uncontrollably as his daughter-in-law had earlier.

"Hans...Hans...are you sure? Is there no hope? The letter, do you have the letter, Hans?"

Looking down at the dirt, Hans passed the letter to his old friend. He continued looking down while Niklas read the strange and devastating letter from America.

"I don't understand this, Hans. Who is this American who writes? How did he come to know Heinrich, and why is he sending Anka money? I don't believe this, Hans. I can't believe my son is dead. I can still see him running around this yard chasing chickens as a little boy, and then he walked through this door with a packed bag to go to university. I remember when Herr Schultz brought the letter saying that he'd been accepted to the study of medicine, and how excited he and his mother had been. I lost her, but I can't accept that he's never coming back.

"He wasn't like that Stoessel thug who ran off at his first chance to join the SS. Heinrich was kind, gentle, always happy, and always trying to help others. He only went when those Nazi bastards drafted him out of university. Stoessel ended up in their unit with all the conscripts from here, and it's Stoessel who should've been killed, not my Heinrich!"

Again, the dead man's father crumpled over in tears. "I won't believe it, Hans...I can't believe it."

"I know, Nik, I know. Another strange thing about this American, assuming that he's a man, is that he's sent five more of these money order things, four from Boston, and another from a city in the state of Indiana. I'm not sure where that is, but he gets around. And there's nothing else in writing in the envelopes, just the money orders, one a month since the war ended. They all came at once because they'd been backed up at the central post office in Berlin, and they're just starting to get back in business.

"Nik, I know you don't want to give up hope, but I think we should have a memorial Mass for Heinrich."

CHAPTER TWENTY-FOUR

Meanwhile, Back in South Bend

Wandering back to Cavanaugh Hall, still upset about the events of the afternoon, Dan and Charlie saw a typed note taped to the front entrance door.

"RESIDENTS' MEETING TONIGHT AT 7:00 P.M IN THE VISITORS' LOUNGE ON THE FIRST FLOOR.

ALL ENTERING STUDENTS ARE REQUIRED TO BE THERE AND TO ARRIVE PROMPTLY!

REVEREND MALACHAI FRANCIS FITZGIBBON, C.S.C.

RECTOR, CAVANAUGH HALL"

"Great," said Dan, "we meet and get dumped on by two nice girls in the same day, and to add to it we have to go to a meeting run by the Grupenfuhrer of Cavanaugh Hall. Maybe he's recruiting us to join the North American branch of Hitler Youth. We'd better get there on time so we can get a seat near the door and bolt out as quickly as we can after the meeting.

"You know, Charlie, I forgot that I'm supposed to meet someone after the meeting. When I got to campus this morning, the first guy I met was from a town in Massachusetts, not too far from where I live. He was going to swing by after tonight's meeting and we were gonna head over to St. Mary's. I'm not sure that I ever want to go near that place after what just happened, but if he does show up, do you want to take a hike over there with us? He has a girlfriend at St. Mary's who can fix us up, but I'm not sure that I can handle another St. Mary's girl after what we just went through."

"Well, Roomie, I've heard that the ratio of ND guys to St. Mary's girls is something like ten or twelve to one, so we should probably strike while the iron's hot. There're going to be a lot of lonely freshmen around here on the weekends. If we get an in at Saint Mary's, maybe we won't be among them."

"I hope Father Fitzgibbon doesn't keep us too long. It'd be an all-time first for me to meet and get shot down by two girls in one day, not an insurmountable feat, but one I think we're both capable of."

"You might be right, Charlie, but I'm still confused and very attracted to Yvette...I'm sorry, I mean Yvonne."

"Hey, who's this Yvette chick...your Boston Honey? You've got them all over the place, Roomie, don't you?"

"She's a girl I met in France...a friend of a friend."

"She sounds like more than a friend of a friend to me, Roomie."

Dan's countenance and his whole body turned hard. Costanza knew from the way Dan turned, tightened his face and body, and squared his shoulders that this was an area that he didn't want to share.

"Look, I told you that I'm carrying a lot of stuff around from the war. Yvette's part of that. She's in a little box in my mind. I want her to remain there, and I'm sorry that I momentarily let her escape. Capish?"

"Yeah, yeah, I understand, Dan. I was just razzing you a little bit. I'm sorry if I hurt you."

"No, I'm sorry, Charlie. Her name slipped, but I want to put a lot behind me, and she's part of it."

"I understand."

Dan wasn't sure that he was being honest with himself by saying he wanted to put Yvette behind him. But, she was gone, and there was no feasible way for him to contact her.

For the rest of the day they worked together, unpacking clothing and arranging and rearranging the furniture till it was back in its original configuration from their first move. The hinges on the door to their room were on the left as you faced it from the hallway. As you stepped into the room, Charlie's bunk bed was just in front of you on your left. It ran parallel with and against the other wall that ran perpendicular to the hallway, and which separated Room #151 from Room #153. The back of Charlie's wall locker was against that same wall at the foot of his bunk bed in the corner of the room, with one side touching the outside wall of the building.

Dan's wall locker was to your immediate right as you entered their room, this time with its back against the wall that separated the room from the hallway. Dan's bed was parallel with and against the corridor wall. The sink and mirror were about three feet from the foot of his bed on the wall that separated their room, #151, from room #149.

There were two sets of windows facing out on to the north quad across to Breen-Phillips. Each set of windows consisted of two double hung windows with about ten inches between them. There was one desk under each set of windows, separated by the third wall locker with its back against the exterior wall. The third desk sat by itself on the same wall as the sink, about five or six feet from the exterior wall. Though Dan had originally thought he'd like a desk looking out on the quad, he eventually decided that it'd be less distracting for him to stare at the glazed brown cement blocks of the partition wall rather than at the occasional St. Mary's coed who might wander into view.

As the time for the hall meeting grew near, their third roommate was nowhere to be found.

"I wonder if he changed his mind at the last minute and decided to go someplace where the weather's warmer and the women plentiful," Charlie declared.

"I don't know," Dan said, looking up from the copy of the Hall Rules that he was reading. "Maybe he saw us running around campus today and decided that he could do better. Charlie, did you read these rules yet?"

"No, I figure the Grupenfuherer will go over them at the meeting."

"There are a lot of ways to get kicked out of this place, and most of them have to do with sex and alcohol. I sometimes wonder why Catholic priests are so hung up over sex. Do they think that all of their mothers were virgins, or that they didn't enjoy it when their priest and bishop sons were being conceived?"

"I don't know. I always figured it had something to do with guilt. I don't know if it's the same with the Irish, Dan, but an Italian mother's guilt's a terrible thing to bear when you're growing up. Of course, that's an Italian *Catholic* mother's guilt."

"Yeah, Irish Catholic mother's guilt's pretty bad too, but this stuff's ridiculous. You can get heaved for having a girl or a can of beer in your room. Even my Irish Catholic mother wasn't that strict."

"Oh shit! We'd better get going or we'll miss the meeting."

The visitor's lounge was packed, and the priest had already begun his talk when Room 151 arrived.

"Will the gentlemen who just arrived please identify themselves for the group!"

The large priest in the cassock standing in front of the room had a booming voice. Charlie was uncomfortable, and he replied nervously, "Charles Costanza, Sir." And the whole room began laughing. Unaware that he had said something funny by addressing the priest as "sir", Charlie turned to Dan with a bewildered look. Dan had the locked tight look on his face that he had shown earlier.

"I am not a 'sir,' Mr. Costanza. I'm a priest, and the usual way to address a priest is to call him 'Father.' Do you understand that, Mr. Costanza?"

Again the room broke out laughing as Charlie turned an ever- deepening red.

"Yes."

"Yes, who?"

"Yes, Father."

"Now, that's better. See gentlemen, we're making progress with Mr. Costanza. Now, who might your companion be?"

"My name's Fleming, Father, Dan Fleming, and there's no need to embarrass either one of us because we're a few minutes late."

"Thank you, Mr. Fleming. Now gentlemen, as I was saying before we were interrupted, we have certain parietal rules here that are designed both to help you save your souls as well as to make you better students. There's a typed copy in each room, and copies posted around the hall. We only accept outstanding young, Catholic men here, and if you prove yourself to be otherwise, we'll make it a point to correct our mistake. Do you understand me, gentlemen?"

His question being answered by a few mumbled grunts, the priest bellowed out louder and a few octaves deeper, "Do you understand me, gentlemen!'...it was less of a question than a statement.

This time he was met with a resounding, "Yes, Father!"

"Good! Are there any questions at this time gentlemen?

"None? Well then, you're free to go about the business of setting up your rooms. I trust that by now you've all discovered your way to the dining hall. You're to be back in the hall by ten o'clock, and lights will be out by eleven. Mr. Fleming, I'd like a word with you in my office in ten minutes. Please be prompt, sir."

Charlie turned to Dan on the way out of the room and said, "You're in it now, Roomie. This guy's gonna have us both in his sights for the entire year."

"Charlie, you're a jock and I'm a veteran. There's nothing that this drill instructor of a priest is gonna to do to either of us."

"He can campus us."

"Charlie, you can bench press 240 pounds, and I spent the last three years climbing and jumping over things, so I don't think it'd be too difficult for either of us to climb in or out of our room on the first floor of Cavanaugh Hall.

"I'll go down and talk with him and see what he wants, but I'm not going to cower and take a lot of bullshit from him.

"Look, could you call Ed Burke in Sorin Hall and tell him that I can't make it tonight?"

Cavanaugh Hall was long, with entry doors at either end, as well as in the middle. Student rooms were on either side of the corridor, except for the center door. The visitor's lounge was across from the center entrance, and across from that was the rector's suite of rooms consisting of a living room, a bedroom, and a small bathroom. The rector ate at Corby Hall, the priests' residence, with his brother priests.

Dan thought that the highly polished, brown tile floors reminded him of the many military bases he'd been on over his service career, and then he remembered Notre Dame's deal with the Navy. This was probably a barracks or junior officers' quarters for the midshipmen or their instructors.

Approaching the rector's door, Dan, out of habit, checked his military line, trousers' fly, belt buckle, and shirt, all aligned in a straight line; hair combed; shoes...well they weren't spit shined, dress black shoes, but the scuffed casual loafers didn't take away from his otherwise military bearing.

Knocking on the door firmly and crisply three times, he stood in a position of attention, his shoulders squared and his gut tight, a position of confidence.

"Enter!" Dan almost laughed at the command, and the thought crossed his mind that he should enter the room, stand at attention, render a Nazi straight arm salute and say, "Seig Heil, Mein Grupenfuhrer."

Turning the doorknob and opening the door smartly, Dan entered the room to face the priest seated behind his desk.

"You wanted to see me, Father." Dan said respectfully but confidently, not a question, but a statement.

"Sit down, Mr. Fleming."

"Thank you."

"You don't know why I called you in here do you."

"Father, meaning no respect, but I have no idea."

"You were in Europe, I believe."

"Yes, Father...I landed in Normandy on D-Day and walked all the way across France and into Germany by the time the war had ended."

"I'm trying to find some information on one of the priests in our Order, and I was wondering if you could help me locate him. We don't know whether he's dead or alive, or what became of him. The last we heard was that he was with an infantry unit somewhere in Germany around the time the war ended."

"Father, the Army personnel branch could help locate him, and if you could find out what unit he was attached to, the after-action reports would show if he'd been killed or wounded. By the way, what's his name?"

"Porcelli, Father Anthony Porcelli."

Dan paled and just muttered, "Oh shit."

CHAPTER TWENTY-FIVE

A Mile or So Down the Road, Patti-Jo Tries to Find Out What Had Happened Between Yvonne and Dan

The sun had faded in the west and it got chilly outside LeMans Hall. "Are you feeling any better, Yvonne?"

Patti-Jo was both solicitous and nosy, with a West Texas attitude that said it was her right to know what was in your mind, and that whatever was bothering you, she had the power to make better.

"I'm OK, Patti-Jo. I'm sorry that I got so upset. Were you having a good time with Charlie before I ruined it all?"

"He's all right...you know; ND jock, probably can lift twice his weight and run a hundred yards with the speed of lightning. I do kind of like him. As big and strong as he is, there's something very warm and cuddly about him, sort of like a big teddy bear.

"Could you imagine, though, if Daddy ever found out that I was going out with an Italian boy? He'd be fit to be tied. The thought of having black haired, furry grandchildren would send him through the roof.

"Were you serious about you and Dan going out Saturday night, or were you just saying that to get away from him? When did he ask you out, and why was he holding you like that? That's pretty forward when you just meet a girl, although the thought did occur to me that I'd fit nicely in Charlie's arms. But, he's no beast and he wouldn't grab me like that...like Dan grabbed you."

"It's getting cold out here, Patti-Jo. Maybe we should go inside."

"Why did he grab you, Yvonne? What made him do that?"

CHAPTER TWENTY-SIX

The End of the House of the Lone Ranger
and the Start of a New Life

"Mr. Mayor, we have a problem in town."

"Armand...no problems! You're the chief of police and I don't want to hear about any problems. Make them go away."

"It's the whores, Mr. Mayor. With the American troops in town bidding up their prices, none of the local men can afford to get laid."

"Look, I've got enough problems running the town and dealing with the Americans; I can't take on the problems my constituents have with their sex lives. I have neither the time nor the inclination. Tell your friends and neighbors to stay at home with their wives and make babies for the new Republic...and save their money in the deal. This is ridiculous."

"Well, some of the boys are really upset, and I've heard that a bunch of them are planning on raiding the convent, shaving the heads of the whores for sleeping with the Germans, and kicking them out of town."

"You know, that might not be a bad idea; just do it at a time when there'll be very few Americans in the house. I don't want another hassle with their civil affairs people...they're almost as bad as the Gestapo, and they wouldn't appreciate it that we're trying to save their troops from getting the clap. Can you make sure that no one gets hurt and that the whores have enough warning to pack their things before getting shaved and thrown out of town?

"I've been getting nasty letters from the bishop about evicting the 'current residents,' to use his own words, of the convent and placing it back into the hands of the nuns. This might not be a bad way to accomplish that. I'll still have to deal with the bishop after the Americans pull out, and it'd be good if we could get him back into that piece of property.

"Have them hold off till Saturday, though; I may want to make one final inspection of the site before they go. Is the cute little Parisian still there?"

"She is, but they say she doesn't turn tricks any more. She's pregnant, and works around the house cleaning and cooking, and the boys say that she spends a lot of time in the convent chapel."

"Tell the boys that I don't want anyone to touch her, and I want your men to make sure of that. Also, I don't want to see any of your men taking part in this activity. There are enough frustrated studs in town to carry this off without official involvement."

"Yes, Mister Mayor."

"Brigitte!"

"Yes, Mister Mayor."

"Brigitte, I'm taking off a little early today. If the American major calls, tell him that I'll get back to him as soon as possible, and in any event no later than when hell freezes over."

"Shall I say that you're at a meeting across town?"

"Yes, that'd be fine."

Rene Bourque had survived the Nazi occupation because of his political skills, a high degree of intelligence, and more than a little guile. As mayor, he had the Germans thinking that he was a loyal Vichy politician, while at the same time he was helping supply the Free-French Partisans, guerillas who operated around the town, and helped smuggle downed fliers back to allied lines.

He couldn't save the nuns and he couldn't save all the Jews in town, but there were a lot of men, women, and children still alive and living in the area because of Bourque. He was tired of it though. The Americans liberated his town, and he'd seen to it that the local Free-French unit blocked the SS troops from leaving and killed them all to a man. Not that those Nazi bastards deserved anything less for what they'd done to the nuns and the couple of Jews he couldn't manage to move into hiding. It was just that all of the killing, all of the suffering and pain they'd all been through, made him sick.

He didn't need to be the leader of this town any more. Any number of people could do as good a job as he in dealing with his American liberators. The front line troops who first entered the town were all right. They did the killing that needed to be done to end this whole exercise from hell, but the units that followed them as the front moved forward were terrible. Nobody had elected them, yet they acted as if the town was under their control, which of course it was

180

because they were paying people to work for them and feeding more than half of the town till crops could start being harvested.

In spite of the Army's non-fraternization policies though, it was difficult to keep young American men away from young French women. Two women in town had already been impregnated by American servicemen, and the Army wouldn't allow a magistrate's warrant to be served on the men who were responsible.

When he'd spoken with the local American commander about the situation, the mayor was told that the two soldiers had been transferred to another unit stationed in Germany. The colonel also told him to keep his women away from the American troops. That was when Mayor Bourque told the colonel that he could go fuck himself. This was the high point of their relationship, and the situation had been deteriorating since. He was almost ready to call the Partisans back into service to liberate the town from the Americans, but he knew that would be futile.

"Maybe," he thought, "closing the Lone Ranger would be a good way to get back at those bastards."

"Madam LeMieux, how are you?"

"Mr. Mayor, you've ignored us for so many years. To what do we owe the pleasure of your visit today?"

"Michelle, it's I who owe you for helping us get information on German troop movements and plans. Your ladies did a wonderful job for the French Resistance, and they should all receive commendations personally from De Gaulle. But, unfortunately, that won't happen, and I have some other bad news as well. Some of the boys in town are jealous about your new customers. Apparently, the competition from the American fighting men has driven your prices so high that very few of the local men can afford your services any more. Because of this, their patriotism overwhelms them and they want to rampage in here to shave everyone's head for collaborating with the Germans, and then drive you all out of town, where you'll be ridiculed and harassed until your hair grows back.

"I've got another problem. The bishop wants his convent back, and he's all over me to throw you out so he can bring in another crop of nuns. It'd be nice if you all had vocations, but since that's not likely to happen, I think that you should have everyone out of here by the weekend."

"This weekend, Mon Dieux! Where are we supposed to go?"

"Go back to Marseilles, or to one of the displaced persons camps the Allies are setting up. It'll take a while for this whole thing to settle down, and you and your girls should be able to start new lives out of all the turmoil and confusion the country's in right now."

"But, Mr. Mayor, Yvette LaFleur's about to have her baby; where will she go? She has no one; the collaborationist bastards killed her entire family."

"I know of Yvette's father. I met him once when I was studying in Paris, and he was a junior minister in the Department of Foreign Affairs. I actually dined with him and a common friend. He struck me as a very honorable man and a patriot. My wife and I will take Yvette in and care for her and her child. Please have her packed by Thursday and I'll have Armand send a couple of his men to escort her to our farm.

"Of course, this must be handled with some discretion. I don't want to hear a rumor that I've taken a mistress and moved her in with my wife. Now don't get me wrong; that'd probably help me get votes, but my wife would likely kill me the first time she heard the rumor.

"Michelle, I'm sorry to be bringing you this bad news, but it has to end this way. Start breaking your operation up and get the girls out of town, a couple at a time, with all of them out by the weekend. I hate doing this to you, but this is how it has to be. I'm sorry."

"I understand, Mister Mayor, and of course we'll comply."

"Thank you, Michelle, and good luck."

Rene Bourque left the House of the Lone Ranger with the feeling that he'd killed a couple of birds with one stone. This will get the bishop off his back, satisfy his sexually frustrated constituents, and stick it up the ass of the American colonel and his lap dog of a major. "They don't want fraternization," he thought to himself. "Well, we've just shut this particular fraternization valve tight. Let's see how the stupid bastard feels now!"

CHAPTER TWENTY-SEVEN

Déjà Vu for Dan All Over Again

It was semester break at Notre Dame, and all of the students were looking forward to returning home, all of them that is, except for Dan Fleming. During his meeting with Father Fitzgibbon, Dan was shocked to find out that the missing priest the Order was trying to locate was none other than the Reverend Anthony Porcelli, Major Anthony Porcelli, the very priest that Dan had dragged out of the minefield.

When he had explained to Father Fitzgibbon that he both knew Father Porcelli, and what had happened to him, the older priest looked at him in stunned silence. When Dan had said, "Father, I believe that Father Porcelli intentionally walked into that minefield with the intention of committing suicide," Fitzgibbon buried his head in his massive arms that lay crossed on his desk. The rector thanked Dan and said that he had nothing more to talk about with him.

About a week later, Father Fitzgibbon asked Dan if he could stop by his office one Friday afternoon after classes. When Dan entered the priest's office, the priest went into his bedroom, and Dan heard a refrigerator door open and close. Father Fitzgibbon came out with a couple of cold, frosty bottles of beer. Dan's attempt to move on beyond his drinking days had been successful, and he was somewhat taken aback with the offer of a beer from the priest. Overcoming his shock, Dan and the priest finished a six-pack before Dan left the office.

In the course of their discussion, Father Fitzgibbon told Dan that he had relayed their earlier conversation about Father Porcelli to the university president, who wanted to know if Dan would be willing to spend his semester break in Europe and attempt to locate Father Porcelli. Dan replied that he'd do that, but he wanted the president to contact the head chaplain to find out where casualties from his old battalion were being treated. After finding out that it was the former Wehrmacht hospital where he himself had been a patient, Dan said that he'd return if they could arrange transportation for him. This wasn't a problem for the university president, who used his Navy connections to get Dan scheduled on a flight from Boston directly to Europe. This regular courier flight was part of the first scheduled series of direct flights to Europe after the war

The university president had also arranged for Dan to be flown from Chicago to Otis Air Force Base on Cape Cod as part of a training flight so that he could spend a couple of days at home with his family before leaving for Europe.

His mother knew nothing about the mission to Europe, and wasn't expecting Dan home for the break because of the cost of travel. She looked as if she'd seen a ghost when Dan walked in the front door of the house.

"Dad, is that you? Why are you home so early?"

"It's me, Ma...Dan. I'm home for a couple of days on semester break."

"Oh, my God, Dan, you're going to be the death of me yet. We never expected you home, and all of a sudden, there you are. Wait a minute, you didn't flunk out, did you? You've not been drinking beer again now...have you?"

"Hold on, Ma. No, I haven't flunked out, and they've not thrown me out either. I've had three beers since I left home in August, and those were all in one night with a priest. I should have all 'A''s in my first semester courses when the grades come in, and so far I have an 'A' average in the year-long courses."

"Oh, blessed be God, Dan, blessed be God. I'm sorry, I'm sorry that I doubted you. I just worry about you, Dan...I still do. It's the mother in me. All mothers worry about their children, no matter how grown up they become. Maybe our fears are irrational, but it's because we love all of you so much, and fear losing you. I'm sorry, Dan, I'm sorry."

"Ma, don't worry about it. I'm doing OK at school, and the priests asked me to do something for them over semester break. I have to go to Europe to look for a member of their Order who we think is in a hospital in Germany. They arranged to fly me home from school, but I'll only be here for a couple of days because I'm flying to Europe on Saturday on a courier flight."

"They flew you home; they're flying you to Europe? I didn't know that planes could make it all the way to Europe. Dan, you're not going to be in any danger, are you?"

"No, Ma, I'm just helping them look for this priest. It's a coincidence, but I know who he is. He was my battalion chaplain, and I was trying to drag him out of a minefield when we both got wounded. I had no idea what happened to him, but the hospital that I was in has an amnesia victim, and that could be him...Father Porcelli, the priest they're looking for. I had asked about him, but no one knew anything, and we all assumed that he'd been killed. I'm going to the hospital to see if the amnesia patient is Father Porcelli. If he is, than the Order will see to it that he's shipped to the States, where he can get better treatment."

"Oh, that's quite a story. You're telling me the truth, Dan? Now look me in the eye and tell me it's true."

"Ma, it's true, and I did get all 'A's, and I'm not drinking any more, and I've been dating a Saint Mary's girl. Her name's Yvonne Chrysler and she lives in Detroit. We've been getting very involved with each other."

"Dan, that's wonderful, but be sure that you don't get too...too physically involved, you know what I mean? What I mean is that I wouldn't want you to be in a situation where you would have to leave school to get married or anything like that."

"Ma, I'm not going to knock her up. Ma, stop blushing; you know that's what you were referring to. She's an ex-nun, for crying out loud. When I'm with her I feel like I'm dating the Blessed Virgin. If she ever gets in a family way, there'll be a star in the East, and I'll take up carpentry."

"Yeah, Ma, like Saint Joseph," said Dan's brother, who had just entered the room.

"Right, that's what I've been trying to say; I haven't touched her. She's very special and I can tell her things about what happened to me in the war, and she's very understanding. She's helping me work out a lot of things, Ma. She listens, Ma; she listens and helps me...like you, Ma. Ma, I like her very much, and I think she likes me."

That evening his family celebrated Dan's success, and for the first time in a long time, he slept in his own bed without any demons chasing him around the room. He dreamed of Yvonne and holding her in his arms, and feeling her warm body next to his. He knew what he wanted to do with her, but he loved and respected her too much to try to seduce her. Now he knew how Smitty had felt about Yvette, and how much it was necessary for a man to have a woman to share his life with....to be complete. He had learned more about the meaning of life in the arms of Yvonne Chrysler than any philosophy or theology course could teach him.

CHAPTER TWENTY-EIGHT

Germany and a Search for Shadow

His time at home went by too quickly, and it was on a very cold Saturday morning that a Navy car pulled up in front of the Fleming house at 6:00 A.M., or "06:00," as Dan would have referred to it a couple of years earlier. The car drove Dan to the Squantum Naval Airfield in Quincy, where he was given a flight suit and a warm pair of gloves. He got into a jump seat behind the co-pilot. The seat was made of canvas and folded down from the side of the plane. Dan didn't think it looked very comfortable, and he was right. He had to change planes in England and take a second flight to Germany. By the time he had arrived at the former German Army Hospital, he could barely stand with the pain in his lower back. Walking into the reception area, he noticed that all of the signs in German had been taken down and replaced with English signage. Dan was told that the hospital commander was expected in shortly, within the hour, and that he could either wait in his outer office or come back in an hour. The secretary, a red headed, freckled corporal who looked like she had come directly out of a corn field in Iowa, suggested that he might want to get lunch or a cup of coffee in the hospital cafeteria.

"Thank you, Corporal, I'll do that.

"Corporal, you know...when I was on active duty during the war, I was wounded and was a patient in this very hospital. There was a nurse, Mary O'Daugherty, who helped me considerably. You wouldn't know what happened to her, would you?"

"Major O'Daugherty, yes sir. She's the director of nursing. Her office is on the floor above us, kitty corner to this office. Do you want me to call her, Mr. Fleming, and tell her that you're here?"

186

"No...no...please don't do that. I'm sure she wouldn't remember me...it's been almost two years now, and I wouldn't want to disturb her. Maybe I'll take your suggestion and go upstairs to the cafeteria. If we run into each other and she remembers me that's fine, but I wouldn't want to disturb her."

"Yes, sir, then Doctor Casey should be back here in about an hour. When he gets in, I'll tell him to be expecting you."

"Thank you, Corporal, that's very nice of you."

Taking his leave and riding up a floor on the same elevator, Dan noticed that even though they hadn't changed the floor designations on the elevator control panel, someone had taken a thick marking pen and written the American floor designations next to the brass floor numbers the Germans had originally installed.

...

"Major O'Daugherty, please. This is Doctor Casey's secretary, Corporal Faulkner.

"Hello, Major....yes, thank you, Major, we did have a wonderful time, and I'm going to meet him again this Saturday. We'll take a jeep into the mountains for a day to do some exploring on snow shoes. Thank you for introducing us. I do like him.

"Major, a civilian by the name of Daniel Fleming just showed up early for an appointment with Doctor Casey, and he asked for you, wanted to know if I knew what had happened to you. When I told him that you were the director of nursing, he blushed deeply, and didn't want me to call you. He said something like you probably wouldn't remember him, and that he didn't want to disturb you."

...

"Yes, Ma'am, thank you, Ma'am; I thought you'd want to know."

...

"Yes, I sent him to the cafeteria a couple of minutes ago."

...

"Yes, thank you, Ma'am, goodbye."

Leaving her office, Mary O'Daugherty hurried down the hall to the hospital cafeteria at the same time that Dan was getting off the elevator. He noticed the new sign on the wall with an arrow: "Cafeteria." He thought to himself that the Army was getting decidedly more civilian oriented when they call a mess hall a cafeteria.

While he was looking at the sign, he literally bumped into Mary O'Daugherty as she was striding down the corridor.

"Oh, excuse me."

"Sorry!"

187

"Mary...?"

"Dan Fleming...Dr. Casey's secretary told me that you were looking for me. You've survived the war and you're a civilian; I'm happy for you.

"To be honest, I'd forgotten your name until I got the call a few minutes ago. But, I'll never forget you and what you did for me."

"What I did for you? I was your patient; you took care of me. I'll never forget you or what you did for me.

"How did the men in your triage ward do that day?"

"Miraculously, two of them survived."

"The fellow who asked you if he'd be all right..."

"He died shortly after you left. He did go home, but...sometimes in the middle of the night, he comes to me and asks me again whether he'll be all right."

Major O'Daugherty's eyes began to fill as she relived this for Dan.

As she spoke, Dan felt the presence of Yvonne Chrysler slip out of his mind. Yvonne was from another time, another life...a wholly different reality. He'd just gone back in time, as it were, to a place...a world that he thought had been over for him.

His bond with Mary O'Daugherty formed when fate threw them together. An exploding ammunition truck and seven dying young men had brought them into a brief but intense relationship, closer than for many couples who've been together for years.

"I never thought that I'd see you again," she said. "I often wondered if you were killed as the war was winding down, or if you were still alive.

"I was on the verge of breaking down when you came into the triage ward. Someone must have sent you...someone...somewhere...knew I needed you very badly at that moment. When you appeared, you saved my soul. You were my bridge out of hell. I felt that then, but I need another bridge now."

Looking deeply at her, Fleming again felt their unity, a unity bred out of the same insanity that initially brought them together during the war. She had cared for him then when he was wounded, and he'd showed up when she was on the verge of an emotional breakdown. Now she needed someone again, and the same fate that had thrown them together earlier was responsible for them now facing each other in the middle of a busy hospital corridor in Germany.

He put his hands out and held her forearms, and they stood there wordless for what seemed to be an eternity. The daily life of the hospital passed around them and they were oblivious to it.

"Can we go somewhere and talk?" he asked.

"My office is just down the hall...we can go there."

Following her back down the hospital corridor, they entered her office.

"Corporal, would you see that we're not disturbed unless Dr. Casey calls for Mr. Fleming?"

"Will do, Major." "Thank you."

Going into her office and closing the door, the two sat facing each other in chairs in front of her desk.

Dan spoke first, "I know you were having a tough time caring for those guys because they were sent to you to die. We all lived death then; we were surrounded by it. We breathed it, we ate with it, and slept with it. We were all death then...major cogs in the dying machine, a machine that we somehow escaped. It was death that brought us together, death grown out of evil.

"I almost died so many times and I saw so many dead men, women, children, and animals that I nearly went insane myself. After I left you I returned to my unit, and just as the war was ending, I killed a man on the end of my bayonet when he fell into my foxhole. I was in a forward observation post. Apparently, he was approaching our lines to surrender, but I didn't know that. I thought he was attacking me. He died in my arms with my bayonet in his stomach and both of us praying together."

"Dan...that's horrible!"

"Then I got caught in a minefield. Luckily, only the detonator charge exploded when I stepped on the mine. It damaged one of my feet, but I recovered, and then they discharged me from the hospital shortly after my unit was demobilized.

"I was separated with a 30% disability, money that I used to drink myself silly at the local Legion post. Mary, it was terrible. I'd wake at night screaming. One night I tried to strangle my father when he came into my room while I was sleeping. I thought he was a Nazi storm trooper. That ended me up in a psychiatric ward, and when I got out of there, I went back to trying to kill my demons with alcohol."

"Dan, I'm sorry to hear that. You look...how do I say this...you look normal. Are you still drinking? Have you found a way to deal with your demons? I have my own demons, and the only way I deal with them is to work myself into exhaustion and to sleep with every man I meet. I'm looking for someone like you to rescue me from hell. But the only escape I can find is in a bottle. If I have any time out of work or out of bed, I usually spend it at the bar in the "O" Club.

"Maybe the same fate that threw us together two years ago has done it again today.

"I know you've beaten your demons; I can tell by looking at you. How do you do it? Can you help me with my own demons?

"Dan, I don't know what brought us together again, but I need you now as much as I needed you then. When I sleep, I hear the cries and moans of those dying men. They die over and over every night. I can't get them out of my mind...their screams, their struggling, gasping breaths, their sobbing, and their pain...they follow me everywhere...everywhere."

"Mary, you can't run away from this; there's no escape, but you have to move on. One V.A. psychiatrist told me how I could deal with my own demons...a screaming German tank crew burning to death inside their steel coffin and my closet friend who died in my arms. He said to gently place my demons in a box, reverently tie the box with a red velvet ribbon, then put the box in the ocean, and let it wash away.

"It was certainly easier for him to say than it was for me to do it. But, I've tried and now I take it one day at a time, and try not to look back. You're the exception though. I often dream about you, about waking from my coma and seeing your face looking down on me from over my bed. I see you as I fade back into unconsciousness, and then I hold you in the triage ward. I see the fear in your eyes and you bury yourself in my arms. And then...and then...I wake up.

"You're forever a part of my life, Mary, in a chapter that will never close. It can never close because it shaped our lives and is so much a part of who we are now. But in another sense it has to close because it also controls our lives. A chapter that's never finished is only going to torment us for however long we allow it to stay open. Maybe we can close that chapter in both of our lives; maybe I can help you with your demons.

"My former CO lives in Indiana. He's a Notre Dame graduate. He called me one day and told me he could get me admitted if I wanted to go. I didn't know if I could stop drinking, but I told my parents that I'd try. I enrolled this past September. I've been doing really well, and my demons seem to have just slipped away. I know they're floating around out there ...somewhere...in that box with the red velvet ribbon. I know they can come back, but I don't struggle with them anymore. I just leave them. I can't control what happened in the past. I can't undo what's already been done; it's part of me, a part of who I've become, but I don't have to stay frozen in time, anchored to the horrors of that life.

"You weren't a demon in my mind, Mary. You were an angel, formed out of the cauldron of that war, forged out of the molten metal of the pain and suffering of the wounded men you treated. You were an angel to the men you couldn't save. You eased their pain and you made their deaths more tolerable with your kind words and attention. You helped bring me back to life, and you gave me an anchor for my own sanity.

"Mary, I can help you with your demons if you want me to."

Dan stood as he was saying that, and for the second time in his life, he provided a pillar of strength for Mary O'Daugherty as she buried herself in his arms.

Wiping tears from her eyes, she said, "Some people know each other for a lifetime and never develop the intense relationship, the intimacy, which you and I had in just a few minutes together.

"I have a superficial relationship with most of the people I deal with. I hear the enlisted men and the other nurses call me 'the ice queen' behind my back. I've never had...maybe I'm afraid to have...as intense a relationship as you and I shared that day."

"Mary, we have to close the chapter on that day. We needed each other in different ways then and we were there for each other. You cared for me, and I was with you on the triage unit when you needed someone. The fate of war brought us together then, Mary; just one of the random things that grew out of that insanity. We came together in a very deep and profound way, a way that neither of us had plotted, and a way that ended as suddenly as it began. Our relationship lasted less than 24 hours, or at least I was only aware of it for less than 24 hours after I regained consciousness.

"But, that's over. That was then and this is now. Mary, you don't need to hang onto your demons. You can let them go. I know that it's not like getting a parking ticket that you can pay and forget; they'll always be there...floating somewhere, maybe in the Atlantic Ocean or the Rhine River, but we don't have to wallow in them and continually relive their pain every day of our lives.

"Mary, our demons and our ghosts are a part of who we are and we have to acknowledge them, but we don't have to wear them like chains around our necks forever.

"We're survivors, Mary, and we shouldn't let the chains of the dead force us to envy those who didn't survive. We're alive, through what quirk of fate God only knows, but we have lives to live, relationships to develop, and careers to follow.

"We can grow, Mary; we can love again, and we can live. Our trip through Hell can't deny us that unless we let it."

Dan Fleming felt the presence of someone or something while he was talking. It was as if he were mouthing the words that someone else was speaking. The voice was his, but the words weren't his own; they came from somewhere, from some higher power, from somewhere beyond himself. He was the instrument that gave voice to those words, and though they came from within him, he didn't control them or create them.

When she stopped crying, Major O'Daugherty wiped her eyes with a tissue from the box on top of her bookshelf. Her face was red and she was soaked from sweating, as if she had run a race. But, exorcism's never easy, and Dan was sweating profusely too.

"I'm exhausted, Dan. I don't know if I'll be able to do what you've done. I'll try....but...."

"You can't try, Mary. The harder you try, the worse they'll get. You just have to let them go."

At that, Dan opened his closed fists, palms turned upward, and threw them as if he were tossing confetti into the air. "Poof," he said. "Let them go, escape and fly away. You don't have to own them or fight with them anymore."

Looking intently at him, she asked, "Why did you come here....to find me, or for some other reason?"

"Mary, it's good that we found each other again, but I'm here on a mission to look for my old battalion chaplain who belongs to the same order of priests that teach at Notre Dame. He may be a patient in your hospital suffering from amnesia..."

"Major Shadow?" she asked, blotting at her eyes with the tissue.

"I'm sorry....what?"

"Major Shadow...he was in tough shape when they brought him in. It took a long time for him to regain consciousness, and no one knows what to do with him. All we know about him is that he had a major's insignia on his collar, no dog tags, clothing in shreds, and multiple wounds of the lower extremities, consistent with injuries from a partially exploded landmine. No fingerprint match and we don't know his name or what unit he was from, only that he lives in a shadow world. He's recovered physically, but he has no idea of who he is or where he comes from. He lives in a room off the main ward on the second floor. The CO assigns him duties consistent with his rank that don't involve heavy lifting."

"If he is who I think he is," responded Dan, "I can tell you that it *was* a partially exploded landmine. The battalion chaplain had tried to commit suicide by walking into a minefield. He triggered a landmine that only partially detonated. I was carrying him out when I slipped and set off another antipersonnel mine. Fortunately, that was defective too. I lost consciousness though, something I seem to have a predilection towards. When I came to, I was in another hospital. I never learned what had become of Father Porcelli, and presumed that he had died from his wounds.

"While I was at Notre Dame this semester, I learned that Porcelli's Order was looking for him. They arranged with the Navy to fly me over here to learn what I could about his whereabouts. I may have just hit pay dirt."

Mary spoke, "A Catholic priest trying to commit suicide....that's strange. Shadow's suffering from severe shell shock. The thought never occurred to us that he could be a chaplain, but he's a kind and docile person....I suppose that's plausible.

"Do you think he'd recognize you?"

"Well, I'd know him for sure, but I don't know what his reaction would be if he sees me...maybe nothing."

"I'd be afraid that seeing you might trigger some sort of adverse psychological reaction. Shadow doesn't seem to have any demons; he's just calm and placid and in his own world.

"We've seen a lot of guys who are shell-shocked and many of them seem almost as if they had a lobotomy...no affect, flat personality, and that describes Major Shadow to a 'T'.

"Well, look, why don't I call Dr. Casey and ask if he can see you now. I'll take you up there and we'll see what he has to say about whether your Father Porcelli and our Major Shadow are one and the same man.

"Hi, this is Major O'Daugherty again. Is the colonel back yet?"

. . .

"Yes, I know about the meeting. Mr. Fleming's here in my office."

. . .

"OK. Tell Dr. Casey that I'll bring him right up. If it's all right, I'd like to sit in on the meeting. Mr. Fleming and I know each other, and he's told me why he's here.

"We'll be right up."

Turning to Dan, the major was all business and said, "Let's get up there on the double. Casey has been waiting for you. And Dan....let's keep the ghosts and demons between the two of us. I wouldn't want Casey to send me for a fitness for duty exam because of them."

It almost seemed surreal to Dan that he was back in this place with Mary O'Daugherty and maybe Father Porcelli, people from another life and another world that was as far away from the world that he and Yvonne Chrysler were living in as Mars is from Jupiter.

He thought that he'd managed to set all of his demons adrift on the tide. The only problem was that now the tide was turning and starting to bring the whole thing back to him. Meeting Mary had reopened one chapter of his book of horrors; he hoped that meeting Porcelli wouldn't open others.

"Colonel, Major O'Daugherty's here to see you, Sir, along with Mr. Fleming.

"Yes, I'll send them in.

"The colonel said that he'd see you now, Major."

"Major." The colonel rose at his desk to greet his visitors. "Dr. Casey."

"Sir, this is Dan Fleming. He was in the 805th and we had a brief encounter during the war when he was a patient here."

"Nice to meet you, Fleming. What can we do for you?" The colonel, Dr. Casey, extended his hand and Dan shook it, noticing the strength of Casey's grip, a steady surgeon's grip, he thought.

Mary, undaunted, continued talking, "Mr. Fleming has been sent by the priests at the University of Notre Dame to interview Major Shadow. Dan suspects that Shadow may be the former chaplain of the 805th. Mr. Fleming could identify him, but I'm concerned with how Shadow will react when he sees someone from his former life."

"Good point, Mary. We should arrange for Fleming to see Shadow without Shadow getting a look at him."

"What if you asked Shadow to accompany you in your staff car? Mr. Fleming and I could sit in another car parked between the office door and your car. Mr. Fleming could observe Shadow as he walked past with you and the major probably wouldn't notice us."

"Brilliant, Mary...I'm glad you didn't go to med school or I'd be working for you instead of the other way around."

Shooting Casey a knowing look, O'Daugherty said in a low and sultry voice, "I guess it depends where we are, Sir."

At that, the Colonel blushed profusely.

Looking only a little relieved, Casey harrumphed and said, "That's a good idea, Major. I'll ask Shadow to meet me here at 13:00 hours."

Picking up his phone, the Colonel asked his secretary to call the motor pool and have a car and driver dispatched immediately to the hospital's main entrance to pick up Major O'Daugherty and another passenger.

"OK, I'll tell Shadow that I'd like him to come with me to check out the new enlisted barracks. I'll try to delay him as we walk past your staff car."

"Sounds like a plan, Sir."

"Colonel, the motor pool just called. The car will be in front of the hospital at 13:00 hours."

"Thank you, Corporal."

"Sir?"

"Yes, Mary."

"What if Shadow goes into a flashback when he sees Fleming? Should we have a couple of corpsmen standing by to restrain him?"

"Well, I don't think that's likely. It assumes that Shadow is Porcelli, that Shadow sees Fleming, that he recognizes him, and that his recognition triggers an adverse psychological response.

"But, I agree that an ounce of prevention's worth a pound of cure." Picking up his phone, Casey again spoke with his secretary.

"Corporal, I'd like you to have two corpsmen with a straight jacket standing by off to the side of the main lobby at 13:00 hours. Tell them to keep an eye on me and Major Shadow. If Shadow becomes psychotic, I'll signal them to restrain him."

"Is that clear?"

"Yes, two of them. How about Jankowski and Russo? They're probably the strongest men on the base.

"Right, thank you.

"OK, let's get rolling. Mary, I'd like you to draw up a syringe of Thorazine. If Shadow does turn psychotic, wait till the corpsmen restrain him, then give him a bolus of about 25 milligrams in his butt. I'll tell you if I think he needs it.

"Your car will arrive at 13:00 hours and I'll keep Shadow here till at least 13:05."

"We'll see you then, Sir," Mary said, standing to leave the office.

On cue, Dan rose to walk out with her and they headed downstairs back to her office. Dan noticed that even though they had renumbered the elevator signs in the hospital, the corridor signs still had the same European floor designations.

"Crazy place," Dan thought to himself. "These people are all nuts; they don't even know how to number hospital floors. I hope my box of demons doesn't open up again if Shadow does turn out to be Porcelli."

They weren't in Mary's office very long when her secretary entered the doorway.

"Your car's here, Ma'am."

"Thank you.

"This is it, Dan. Let's go see if Major Shadow's your Father Porcelli."

As they left the front door of the hospital and headed towards the waiting car, Dan broke the silence he'd been keeping on the elevator ride down from Mary's office.

"You know, Mary, I'm concerned about myself as well as Porcelli if it turns out to be him. I'm still carrying a lot of baggage and I don't want any more of it to surface. I've been going one day at a time and I hope this is a good day for me."

Opening the car door, Major O'Daugherty spoke to the driver, "Thanks for picking us up, Corporal."

"You're welcome, Ma'am. Where to?"

"Well, no place for right now. Two officers will be coming out the front door of the hospital in a few minutes. We want to observe them momentarily without being seen by them. I'd like you to be prepared to drive away when they're about halfway to the car."

The driver gave her a puzzled look and said, "OK, Ma'am, whatever you say. You're an officer; just tell me what to do."

"Nervous, Dan?"

"A little more than I'd thought I'd be. This guy attempted suicide right after trying to help me. I was having a rough time after killing that German soldier who was trying to surrender. I didn't know that, and when he stumbled into my foxhole, I killed him with my bayonet. I may have given Father Porcelli too much to handle."

"You mean the straw that broke the camel's back?"

"Yeah, maybe that's it. We were always walking by bodies lying in or beside the road: Germans, French, American, soldiers, women, men, and children. After a while, you just became numb to it. You may have just passed a couple of grotesque dead bodies, and twenty minutes later you stopped to eat chow without even thinking about it. But for Porcelli, he couldn't just pass them by. For the most part, he was close to the front line, but behind the killing zone. The bodies were still in place when he came along, and as a priest, he felt it his duty to anoint them. I guess it took a toll on the poor guy. Maybe you're right; maybe I was the straw that broke the camel's back."

"Here they come now, Dan. Can you see Shadow's face?"

"Yeah, that's him, Mary. No doubt about it, that's Porcelli."

"OK, driver, let's go!"

"Yes, Ma'am. Where to?"

"Just take off, soldier! Get out of here! Move! On the double!"

Nervous about his charge, the driver popped the clutch too quickly and the car stalled. In his hurry to start the car, he flooded the carburetor and sat there cranking the ignition as Colonel Casey and Porcelli approached.

Drawn by the noise of the ignition, Major Shadow turned to the colonel and said, "That car seems to be having some problem starting. Let's see if we can help the driver."

"No, Major, we'd better get along. I have to be back for a meeting at 14:00 hours. If he can't get it going, the motor pool will send someone to help."

"It'll only take a minute, Sir. I'll hold the butterfly valve open with a screwdriver to get more air into the carburetor."

Approaching the car, Porcelli froze, staring with an intense and painful glare at the passenger in the back seat.

"Oh shit, Mary...he sees me! What do we do now? He recognizes me!"

"I think the only thing you can do is get out of the car and say hello. Act as if there's nothing abnormal about the situation...just a coincidental reunion."

Nervous as he was, Dan did as she suggested. Saluting Porcelli as the priest approached him, Dan said, "Good morning, Father."

Porcelli looked like a deer caught in the headlights. Dan didn't look much better. The priest mumbled an incomprehensible greeting: "....Third Platoon....Captain Miller...Corporal Fleming...."

Now the priest's voice started rising, "Your god loves you, Fleming! He does! He's not responsible for this madness, Fleming! Do you understand? Do you understand? You didn't kill that man, Fleming, the war killed him! They killed him! Not you! You're innocent, Fleming! Your god loves you! He forgives you, Fleming!"

The priest was screaming now, and Colonel Casey was nervously looking back towards the hospital door to see if he could get a glance at the two medics who he hoped would see what was going on.

"Fleming! Damn your soul to hell! You bastard, why didn't you let me die? You bastard, Fleming! You bastard! Why didn't you let me die? Why? Why?"

"I tried to save your life, Father! I saved your life!"

"You killed me, Fleming! You killed me! You killed my soul, you ungrateful bastard! You should have let me die! I wanted to die!"

As the two men stood their ground, the one screaming at the other, Casey turned fully toward the hospital and motioned the two corpsmen forward. They came out quickly, not running, but walking smartly, almost on the verge of a trot.

"We're standing by, Sir," one of them said to Casey.

"Hold fast for a moment. See if he calms down and comes out of it. If he doesn't, try to be gentle with him and get him to the psyche ward under restraints."

"Yes, Sir!"

By this time, Mary O'Daugherty had gotten out of the car, leaving the flustered driver cranking and cranking the ignition, still trying in vain to turn over the flooded engine.

"Doctor, I have the Thorazine."

"Stand by, Major, let's see if Shadow brings himself out of it."

But, oblivious to everyone else, Porcelli remained fixated on Fleming, staring at him and screaming like a man possessed. He started ripping his clothes, crying, and now speaking to a presence that wasn't there, unseen by anyone but the priest in his delirium. Throwing himself on the pavement at Fleming's feet, Porcelli called out to the invisible presence, "I didn't want to do this! I did this in your name! I did this for you, but you wouldn't let me die! Why? Why? Why wouldn't you let me die?"

At this, Colonel Casey motioned the two medics into action, and though Porcelli fought with the strength of ten men, they quickly subdued him, holding him in the prone position on the front lawn of the hospital as they tied the arms of the straight jacket behind him.

Mary O'Daugherty came up behind the writhing, squirming form pinned on the grass. She held the needle up to eye-level and forced a bubble of air from the syringe. She squirted a drop or two of the medication into the air from the barrel of the large bore needle, flicking the tip with the back of one of her finger nails. She kneeled and expertly injected the Thorazine through Porcelli's trousers and into his gluteus.

Slowly and gradually, the priest's resistance subsided till he lay on the grass, as if at peace. He was asleep, though tormented by his restored memory. The bliss and innocence of Major Shadow had succumbed to the torments of Father Porcelli in the restored memory of this haunted man.

In that haunted place that had become his mind, Porcelli's dreams and his demons were back, and not dissimilar to Dan's. Schmidt, the dead German soldier, repeatedly came up to him and thanked Porcelli for picking his field cap up off of the road in the Hell's forest where he and all of his comrades had died at the triple click of Corporal Fleming.

"Click it again, Dan," Schmidt would say over and over in the haunted priest's mind as Dan Fleming, sitting in his foxhole, would smile and respond, "Sure enough, Fritzie, here it comes." At this, the priest's brain would explode with artillery fire ten times more intense than the loudest Fourth of July display he'd ever seen.

"More for you, Fritzie," he would hear Dan Fleming say, and he could see his smiling face.

"You didn't kill him, Dan, they killed him. The hand of Evil placed all of you there. He would have killed you if you didn't kill him. He may have wanted to surrender but he would have resisted you. It's evil, Dan, it's evil that leads us into this insanity...."

It all came back to Father Porcelli in a flash once he recognized Dan Fleming's face.

By this time, Jankowski had returned from the hospital with a stretcher, and the two medics gently placed the now subdued priest on it and were carrying him off to the psychiatric ward.

Chapter Twenty-Nine

Dan and Mary Reconnect
and Confront Their Demons

"Well, I guess the mystery of Major Shadow has been solved," Casey said.

"How are you doing, Dan?" Mary asked the pale and sweating young man in front of her.

She was about five years older than he and she sensed that, more than anything, Dan needed mothering now. He had been there for her when she needed it, and now it was her turn to help him. He was fragile and vulnerable and on the verge of succumbing to his own newly invigorated demons. Dan stood motionless, consumed in his own mind over what had just happened.

"Fleming, I'll arrange a billet for you."

Casey's words came less out of concern for Fleming than a concern that his head nurse and occasional mistress would bed this young civilian.

"That's OK, Colonel, I'll see to Dan's quarters."

"I won't have it. I'll see that he's properly billeted."

"You know, Brian, why don't you leave us alone?"

Dan was oblivious to all of this. He was numb and back in the minefield carrying Porcelli when the defective charge exploded, again knocking him unconscious. And then again in his mind, Porcelli was hearing his confession.

"Don't let yourself go there, Dan. Don't wrestle with your demons. Let them come into your mind and then pass on through. Don't trap them, Dan. Don't wallow in them."

"I'm trying, Mary. I'm trying." Dan was sweating more profusely now than when they were in her office. "I can't stay in this flash-back with Porcelli. I have to put him in my past."

By this time, with the dying gasp of the nearly drained battery, the motor pool driver managed to start the staff car.

"Get in, Dan."

Too numb to protest and too exhausted to care, Fleming dumbly followed her instruction and got in the rear seat behind the driver.

"Where to, Ma'am?" the driver asked Major O'Daugherty, replaying the question he'd asked just before he stalled the car, about three hundred years ago.

"15 Wilhelm Strauss Avenue."

"Yes, Ma'am."

Dan and Mary didn't speak on the twenty-minute ride to her apartment. She held him close to her, cradling his head on her chest.

Exiting the car, Mary addressed the driver, "Corporal, there's a suitcase in my office at the hospital, on the second floor in the head nurse's office. I'd like you to pick it up and bring it back here. We'll be on the third floor of this building in the rear, Apartment 3-R."

"That was three-Romeo, Ma'am?"

Blushing at his use of the phonetic alphabet to confirm her apartment number and what she had in mind, Mary smiled and said, "Yes, soldier, three-Romeo."

Dan just followed her; still numb and oblivious as they entered the old stucco apartment building.

Entering her apartment on the third floor, Mary said, "Why don't you go lie down. You've been through a lot and need the rest."

"Mary, they're coming back now. I'm in the foxhole again and I hear the noise of people walking through the underbrush. I thought it was gone…but it's back.

"Hold me, Mary, hold me…."

She took him in her arms and pulled him close to her. "It's OK, Dan. It's OK. It's all over now!"

"I know it's over, but deep inside me it'll never be over. It'll always be a part of me."

"I know that, Dan, I know that. I see those men in my triage unit dying….one at a time. I hear one of them over and over asking me if he'll be all right, and I hear myself telling him that he'll be OK, and that he'll be going home soon.

"That's all he wanted, Dan, was to go home, and that's what he wanted to hear from me. And I lied to him, Dan; I lied and told him that he'd soon be going home. That's what I can't get rid of; the feeling that I betrayed him, that I gave him false hope where there was none. I see his face in every man I sleep with, and they all ask me why I cry when we're doing it. I...I...don't know how to control this. I can't control it, you're right. I have to accept it and just let it move on out of my mind, and that's what you need to do right now.

"Seeing Porcelli triggered your demons, but like you told me, you don't have to wallow in them. Let them go.

"This *is* evil, Dan. Shadow is right. We're reliving the evil we've experienced. We can't escape its presence, but we don't have to succumb to it. I don't know how to control it. But, I don't have to wallow in it either. I know it's there and it's consumed me in the past, but it doesn't own me. You were right earlier, and now you have to listen to your own advice.

"They were boys, Dan, and there was nothing I could have done to save them. I have to accept that. They were killed by Evil; I can't be obsessed by that for the rest of my life."

"Mary, we crossed France and into Germany, and I kept wondering when I'd get it...we all did. And as we got picked off, one by one, I just figured that my time would come eventually, and sooner or later the war would end for me. I just hoped that it'd be quick and over with quickly, and that I wouldn't suffer a lot. I've seen men die horrible deaths; Germans, Americans, all of them some mother's son....a mother who didn't raise her child for this. No mother raises her child for this.

"Death, our companion, was always with us on our walk through Europe. It happened to so many others that it seemed inevitable that it'd happen to me. I'd be shipped home in a box with a couple of medals and a letter from the C.O. telling my mother what a wonderful young man I had been, that I'd died quickly, as a hero, and without suffering. That's what they all said.

"But, it didn't happen to me. At some point after the killing had ended, my anticipation of dying stopped. But now, something else has taken over. Now I have an overwhelming sense of guilt and evil ....guilt that I survived, and evil because that's who was leading us around, orchestrating the whole thing. Evil made me kill, and the killing, death, and suffering made me insane. Evil became one with me. And now that Evil has consumed himself, he doesn't want me, or the thousands like me, to forget him and the part he's played in our lives.

"I waited for death, Mary. I would've welcomed it, and I came close more than a few times. Was I spared for Evil to play with me for the rest of my life? Did he want some reminder of his past glory, some vestige from the days when he'd enflamed the entire world? Is that why he spared me; to torture and toy with me till he drives me mad like Porcelli?

"Smitty got it. Those poor bastards in the German tank crew got it, and I killed Hans Heinrich, all in the last month of the war; but I survived....at least I think I survived, Mary, I think I survived.

"And Porcelli....why would a priest try to commit suicide? That's against everything he stood for, everything he believed in. Is Evil stronger than the god that Porcelli tried to serve...an angry god and an evil god? Sometimes it seems that way."

The day turned to evening now as they tried to talk out the struggle with their demons. As one of them would become obsessed, the other would grow rational, a ping pong match of the absurd, a balance between reason and insanity, overseen and conducted by the person they both acknowledged and feared most, the presence of Evil.

"I don't know why you survived, Dan, or why the others died. I don't know how either of us will break out of this and live normal lives. 'Normal' has changed forever for us, Dan. 'Normal' to other people is fantasy to us. 'Normal' is killing, suffering, and dying, and we have to let that go; we can't let it haunt us forever."

"Mary, do we each create our own sense of 'normality, of reality?

"In Porcelli's mind, there was an all-just, all-knowing, and all-powerful God, a god who was all-loving. Porcelli devoted his life to that god. He had a personal god, one who looked out for him and took care of him. At some point in his life, he must have created his own reality around that god: Do this; don't do that; Mass on Sunday; no meat on Friday; Confession on Saturday, and above all...no lust. Then, on to the seminary."

"I was brought up Catholic, Dan, and I can't understand why a priest would attempt suicide. The madness must have overwhelmed Porcelli and destroyed his sense of reality. How could he believe in an all-knowing, all-powerful, all-just, and all-loving god who'd let this happen, or, even worse, who caused it to happen?

"He couldn't. He was overwhelmed by the raw evil and cruelty, and it destroyed him. His vision of life was shattered, and in response, he tried to kill himself. When he didn't die, it was only through becoming Major Shadow that Porcelli could escape from the horror that had overtaken his mind and destroyed the reality of his god. He became a blank slate.

"We're no different, Dan. You and I had each created our own realities before the war. I spent my time in a maternity ward after nursing school. When the war first broke out, I paid little attention because I was surrounded by newborn babies and new moms. Like Porcelli, we both had those nice neat constructs of normalcy destroyed when we became involved with the evil of that hell.

"The difference between us and Porcelli is that we never thought about evil as we went through the war; we just lived it and tried to survive it. The sheer power of that evil, and the inability or unwillingness of his god to control it, is what drove Porcelli mad.

"We didn't go mad, at least not yet, but after the war, we both started drinking to get away from that evil. That didn't work for either of us and we couldn't escape our ghosts. I tried to consume myself with work, sex, and alcohol. And you went on to college.

"Dan, I don't know how we'll escape this, but you were right this afternoon; we have to let it pass when it starts to overwhelm us. These flashbacks are like unexpected waves at the beach when our backs are to the ocean. They break on us, knock us down, and overwhelm us, but we have to let the tide carry them back out to sea. You said it to me; we can't let ourselves wallow in them!

"Porcelli escaped from his ghosts by becoming a simpleton whose life consisted of getting out of bed in the morning, cleaning his quarters, and showering. After breakfast, he helped out on the wards. Day after day, week after week, he went on like this in a routine that he could live with, never turning that blank slate of his mind to see the horrors that were written on its other side. But, today when he saw you, the slate turned; the horror of it overwhelmed him, and he exploded."

Their passion over their respective ghosts had almost spent itself, leaving them both exhausted, when there was a knock on the apartment door. Mary stepped away from Dan and held him at arms-length by the shoulders. "We'll be all right, Dan, you and I, we will make it!" she said, emphasizing the word "will."

"Who is it?"

"Mr. Fleming's suitcase, Ma'am."

Opening the door, Mary accepted the heavy bag from the driver's hand. "Thank you, Corporal," she said as she started to close the door. Then suddenly, she opened it again.

"Corporal?"

"Yes, Ma'am."

"You said the suitcase belonged to Mr. Fleming. How did you know that?"

"Colonel Casey, Ma'am. The Colonel told me and he asked me to give you this."

Having said this, he handed her a heavy paper bag stuffed with crumpled newspapers, a large bottle, and an envelope.

"Thank you again, Corporal. Will you come by around ten tomorrow morning to pick us up?"

"Yes, Ma'am, I'll tell Sergeant Hamrock that when I get back to the motor pool."

"Corporal, one more thing, what took you so long?"

"Ma'am, Colonel Casey told me to wait till 19:00 hours before returning."

"Oh...we'll see you in the morning, Corporal."

Closing the door, Mary opened the bag to find a very large bottle of champagne packed in the newspapers. She opened the envelope, took the note out, unfolded it, and read it to herself: "My dearest Mary, I liberated this bottle of vintage champagne for you. Take care of your new friend, and I'll be waiting for you when he leaves."

It was signed, "All my love, Brian."

Mary's face turned hard. She'd been sleeping with Casey and others to escape her demons, but she was drawn to Dan out of their shared pains in hell. Casey was married, and she bristled at the thought that he was trying to play with her emotions: "...all my love – bullshit!" she thought to herself.

She could love Dan Fleming because her love was pure, born of the cauldron of evil they'd both shared and survived. Casey was taking out gall bladders in the States for most of the war and had volunteered for this assignment because he was bored. He was anything but bored with his head nurse. All of his love meant nothing to her, just another escape from her demons.

She did love Dan Fleming, though. The passion of her fear when they had first met had turned into lust for him now, rekindled out of that same passion which had drawn them together two years ago. Their dealings with evil had fused their souls, and now they each knew intuitively what the other was experiencing as the tide changed, washing that box with the red ribbon back out to sea.

"Dan, the colonel sent us a bottle of champagne...are you interested?"

He noticed that her voice had changed now. The intensity she had when they were struggling with their demons was gone. She was softer now, enticing, gentle, and inviting. He could sense the lust in her voice and it excited him.

"Mary, I've only had three beers since I started school...I know I shouldn't."

"Oh, what the hell, Dan, if we're going to be alcoholics, at least we can enjoy the good stuff. This would cost close to a hundred dollars a bottle back in the States."

She could sense that he was softening; his demons had left him for the moment, and he was more responsive to her as a woman than as his soul mate in agony.

"Mary…" he wanted a drink almost as much as he feared having one, and he wanted Mary. Yvonne Chrysler was not very close in his mind at the present moment.

"Dan, come on, just one glass."

"Well…maybe one glass." "One apiece."

Mary poured the first glass, and it was not long before they had emptied the very large, though not quite a magnum, bottle of champagne.

"I feel good, Dan, how about you?"

"I'm OK, Mary…a little drunk, but very relaxed. When I'm with you, my ghosts seem to melt away."

"I feel that way too. Let me get into something more comfortable."

"More comfortable, Mary, or more seductive?"

"You are a cocky bastard, Dan. You want to sleep with me…I know that!"

"Right now, Mary, I'd love to sleep with you, but I'm so drunk that I'm afraid I couldn't give you much satisfaction. You're a special woman in my life. You kept my ghosts at bay today, but we shouldn't be lovers; that'd ruin it all."

CHAPTER THIRTY

Semester Break Is Over
and Dan Goes Back to Class

"Well, Mr. Fleming, welcome back. I understand that you had a fruitful semester break."

"I did, Father, but it almost seems unreal.

"Meeting Father Porcelli, or 'Major Shadow,' as the hospital staff called him, because he'd lost his memory after he stepped on the mine; that was strange, Father."

"I can imagine. I heard that Porcelli is being sent back to the States and will be treated at Walter Reed Army Hospital in Washington.

"I was Dean of Discipline at Moreau Seminary when he was a student; a little bit of an odd duck, but a decent fellow; a good sort, and from what I've heard, a caring priest."

"You know, Father, I didn't know Father Porcelli that well. After all, he was a major and I was a corporal. But, I'd served Mass for him a couple of times, and he listened to me when I had problems about all the killing and suffering.

"You know, I never asked to go; they told me to go and I went. I saw it as my duty. What I didn't see was the madness, the complete and utter futility of random death, the evil of it all. I was an instrument of that madness and evil, and so was Father Porcelli. His job was to tell dog-face soldiers like me that we were doing God's work; that killing those poor bastards in different uniforms was somehow noble and patriotic.

"My country calls and I have to leave my family and march off to war to kill some poor son-of-a-bitch who left his wife and child to do the same thing for his country.

"I tell you, Father, it's evil and insanity, and it almost broke me. It still might do that yet. But, Father Porcelli helped keep me sane. I think he realized that he'd been used by the War Department, that he'd been given the rank and privileges of a field grade officer, and then expected to encourage, or at least facilitate, every soldier's willingness to kill others, or to be killed, if necessary, all to benefit the war effort. Kill the savage Hun, they told us. Fight for country, motherhood, and apple pie. You know that when he's dying in your arms, the savage Hun looks a lot like one of the kids you went to school with.

"I think the weight of my problems, and the problems of others like me, broke Porcelli when he tried to take all of us on his back.

"Father, you're a priest, tell me how a Roman Catholic priest cannot be a pacifist? How can a priest put on an Army uniform and encourage gullible and innocent kids like I was to go out to kill and die? He drinks at the Officers' Club and has the pay and privileges of his rank, but how can a chaplain reconcile his vocation with his military duties?

"How many Catholic priests were chaplains in the German Army, telling young German kids that they should go out to kill and die for their Fatherland in the name of Jesus Christ?

"It's evil, Father, an evil borne out of madness....pure insanity!"

"Mr. Fleming, I don't know the answer to that, but be assured that you'll have an "A" in my Moral Theology course should you decide to take it. Registration's over, but if you go to the Dean of Administration's office to request a change, I'll see to it that you get in. The course is closed, but I suspect that the other students will learn more from your class discussions than from my lectures."

"I'd like that, Father, but I'll earn the 'A'.

"It seems unreal, almost surrealistic, to come back from war to Notre Dame, then back to Europe, and then back here. It's a total suspension of my disbelief that any of this could have happened."

"You'll find that we suspend our disbelief for a lot of things in life, Mr. Fleming; hopefully none as gruesome as what you've been through."

"Father, I'm dating a Saint Mary's girl who had come out of the convent. But, I left her to go to Germany, and I reconnected with a nurse who ran a charnel house and who's going through the same psychosis as me..."

"That's not a psychosis, Mr. Fleming," the priest cut in, "that's a normal reaction to a psychotic situation. The world has gone mad, Mr. Fleming, not you.

What normal human being could go through the hell that you've experienced and come out of it the same as when he entered?

"No, Mr. Fleming. Your reaction's normal. Your world's different now. In class, we'll discuss the problems of human nature that lead to wars, now that we're no longer instruments of that madness you describe. Poor Porcelli, he had no one to unburden himself to, and it broke him. I wonder what his life will be like when, or I should say, if he returns. Will he sit in a corner of Corby Hall all day cutting out paper dolls with a scissors? On the other hand, maybe he'll recover and end up running the place.

"But, for you, you're not a part of the horror of war any more. The erupting volcano has quieted now, content with the volume of its human sacrifice. It'll probably remain that way for another twenty years or so till some other generation full of piss and vinegar sends its young men off to die for some other patriotic cause fueled by arrogance, and stoked by the evil side of our human nature.

"You'll contribute to our discussions in Moral Theology, Mr. Fleming. We'll discuss evil and how an all-powerful and all-just God can let evil run amok, as we've just witnessed. I can give the lectures, Mr. Fleming, but you've already worked in the laboratory of human nature on the good, evil, and random madness of war.

"This is a course for life, Mr. Fleming, a course where we share our common experience, a participatory exercise for both of us. We'll try to share our experiences with your fellow students, and the questions that've grown out of those experiences. Most of those students will look on the course at best as merely philosophical sophistry, and at worst a required course that must be tolerated on the road to graduation.

"If history is any guide, this madness does seem to repeat itself every twenty years or so. Having been through it, I hope you'll be able to prevent it from happening in the future.

"But, for now, Notre Dame is your world. Study, read, play interhall football if you wish; court your Saint Mary's friend and try to put that other world behind you. No more mines, snipers, machine guns, or high explosives. Your focus now is to develop your mind, to prepare for the rest of your life in service to our God and humanity."

"Father, that sounded like a final exam answer from one of your courses."

"It is, Mr. Fleming, it's the answer to the final exam that each of us takes in life. There's only one exam, and they don't grade on a curve. We can only pass or fail the course, and it's the one exam that determines whether your Notre

Dame education was well received. Passing that exam will validate the diploma you received after four years at this place."

"Father, I understand what you're saying, but I'm exhausted and can barely keep my eyes open. I need some sack time. I'll go to the admin office tomorrow and switch into Moral Theology."

"Good night, Father."

"Good night, Mr. Fleming."

It wasn't a good sleep that Dan had that night. The trip back to Europe had given his demons new life. Smitty, the German tank crew, and the son-of-a-bitch of a captain who had wanted to see him killed all came to him on the front steps of the Main Building, the one with the golden dome. The Panzer was burning half way up the steps, and the crew was in front of it, arm in arm with Smitty and the captain, singing Silent Night together. Then, Yvonne Chrysler came to him and pulled his head softly onto her chest. "Why are you so troubled?" she asked. He ran from her toward Sorin Hall and almost knocked over the dead German soldier that he'd killed, walking with his wife and daughter on the main quad, Dan's bayonet still sticking out of his chest. His wife smiled at Dan and asked, "Why did you kill my husband? What did we ever do to hurt you?" And finally, as the long and lonely fingers of dawn crept slowly across the North Quad and into his room, Dan saw Yvette, the French nun turned prostitute, come and sit on the end of his bed. Unbuttoning her blouse, she told him that he was special, that she loved him and wanted to have his babies; that she wanted to come to America to live with him.

This time, the pain of his delusions was not so intense, the burning flesh not so pungent, and the color of fresh blood not so vivid or deep. There was a new actor in his dream though. Major Shadow, the man with no mind, came walking through a minefield toward Dan. The major was a man whose nervous system had hit "overload." And like an electric motor that had popped its internal fuse, Shadow would have to be reset.

"Where am I going now, Corporal Fleming? Why did you save me in that minefield? Didn't you understand that I wanted to die, that I wanted to meet God who made me and to tell him of the insanity that he'd created? Why did you bring me back to all of that? I didn't want to remember, but you brought me back to hell just now. Why? Why did you do that? Why wouldn't you let me die? Christ died for your sins, Dan, and I wanted to die for his."

The fingers of dawn were still long, but not so lonely anymore, as the beams of sunlight flooded into Room 151 of Cavanaugh Hall. Dan still had the single bunk in the forced triple and it was a comfort to him that the sun had rescued him, at least temporarily, from his demons.

It was barely 6:00 A.M. when he quietly dressed and tiptoed past the snorting, snoring hulk of Charlie, who looked for all the world like a beached whale.

"You're early for Mass, Mr. Fleming." The booming voice of the rector shocked Dan out of his stupor.

"Hi Father, I'm afraid that I won't make it this morning. I'm heading over to the caf for breakfast, and then I want to be the first one in line at the Admin Office for 'drops and adds.'"

"Good, Mr. Fleming, good! We're having our second meeting this afternoon at 2:30 in room 105 of the Engineering Building. I looked at the class list and I see that your Miss Chrysler from Saint Mary's is taking the course, since they don't offer moral theology over there. She had requested and obtained permission to take the course at Notre Dame."

Dan turned beet-red at this, and the priest continued, "Well, Mr. Fleming, maybe this course will improve your social life as well as your mind....and your faith."

"Father, I don't know what to say. I've not had a chance to talk with Yvonne, but I've left her a message. I asked if we could meet for lunch today.

"I had a tough time last night because some of the baggage I thought I'd left behind came back to me in the middle of the night. I'll tell you about it sometime, Father, but it's really too horrible to share with any other human being."

"Too horrible, Mr. Fleming? But, maybe not too horrible to share with your fellow students; to knock some of the royal peacocks in our class off their thrones.

"Men who face death in war are different from other men; we face life from a perspective different from anyone else."

"You know that, Father, you were in the service?" Dan asked quizzically.

"The reason I became a priest was because I had faced the same horribles as you in the trenches of France in the last war. The 'Great War' they called it then, the 'War to end all Wars'. Like you, I carry those horribles inside me, and I want to do whatever I can through my prayer and my teaching to make sure other young men don't go off to kill and die.

"Are we the lucky ones, Mr. Fleming, or should we envy the dead? I do know where you've been, Mr. Fleming. I think we'll explore in class where we both should be going.

"Most of your classmates were too young to have served in this past war, and they're swept up with romantic notions about war, notions that no doubt have been fed by too much beer with too many barracks soldiers. We'll dissuade them of these fantasies, Mr. Fleming. They've not had the pleasure of watching one of their comrades die a slow, lingering death on barbed wire because it would have been suicide for anyone to try to save him. And then....and then...watch over a period of weeks as his body was slowly eaten away by rodents and other animals in the night.

"Yes, Mr. Fleming, we shall reveal the glory and romance of war for all that it is to these young men through the medium of Catholic moral theology. And we shall hope that by doing so we, in a small way, may help prevent this horror from recurring, at least in our lifetimes.

"I'm afraid that I got carried away. Look at the time. I should finish saying my office now before the seven o'clock Mass. Two-thirty then it is; I'll see you there, and your Miss Chrysler."

Having said that, the priest turned abruptly and started walking purposefully down the corridor in the direction of the chapel, his eyes fixed on the breviary he held before him.

Breakfast wasn't bad, better than the Army food he'd been eating for the past few weeks. But, just a little bit better, and nothing like what his mother cooked.

The first one at the door, Dan blew through the Dean of Administration's office with no trouble once he showed the note from the professor authorizing him to register for this otherwise closed course.

Chapter Thirty-One

Dan's Life Changes Again
and Becomes Much More Mundane

He found it difficult to stay awake in his 9:30 chemistry class. The professor started out saying that if you understood the difference between tennis balls, golf balls, and baseballs, you could understand chemistry. Dan wasn't even sure why he needed to study chemistry. He had no interest in it, and it would, he thought, have no practical application in his life.

Even if he hadn't been up all night wrestling with his demons, he would've found it hard to keep his mind on this class because all he could think about was his lunch date with Yvonne.

"You'd agree with me on that wouldn't you, Mr. Fleming?"

The student next to Dan gave him a sideways kick under the desk to wake him and Dan, startled, jumped to his feet.

"Yes...yes, Doctor, I would indeed."

"Very good, Mr. Fleming. It's a wise student who agrees with his professor and a foolish one who argues with him or...." and he paused, "who pays him little mind," he said, slowly dragging out each of the last five words.

"Which are you, Mr. Fleming?"

Embarrassed and blushing red, Dan tried to think quickly on his feet.

"No...no, Mr. Fleming, please don't sit down. You and I can have a little dialogue that might educate both of us, and perhaps provide some slight amusement for the class.

"Now, Mr. Fleming, which of these two students are you?"

213

Dan's redness deepened as a couple of his classmates chuckled at his predicament. It was no longer embarrassment that caused him to blush, but the anger welling up inside of him.

"I could take that arrogant little son-of-a-bitch down and kill him in a minute," he thought to himself.

"He wants to make me the butt of his humor in front of the entire class just because I'm over-tired and not paying attention."

"Keep in control!" He said to himself a couple of times before responding.

"Cat got your tongue, Mr. Fleming?"

"Well, Doctor, I don't know. I think that most of the time I would agree, and some of the time I might disagree, if I had good reason, and I'd always pay my professor good mind...." Here, Dan paused and his jaw tightened as he spoke, and like his protagonist earlier, the last part of his sentence was spoken slowly and firmly. "I would pay him good mind if he respected me and the other students in his class." Dan went on, "I would pay him good mind if he challenged us intellectually and didn't pick on occasional wanderings to make an example for the rest of the class."

"You are as articulate as you are insolent, Mr. Fleming. See me after class!"

"Christ, here I go again," Dan thought to himself. "Why do I always end up screwing with Authority?"

The 10:30 bell sounded; the professor assigned reading for the next class, and Dan remained dutifully in his place as the rest of the class filed out.

"Mr. Fleming, I do a lot of work to prepare for class. Teaching chemistry to students is my passion in life. If you don't want to be in my class, I suggest that you drop it. I don't want to see you sleeping in class again or you'll fail for the semester.

"It's a profound disrespect to a teacher for a student to sleep in his class, and I will not tolerate it!

"Oh, and should you not drop the course, you can expect me to call on you each day that we meet."

"Sir, I'm sorry, I had trouble sleeping last night."

"We all have our troubles, Mr. Fleming, but I expect preparation and participation.

"You look older...are you a vet?"

"I am, Sir."

"Well, no matter to me; we're here to study chemistry, not to tell war stories. If you have trouble sleeping, maybe you belong in the infirmary. The University Chaplain's office is in the Main Building if you have to work something out with him. But, if you're going to stay in this class, you damn well better perform, sleep or no sleep.

"Am I making myself clear, Mr. Fleming?"

"Yes, Asshole, you are," was the response that leaped to Dan's tongue. Fortunately, he did bite his tongue before meekly muttering, "Yes, Sir."

"The decision's yours, Mr. Fleming."

Having said that, the professor placed his class notes in his brief case and walked out of the room through the mob of students who had begun filing in for the next class.

"Jeez, Dan, you look lower than whale shit." The voice belonged to Charlie, who was coming in with half of the freshman football squad for a math class that was being taught by a professor, who incidentally was the baseball coach.

"Christ, I screwed up again, Charlie. I fell asleep in O'Brien's chemistry class and he tore into me. Boy, I must have a sign on my back that says 'Kick me.'"

"It's the first day of the semester, Dan. I wouldn't worry about it. You've got a long time to work it out with him.

"How was your semester break?"

"I'll tell you back at the room but it's a long story and I've got to get across campus for lunch.

"I'll see you tonight."

"Yeah, it's nice to have the evenings off without team meetings. I'll see you later."

"Thanks, Roomie; I'm glad I ran into you. I needed to see a friendly face."

"You'll see an even friendlier one pretty soon. There's a note on the door saying that Yvonne called this morning and that she expects to meet you for lunch. When you see her, ask her about Patti-Jo and try to find out how she feels about me."

"Will do...you big, furry bear. I'll see you later."

The news about Yvonne buoyed Dan and he hurried over to the caf so she wouldn't have to wait for him. Sitting next to her for the whole semester during Moral Theology was the best thing that had happened to him in a long time. Maybe they'd study together after class at the library, and he'd walk her back to Saint Mary's in time for supper.

Dan's mind was bouncing around these days, but at least he thought he had the tools to deal with his ghosts. His time with Mary O'Daugherty had helped him sort out a lot of things. They were both good for each other, but there was something about Yvonne...He hoped that Mary would be able to find someone who could love her the way he was beginning to love Yvonne. He loved Mary too, but in a different way, like a big sister, one who you could share things with, who'd always understand you and who'd never scold you or hurt you. Yvonne was different.

His run-in with the chemistry prof didn't amount to a piss-hole in the snow compared to what he'd been through the last couple of years. He was developing a special relationship with Father Fitzgibbon because of what they'd both been through in their respective wars, and because of Dan's jaunt to Europe to discover the missing priest. That relationship was one that he wanted to preserve and to grow, along with his relationship with Yvonne.

In none of this was there a sign of evil. Surely, they'd talk about evil during class, but talk was different from experience, Dan thought. Evil wouldn't be everywhere, permeating the air he breathed, the food he ate, and the water that he drank. Evil wouldn't be soaking into his every pore, consuming him as it slowly destroyed him, eating away at him inch by inch.

"The living don't envy the dead. You are a misguided son-of-a-bitch," he thought to himself. "The living have another chance....another chance at creating new and better lives for themselves, lives without evil."

Dan felt good. He was drinking coffee and relishing the anticipation of seeing Yvonne.

"Hey, good- looking!"

He heard her voice behind him at about the same time that he smelled her perfume. He wanted to leap up, wrap his arms around her, and hold her next to him forever. But, slowly – or so it seemed to him – and ever so restrained, he rose and turned to face her. But, in reality, he did rise somewhat abruptly and managed to knock over the table, chair, and a cup of coffee in his enthusiasm.

She threw her arms around him before he could do anything and kissed him on the lips deeply and passionately, more than refined, dignified Saint Mary's girls were wont to do in those days.

Their embrace, especially after the commotion of knocking the table chair and coffee over, hardly went unnoticed and was greeted by applause, cheers, and catcalls by the predominantly male patrons of the caf.

"I missed you, Dan! I worried about you."

In spite of the commotion, they were oblivious to anyone but each other.

"I said a novena for your return. Father Fitzgibbon called to tell me how you were flying to Europe at his request, and he invited me to join his class on moral theology. He said that he thought you might register for it as well. I'm so happy and excited that you're back and didn't get hurt. I'm afraid to ask you what happened. If you don't want to tell me, I understand.

"Dan, you're very special to me. I realized that even more when you were gone and I was afraid that you wouldn't come back. I had nightmares that you were in a plane crash and I couldn't get to you. I woke up at night crying because I thought I'd never see you again.

"Dan...I love you."

This overwhelmed Dan and all he could do was to hold her and try to keep her from seeing the tears that were welling in his eyes.

He held her hand...in public...as they walked over to join Father Fitzgibbon's class. As people shuffled into the room, they got two seats in the front row on the end away from the door. Oblivious to everyone but each other, they talked quickly, trying to say so much before the bell rang.

Father Fitzgibbon strode into the room and arranged his class notes on the small portable podium that sat on top of the class room desk.

The bell rang and the priest intoned in a loud voice, "In the name of the Father, the Son and the Holy Ghost," he said, while making the sign of the cross on himself. All of the other students blessed themselves in unison.

"Loving and gracious God," he said, "we come together today in your name to learn from you, to share your goodness, and to grow in your love. We ask this through Christ, our Lord."

On cue, the assembled class muttered "Amen" in unison.

"Now gentlemen...and Miss Chrysler..." he interrupted himself to say, "We're graced this semester by the presence of a Saint Mary's student in our class, and I expect each of you to act accordingly, and to refrain from some of the boorish behavior I've witnessed in some of my other all male classes."

Going back, he started again, "Now, class, we'll be discussing Catholic moral theology this semester. That may be a surprise to some of you. Anyone who thought this might be a jock course should probably reconsider how to spend this period over the semester. We will look at the world in terms of the struggle between good and evil, and how our individual actions fit into that context.

"We all make hundreds of decisions every day in our lives. Most of those decisions have little or no moral content to them, but some of them do. Surprisingly, more do than we sometimes recognize.

"We'll study Thomas Aquinas and try to place his teachings in the context of both his time, and of our lives today. Saint Augustine will guide us. He said something in prayer to the effect of asking God to make him chaste, but not just yet. What does this mean for us today, here at Notre Dame, as we live our lives, prepare for our future, choose our careers, and for many of you, decide to marry and raise children? Should we be concerned with our salvation and the salvation of the world now, or is that something we should put off till the day we confront our own deaths, individually and alone?"

Dan was mesmerized as his hall rector went on, and it was close to the end of the period when Father Fitzgibbon said, "And we shall look at much of this in the context of the most recent exercise of the dark side of human nature. We have a couple of veterans in our class who have experienced the dark side of life at its worst in both the Pacific and European theatres of war. We'll explore with them how Catholic moral theology failed to make a difference in that conflict, or whether it did in fact have an effect."

Turning to the student in the front row closest to the door, the professor said, "Mr. Dalrymple, you served in the Pacific. Briefly, because the bell's drawing near, tell us how your Catholic faith was affected by your experiences."

Clearly embarrassed at being called on, the student began to mumble a response.

"Can't hear him!" a voice rang out in the back of the room, and the student turned to face the back of the class.

Looking up, Dan was stunned to see that face again.

Dalrymple went on, "It was like being a passenger in a cah racing along a narrow dirt road at sixty miles an hour. You had no control, and you didn't know how the road curved, or what was coming in the other direction."

"Thank you, Mr. Dalrymple. For those of you who don't know Mr. Dalrymple, he's from Boston, and a cah is an automobile. We'll continue this discussion at our next meeting. I'd like everyone to be prepared to discuss the first three chapters of the Aquinas book, especially in the context of the issues raised by Mr. Dalrymple. How much are we in control of our lives? What decisions do we make that have future unseen consequences for us? What are the moral dimensions of these decisions? How do they affect others, and what's reality for them and for us?"

After Father's last question, the bell rang, and students began to move out of the classroom, preparing to turn it over to the next group that would be using the space.

Yvonne had noticed the stunned look on Dan's face when Dalrymple had turned around. As they gathered their notes she asked him, "Dan, are you all right? You turned pale when the fellow at the end of our row turned to answer that question."

"I know him, Yvonne. Dalrymple and I used to sit on the opposite ends of a bar at the American Legion Post in Brighton Center where we both went to drown our demons. I never knew his name, and we only spoke once when he had tried to kill a braggart who was lying and boasting about his war experiences. I never saw him after that until just now. Now we're on the opposite end of a row of students trying to sort all of this out in a way that makes sense. I want to talk with him. I know what he's going through, and maybe I can help him sort some of this out in his own mind."

CHAPTER THIRTY-TWO

Winter Becomes Spring in a French Village and Dan Fleming Has Become a Father

The French winter had been mild, and the young woman with the year-old infant went about her morning chores, singing hymns to the child in the cradle beside her. The blond haired Daniel Charles LaFleur was named after his father and Charles De Gaulle, the hero of the French resistance movement, the "Free French".

"Yvette, you don't have to do that; I'll finish cleaning the kitchen."

"No, Anna, you've been too good to take me in. The least I can do is to help you with your house work."

"Daniel gets prettier and prettier by the day. Rene was asking me the other night if you'd been able to contact his father."

"You know, Anna, I've not done that, and I don't know why.

What I did that night with the American soldier wasn't for money and it may sound funny, given what I had to do to survive during those years, but it was because I was deeply and seriously attracted to him."

"And apparently, he to you, if he gave you his name and address in America, assuming he was honest."

"Oh, Anna, I have no doubt that he was honest. He reeked of integrity and decency. Maybe that's why I was so attracted to him.

"I tried to remain uninvolved with my customers. I had lived a life of total commitment to Christ. Then I became an absolutely uncommitted vehicle to relieve the sexual tensions of a group of young men who were going off to kill one another. French, Germans, Americans; they were all consumed by the great madness. The only respite they had from it was when they were consumed in their lust for me. Most of them weren't bad people, though a few were. Pillow talk with a couple of German officers did give me good information to pass on to the Resistance, but I had revulsion toward those men and their love of killing.

"Most of them on both sides were conscripts though, conscripted to go off, kill, and die for some greater social cause. For many of them, I was their last human comfort this side of death. I knew this when I slept with them, that they'd likely be killed very soon. So, I tried not to get involved; I don't know how I could go on if I ever did get involved with them as human beings, rather than as animals who needed to ejaculate into a woman's body. I just did what they wanted me to do and tried to get paid enough so that I could survive.

"But, Daniel's father was different. He came, not to sleep with me, but to deliver a letter from a dead comrade of his who'd fallen in love with me. I tried to maintain my façade with him, but there was something about him, a purity, an intensity, that made me want him. I wanted him in a way that I'd never wanted a man before, though I'd slept with hundreds of them.

"He hated me and wanted nothing to do with me, but he eventually succumbed. I've not slept with another man since that night, and I knew right away...I knew that I'd have his baby....and...I wanted to have his baby. And now I have little Daniel Charles, a gift from the Blessed Virgin."

"But why don't you try to get in touch with him, Yvette? Maybe he could help bring you to America?"

"Part of me wants to do that, but part of me is afraid that he'd try to take my baby away from me if I did. I know deep in my heart that he wouldn't do that, but I'm afraid that he would see America as a better place for his son to live, and that he'd try to take him from me because of that.

"There was something very special between us that night, very intense and very unusual. He hated me because I didn't remember his friend, and I wanted him because of his pure hate for what I was. He mirrored my own hate for what I'd been doing. But, I never allowed myself to become what I had to do to survive. He couldn't have known that, but he was the only man I've ever slept with who didn't want to sleep with me. It was his first time with a woman, and the fire of his hate with the passion of his lust was overwhelming for both of us. For me, it was the only time that I ever found complete and total satisfaction from sleeping with a man. He, too, was totally consumed by it, and I end up with this beautiful treasure of a child."

"What will you do, Yvette? Of course you're welcome to stay here, but you're a beautiful, intelligent, well-educated young woman. I don't suppose that you want to spend the rest of your life living in a small French farmhouse. But, you know you're like a daughter to Rene and me, and you're most welcome to do that."

"I know that, Anna. I do love it here, and both you and Rene have become like parents to me. Rene goes off to his office every morning, and you and I do the house and farm chores. He tells us what's going on in town, and...I do love it here. You're right though, Anna. I know that it can't go on like this forever. I just don't want it to end though."

"It's very comfortable for all of us. Rene and I love having you and Daniel in our family. And now there's plenty of food.

"It's also better now that the Americans are reducing the number of troops in the area. Thank God they had replaced Michaelson, the American commander. He was giving Rene such a hard time. This new commander's a gentleman and he maintains a good degree of discipline among his troops. Michelson was leading a drunken rabble by comparison. I've not missed him since he left."

Before they had finished, young Daniel Charles started making little coughing noises and stretching his arms and legs, signaling that he was in the process of waking from his nap and would soon want to be fed. Nursing him was one of Yvette's great pleasures in life, as she would sit in a rocking chair by the stove in the kitchen, singing gently and sweetly to him as he suckled.

After he had finished nursing, young Daniel bit his mother's nipple playfully, looking up and smiling as she pushed him away from her breast.

"Well, young man, that means you're done. Keep it up and you'll be done forever. You'll go from Ma-Ma to mashed potatoes in a heartbeat."

"Ma-Ma!" he replied, with an impish grin of delight.

"Anna, I'd like to go down to the village to do some shopping. Could you watch Daniel for me for an hour or so?"

"Go child, you need to get out of here more often for your own sake. Take your time. Enjoy the afternoon, and don't hurry back.

"What are you shopping for?"

"I just thought I'd check out the vegetable stalls to see if any of the early produce is in. Even though we do have plenty of food, I think the potatoes and squash left from last year aren't in the best of shape. Maybe one of the other farmers had some good luck and some good sun and got a jump on the season."

"I do think it's still too early, and besides, the vegetables in our root cellar aren't that bad. But the walk would be good, and maybe you could drop in on Rene and tell him to be home in time for dinner. He's working too long these days and he's starting to look older and tired. I tell him this, but he doesn't pay any attention to what I say. Maybe if you mentioned it to him...."

"I'll drop in on him and try to get him home in time for dinner."

It was a pleasant, sunny spring day and Yvette found the walk into town to be refreshing. The cool spring breeze was clean and sharp, and the fresh air filled her lungs with the taste of the new season each time she inhaled.

"It's wonderful to be alive!" she thought to herself as she walked down the town's main street to where the pushcarts were set up.

"Good morning, Yvette, you've not been in town for a while." The voice belonged to an old friend, Charlotte Legas, who was a regular at the market, and the godmother of all the other vendors in the town square. Charlotte was better than the parish priest in helping people with their problems, and spent more time doing that than hocking her vegetables.

"Charlotte, what a beautiful day!"

Before they could continue, they were interrupted by the drunken young man standing at the cart next to Charlotte's. "And how are you, Missy? Turned any good tricks lately?"

Charlotte turned crimson red as she wheeled to look into the bloodshot eyes of the face that had cruelly set out to hurt her friend. "You know, you were the best lay I ever had." The words were muddled in his alcoholic haze.

"Get out of here, you pig!" Charlotte's rage exploded on the drunk standing next to her as she began pushing him away down the street. After a few steps, he stumbled and fell.

Lying in the dirt, he yelled, "You're both fucking whores!" He then staggered to his feet and continued lurching down the street, away from the two women.

"Don't cry, Yvette. He's a pig, a loser who's only sober long enough to hurt anyone around him. No one can stand him."

"Charlotte, this is why I don't come around very much. When some of them see me, they mock me. Most of them look down and pretend that they don't know me, but a few like that one deride me and abuse me.

"Why, Charlotte? Why? I don't know how much more of this I can take. Why do they torment me? I did nothing to hurt any of them."

"Rochambeaux's a little shit. When the Nazis were in town he was a big man, kissing their asses and feeding them trivial bits of information. The Resistance would have killed him then, but they used him to feed disinformation to the Germans. We knew he was a regular at the Garden House with the money the Germans paid him. When the Americans came in and the Garden House became the House of the Lone Ranger, you didn't see him anymore. The only reason the townsmen didn't kill him then was because everyone liked his old, sweet, widowed mother. Now, no one will hire him. The only thing he can do, when he's sober, is to clean out cesspools and pigsties. When his mother dies, and if he's stupid enough to stay in the area, they'll find him some morning either with his throat slit, or swinging from a tree.

"Ignore him, Yvette; he's a little shit, not worthy of your trouble."

"Yvette!" The mayor stood in greeting as his honorary stepdaughter walked slowly, almost sulkily, into his office. "I'm honored. Don't you see enough of me around the house?

"Your eyes are all red...you've been crying?"

"Rene, I was just in town and was confronted by that Rochambeaux fellow who had been one of the regulars at the Garden House when the Germans were here. He was drunk and insulting. I was talking with Charlotte at her stand when he started on me. She pushed him away and he eventually staggered down the street..."

Yvette was interrupted by Rene's rage as he yanked the telephone off the hook. "Brigitte, could you get Armand on the line right away. If he's in the building, could you have him get up here as soon as possible? Thank you.

"That little shit! I'll kick his ass out of town so hard that he won't stop till he reaches the beaches at Dunkirk, the collaborationist bastard. I'll slice his nuts off and feed them to the dogs!"

"Don't, Rene. I know what I have to do though, I've got to leave here, go somewhere where I can make a new life for myself without always having to confront my past. I gave them pleasure for their money. I needed the money to survive. They got what they wanted out of the transaction, and I got the money that I needed to stay alive. Why do they mock me now? I didn't like doing what I had to do, but I don't feel any shame or guilt because of it. Why do they want to hurt me now that things have changed?"

"You have to understand, dear, they're not mocking you because of who you are or what you'd done with them in the past. They're mocking you because of their own shame over what they'd done to you. When they see you, they're reminded that they'd exploited a destitute member of the church to satisfy their own sexual drives.

"The shame is theirs, not yours. Ignore them or confront them as you will, but don't waste a moment thinking about them.

"I understand how you feel and why you want to leave. Anna and I would like nothing better than for you to stay here and marry, and then we could build you a place across the fields where you could bring up your family as our world changes, and we develop a more normal rhythm of life."

"Rene, I do love you and Anna as parents; you couldn't have treated me better or loved me any deeper than you have, and you'll always have that place in my heart, but I have to leave. I'd like to go to America, but not to live off young

Daniel's father. I want to support us myself. I'm fluent in English, and it'd suit me if I could get a position teaching French, hopefully at a school for Catholic girls or women. I haven't any records certifying my education, but I could pass any proficiency test they could give me, either in French or English."

"Child, I'll see what I can do. Edgar Marceaux, a close friend of mine, has just been assigned as Counsel for the Republic in the City of Boston. If memory serves me correctly, that's the purported home of Daniel's father."

"Oh, it is his home, Rene! Daniel Fleming is an honorable man who said he'd help me. I don't want to ask for his help though, and I'm afraid to let him know that he's young Daniel's father. But, I would like to see him again. I was very infatuated with him then, though I don't know how I feel now. I was young and in an extreme situation then...

"When I think of Daniel's father now, I have a brief fond memory of him, but I realize that the infatuation was mine alone, and not shared by him. I've changed, Rene. Young Daniel has made me realize how beautiful life is, and how beautiful life can be. Whenever I run into a lout like Rochambeaux, I'm dragged back into my past. I have to struggle to escape, but then I see this beautiful child, and you and Anna, and I know there's a god who loves me.

"But, I know I've got to leave, Rene. I'd very much appreciate it if you'd write to your friend and ask if he could look for a position for me, if there are any Catholic girls' schools in the Boston area."

"I'll do that child, but for now, I think you'd better get back to Anna and young Daniel before he needs to be fed again and Anna goes into a panic. Tell her that I may be a little late for supper."

CHAPTER THIRTY-THREE

Dan and Yvonne Hunt for Dalrymple

"Can we walk over to the Registrar's office for a minute?

"We can stop for a shake, or a frappe, or whatever you call it. And after that, I'll walk you back to St. Mary's. But, I don't want to walk you back; I want you to stay here with me. We have the extra bunk in our room. Maybe you could move in, and we'd ask Charlie to move into the Field House?" He was whimsical, but as he said the words, he wished he could make them happen.

"And what would Daddy say when he found out I was living on campus with some Notre Dame guy? He'd probably shoot both of us, or at least force us to get married. Maybe that isn't such a bad idea. Do you think Charlie would go along?"

"I don't think Father Fitz would go for that at all, but I do like the idea."

The Registrar's office was still open, and Dan approached the secretary at the desk by the front door.

"Excuse me."

"Yes," she answered, "can I help you?"

I saw an old friend on campus recently, but he was off at a distance and I didn't get a chance to talk with him. His name's Dalrymple and he's from Boston. Can you tell me where he's living?"

"He just registered this week. He's a transfer from Boston College, starting in the middle of the year. He hasn't been assigned a room yet. They want to put him in Vetville, but there's nothing there. He's staying off-campus up on Angela Boulevard until we can get everything sorted out."

"Well, I'm living in a forced triple in Cavanaugh, 151, and there are only two of us. Do you think you could move him in with Charlie Costanza and me?"

226

"Let me talk with Father Collins. This layout of Cavanaugh Hall shows 151 as a double."

"It may be a double, but there are three bunks and three lockers in it."

"Why don't you check back here tomorrow afternoon and I'll see what I can do after I talk with Father?"

Yvonne spoke first as they were leaving the Registrar's office, "If you don't know him well, why do you want to bring him in as a roommate?"

"I don't know. All I know is that in one brief episode, I became closer to this guy than I've been to people I've known all my life. I can't explain it, Yvonne, but you know that remark Father Fitz made as we were leaving class this afternoon? This guy Dalrymple and I have shared an experience that very few people around here can understand. You know how I feel about you, but you could never understand what my life has been like; I wouldn't want you to be able to understand it. I'd do everything I could to keep you from understanding it. It was just so horrible, and it still affects me, and it'll continue to affect me till the day I die. You know about some of my ghosts, and I can tell you that Dalrymple has some powerful ghosts he's carrying around. Also, and this is between the two of us, Father Fitz has some of those ghosts too. He alluded to it one night after we had a couple of beers together…"

"You went drinking with your hall rector, a priest?"

"Actually, we were drinking in his room. He was in the service during the First World War and has some ghosts that he owns and is still dealing with. He told me that this morning.

"Yvonne, I want to help Dalrymple! His situation, I suspect, is close to my own. At one point, we shared our demons and gave silent witness to them from stools at the far ends of the same bar. My world has changed, in great measure because of you. He may still be mired in the horror and carnage of what he's seen and done. I want to help him, Yvonne, and I think the best way to do that would be to get him into the room with Charlie and me."

"I'm sure Father Fitz would support that."

CHAPTER THIRTY-FOUR

Yvonne Meets the Millers

"Janet, this is my friend, Yvonne Chrysler," said Dan. Yvonne's a Saint Mary's freshman, and we're taking a course together on Catholic Moral Theology. It's nice of you to have invited us out for Sunday dinner, and it was good of Ed to offer to drive onto campus to pick us up, but we were able to get here pretty easily by bus."

Just then, Ed Miller entered the room. "Dan, how are you? I'm glad you made it. Half the buses in the fleet are out of service at any time because they don't do any preventive maintenance on them." Then, turning towards Dan's companion he said, "This must be Yvonne. We've heard so much about you."

Both Yvonne and Dan blushed from ear to ear. Janet ushered them into the living room and asked if she could get them something to drink. Yvonne asked for a glass of water, while Dan and Ed had a beer. After chatting for a short while, Janet stood up.

"Well, I've got a roast going in the kitchen and I'd better get in there."

"Let me help you, Janet," Yvonne said, rising up out of her chair. "Daddy always says that a woman's place is in the kitchen. I really want to become a good cook."

"Well, I don't think you'll learn much from me, Yvonne, but come in and I'll see what we can do, and we can leave these two to talk about their war stories."

"She's still upset?" Dan asked, after the two women had left the room.

"I'm sorry, Dan, but she still doesn't understand. How could she? How could anyone who hasn't been through it understand what our lives were like then?

Sometimes I feel like I want to go back to that world, because I don't seem to be able to adjust to this one."

At the same time in the kitchen, Janet and Yvonne were also talking, "See, it's important to baste the roast to keep it from drying out."

"Janet, the fatty part of the meat's on the top; does it always have to be there?"

"Oh dear, yes, that's so it can melt and drip down and flavor the rest of it. Otherwise, it would just drip to the bottom of the pan without coming into contact with the rest of the meat."

"Janet, you have the perfect world here. This is what I'm looking for in my life: a husband, a family, and a home together. I know that if Dan and I ever get married...." Yvonne stopped momentarily and blushed, "...I mean, if we ever got married, not that we're planning to do that, but if we ever did, I know that Daddy would set Dan up in business and that we'd have a life like this. It just looks so wonderful.

"Janet, why are you crying? Janet...?"

"I'm sorry, Yvonne, I'm sorry. I don't mean to. It's just that things here aren't as perfect as they look. You and Dan are young and in love, and I don't mean to spoil that for you, but being married to Ed....he goes off to work all day, and then drinks all night till he falls asleep. That's not what I had bargained for out of life. I'm home all day with the kids, washing diapers, cleaning the house, and cooking the meals, not to mention washing and ironing all of Ed's work clothes, as well as my own. And the war...he can't get away from the war. He's killed men, seen men die, and experienced other horrible things that he doesn't seem to be able to relate to me, or maybe I just can't understand. But, he drinks, and the more he drinks, the more he talks about the war, and one person in particular. I think it was his former commanding officer, a fellow by the name of Stadholm, who I believe was killed early on. He's obsessed by this Stadholm person and starts cursing and swearing at him after he's drunk too much.

"Yvonne, I really didn't mean to unburden myself on you this way. I've married this man. I loved him, and I think that I still do love him, but he's not the same man I married, not the same man who went off in glory to fight for his country. I don't know who he is, Yvonne. I just want us to have our lives back again."

"Janet, I'm sorry...I'm so sorry." Yvonne moved toward the older woman and pulled her head onto her shoulder. "It's all right, Janet. It's all right. Things will work out. It's going to be all right."

"Is everything all right in here?"

Ed Miller and his guest had heard the sobbing, and Ed went into the kitchen, trailed by Dan, to see what was going on.

"Oh, for the love of Christ, Janet!"

Ed had been drinking before Dan and Yvonne arrived.

"For Chris' sake, Janet, can't you keep it to yourself? Do you have to lay our problems out for our guests?"

Ed pounded on the table before rushing out of the kitchen into the living room.

"I can't take you! I don't want to be married to you anymore! I want this over, and I want you out of my life!"

Yvonne left Janet, who was in tears, crying loudly and gulping for breath. She ran over to Dan and threw herself into the shelter of his arms.

"Ed...Ed..." Dan spoke softly, "you'll scare the children. Calm down. It's not combat, Ed. You and Janet can work this out without screaming and crying."

"I can't, God damn it, Dan! I can't! I've tried, but this is the straw that broke the camel's back! How could she suck Yvonne into something that's between the two of us? It's nobody's business but our own, and she had no right to dump it all out on Yvonne!"

"Ed, it'll be all right, but you've got to work it out. As hard as it is, you've got to put the war behind you. Have you talked to a priest or someone who could help you?"

"I dunno...I dunno, Dan. I'm so confused, so angry. I just don't know what's happening. I don't know what to do or where to go. I just want out! I don't want to keep hurting her, but I can't help it. I don't know what's happening to me; I don't know...."

Janet had gotten somewhat back into control and was sobbing softly. Ed had calmed down, and Yvonne clung to Dan.

"Ed, I think it'd be better if Yvonne and I left. We can walk down to the bus stop and take the bus back to campus. I think we should leave you and Janet to work things out between yourselves. You can do this...you can make this thing work, but you need to talk to someone to try to work it out."

Going to the hall closet, Dan took out Yvonne's coat and his own. Moving to the door, he turned to Ed, who by this time was leaning on the back of the living room sofa. Janet was still sobbing softly, standing in the kitchen doorway.

"Look, Janet, you both have to work at this. Talk to your priest, he can help you. I'll give you both a call on Tuesday. I'm sorry about the way things happened today. This will work out; I'm sure it will."

After they left the Millers' house, Yvonne and Dan turned up the street for the four block walk to the bus stop.

"Dan, I'm sorry. I just was telling Janet what a beautiful home and family she had, when she started crying and told me about the problems she was having with Ed. I wish I hadn't said anything; I didn't mean to start this...."

"Honey, you didn't do anything to cause this; they've been having problems since Ed came home. I suspect that Janet was on the verge of breaking and you just happened to be there when she eventually did pop."

"Oh Dan, I feel so bad for them. I can't begin to understand what they're going through. It seems like a nightmare that they're living in. No one's at fault, but they're both trapped in their marriage."

"This is what I worry about with myself. I've been where Ed is, stuck, and I don't want to go back there. It's still part of me, and I'm afraid of it returning. I know a lot of other people besides Ed and myself who suffer from this. The problem is that everyone thinks you're a hero and they want you to tell war stories, but all you want is for the nightmares to stop.

"You want to put the whole thing out of your mind because you know the glory of war's a lie. Watching men, women, and children die, and in some cases knowing that you had killed them...that's too much for anyone to carry around inside themselves. Ed can't deal with it, and Janet doesn't understand what he's going through or how to help him.

"I've told you, Yvonne, that I've had a lot of trouble dealing with this myself. I pray that my ghosts and demons never return. I'd never want to inflict them on anyone else, especially you."

"I don't understand. Why does this only affect men? Why are women immune to this?"

"They're not, Yvonne! I know a nurse, still on active duty in the Army, who's going through the same sort of thing you just saw in Ed, the same sort of thing that I've been going through, something I pray that you never see in me.

"That nun I had told you about will also have to live the rest of her life running from the ghosts of her past. Unless you've been there, you can't understand what I'm talking about. This is a very personal thing that never leaves you. It's like a scent or something that you can't get rid of. You want to forget that it happened; you don't want to bring it to mind, but sometimes you're powerless to keep it from overwhelming your whole being."

Chapter Thirty-Five

Dan Gets Surprising News From His Past

"Dear Daniel Fleming," the letter read, "you may not remember me, but we had a brief encounter in France one evening at the House of the Lone Ranger. That encounter has resulted in both of us becoming parents to a beautiful baby boy, Daniel Charles LaFleur, named after Charles DeGaulle, the famous French general, and his father, Daniel Fleming, the infamous American corporal.

"I don't write to seek your financial support; in fact, I shall return any monies that you attempt to send me. I do write, though, to share the beautiful presence of your young son with you, if you're desirous of meeting him. I hesitated to write this letter for fear that you'd try to take our son away from me, but I couldn't let myself go through life without giving you the opportunity to see and take a part in the life of this beautiful child who we both helped create.

"During the war, I did what I had to do to survive. I was very infatuated with you the night we met. Your integrity and purity, your anger and passion, aroused me, and I'm very grateful to you for fathering our child. I pray that he has the character and personality traits of his father.

"I've taken a position teaching French at a Catholic Girls School in Brighton called Saint Mary's School for Girls. I've also arranged to rent an apartment on the second floor of a house on 37 Murdock Street, very close to the school.

"If you'd like to meet our son and to see me again, you can reach me at that address.

"I realize that what happened between us that night grew out of my infatuation with you and your passion for me. I expect nothing further from you as a result of that; I only want to give you the opportunity to share in the beauty of the life of your son."

The letter was signed:

"Fondly yours,

Marie LaFleur, (Yvette)"

Dan Fleming sat stunned on the bed in his dorm room.

"Marone!" he screamed at the top of his lungs, startling Charlie, who had his back to Dan while studying at his desk facing out the window.

"Jesus Christ, Fleming, are you trying to give me a fucking heart attack?" Recovering his composure and his sense of humor, Costanza added, "By the way, why are you cursing in Italian anyway? I've never heard you say that before."

"Charlie, you're not going to believe this, but I just found out that I'm a father."

"You're shitting me!"

"No, it's real, a French woman that I slept with during the war just sent me a letter telling me that I knocked her up and that we have made a beautiful baby boy together.

"Holy shit! What do I do now?"

"Wait a minute, wait a minute, how did she get your address here? And besides, how does she know the kid's yours, if there is a kid? She's probably just trying to use you to get into the country or to shake you down for money."

"No, she's moved to America; in fact, just a couple of streets away from my parents' house. She has a job teaching French and she sent the letter to my home address because I'd given it to her, and my mother forwarded the letter to me. She says that she'll return any money that I try to send her, and that she's writing because she doesn't want to deny me the opportunity of seeing the beautiful child that I fathered.

"I believe her. I think she's sincere. I just don't know how to deal with all this. What do I tell Yvonne? How can I afford to help Yvette support the child?"

"This is Yvette, from the former life you've been trying to deal with...part of that war baggage you've been carrying around?"

"Yeah, Charlie, this is part of the baggage. I can't begin to tell you what this poor woman has been through, the horrors she's seen and experienced, and now she has a child to worry about...my child. Wow! I'm floored. I don't know what to do. This is unreal."

"Why don't you talk with Father Fitz. He's been a big fan of yours since you found the missing priest over semester break. You certainly do have a new world to look at now....Daddy."

"Charlie, don't bust them. This is serious. I wonder if I should drop out of school and get a job to try to help support them."

"If she's got a job teaching French, she must be making a couple of bucks, enough to support her and the child. I think the bigger question for you is how's this gonna affect your relationship with Yvonne. Also, who's this Anka in Germany that you send a letter to each month? None of my business, but do you have a relationship with her too?"

"Charlie, I can't do this with you. I can't open that can of worms in front of you. I killed Anka's husband, leaving her a widow with a child. Think of that, Charlie! Believe me, Charlie, you don't want to know a tenth of the shit I'm carrying around."

"Ooo...kaaay" Charlie said, expelling his breath slowly, drawing out the letters, and wondering just what his roommate had gone through during the war.

It was Friday afternoon, and Dan was shaken in a way he had never been during the war. His entire world had just been turned upside down, and now he didn't know what he should do....how to deal with it. His interest in Yvette had remained in the back of his mind, not as something he wanted to actively pursue, but as a part of his past that continued to intrigue him and pique his imagination. He'd wondered from time to time how her life must be going, how she'd survived the war, but now she'd come full force back into his life and had turned his world on its head. Dan spent a lot of time over that weekend praying at the Notre Dame Grotto, a replica of the grotto at Lourdes. He agonized over what he should do. By Sunday afternoon though, he tried hard to put his new paternal status into a compartment in his mind. He reasoned that, whatever he ended up doing, it would be better for him, his child, and the mother of his child if he continued to do well in college for however long he remained a student.

CHAPTER THIRTY-SIX

Father Fitzgibbon's Moral Theology Class –
The Second Day

Dan had spent the weekend trying to adjust to his new situation in life, struggling with himself about what he should do, and how he should deal with his new son and his son's mother. Now it was Monday, and he was again sitting in Father Fitz's Moral Theology class, a changed man living with his new awareness.

"Gentlemen and Miss Chrysler, when last we met, Mr. Dalrymple had started to tell us what his faith had meant to him when he was stationed in the Pacific Theater. He had started to tell us that it was like being in a car going out of control at sixty miles per hour. "Did I get that right, Mr. Dalrymple?"

"You did, Father, and what I meant was that none of us had any control. It was just a whole series of random horrors and you just skated through from one to the other without being aware of a god, without having any hope whatsoever that someone was in control of the situation. Then it's as if someone blew a whistle at a basketball game and said that time had run out. They put us on ships and sent us home.

"If there's a god, Father, he wasn't in the South Pacific area of operations."

"Mr. Flanagan, what think you of Mr. Dalrymple's observation?"

"Father, I respect Mr. Dalrymple's service, but he has it all wrong by denying the existence of God. It sounds sacrilegious to hear that at a Catholic college like Notre Dame."

"Thank you, Mr. Flanagan. Miss Chrysler, would you like to weigh in on this?"

"Well, Father, I think we all feel the presence of God in different ways, and I think that Mr. Dalrymple experienced the absence of God. I think that's personal to Mr. Dalrymple and there's nothing sacrilegious about it. Also, I think it's courageous of him to say that, especially at Notre Dame."

"Christ spent forty days in the desert, and when he was at his weakest, he was tempted by Satan. Let me ask each of you whether what Mr. Dalrymple describes, and what Ms. Chrysler so aptly defines as the perceived absence of God, is a reflection of that temptation experience?"

"What do you mean, Father, that the perceived absence of a god is a 'reflection' of Christ's temptation?" asked Dan.

"Perhaps the word 'reflection' is a poor choice, Mr. Fleming...or is it? Is it the word 'perceived' that concerns you?

"Let's start with the last question first. Does perception equate with reality at some level of consciousness? Certainly not at the level of existence that Mr. Dalrymple and yourself have so recently been through. Reality in that experience is very basic, living and dying, and very little else in between. But for us, Mr. Flanagan, would you agree that in many areas of life, reality is as we perceive it? Do we create much of our reality as human beings in our minds...between our ears?

"Is it true that, in many situations, perception equals reality?"

"Father, all reality is basic; otherwise it wouldn't be reality, only illusion. The reality of Our Lord, Jesus Christ, is an ever-present, all-transcending reality."

"Is the temptation of Christ physically accurate, or merely allegorical, Mr. Flanagan?

"If it were allegorical, would it be mirrored in Mr. Dalrymple's experience? Does the perceived absence of God in a situation consumed by evil mirror what the Bible story is telling us about the temptation of Christ?

"Is the great evil that we've just witnessed or participated in analogous to Christ's forty days in the desert?

"Another question to ponder: Where have you seen Christ in your lifetime? When was the last time you saw Christ?"

Pointing to the young man waving his arm in the air, the priest said, "Mr. Flanagan, I'm sure there are other members of the class involved with this exercise, though I must say none as enthusiastic as you."

"Thank you, Father. I see Christ every morning in his transcendent radiance in the purity and glory of Holy Eucharist."

"Mr. Dalrymple."

"This might sound tough to understand, it's tough for me to live with, but the last time I saw Christ, I immolated him."

Yvonne let out a slight gasp in surprise, covered her mouth, and recoiled slightly toward Dan and away from Dalrymple.

"We were in the third day of our landing on Guadalcanal and the fighting was ferocious, with men dying all around me, American and Japanese. I was operating a flame-thrower. You've probably seen them in the movies. I had two tanks strapped on my back, with a hose to a handle that had a nozzle and a trigger. When I pulled the trigger, a plume of flame shot out about twenty feet in the direction I was pointing the weapon. We were taking fire from a camouflaged pillbox when I tried to move around it to get a clear shot through one of the gun ports.

"I thought that none of the enemy had spotted me as I crawled closer and closer to the pillbox. I got around beside it when I looked up and saw that a young Japanese soldier standing no more than ten feet in front of me had drawn a bead on me with his rifle. I was looking down the barrel and saw my life on the verge of ending. He said nothing and he did nothing. He had it in his power to kill me. He looked serene and at peace as I discharged the flame-thrower at him and watched as he crumpled to the ground in flames. He was dead before he hit the ground because the fire had sucked all of the air out of his lungs. He could have killed me, but he didn't. I went on to kill the others in the pillbox so that we could advance and then, wondering why he hadn't killed me when he had the clear advantage, I picked up his rifle, thinking that perhaps it had misfired. It hadn't. I shot the round and it discharged. I chambered another round and that one discharged also. I'll never forget his face. He had the power of life and death in his hands....my life and death...and he spared me. He must have known that by doing that, he'd lose his own life, that I'd kill him if he didn't kill me. He looked to be younger than me at the time, and his face had a purity and serenity about it that was so odd to see in the middle of the carnage. We were mad men then, both sides in a killing frenzy, no order, no plans, just random periodic encounters that left some men dead and others still alive.

"I saw Christ in that Japanese soldier. He died for my sins and because of my sin. I killed Christ that day; I killed him after I had recognized who he was. I killed him because I was afraid. I killed him because I was consumed with killing people so they wouldn't kill me."

"Mr. Flanagan, can you relate to Mr. Dalrymple's encounter with Christ?"

"Well...ugh...I'm, ahh...no, Father; I can't."

"I suspect that Mr. Dalrymple has encountered Christ at a far deeper level of reality than most of us, who merely encounter him in the Mass and then forget his face when we leave church. Mr. Dalrymple's perception of the divine presence far transcends whatever we encounter when we see Christ at Mass."

Dan raised his hand and started talking at the same time.

"Father, I had a similar experience to Dalrymple's, and it involved the death of an enemy soldier...actually many of them, because of my doing. One in particular...I never saw Christ in his face until now. I had felt consumed by a great tragedy, that I was the instrument of evil, beyond redemption for having caused their deaths. But, I've come to realize that it was the presence of this evil, much like the presence of Satan during the temptation of Christ, that was surrounding me. I did what I did at the time. I did what I had to do, but I never surrendered to the hate that evil brought. Dalrymple saw Christ in the face of the man he killed. I saw peace and love and resignation in the face of the one man I killed directly. I never saw hate or malice of any sort toward me, but I killed him out of that same fear that Dalrymple spoke of.

"Maybe for Dalrymple and for me, our experiences with Evil during the war were akin to Christ's suffering and temptation at the hands of the Devil. Though I don't think that story's literal, I can see how it affects my perception of this horrid situation that Dalrymple and I were in."

"Mr. Flanagan."

"Of course, the Bible story is literal. We believe it because it happened, and we know it happened because the New Testament says so."

"It's as simple as that, Mr. Flanagan?"

"It is, Father, basic black and white. Read the Bible and it gives you the answers, unequivocal; no doubt."

"How then would you relate the story of Christ's temptations in the desert with the stories we've just heard?"

"I don't know, Father. All I know is that there's an all-loving, all-just God who looks out after each of us day and night. The Bible story is the Bible story as the words were written, nothing more, nothing less. Christ was tempted by Satan in the desert. It was a valuable lesson for us to learn, but I don't think it has relevance for us in our modern-day lives."

It was a long semester. After Fr. Fitzgibbon's class, Dan, Yvonne, and Dalrymple would frequently move to the campus malt shop to continue their discussion. The three of them became very close over that semester, with a bond that none of the others in that class shared. For Yvonne, listening to the two veterans of the killing fields recount their war experiences opened her to a new and ugly world, one from which she'd been sheltered, first by her father, and then by the convent and her Mother Superior. She loved Dan, but she was more and more becoming attracted to the purity of Dalrymple. Dalrymple, for his part, had refused Dan's offer to move into the triple in Cavanaugh Hall, and preferred to live alone in a rented room off-campus.

Both of these men participated in the class discussion from the depth of their souls, their very cores were open and exposed in that class with no hold-back, no concern about whether the professor or their classmates would accept or reject their observations, their ideas, or their conclusions. They were using the class to help them deal with what they'd been through, and Father Fitz was using them to show the other members of the class what life's like when it's lived at its very essence. No pretense, no show or posturing; these men told you what they thought and what they'd lived as if they'd torn open their chests and bared their hearts to the professor and their classmates.

You pass through many layers of yourself during the course of a life. Those layers run from the day to day superficiality most of us live, to the core of your soul. After their same trip through Hell, Fleming and Dalrymple shared all of those layers, from the trivial to the intense. For them, it was cathartic; for their classmates, it either inspired them in their search for their own reality, or repulsed them to the point of denial.

CHAPTER THIRTY-SEVEN

Summer Vacation Brings an
Exciting Twist in the Road for Dan

The school year had ended well, and the three of them were ready to break up for the summer: Dan back to Boston and a job at the Dean Rubber factory; Yvonne to her family's summer cottage on Lake Michigan; and Dalrymple to Detroit where he had a summer job working construction.

Dan had been in touch with Yvette. He offered to leave school and get a job to help support them. Yvette had answered back that she appreciated his willingness to do that, but that she was making out all right financially. She just wanted to share the excitement of their child with Dan, and to let young Daniel get to know his father.

Dan had not shared his new status in life with anyone other than Charlie and Father Fitz. The latter had suggested that by staying in school, Dan would ultimately be in a better position to support all of them, if that was what the cards had in store for him.

At the time, Dan had thought that referring to an astrologer's game was a funny way for a Catholic priest to invoke concepts of fate and destiny.

He did return home at the end of his freshman year, having earned a straight "A" class average for both semesters. He was concerned about how to tell his family not only that he had become a father, but that their new grandson was living just around the corner on Murdock Street.

He'd been back in Brighton for just a day when he found himself on a Saturday morning outside the vestibule door at 37 Murdock Street with a bouquet of flowers and some toddler's clothing and toys that he'd purchased in South

Bend. He had wanted to ring the doorbell, but found that he was powerless to do that. He stood there for a while before he gulped and pressed the buzzer.

He could hear footsteps as someone on the second floor was running down the stairs to answer his ring.

"Daniel, Mommy will be right back," he could hear through the closed door, and later words addressed to him, "Wait a minute! Wait a minute! I'm coming."

"The door opened and the exuberant person behind the voice stood motionless looking at Dan, who also stood motionless looking at her. They were both frozen for what seemed to be an eternity. Awkwardly, Dan thrust the flowers out. "I brought these for you, Yvette."

"Well, Daniel Fleming, Corporal Fleming, here to see your son, I suppose?"

"Yvette, I'm here to see my son as well as his mother."

"Come in, Daniel Fleming. I don't use the name Yvette here. That was from a time and a place long ago, a place that was different from what I'm living here. I go by my baptized name, "Marie."

"Marie, I don't know what to say. I felt awkward before I came, but I'm not uncomfortable being here. Can I see Daniel?"

"Of course you can, you're his Papa, and he's a beautiful child. Come in, Daniel Fleming, you're welcome here."

Dan picked his son up in his arms, hugged him, and started crying when the baby said "Da-dee", after his mother had said, "Here's your daddy."

Looking at the child, there was no doubt in Dan's mind that he was looking at his biological son. "Yvette...err...Marie, can I continue to see you over the summer while I'm here."

"Of course you can; you're his father, of course you can continue to see him."

"I mean, can I continue to see his mother. Marie, I'd like to get to know the mother of my son."

Marie La Fleur blushed, the first time she'd blushed since leaving the convent.

"Your son's mother would like that."

"Marie, I've not told my family yet...I mean about Daniel. I'll do that after Mass tomorrow, and then I'd like you to meet them."

"Won't they be upset and angry at me for having seduced their son and gotten myself in a family way because of that?"

"They're not like that. They'll be surprised, and maybe a little bit upset, but that won't last after they meet you and Daniel.

241

"I don't think we should share our secret beyond them though. This can be a severe community as far as Catholic morality is concerned, and I wouldn't want to see any repercussions because you had a child out of wedlock."

"People think that Daniel's father was killed during the war; I don't see any reason to change that story. You're my child's father, Daniel Fleming, and you'll always be welcome in my house."

"I want to get to know you, Marie. We're so far away in time and distance from that madhouse where we first met. I've thought about the pressures you must have been under at the time, and I apologize for being so angry with you then."

"I apologize to you too, Daniel Fleming. I was the one who seduced you. I enticed you into bed with me, and this is the beautiful result of our one-night coupling. It was a different time and a different place, a totally different life than what we're living now. Young Daniel is my life now, and I invite you to include him into your life."

Dan went to the ten o'clock Mass on Sunday with his parents and Tommy, his brother. Walking down the hill from the church next to his father, they were talking about the Red Sox and how the various players were doing, the kind of father– son discussion most males engage in over the years, either as father, or son, or both.

"Dad, are you and Mom really happy with the way your lives have gone up to this point?"

"Are we happy? Well, to be honest, I've never really thought much about it. I guess you'd say that we're content. We've..."

"Dad, let me change the subject...OK? I have something important I want to tell you; good news, but it might be upsetting."

Dan's father stopped and turned to face Dan, "I'm all ears...so what is it?"

"Dad, when I was in Europe, I got into a relationship with a French girl, and I've recently found out that you're a grandfather as a result of that relationship."

"What? You're not serious are you?"

"I am."

"Nooo...not my son knocking up some French woman; I don't believe it. Is she looking for money or for you to get her over here?"

"No Dad, she's already here. She lives around the corner on Murdock Street and has a job. I offered her money, but she wouldn't take it.

"Dad, you've got to see this child. He's beautiful! He is about two years old and he calls me 'Da-dee'. I can't tell you how I feel when I see him. I've never felt so complete, so fulfilled before in my life.

"I offered to marry his mother, but she said, 'No, not under these circumstances.'

"I hope that you and Mom will come over and see him. He's absolutely the most beautiful baby on the face of the earth."

"How about his mother?"

"She's a former nun who got displaced by the war. She teaches French at St. Mary's School and pays her landlady, a widow, to watch young Daniel while she's at work."

"Daniel...she called him Daniel? Are you sure that you're the father?" "Dad, when you see this kid, you'll have no doubt."

"You're happy about the situation?"

"Dad, it isn't the way I would have planned it, but yes, I'm delighted. And you'll be too when you see him."

"Congratulations, son! If you're happy about it, I'm happy about it."

"What are you two doing? Are you coming home or what?" Dan's mother Marge turned back to her husband and son, who had lagged behind her.

"Just go home, woman, we're having a man to man talk here."

"You're gonna pay for that when we get home," Dan said.

Dan's mother had turned at her husband's remark and started storming home, her face turning beet red as she went.

"I'll talk with her when we get back, but how are you going to break the news to her, and when can we see the baby?"

"Well, I was kind of hoping that you'd tell Mom, and that we could have Marie over for dinner this afternoon. I talked with her about it, and she'd like to meet you and introduce you to your grandson."

"You want me to tell her? No way!

"I'd like to meet her and the baby though. What's her name, and what type of relationship is there between the two of you?"

"Marie LaFleur, and her father used to be the French ambassador to the United States before the war. At this point, I'm not sure what our relationship is. We knew each other briefly in France, and neither of us expected this to happen.

"As you know, Yvonne Chrysler and I had been getting pretty serious, but I think that's starting to cool off somewhat. Yvonne's a lovely person, but I've seen too much and done too much that I can't share with her, so much so that I think we'd be living separate lives, living in two different worlds. I think that'd always make our relationship difficult.

"I see the problems that my old C.O., Ed Miller, is having with his wife, Janet. She's a lovely woman, a good wife and mother, but they're having problems because their lives are based on two separate ways of looking at the world. Ed has seen the raw brutality of life, but Janet sees life in terms of family and babies, paying the bills, and cooking meals. Their lives are based on parallel realities. His is tunneling down deep under the surface, while her life is more transparent, superficial to us, but real and overwhelming for her. And she feels that she's living it alone because he's so wrapped up in trying to sort out the different lives he's led while supporting her and their children. He works to provide for his family, and at the same time, he's trying to make sense of the insane world we both inhabited.

"I know what Marie has been through. We can relate to each other because of that, but we only knew each other briefly. I'd want to get to know her better, and to be honest, I don't know whether she wants anything to do with me. She wrote that she initially didn't want to tell me about young Daniel because she was afraid that I'd try to take the child away from her. But, ultimately she concluded that it'd be wrong to deny me the opportunity to meet and grow with my own son, and it'd be wrong to deprive Daniel of his father. That's the kind of person she is. She's a good woman, and we've both been through the same horrors of hell in different ways. She's sorted it out and finds life through our son. She's been through far worse than me...if that's possible, and we each understand the horror that the other's been through. We speak the same language in that regard. We're unlike Ed Miller and Janet because both of us have been through hell.

"Dad, I don't know what's going to happen. I've got the job at the plant this summer, and I want to get to know the mother of my child and just see how our relationship develops...if it develops at all.

"Will you tell Mom, and get her to cook dinner?

"I'll go get Marie and young Daniel and bring them over to the house."

"I don't know how I'm going to do this. She's already upset at me because of telling her to go home, but I'll do it. Why don't you get over to Marie's house and call me in about half an hour to see what the lay of the land is.

"Now I really want to see this kid, my own grandson, and I want to acknowledge that to the world, but I can't; there's got to be something wrong with that?"

"Thanks, Dad! You're Aces! I'll go to Marie's place and call you in half an hour."

Dan headed directly to Marie's, while his father did the dirty work of informing his mother of her new status as a grandmother. Dan noticed Marie's voice coming from the open window on the second floor as she sang to young

Daniel Charles. He knew he would feel very comfortable being there with Marie and the baby.

Marie and Dan both had an endless stream of questions to ask each other; so much so that Dan totally forgot to call his father, until it suddenly dawned on him that it was 4:30 in the afternoon.

"Marie, I forgot to call my father, we got so wrapped up in talking. Is it too late to go over there now?"

"I have a lesson to prepare for school tomorrow and you have a job to get to in the morning, but if you think we could be back here by 7:30 and I could get Daniel a bath and put him into bed, we could do it."

Dan then called home. "Dad, yeah, it's Dan.

"Yeah, yeah, I did forget. We were talking and I lost track of the time."

. . . .

"Yes, I'm sorry. How did she react?"

. . . . .

"Oh, my god! She didn't?" . . . . .

"She did. Wow, that's a surprise!"

. . . . .

"No, we're not gonna' have a shotgun marriage. We really have to get to know each other before we decide what we're gonna' do."

. . . . .

"OK, OK, give us ten or fifteen minutes and we'll be there. Yeah, just warm everything up in the oven. I'm sure it'll be fine."

"What happened? What did your mother say?"

"Dad was shocked because she was delighted. She wanted to see if one of the priests would marry us this evening in the rectory. He explained to her that they couldn't do that, and besides, he didn't know whether we wanted to be married."

"It sounds like you get your impetuosity from your mother."

"Yeah, maybe. She's a spunky lady. My dad's more deliberative, afraid almost to make a decision, but Mom thinks quickly and acts even quicker. When she was young, she had put a ring on layaway at one of the jewelry stores downtown. The way that works is you tell them that you want to buy the ring and they put it away for you. You give them so much a week till the ring's paid for, and then they give it to you. Well, and this was long before she met my father, she had the ring on layaway and had been making payments. But, one day her boss at work came up to her with a note from the jewelry store addressed to the company where she worked, telling them that she was behind in her payments, and asking them to see that she paid up.

"She was bullshit! She took the note, tied it to a rock, and threw it through the store window. They brought her to court, but the store dropped the charges after she threatened to go to the newspapers with her story."

"I think we'll get along fine...your mother and me."

"I thought that she'd be upset, but it sounds like she's more interested in her grandson than whether or not we've given rise to scandal."

Marie dressed young Daniel and placed him in his stroller. Almost two years of age, he was a good child, interested in everything that he saw, and full of energy. Prompted by his mother asking "Where are we going?" he said, "Gramma's house?"

"Boy, you know how to get her approval, don't you? One look at Daniel and she'll melt. If he says 'Gramma,' she'll forget all about us."

"I'm still nervous, Dan. What if she doesn't like me? What if she's angry about my having seduced you and getting pregnant?"

"She won't be angry; she's not like that."

CHAPTER THIRTY-EIGHT

Meanwhile, in Michigan, Things Were Changing for Yvonne and Flanagan

While Dan was getting acquainted with his son and his son's mother, Yvonne Chrysler was settling into summer at her family's summer home on Lake Michigan. Tennis, golf, and sitting in the sun by the pool took up most of her time. In the evenings, she would read and often wrote letters to Dan, letters that she never had the courage to send. She wrote those letters because, on the first week of her vacation, she'd received a telephone call from John Flanagan, Dan's protagonist through much of last semester's Moral Theology course. Flanagan had told her that he was spending the summer at his aunt and uncle's house on the lake, not too far from where she lived, and he was wondering if she'd like to go to a movie with him some evening.

Although Yvonne admired and loved Dan for his honesty and openness, she'd been troubled by his views on God, life and death, as well as heaven and hell. At one point in Father Fitzgibbon's class, John Flanagan had called Dan an apostate in a fit of rage after Dan had denounced the concept of an all-loving god because of what he'd been through in the war.

Yvonne believed in an all-loving God. This was the main reason she'd entered the convent in the first place. And even though she had left the Order when she realized that a religious life wasn't for her, she remained strongly convinced of the redemptive and salvific qualities of God's love. This was the pillar that her faith was based on...the way she lived her life. She'd secretly admired John's courage and righteous anger in response to Dan's assertion that there was no all-loving God. Dan had just shrugged off John's rage, and the class proceeded with John simmering until the bell rang, after which he stormed away to vent his anger somewhere else.

Now it was this same John Flanagan who was asking Yvonne out on a date.

"Yvonne, I realize that you and Dan Fleming are really involved with each other, but I'm here for the summer, and I thought that you might be good enough to introduce me to some of your friends. With the exception of you, I don't know a soul here."

Yvonne thought to herself that it would be the hospitable thing to do, for her to go out with John. After all, it wasn't like she was cheating on Dan; they had no agreement that they wouldn't date other people, and she and John did share Father Fitzgibbon's class together. Maybe they'd have some interesting discussions about moral theology.

"Well, that'd be nice, John. I'd like to see you again. Maybe we could go out after the movie for a malt. You can tell me how things are going in New York."

"I'd really enjoy that, Yvonne. What movie would you like to see, and when should I pick you up?"

"Well, the 'Bells of Saint Mary's' is playing at the Bijou. Bing Crosby plays a priest in it and it sounds like a wonderful movie."

"That'd be great. I'm tired of all this moral relativism we've been hearing over the past semester. I think I'd enjoy a movie about a priest who acts like a priest instead of an Indian mystic. I sometimes wonder if Father Fitz goes back to his room and sits on a bed of nails."

"Why, John Flanagan! I'm surprised to hear you talk that way," Yvonne said in mock shock. "I heard that he gave you an 'A' in the course, and it's true that you were no shrinking violet in class. The truth is that I agree with you on most of what you say. Dan's been through a lot, though, and I understand his point of view, even though I don't always share it with him.

"Why don't you come by about 6:30 and you can meet Daddy." Daddy liked John Flanagan from the moment he met him that evening.

John had always been attracted to Yvonne, and after the movie, their relationship deepened. The next day, Mr. Chrysler had asked Yvonne to "...bring that nice young man along for Sunday dinner some time."

By the end of the summer, Yvonne feared going back to school. The distance from Dan, and her growing relationship with John Flanagan, had left her very confused.

Chapter Thirty-Nine

Marie Learns the Meaning of Trust

In the meantime, on the East Coast, Dan was equally confused, as his relationship with Marie had deepened. She had the summer off and was a fixture around the neighborhood with young Daniel in his stroller.

"Good morning, Mrs. Fleming."

"Hello, Marie. How are you and young Daniel doing this morning?"

"Fine, Granmere, fine. He's a very busy young man and keeps me going all day. When he naps, I often go down for a little rest as well.

"And you...are you busy with your garden? It looks beautiful, like so many of the gardens we have at home in France. Your green beans, haricot vertes, we call them in French, are making a green wall out of the fence in your back yard."

"I like 'haricot vertes,' Marie; that sounds so much more elegant than 'green beans'. I hate seeing the summer come to an end though. Is Dan going back to Notre Dame in the fall? Do you know?"

"We've not talked about it. He likes it when he's together with young Daniel and me. I feel very comfortable with him. He's very good with Daniel. I assume he's going back. He told me that he'd been involved with one of the students at a neighboring college, Saint Mary's. I don't know what he's going to do.

"I'm planning on going back to Saint Mary's in Brighton. I love teaching French, and the girls are...I'm not quite sure how to say it...they're girlish...young and innocent, attracted to boys, but not quite sure why, most of them that is. They remind me of myself at that age; innocent and naïve. Someday they'll lose that innocence and naiveté, and I want to prepare them for that so it's not the same shock to them as it was to me."

249

"Marie, it's none of my business, but why don't you and Dan marry and give that child a proper home?"

"Well, in fact, your son hasn't asked me to marry him, and I'm not sure what I would say if he did. I was madly infatuated with him when I first met him. But, I realize now that marriage must be more than infatuation. I feel very comfortable with you and your family, and I sense that you're comfortable with me as well, but your son and I have to get to know each other more deeply before we can think about marriage.

"And, in terms of a proper home, I think I take proper care of my son. He's always clean, dry, well fed, and very loved. It would be nice if I could be home with him all day, but he's not loved any the less because I can't do that."

"Marie, would you like me to care for Daniel when you go back to school?"

"That would be good, Granmere, good for Daniel to get to know his grandmother."

"It'd be good for me, Marie. I'd love for him to get to know me...and for you and me to get to know one another.

"Marie, I'd like to get to know you better too." "Mrs. Fleming..."

"Please, Marie, call me Margaret or Marge."

"Margaret...Granmere...I am, as you probably know by now, a very private person. I've been through many horrible things during the war, and I find it difficult to trust anyone...to get close to anyone...

"Please don't think me rude; I want to get to know you too. You're Daniel's grandmother. I know my own grandmother was very special to me before she was killed in the war.

"You in America didn't suffer the horrors that we went through in Europe. Most of my family was killed by the Nazis. The ones that managed to survive initially became partisans and were eventually killed in the fighting. It's very hard, Granmere, very hard." Marie's eyes filled as she spoke.

The two women stood in Margaret Fleming's garden, motionless and speechless for an instant, their eyes swelling on the verge of tears. Margaret Fleming reached out to the mother of her grandchild, and the younger woman moved softly into her arms, burying her head unspoken into the other's shoulder.

"Marie...Marie...I had no idea of what you'd been through. I'm sorry...so sorry about your pain. I want you to know that I'll always be here for you when you need me. I would like to see you marry my son, but whether you do or don't, I want you to know that I'm your friend. You're the mother of my grandson. I'd love you for that reason alone, that special bond that brings us together. It was a random act of fate that brought us together in that bond, the special relationship between two mothers, the mother of the child and the mother of the child's father.

"Learn to trust me, Marie. I can never know what you've been through or undo the hurt you've suffered. In many ways, I don't even know my own son, from all that he's been through. This war has been the catalyst that changed people, good, normal people, and deprived them of a part of themselves, as if a surgeon had removed something from them. It's taken the good and the decency of their lives away from them...their innocence...and replaced it with a vision of evil. I see that in my son, and I know that's the reason for your reserve. Little by little, Marie...day by day, we'll rebuild our family, you and Dan with the rest of us. And young Daniel will be the glue that pulls us all together.

"Little by little, Marie, you'll learn to trust us, and the horrors that you've lived through will give way to a new life based on love and trust."

"Little by little, Granmere, little by little," Marie said, as she lifted her head off of the other woman's shoulder. Marie remained close to her son's grandmother, holding Margaret's arms behind each elbow as she spoke.

"I'm sorry I cried, Margaret...I'm sorry...It would be wonderful if you could care for young Daniel during the school year. I'm sure that Mrs. Gemelli wouldn't mind. I've sensed that she's more concerned with helping me than she is with earning the pittance I pay her for watching Daniel.

"I'm sure that we'll get to know each other, as you said, little by little. Your son and I have to make that journey too, though there's nothing I've learned about Dan that lessens my infatuation with him. Honestly, that gets deeper and deeper every day. But, my showing up like this with a son that he never knew he had is a shock to him. I've also changed since Dan and I first came together. I want us to go slow and I want him to finish college.

"I have a life here, independent of Dan. He has a life at Notre Dame independent of me, and a girlfriend, I understand. We'll both sort this out and if it's meant to happen...for us to be together...then it'll happen. If we're not meant to be together, we'll find that out by taking one day at a time until we reach that conclusion."

Now it was the older woman who was sobbing.

"Marie, I so much want to see the two of you together..."

"One day at a time, Granmere, one day at a time. If it's meant to happen, it will."

CHAPTER FORTY

A War Widow Mourns Her Father-In-Law

It was a cool and cloudy day as the procession wound into the small church in the mountains. The priest was preceded by an altar boy carrying a crucifix, and followed by two more carrying three-foot high, lighted candles in brass stands. The pallbearers carried the rough-hewn, wood box behind the priest, and the fourth altar boy who was carrying a smoking censor walked in back of them. The coffin was followed by all of the residents of the small German town who had come that day to pay their last respects to the soul of Niklas Richter. Their neighbor, the man who had died of a broken heart, was to be buried today. His daughter-in-law, Anka, his granddaughter, and Anka's family moved in procession behind the acolyte with the censor. The smell of incense filled the church as the ancient Catholic burial ritual was enacted for the repose of the decedent's soul.

As they approached the entrance to the church, the cantor inside began singing the hymn of Catholic burial, the mournful Dies Ire, the day of wrath. The priest, wearing black vestments, welcomed the body to the church and began the Mass.

Anka sat in the front pew with her mother, her father, and her young daughter. She was sobbing softly as the priest said the Mass in Latin, facing the altar with his back to the assembled congregation.

Totally overwhelmed by the death of his only child, Niklas Richter had willed himself to die because all that he had to live for had been taken from him. Anka had tried to console him in her own grief by her presence and the presence of his beautiful granddaughter, all to no avail because he was forlorn and desolate. He'd stopped eating and drinking, though he'd have something each day when Anka, sometimes accompanied by her mother or father, would come across the valley and climb up to his farm.

"Father Niklas," she'd say, "young Katherine and I are here to visit you."

"Go away, my child," he'd say in a gentle, resigned tone, "leave me to die; let me join your husband, my son, and his mother, my wife. There's nothing here for me anymore, nothing to live for."

"You're wrong, Father Niklas," she'd say. "You're wrong. We're here, Katherine and I, and we need you to be with us to honor Heinrich's memory and to help us survive."

"I am with you, child. I love you and your beautiful daughter, but I belong with your husband and his mother. I won't leave you; I'll always be with you; my spirit will always be with you, but it's time for me to go, to pass on...to leave this place."

He'd take some slight nourishment and water from Anka, though only for the purpose of satisfying her, and not for the purpose of sustaining his life. Alone at night, he cried until he could cry no more and waited for the dawn, exhausted and drawn. Then he'd collapse again in tears, lying in the dirt in front of his home, till she'd find him and revive him.

The priest and the town doctor had talked to him and tried to convince him to live, but to no avail. He willed his death, and his death came in short order. The whole town had come out as they had for the funeral Mass in absentia for his son, killed in the last days of the war.

After the Mass, they carried his body to the small town cemetery. Some of the men in town had already opened the grave where his wife was in her own eternal rest. The top of her coffin could be seen in some places where the dirt had been scraped away. They placed Niklas' coffin in the hole beside hers. There were two ropes under his coffin, and the pallbearers and others raised the long wooden box and carried it over the open grave. Then they gently lowered him into the ground. All the while, the priest in cassock, surplice, stole, and berretta chanted prayers in Latin. When Niklas was positioned, resting beside the coffin that held his wife, they pulled the ropes up and the men began shoveling in the hole.

Anka cried softly. Holding Katherine in her arms, she turned to her father and said, "Father, I have to leave this place; I can't stay here. As much as I love you and mother, this place smothers me with death and loss. Everywhere I turn, I see reminders of Heinrich; his face is in the mountains, and I feel his presence everywhere I go. Sometimes, when I'm in front of the house in the early evening, I look for him to come up the path like he so often did. And then...then...the awareness that he'll never come up that path again sweeps over me like a wave, a huge wave of emptiness, loneliness, and pain. I have to go, Father; I can't stay here."

CHAPTER FORTY-ONE

Father Fitz Reveals Part of His Past
to Father Porcelli

It was hot in South Bend that summer and Father Fitzgibbon, when he was not teaching his Theology I summer course, continued his research, reading, and writing on Zen Buddhism. It was early on a Thursday morning and the priest had finished the seven o'clock Mass and was walking around Saint Mary's Lake saying his office, silently mouthing the Latin words to the wood ducks and geese in the lake. He looked around and saw a figure approaching him in the distance, coming from the opposite direction.

As the other drew closer, the features of Father Porcelli came into view. The shell-shocked ghost that was Major Shadow, discharged from Walter Reed Hospital and the Army, was slowly starting to regain his self-confidence. Once a week he took the train to Chicago to talk with a VA psychiatrist as he tried to rebuild his shattered personality.

The older priest spoke first.

"Good morning, Father. You're up and about pretty early on this beautiful summer morning."

"And you, Father, you're up early as well."

"They had me down for the seven o'clock Mass at Sacred Heart, and I figured that I'd start my breviary before the day got too far along."

"Your office...yes, your office...I don't know the last time I prayed my office. At some point in Europe, I stopped saying it because I was overwhelmed with everything...I must start up again...soon, but I'm not sure that I want to remain in ministry. I've not said a Mass since I've regained my consciousness, and I've not looked up Fleming, Corporal Fleming, to thank him for saving my life and helping me regain my memory.

"The truth is, Father, that I'm afraid to undertake my priestly duties. I'm also afraid to face Fleming. I know that at some point I'll have to do both of these, but I'm not ready yet."

"Tony, you have to take your life slowly, one day at a time. Eventually, you'll decide whether you want to resume your clerical duties, but for now you have to adjust to your new life. You're not in battle; you're not suffering from amnesia. This is a beautiful summer day in Indiana. The corn's growing and you're walking around this beautiful lake with the ducks, the geese, and me."

"Easy for you to say, Father. The truth is that you don't know what I'm going through!"

"I do know what you're going…"

"No, no one who hasn't been there could ever understand the hell I've lived, the hell I'm still trying to escape!"

"I've been there, Tony. I've been there myself. Yours wasn't the first war of this century you know."

"Not the first, Father, but the worst...the worst for me."

"For you, maybe, but you're wrong about it being the worst. They're all horrible. They all represent the failure of human nature and the blossoming and fulfillment of evil in the world.

"Tony, I've inhaled the stench of death. I've tasted the flavor of death, and been an instrument of death and evil myself...along about the time that you were born. No, Tony, I've experienced your reality."

"You fought in the last war?"

"Yes. The trenches of France...the same insane asylum that you experienced...the senseless killing and destruction...the whole ball of wax...all of it."

"You were in combat then?"

"If you call being pasted in the middle of someone's bulls-eye target combat...yes, I was in combat. We lived in mud, ate rations that made us vomit, got picked off by a Kraut sniper who we called 'Dead-Eye', and got blown up when the Fritz gunners happened to lob a lucky artillery shell into one of our trenches."

"You weren't a priest then, were you?"

"No, Father, I wasn't. I spent my time in the trenches with my menagerie of pet rats and my bunker mate. We had carved a mudroom off of the main trench. We spent most of our time bailing the trench, dumping water and mud eventually.

worked its way back in. We usually had at least four inches of water under the duckboards"Maurice, my bunker mate, was killed after a while when he went out to no-man's land to try to get a shot at Dead-Eye. Dead-Eye had set up a helmet and a rifle where he usually did his mischief, but he'd moved to the other end of our sector. He didn't kill Maurice right away though. He wounded him and let him hang on the wire as bait for any of us who were stupid enough to go out after him. I was stupid enough, and Dead-Eye almost got me too. But we couldn't reach Maurice. He lay there hanging on the barbed wire for about three days, trying to fight the rats off that were nibbling at him. When he eventually did die, they gnawed at his face, chewing half of it away before we were able to retrieve his body after we'd captured that sector.

"Dead-Eye taunted us in English. He had a very distinctive voice, very nasal. 'What's wrong, Americans? Are you going to leave your comrade there to die? Why don't you go get him? I won't shoot you.'

"Another of our trench mates decided to try to get Maurice. Dead-Eye got him through his helmet...straight on before he'd even gotten all of the way out of the trench. His feet were still hanging over the top of the trench and we were able to pull him back in. Later that night, the rats were drinking his blood that had pooled under the duckboards.

"Yes, Father Porcelli, I do know what you've been through."

"How did you deal with it...I mean, the ghosts...what did you do?"

"At first, I drank a lot; then I became a priest and a theologian to help me find answers to the same questions and doubts that you have.

"Mr. Fleming, your savior or nemesis, as the case may be, has ghosts and demons of his own. I've been working with him and I think we're making progress, both of us."

"When I first met him in France, Fleming used to serve Mass for me. Then, in Germany, he told me that he'd killed a man in hand to hand combat. He told me that in conversation...I'm not breaking the seal of confession...though I did hear his confession."

"I've killed men, too, Tony. Unlike Fleming, I've murdered men, one man in particular. We were told one afternoon that there'd be an artillery barrage that night, and that at the first light of dawn, we'd advance over the top.

"The barrage was a cacophony from hell. I still have nightmares from time to time about that shelling. When dawn came, whistles started blowing all up and down the line, and we started moving out over the tops of our trenches, advancing toward the Jerries' line. It was a weird feeling; men walking and stumbling through a heavy morning fog in the mud toward the enemy trenches, no sound of firing, just the noise of an occasional canteen or shovel clanking as their owners tripped or bumped into a barbed wire post or something...very surreal. The tension was terrible. We all felt in our bones that the Germans were holding off long enough for us to get close to their lines so they could slaughter us.

"When we got closer, I could hear the sound of groaning coming from one of their trenches. Our gunners were either very good or very lucky because the Germans who had survived the bombardment had pulled out during the night, leaving their dead and wounded behind them.

"Again, I heard moaning, and with the first sergeant covering me, I cautiously approached to see if it was one of our men, or maybe a Hun trying to lure us into a trap.

"I stood over the top of the trench and looked down at the figure lying in the mud beneath me. His leg was shattered, and he was holding a white cloth in his right hand while crying, 'I surrender, American! Don't kill me! Please don't kill me! I looked into his eyes and saw the terror they reflected back at me. 'I surrender! I surrender!' He said again, in that distinctive nasal tone that I had heard so often.

"It was then that I succumbed to evil, became an instrument of evil. Consumed by evil, I took a hand grenade off my kit, pulled the pin, and counted to three as I backpedaled quickly away from the trench. When the fuse had run down three seconds, I tossed the grenade underhanded into the trench, and then dove to the ground.

"After the explosion, I saw that Dead-Eye's skull had been split in two by shrapnel. Before I moved on, I stopped, unbuttoned my trousers, and pissed into his brains.

"I do know evil, Father, and I'll be spending the rest of my life trying to atone for my actions that day, a day that I really came to know evil, a day when I had become one with evil.

"I'm sorry to burden you with this, Father, but that's my world, and that's why I became a priest. You're the only person alive to know the full story of what I did that day. The first sergeant who was covering me looked in horror while I was pissing in Dead-Eye's brains, but he was killed later that afternoon."

"I had no idea..."

"No one did. The only person who could understand what I did and what I'm going through is someone who has been through it himself."

"Then you know what I'm going through."

"More than almost all of the people on this campus."

"I feel that I'm slowly getting better," said Porcelli, "but I've not restored my faith in God or my vocation. I feel like I was a tool of evil myself, encouraging young men to kill and to die in the name of their god. I never understood that this is what I was doing until I met Fleming that day in Germany. I heard his confession while I was sitting in a porcelain barber chair in a bombed out barbershop. The more that he and I talked, the greater my understanding became, and the clearer my reality became until it overwhelmed me, and I tried to take my own life by walking into a mine field."

"We were all tools of evil, Tony; that's what war's all about. Good people thinking they're doing the right thing on both sides of the battle, killing each other indiscriminately and with glee...that's until they return to a normal world. Then their ghosts start to haunt them, to possess them, and take control of every waking and subconscious thought that passes through their minds. Dead-Eye was a monster when he was killing us, particularly cruel and vicious in the way he shot Maurice, leaving him there as bait so that he could kill more of us. But, when he was wounded and could neither fight nor escape, he became a frightened animal, like a dog that is being taken to the kennel, knowing that he's going to be put down.

"It's evil, Tony, but you aren't any more responsible for the killing and brutality in the past war than you were for the so-called Great War, the war to end all wars. You were only an infant then, but it's the stain of original sin, the stain of our human nature, that causes war. It's human nature, Father, the evil side of our human nature that causes wars.

"It's evil that leads someone to piss on the brains of a man he's just murdered in cold blood. It's evil that causes wars, but what you did was out of a love of God to serve those young men who went into combat. You were deceived, Father, and the realization of that deception made you want to kill yourself. Your war grew out of evil, but your actions grew out of love. You have to realize that and see it for what it is instead of continuing to torture yourself over and over.

"Christ died for us, Tony; he died for my sins and yours. I dare say that my sins are greater than yours though. I need a larger chunk of Christ's inexhaustible mercy than you do."

"After the war, how did you decide to enter the priesthood?"

"I kept having nightmares. My horror and grief were overwhelming me. I started drinking more and more. Finally, I hit bottom. I called a friend of mine who was a seminarian. He suggested that I could find forgiveness through Christ if I truly repented of my sins. Of course, I repented; I would have erased three years from my life if I could have.

"Surprisingly, my friend suggested that I read a book on Zen Buddhism written by a Japanese scholar, D. T. Suzuki. I started going to daily Mass and stayed in the church for an hour or two, meditating like Suzuki suggested. As I sat there, I slowly came to realize and experience the grace of Christ and the peace that comes from accepting yourself and your bad acts in the past, but being mindful, aware, and compassionate in the moment.

"I can never undo the evil that I had become, but I can accept it as something I can't change, and move on as I experience God's infinite forgiveness, day by day, one day at a time.

"I did what I did, Father, but I am who I am today, and that evil side of my human nature is in check, contained at least for today. Tomorrow is another day that I'll live, if and when it comes, and hopefully I'll continue to be able to contain the evil that I'm capable of becoming.

"Tony, I pray that I'm capable of suppressing that evil side of me, better yet, that it never manifests itself again...once in a lifetime's enough...no, once in a lifetime is too much."

"My God, Frank, could I confess to you while we walk?"

"You can do that, Tony. I just confessed to you. Not even my confessor knows the full evil of my sin. I've always made my confession by saying that I've committed a mortal sin too great to confess, that I killed a man in the course of committing that sin, but that I couldn't tell any more than that.

"Tony, before I hear your confession, could you give me absolution and help me to resolve this one remaining piece of my human nature...?"

"I'll do that, Father. For your penance, I want you to continue to help the former servicemen and chaplains like me who are consumed by their own guilt, and who providence sends into your life.

"Now, make a good act of contrition."

As the older man made his act of contrition, Father Porcelli absolved him of his sins. "Absolvote in nominee Patris et Filius et Spiritus Sanctus, Amen."

After absolving Father Fitzgibbon from his sins, Father Porcelli began to cry softly. This was the first confession he'd heard since absolving Dan Fleming, Corporal Fleming, of his sins while sitting in a porcelain barber chair in a bombed out building in another world.

CHAPTER FORTY-TWO

The Summer Vacation Was Coming to an End

The New England summer drew slowly to a close as the days of August grew shorter. The evenings were cooler, and the cricket chorus incessant as they sought to mate before they succumbed to that first deep frost that they instinctively knew would lie before them.

Dan and Marie seemed to spend every free moment together. During the day, while Dan was at work, Marie frequently walked around the corner to Cushman Road to spend time with her child's grandmother. Marie was slowly and perhaps unconsciously, being absorbed as a de facto member of the Fleming family.

The Michigan summer was winding down as well, and in Michigan, Yvonne and John Flanagan had grown into a far deeper relationship than the one between her and Dan Fleming.

"John, I don't know how I'm going to tell Dan about us. I like him; I always will, but he was the first man I ever had the chance to get to know after I left the convent. I was infatuated with him. I can see that now. I'm confused, John. I know how I feel about you, but I don't want to hurt Dan. I've not written to him all summer, and that bothers me too.

"It's not like I never want to see him again. I do admire him, not only for what he's been through, but for his sincerity and honesty. I realize now, though, that Dan could never be happy as a part of the Chrysler family. John, you're like us; you understand us. You have the same Catholic values, the same faith that we have. Dan's not like that. His beliefs are different from what you and I believe in. He could never be comfortable as part of this family. He could never do that because he comes from a totally different world. When Daddy first met you, he told me that I should invite you around more often. When I was infatuated with

Dan, I wondered how I would ever introduce him to Daddy. It'd be like oil and water coming together, like the poles of two magnets facing each other. What should I do, John? How can I gently break up with him so I don't hurt him? And how do I tell him about us?"

"I wish I could help you, Honey, but you've got to do this one on your own. I understand how you find this difficult. You know that I don't care for Fleming...his dismissive attitude when you disagree with him, and his tone of moral superiority, to say nothing of his sacrilegious view of the Catholic faith and Holy Mother Church.

"You know, he hasn't written to you either. The last time I checked, the post office was selling the same stamps in Boston that they sell in Grosse Point. Maybe your relationship has cooled in his eyes too."

"I know you don't like him, John, but he's a good guy, a friend. I can be his friend, but I wouldn't want to be married to him. Besides, after coming over for dinner so often, Daddy'd be upset if I ever came home on the arm of any other man than you."

"Yvonne, you know that I feel the same way about you, but you've got to let him know that, and that things have changed between the two of you. I think it'd be easier to do by letter than by having to tell him in person."

"I know you're right, John. I'll start another letter to him tonight, and I'll go to the post office tomorrow and find out if they can get it to him before he heads back to campus."

Dawn's light was starting into Yvonne's room as she finished the final draft of her letter to Dan. The wastebasket beside her desk was half filled with crumpled, peach colored stationery, where she'd tried to express her feelings in words, but didn't like what she'd written. Her feelings for Dan, unlike her feelings for John, were very nuanced. She had difficulty in capturing those nuances with words in a way that would let him know that she valued him as a friend and as a wonderful human being, but that they couldn't continue beyond being friends. It was one of the most difficult things that she'd ever done and she prayed to the Virgin Mary that she'd be able to capture her feelings and thoughts in a way that he'd understand, and in a way that wouldn't hurt or upset him.

The letter began: "My Dearest Dan,"

Yvonne had anguished over that greeting, afraid that it would hurt him more to read that at the start of the letter, and then to find that she was breaking off the romantic aspect of their relationship in favor of John Flanagan. She'd decided to tell him up-front about John because she and Dan had always been honest with each other, and it was important to her that no matter how distasteful it was to write this letter, she should continue to be honest with him. In the end, she decided to use that greeting because he'd always be dear to her. They had a very special relationship that magic freshman year, but that relationship had changed. She felt towards Dan as she would feel towards an older brother, someone she could always trust, someone who would never try to hurt her, and who'd always be there for her if she needed help. She wanted to maintain that aspect of their relationship. This time, she knew that her love for John was real, and that she'd just been infatuated with Dan.

Yvonne realized that she and Dan could never have a happy life together because they came from such dissimilar backgrounds. They were simply too different; to use Dan's words, their worlds were too far apart. It's not that she thought her family life in Michigan society was better than Dan's working class background; it was just that he wouldn't feel comfortable with her family. Cotillions, dinner at the club; things like that would make him feel awfully uncomfortable. And in spite of Dan's assurances to the contrary, she wondered how Dan's family would accept her. Finally, there was the matter of religion. Christ, the Blessed Virgin, and the saints were very real to Yvonne. She saw in the Roman Catholic Church the path to her eternal salvation. She knew that heaven existed and that it must be a wonderful place. She had constructed an image in her mind that heaven must be like the Garden of Eden before the fall; all goodness and plenty; no wants, no hatred, no wars, and no evil. Most of all, she looked forward to spending eternity in the presence of the people she loved, and who had gone before her.

John felt that way too, but that vision of eternity just didn't exist in Dan's mind. Heaven to Dan was just unknowable..."ultimate reality," he had called it, sort of like "it is what it is." Yvonne couldn't spend the rest of her life with a man who thought like that, no matter how much she respected and admired him. His doubt would undermine the clarity of her vision of God and salvation. She would always be on the defensive with him about the reality of salvation.

John and Yvonne saw eye to eye on religion and other matters. Dan, she hoped, would be her friend – if he would – but John would be her husband, or so she prayed.

"My Dearest Dan, it pains me to write this letter, more than I could express to you in words. I've decided that we should change our relationship, that we should not go on as we did last year because the way we were going, we would have ended up marrying after graduation, a thought I once held very dear and very close in my heart.

"I realize now that I was infatuated with you. (All of the girls on my floor were too, but I was the lucky one.) The love I felt for you was honest, pure, and deep, and I know that you felt the same way about me. But, it could never last through a marriage. I'll always love you as a friend. I hope that we'll always remain close friends, but in the area of our religious beliefs, we're far too different, too far apart to spend our lives together. How would we bring up our children if I taught them that heaven was a beautiful place to go after death, and you told them it was merely 'ultimate reality'?

"I did love you, Dan, and I hope that I can continue to love you in a different way with a goal of continued friendship, rather than a goal of marriage and children.

"I know that this will hurt you, Dan, and I'm truly sorry for that. Also, I've been seeing John Flanagan here in Michigan over the summer, and he asked to be remembered to you when I wrote.

"I'm sorry, Dan; I'm truly sorry that our relationship has to change like this. I pray that it doesn't end. I've been trying to write this letter for a long time, but have found it very difficult to do. I apologize for not being able to muster the courage to do this until now.

"I'm sorry, Dan. I'm truly sorry!"

It was signed: "Fondly, Yvonne"

The man at the window in the post office had assured Yvonne that the letter would reach Boston at a point in time at least two weeks before upperclassmen were due to report back to Notre Dame. Unknown to Yvonne, though, Charlie Costanza had been writing to Dan over the summer trying to convince his roommate to try out for the football team. Dan had agreed, and on the day that Yvonne had posted the letter to Dan in Boston, he had already been in South Bend for two weeks suffering through double sessions of football practice in the hot Indiana sun.

"Charlie, what should I tell Yvonne?"

Dan and Charlie had just finished the Friday morning session, the only practice session of the day, and were sitting beside each other in the locker room, pouring sweat on the bench in front of their lockers.

"I'm very fond of her as a friend, but after seeing my son, I'm very interested in developing my relationship with his mother. Yvonne's a wonderful girl, pure and pretty naive; she'll make someone a wonderful wife and mother, but that someone can't be me. I like her as a friend. We found each other last year and the whole year was magic because of her. I loved every minute that we were together and I wouldn't have changed any of it. I'd like to keep our relationship going, but as close friends, not as potential lovers.

"I don't know how to tell her about Marie and Daniel.

"Charlie, what should I do?"

Costanza, the bear, they called him, thought for a while.

"Maybe you should just tell her the truth, Dan. Tell her that under the stress of the war, you had a brief but intense relationship with a French woman...everyone knows the French are that way...and that you just found out over the summer that you'd fathered a child by the woman. Tell her that you've confessed it; that'll make her feel a little better.

"Just lay it out for her. Let her absorb it; hold her when she cries, and then tell her that you'd like to remain friends with her, good friends, but as Father Fitz would say, 'Platonic Friends.'"

"You know, Roomie, I never...not for an instant...ever thought that you were a dumb jock, regardless of the rumors around campus. I think that's the only way to do it. I just hope that I have the balls to say it like you just did, especially if she starts crying."

"I don't know how else you could do it, Dan. I want to shower and get out of here though. I'm a little nervous about opening against Purdue next week. I'd just like to forget about football for a little bit; maybe we could go to a movie tonight at Washington Hall."

"Nah, 'The Bells of Saint Mary's' is playing there. From what I hear, it's a sickly sweet story about a parish priest...I don't think so, Charlie. I'll just go back to the room after chow and go to sleep. If you do go to the movie, try not to wake me up when you come back."

Double sessions had ended the previous week, and the rest of the school had reported that Monday. You could feel the excitement in the air, the energy of anticipation permeated the campus as the people who managed the school prepared everything for the returning students. It was like the return of the swallows to the mission at Capistrano.

Friday afternoon, Dan called over to Le Mans Hall at Saint Mary's and asked the girl who answered the phone to leave a note on Yvonne Chrysler's door, asking her to call him at the second floor Zahm Hall campus phone.

Dan kept practicing what he'd say when he met Yvonne. It never seemed to come out right when he practiced it. He was sure that he'd sound like a blubbering idiot when he eventually did meet her. He dreaded his first encounter with Yvonne; he dreaded hurting her, but he had to do what he had to do. He also had trouble keeping his mind off of Marie and young Daniel. He'd already called them twice and was afraid to see what his phone bill would look like.

Dan hadn't wanted to come back early, but if he received a football scholarship, he'd be able to use the remaining portion of his GI Bill benefits to pay for law school.

Over the summer, working in the vulcanizing room of the Dean Rubber plant, he'd decided that he wanted to be a lawyer. Lawyers, he thought, knew how to use power, the power of words and the power of logic, and he could use that power for good. He also thought that he could earn a decent living as a lawyer and be better able to provide for Marie and their son.

The double sessions had gone well, and Dan was the number two halfback, playing on the right side and usually lined up behind Charlie, who was being touted in all of the newspapers as an All-American candidate, unheard of for a sophomore. The athletic department had offered Dan a scholarship, on the condition that during the off-season, he would help out with the boxing program. One of football coaches had organized a boxing program for the Navy during the war. He was now back at Notre Dame and wanted to restart this same program which the team's coaches had formerly used during the off-season to keep the football players in condition.

Dan would get free room, board, and tuition, but he'd be expected to lead the workouts for the boxers. They'd start training after Christmas and would fight in a single elimination tournament, with the championship bouts to be held on Saint Patrick's Day.

In spite of the repugnance he felt when he recalled Stadholm's impromptu boxing matches, Dan agreed to the arrangement. The fights were called the "Bengal Bouts" and were promoted by the campus chapter of the Knights of Columbus. All of the proceeds were sent to the missions in the Indian subcontinent in the Bengal region.

It had seemed like a good deal to Dan, and he was thinking more and more about law school as an option after graduation.

After accepting the scholarship offer the week before the start of the season, Dan got the news that he'd be starting at right halfback for the Purdue game. Rocky Sienkewicz, the senior who was supposed to start, had broken his leg that week in practice, and would likely be out for the entire season.

Dan hadn't heard from Yvonne, and he'd not called her again.

"Maybe she's rethought our relationship," Dan wondered to himself. At any rate, the Purdue game was very early this year, the second week that Notre Dame and Saint Mary's were back in session. He had to keep focused on his plays and formations and couldn't afford to be distracted because of Yvonne.

Dan had explained his situation with the football team and his scholarship to Marie, but she didn't understand American football and thought it amusing that they'd give the father of her son a free college education to run with a ball while eleven men on the other team tried to stop him.

"The entire German Army with tanks and machine guns couldn't stop you, Corporal Fleming. Why do these eleven boys on the other team think they're better than the entire German Army?" she asked him and laughed.

He laughed too.

"It's a different reality," he thought to himself, "fighting for your life and then going out to play a boy's game."

"She's right," he agreed. "The whole German Army couldn't stop me, and I sure as hell won't let some kid from Muncie or Bloomington, Indiana, do what the Krauts couldn't."

CHAPTER FORTY-THREE

Father Fitz Helps Ed and Janet Miller

It was early Sunday morning the day after the Purdue game. Father Fitzgibbon had finished saying his office and was stepping out of the shower when the phone in his Cavanaugh Hall suite rang.

"Father Fitzgibbon? This is Ed Miller. I was in your Moral Theology course before the war and..."

"Yes, Mr. Miller, and very instrumental in having Dan Fleming admitted to Notre Dame, as I understand it."

"Dan has spoken to you about me then?"

"Mr. Fleming's one of my best students. He tells me from time to time about some of your exploits together during the war, and of course you both knew Father Porcelli. I'm forever indebted to Mr. Fleming for locating and returning Father Porcelli to Notre Dame."

"Did he tell you that I'd be calling on you for advice?"

"He did ask me if it would be OK for you to call me with some issue, but he was less than vague in describing what it was.

"I do remember you, by the way. Yours was the only term paper, until your protégé, Mr. Fleming, came along, that I gave an "A". By the way, I grade the papers blindly. I had no proof that it was your paper, though frankly, I did suspect that from the clarity of the writing."

"Thank you, Father, you're doing wonders for my failing self-confidence, and you make it easier for me to ask your help. I've been having some difficulty after returning from the war, especially in the relationship between my wife and myself. Frankly, Dan suggested that I call you. He told me that you were a combat vet as well, and that you were a good person to talk with."

"He flatters me, Mr. Miller. I did see combat in the First World War, but any advice on marriage I might be able to impart, you must remember, is coming from a celibate. My experience is vicarious, but my knowledge from that vicarious experience is extensive."

"Father, could I sit down with you some time to talk about my situation?"

"That'd be fine, Mr. Miller. I'm free today, but I'm afraid I'll be pretty much tied up for the rest of the week."

"Today would be fine, Father. Dan tells me that you're still the rector of Cavanaugh Hall."

Half an hour later, Ed Miller showed up at the main entrance to Cavanaugh Hall, thinking that it'd been at least five years since he'd been this deep into the Notre Dame campus. Memories flooded his mind from the days he was a student here, memories that struggled to the surface through the horrors of the war and the difficulties he was living through now.

"Come in!" The deep voice boomed.

Ed Miller opened the door and stepped into the room, remembering a time eons ago when he'd last entered Father Fitzgibbon's office the day of his graduation from Notre Dame. Then he was wearing his new Army uniform, with the second lieutenant's gold bar pinned proudly on his shoulder.

"It's been a long time, Mr. Miller."

The two men exchanged a firm handshake.

"It has, Father, and there's been a lot of water over the dam since then."

"A lot has happened in the world since then, Mr. Miller, and I'm afraid you've been a victim of that in many ways."

"I don't know if I'm a victim, Father; I'm awfully lucky....or blessed...to be alive.

"I do have problems though; parts of them are from the war, and parts of them are from my marriage. I know they're both related, but I don't know how to deal with them.

"I work hard all day trying to make enough money to provide for Janet and the kids. When I get home, I'm worn out from the day, and when I'm tired or run down, I start having flashbacks to the war. So, I have a drink to calm my nerves. Then Janet gets upset with me. She says I don't understand what she's going through, and that all I do is work and drink.

"Father, it's not like I abandon them, but I've got to be able to provide for them, and that takes up so much energy.

"Father, I can see that Janet and I are pulling away from each other. I don't want to lose my marriage, but I don't know what to do to save it."

"I see, Ed. It may seem unique to you, but I've counseled other returning veterans who are having similar problems with their marriages. You must remember that there's no way an American woman who's lived all of her life in this country could come close to understanding what you've been through. Add to that the dynamic that occurs between a couple in any marriage.

"Spiritually, every marriage is a mixed marriage because everyone's faith is different, and when two people come together, they have to accommodate each other's unique relationship with their creator. Marriage is like that in other ways as well, particularly today. Women, especially American women, have culturally been subservient to their husbands. When the husbands went off to war, women filled their places in the factories, managed household budgets, and brought up children by themselves. After that, American women and their daughters will never again be contented to be 'house-wives', solely responsible for cleaning, cooking, and bringing up children. Now American women want more, and that's a good part of the relationship problems that returning servicemen face.

"There are the normal relationship problems that develop when two people come together and pledge their lives to each other, and the war certainly exacerbated them for returning vets like you. Janet ran the household while you were away, and it's probably not fair to expect her to slip back into a subservient role. I think you have to recognize that those days are over for the two of you.

"The key to a good marriage, from what I've been able to observe over the years, is the ability to communicate with each other so that Janet knows the fears and struggles you're going through. It's equally important that she knows you're interested in hearing her fears and struggles...in trying to understand her and what she wants out of her life."

"Father, she tells me that I don't hear her. I listen to her, but I don't know what to say. She wants me to spend more time with her and the kids. I try to do that, but she doesn't understand how much time I have to put into the business. She says that the war changed me, that I'm not the same man she married...I don't know how to answer her. Usually our discussions like that end with me losing my temper and calling her a selfish bitch; she cries, and then I feel like a heel. She runs upstairs to the bedroom crying, and I sit in the living room with a bottle of Jack Daniels until I fall asleep.

"Father, I don't know how much more of this I can take. I love her, but I can't keep living like this. I don't want to do this to her, and I don't want to keep going through it myself. Can you help us?"

"Well, maybe I can, Ed...But maybe I can't. Where's Janet now?"

"She's home with the kids."

"Do you think she could get a sitter and have the two of you come back this afternoon? It's certainly better to do marriage counseling with the couple present rather than with just one of the partners."

"Let me call her, Father, and see if she can get someone, or if she even wants to try to save the marriage."

"Here, use the phone in my office. It's almost time for me to show my face on the hall. This is still a freshman residence hall, and if I don't start out strict, it won't take long for me to lose control. They got all worked up yesterday over the Purdue game. By the way, what did you think of Dan Fleming running for 146 yards in his first college game?"

"I heard the game on the radio, Father. I was going over some accounts at the office. I knew Dan was having a good game from the announcers, but I never heard the statistics and I've not read the Trib this morning.

"Good for him! He's a tough kid, a good kid, and when I met him I knew that he belonged at Notre Dame."

"Take your time, Mr. Miller. If Janet can make it this afternoon, you don't have to wait for me to return from my rounds. Just leave me a note if you're going to pick her up."

"I will...I will, Father. Thank you for your help, Father. I'll try to get her here as soon as I can."

At that, the priest turned and walked out into the hall. At the far end away from his office, the south end of the hall, there was a ruckus in the entryway.

"Mr. Jacoby!" The priest bellowed, and the four students froze. "What in the name of God do you think you're doing?"

Poor Jacoby was standing on the night watchman's chair, which was on the night watchman's table, and he was in the act of hanging three water balloons in the doorway.

"Mr. Jacoby, you will break each of those balloons on your head, and I expect that after you do that, you and your comrades will clean up the floor and replace poor Oscar's table and chair. You will then take a shower, and I expect to see you report to my office promptly in twenty-five minutes.

"Do you understand me, Mr. Jacoby?" the priest bellowed. The look of terror on poor Jacoby's face was as if he'd been told to face a firing squad.

"Gentlemen, I do run a tight ship in Cavanaugh Hall and I want each of you to understand that...go ahead, Mr. Jacoby, break those balloons!"

At that, poor Jacoby broke the water balloons one at a time on his head, drenching himself and getting water all over the entry way floor.

"...And I won't tolerate this conduct. Mr. Jacoby this is your last chance. Any further shenanigans like this from you and I'll be packing you home to your parents for you to explain how you got thrown out of Notre Dame in your first semester.

"Gentlemen...I want the rest of you to take note of Mr. Jacoby's predicament and also note that you've each been duly warned; any more pranks or problems, and I'll send you packing too.

"Do I make myself clear, gentlemen?"

His question was met by a few timid mumbled "yes" responses.

"Gentlemen...I can't hear you! I expect you to answer me like you had a pair!"

By now, the priest's face was red and the veins in his throat were throbbing against his Roman collar. His basso profundo would have gotten the attention of anyone standing within a hundred feet.

"Do I make myself clear, gentlemen?" The bulging eyes, the throbbing veins, and booming voice commanded a strong responsive answer.

"Yes, Father!" came the response from four voices, sounding as one.

"That's better, gentlemen," the priest said in as relaxed a manner as if he were making small chat with them.

"Mr. Jacoby, you'd better get a move on. I don't tolerate tardiness." The tone of the priest's voice was now commanding but not threatening, asserting itself but not overwhelming poor Jacoby, who was almost in tears over his failed prank and his embarrassment at the hands of his hall rector.

Returning to his office, Father Fitzgibbon almost bumped into Ed Miller, who having completed his phone call was leaving on his way to pick up his wife.

"Father, I spoke with Janet. She cried again, but they sounded like tears of gratitude rather than hurt. She said that she'd have her sister come over to watch the kids and that she'd be ready to leave by the time I got home. I don't understand, Father; I thought she'd be upset that I went to you for help, but instead, she seemed almost happy. I don't think I'll ever be able to understand women, Father."

"On the contrary, Mr. Miller, I don't know that we'll ever be able to understand ourselves rather than others. It would seem that Janet has found hope in the fact that you're taking steps to try to save your marriage.

"This is a good sign, Ed. It shows her that she's important to you, and sometimes it's that first step that cuts the Gordian knot that locks two people in misunderstanding, or that erases the line in the sand that one of them has drawn.

"Ed, the first step is usually the hardest. But, my experience has been that if you have two people of good will who love each other, they'll work through their difficulties together, no matter how painful it is or how long it takes."

"I'll be back within the hour, Father."

Hurrying out of Cavanaugh towards the circle where he had parked his car, Miller ran into Dan Fleming walking back from Mass at Sacred Heart.

"Hey, Ed! Captain!" Dan shouted.

"Corporal Fleming, how does it feel to be a campus hero? 146 yards in your first game...not bad, and welcome back.

"I can't stop for very long, Dan; I just spoke with Father Fitz, and I'm on my way to get Janet. He's going to work with both of us to help us pull things together. How are you and Yvonne getting along after the summer break?"

"Ed, I know you don't have much time and it's a long story, better told over a cup of coffee sometime, but I've not been in touch with Yvonne since I left campus at the start of the summer. I called once and left a message for her, but I've not followed up on it.

"The other thing is that before the end of school, I learned that I was a father and that my child and his mother were living around the corner from my parents' house in Boston. I became very close to both of them and I'm trying to figure out how to change my relationship with Yvonne to being a friend rather than a potential marriage partner.

"Look, you've got to run; I'm in Zahm Hall this year, 226 Zahm. Call me when you get a chance. I think we both have a lot of catching up to do."

"Wow, Dan, that's a mouthful for a five minute conversation. I'm free Thursday morning. Do you have class then?"

"No...can we get together for breakfast?"

"That sounds like a plan. I'll see you at ten in the caf, off to the right when you walk in the front door."

"That works for me; I'll see you then. Say hi to Janet for me."

As the two men separated, Dan thought about how different their lives had become since they last spoke. He'd gotten into a relationship with the mother of his son, and Ed appears at the precipice where his marriage is about to crumble on the rocks.

"I hope Father Fitz can help pull them back together," he thought to himself. Dan had also become a football hero overnight, and he was amused earlier before Sunday Mass to see the banner across the top of the sports section in the South Bend Tribune: "SOPH FLEMING WINS GAME FOR IRISH!"

CHAPTER FORTY-FOUR

Dan and Yvonne Run Into Each Other

"Hello, Dan Fleming." The soft voice interrupted Dan's thoughts, and he looked up to see that he was walking straight into Yvonne.

"Yvonne...ah...hello. Did you have a good summer?"

"I did...I did, Dan...and how about you?"

"Oh, I was busy working in the vulcanizing room at Dean Rubber; my father knows the foreman there and was able to get me on. I came back to school a couple of weeks early when Charlie convinced me to try out for the football team. Charlie made me a hero yesterday by opening holes in the Purdue line that I could have driven a truck through. It's funny how things work out. They've given me a football scholarship, so now I can save my GI benefits to go to law school."

"You were back two weeks early then; did you get my letter?"

Shocked to run into her and with his practiced script for this meeting lost in his panic, Dan didn't hear her asking about the letter.

"Yvonne...I think we do have to talk about our relationship..."

"Dan...I know, please don't make this any more difficult for us."

"I don't want to do that, Yvonne; I always want you as my special friend..."

"I do too, Dan. We can have a close but different relationship than we did last year."

"That's what I mean. Yvonne, you'll always be a very special woman in my life, and I'm glad you understand and that we'll be able to remain friends."

"Dan, I'm sorry that this is happening to us, but I'm excited that we'll remain friends. It must have been Divine Providence that made us run into each other here this morning.

"Call me when you get a chance and maybe we can have coffee some morning. I'm taking Father Fitz's 'Advanced Problems in Moral Theology' this semester, though I had to miss the first week of class."

"Yeah, me too. Maybe we can stop at the caf Monday after class and catch up."

"All right...I'll see you then."

Walking into Zahm, Dan rattled the bed of the sleeping hulk that shared the room with him.

"GET UP! GET UP! TIME TO RISE AND SHINE AND GREET YOUR ADMIRING FANS!"

"Oh, for Christ's sake, Dan, let me sleep, would you! I feel like I've been run though a meat grinder. Those sons-of-bitches who were double-teaming me kept working me over, punching my stomach and ribs. I feel like a piece of tenderized beef. On the other hand, I guess we showed the bastards a trick or two."

Charlie rubbed his eyes, sat upright, and swung his legs over the side of the bed.

"How are you feeling?"

"I'm a little sore, but I didn't take the beating you were going through in the trenches. You made me a hero though. Those two guys punching you in the stomach and ribs must have pissed you off because you opened holes for me that your little sister could have run through for ten yards a carry."

"Yeah, we do all the work, but you backs get all the glory."

Dan took the paper he was carrying under his arm and laid it out on the bed beside Charlie.

"As a matter of fact, you're right, you know."

"Jesus Christ, Dan...you're the fucking hero of the game. I knew you would be though. I only got you through the line; you picked up the rest of those yards on your own. Isn't this something? You know how you're always talking about different views of reality? Well, yours is about to change now that you've become a football hero."

"Yeah, it's gonna change for the worse if I don't do the reading for tomorrow's classes. By the way, I ran into Yvonne today on the way back from Mass."

"Oh, yeah, did you tell her about breaking off the relationship?"

"I did, and it went pretty well. I didn't know how to say it, but it was almost as if she could anticipate the words. She was very receptive about having us remain friends. Charlie, that's such a load off my back!

"Oh, I stopped and checked the mail on the way back from Mass. You have a letter from Patti-Jo, and I've got one from my mother that's pretty thick, like there's something stuffed inside it. Here you go."

Charlie opened the letter and blushed when he read it

"Holy shit!

"Patti-Jo wrote on Thursday wishing me luck in the Purdue game, then she goes on, out of the blue, telling me that she'd like to be spending the rest of her life with me and having children together with me."

"Hey, not bad, Roomie; wait till you meet her parents though. It's a long way between Chicago and Abilene, and not just in distance. You think you might want to be married to her?"

"I'm scared to think of it. She thinks of marriage as a home and family, with me going off to work in the morning and her staying home bringing up a bunch of kids.

"If I married anyone, Dan, it'd be Pattie-Jo, but I don't think either of us is ready for this yet.

"We're gonna' have to work this out...slow it down a little bit....

"What does your mother have to say?"

Dan paused a bit and opened the unopened letter from Yvonne that his mother had stuffed into the larger envelope that she had sent him. He opened the letter within the letter and started turning crimson as he read it.

"It's funny, Charlie, my mother doesn't say much. She wished us luck in the game too, but she enclosed a 'Dear John' letter from Yvonne that came after I had left to come back for pre-season practice. I see now why Yvonne accepted our breakup so easily this morning. I thought she was anticipating what I was going to say, but she thought that she was breaking off with me. I had no idea that she wanted to end it."

"You're kidding, you thought you were shooting her down, and she thought that she was shooting you down. You know, you are one lucky son-of-a-bitch. Are you going to tell her about Marie and your son?"

"I think that might be a little premature for now. We're both in Father Fitz's 'Advanced Problems in Moral Theology' and we're gonna have coffee after class tomorrow. I'll eventually tell her, and it might not be a bad idea to introduce Marie and Yvonne to each other at some point, but definitely not now.

"Charlie, the good thing about this is now I can work things out with Marie without feeling a load of guilt about hurting Yvonne. It's funny that they were once both postulates in the same order of nuns. Life's funny, Charlie, and I wonder sometimes about coincidence? Do things happen randomly, Charlie, or do they happen by some strange plan that we don't know and couldn't understand even if we did know it?"

CHAPTER FORTY-FIVE

Dan and Ed Miller Meet for Coffee

Thursday morning at ten o'clock, Dan was in the caf sipping coffee and reading his philosophy notes one more time before his 1:00 P.M. class. He kept looking up at the door and the end of the food line. Finally, he saw Ed Miller carrying a tray with coffee and a doughnut on it. Dan stood, waving to catch Ed's attention, and when he'd done that, sat down as the other man made his way to the table.

Miller placed his tray on the table, shook Dan's hand, and removed the food and coffee before he placed the empty tray on the adjoining table. Taking a sip, he sighed, and looking at Dan, said, "Ah, cafeteria coffee, the elixir of life. It's comforting to know that they haven't cleaned the pot since my freshman year about a decade ago. This stuff still tastes the same.

"So Dan, how did your summer go? That was quite a story you told me when we ran into each other on Sunday."

"Ed, obviously it's more complicated than what I'm telling you, but to make a long story short, when you sent me back to battalion with the write-up for Smitty's Medal of Honor, I also delivered a letter he had written to a French prostitute who he'd fallen in love with. She was a former nun who'd been raped by the Germans and spared when the SS killed all of the sisters in her convent. They brought in a bunch of whores, and she lived with them and was forced to turn tricks in order to survive. I was infuriated because she didn't even know who Smitty was, but I ended up spending the night with her and I knocked her up. She got in touch with me after the war, and over the summer I met her and our son, who's now a little more than two years old. She's teaching French in a Catholic girl's school not too far from my parents' house, and we've become very close.

278

After you and I spoke Sunday, I ran into Yvonne, and she apparently got involved in another relationship over the summer. She wants us to remain friends and that's fine with me. I thought that I was letting her down easily and she thought that she was letting me down easily, so it's all working out fine."

"That's quite a story. What's your relationship with the French woman, the mother of your child?"

"I'm very attracted to her. We've both been to hell and back and we seem to have survived the trip. She has the same kind of flashbacks and demons that you and I wrestle with, and we're good for each other because of that...because we understand each other. The baby's beautiful, and when I look at the two of us in the mirror, there's no doubt that he's my son. I want to finish college and go to law school. They gave me a football scholarship, so now I can use the rest of my GI Bill to pay for law school. I think that someday Marie, that's her name, and I will get married, but neither of us wants to rush into it.

"How are you and Janet getting along? Are things working themselves out?"

"It's good that you're not rushing into things yet, Dan, and it's good in a perverse sense that you've both experienced the hell of war. I realize now that part of my problem is that Janet has no idea about what I've been through, and I have difficulties trying to explain it to her. She wants things to be like they were before the war, but you can't go back, Dan; you can never go back! Janet and I are two different people now. I survived the hell that you and I endured, and Janet took charge of the family, managed the finances, and took care of our home without me.

"After I saw you Sunday, I went home and picked up Janet so that the two of us could talk with Father Fitz. I had no idea when I was a student that Fitz was a WWI vet. When did you learn that?"

"He's been counseling me, and from what I hear, a bunch of the other vets on campus. We're all carrying the same shit around with us, Ed, and we've got to learn to live with it or it'll kill us.

"How did it go when you and Janet met with him?"

"Well, Father Fitz talked a little bit, and then he listened, and Janet and I did most of the talking. He sort of steered us and sometimes rephrased what one of us had said, like he was directing us to a place where we both wanted to go, but neither of us knew how to get there.

"He helped us communicate with each other. I told her about first seeing the corpses of that mother clutching her child in death that we had run into toward the end of that first month. Remember, when we were moving inland and fighting about fifteen miles in from the coast."

"I remember that, Ed. How could anyone ever forget the absolute horror of that? It isn't one of my resident demons though. I've got enough of my own that I don't need more, but that's a worthy candidate to add to my stable."

"That struck me, Dan, because I realized it could have been my own wife and child. Well, Janet was shocked when I told her how it had affected me, and she started crying. I couldn't understand that and said to her that we'd seen stuff like that almost every day when we were in combat. I explained that to us, death and suffering were as commonplace as hanging laundry out to dry at home: just another load of wet laundry to hang out...the same as just another pile of immolated or bloated bodies lying beside the roadway as we passed.

"She told me how she worried every time the mailman came to the house that there'd be a letter from the War Department telling her that I'd been killed in action. She was relieved somewhat when Charlie Clancy down the block was killed and the news was delivered by a cab driver with a telegram from the War Department. After that, she didn't fear the mailman any more, but got very upset whenever she saw a taxi turn onto our street.

"She told me about the trouble getting the baby to sleep, and how she was worried that she wouldn't have enough money to make ends meet. She had never told me during the war, but she got a job nights working at the auto plant across town. She'd bring the baby to my mother's house for the night. My mother would feed her breakfast and bring her home about ten-thirty so that Janet could catch a little sleep.

"It was tough for her, Dan, and I never understood that when I got home. I had expected her to be like she was when I left, and she was expecting me to be like I was when I had left. The truth is, Dan, we're two different people now, and we have to get to know each other all over again. I don't know if we can do that. Janet doesn't either. We both know that for the sake of the kids, it would be better if we stay together.

"Father Fitz said that the most important thing for our marriage, for any marriage, is that the two partners communicate with each other. If you and Marie are going to get together, it'll be important advice for you, too."

"That's one thing we do well together, Ed. I know her soul and I let her into mine. It helps that we've been through that same hell together. Maybe we were in different parts of it, but we know the drill; we know what happened, how our lives had changed. And, now that it's over, we realize that our lives are again different, different from what they were during the war, and different from what they'd been before the war. We're working on developing our relationship, one where we both understand what's going on with the other, and one that we're both comfortable with.

"Smitty was infatuated with Marie during a different time, in a different place, and under entirely different circumstances. She and I have to work all of that out; we can never forget it, but we have to recognize it and place it somewhere where it won't interfere with our lives. We can't deny it and we can't make it go away, but we have to learn how to live with it."

"How are you doing with the German soldier you killed toward the end?"

"Ed, that continues to haunt me. I send his widow money every month...conscience money, because I'm trying to atone for killing her husband. I don't know how to deal with that. I've shared the story with Marie and she's very supportive. But, this is so overwhelming to me that I keep trying to put it out of my mind, to ignore it as if it had never happened. I just can't do that though. The VA psychiatrist told me that it'd be good for me to confront his widow and ask her forgiveness, but I can't bring myself to do that. I just keep sending her money. Maybe, someday, Ed...someday, but not now.

"Hey, Ed, thanks for coming out to campus, but I've got a philosophy class that I have to study for, and I should get to it because the test is at 1:00. Can I come out to visit with you Janet and the kids sometime?"

"Sure, Dan, that'd be great...if we're still together. We are trying and we're both hopeful. I think it'd be good for the three of us to get together again, especially after the last visit. I think it'd especially be good for Janet.

"Be well, Dan, and pray for us. I do the same for you every night." They shook hands and Ed Miller walked away.

Chapter Forty-Six

The Nursing Office Hires a New Clerk

"Mary, did you meet the new clerk in the records room yet?"

"I haven't, Brian, what's his name?"

"It's a 'her,' not a 'him.' Anka Richter, a German national who comes from one of the villages in the mountains. Her husband, a draftee, was killed in the war, and she's supporting herself and their child. She's fluent in English and is an excellent typist. She said that she had typed her husband's papers while he was at university. He was planning on going to medical school when he was drafted. She seems like a lovely person."

"That's nice; they certainly could use some good help down there. That name sounds familiar, like I knew someone with the same name or maybe knew someone who knew someone…

"Colonel, there's something I'd like to talk with you about."

Colonel Casey could tell from the tone of her voice that this would be something more than the ordinary or casual conversation between them.

"What is it, Major?"

"Colonel, my enlistment is up in January, and I've been recruited by the Boston General Hospital to be the head nurse on their trauma ward. I'm not sure what to do.

"I've made rank so quickly during wartime that I don't see getting a promotion in the foreseeable future, and this would be a tremendous professional opportunity."

"It'd be a chance to reunite with your friend, Corporal Fleming, as well…"

"Brian, don't be such an old fart. Dan Fleming has gone on with his life; he's living in a different world from ours. Life's totally different for him now. I got a letter from him the other day with a newspaper clipping...wait a minute...I have it in my purse."

Handing the letter to Doctor Casey, she smiled.

"Don't you think I'm a little old to get involved with a college boy?"

"Hey, a football hero to boot. Stay here, Mary; we have a good relationship, and the hospital's almost running by itself."

"You may think so, Colonel, but I'm so understaffed in Nursing that it's no fun coming to work every morning. Files are piling up on my desk, and my secretary can't get to them because the phone's always ringing with one crisis after another. I'd have a full staff at Boston General and wouldn't have to worry about anything except organizing a good emergency room protocol.

"The pay would be considerably more than what a major in the United States Army makes."

"Mary, how about if I transfer the new file clerk to your office...to help you out? If it works out, I'm sure I can get division to authorize one more person in the records room."

"Brian, I don't know. We're overwhelmed, so we do need the help, but the Boston General job is awfully enticing. I just wanted to give you enough warning so it didn't sneak up on you and leave you in a hole if I don't re-up."

"Mary, I'll do whatever I can to keep you here. You know I mean that, and in more than a professional concern."

"Brian, we're two different people. We could never make it together. You're a career soldier; you'll make general one of these days. Someday they'll put you in charge of the entire medical corps. But, for me...for me, I just want this phase of my life to be over. I want to be a caregiver, not an Army lifer.

"Since I was a little girl, I've always wanted to be a nurse, to take care of sick and injured people. I did that during the war, but now I'm an Army bureaucrat, wrapped up with budgets and staffing tables. I know there's some of that in civilian life, but I want to be a civilian. If I work at Boston General.... they refer to it as 'God's hospital'....I'll grow and learn. I'm stagnant here, Brian. How many abortions can the Army perform on its WACs? It's the same thing day in and day out..."

"Mary, let me get you additional staffing and promise me that you won't make a decision for at least a month."

"Brian, I'll give you a month, but I'm not promising anything. When can this Richter women start?"

"I'll have her upstairs first thing in the morning. I've got to figure a way to mollify Captain Collins. He'll be screaming bloody murder that I've taken one of his staff members away, even if she's only been there a short while."

The following morning, Mary was at work, not expecting anything to happen as a result of her discussion the previous evening with Colonel Casey. The private from the mailroom came around at 10:00 hours with a pile of letters and large envelopes with medical records in them. Glancing through the mail, she saw another letter from Dan. It looked pretty battered, and from its postmark, it looked like it predated the one she had just received by a month or more. She was about to open it when her secretary knocked and entered the office.

"Ma'am, there's a woman here from the records room, a German national who says she was told to report here by Captain Collins. I'm not sure what it's about or what she's doing here...."

"It's OK, Sarah, I know what's going on. I was talking with Colonel Casey yesterday about the backlog here and about how we needed more help. He told me that we had just hired a German national to work in the Records Room, but that he'd have Captain Collins transfer her up here, and that he'd try to get someone else for Collins. I think Collins was probably bullshit, but c'est la guerre.

"Why don't you send her in."

"Frau Richter, Major O'Daugherty asked me to take you into her office."

"Frau Richter, welcome to the Nursing Office. I'm Major O'Daugherty, but please call me Mary."

"Major...Mary, I mean, I'm Anka Richter, and Captain Collins told me to come up here...that I'd been transferred and didn't work for him anymore. He seemed quite upset. I'm confused because I don't know what I've done to upset him so...I'm not really sure what's happening, and this job's so important to my daughter and myself that I'm afraid to lose it. I really don't know what I did for him to throw me out of his office when I'd only been there for a week...."

"It's nothing you did, Anka. He wasn't angry with you; he was angry with me. I had complained to the hospital commander that the nursing office was understaffed, and Doctor Casey, the boss, ordered Collins to transfer you to my staff. That's why he's upset, not because of something that you had done, but because he's losing you.

"I'm sorry that you were in the middle, but don't worry; we need your help because we're tremendously backlogged, and I've been told, and can see from talking with you, that you speak excellent English.

"Sarah...rather, Corporal Clark, will show you where you work and how our files are arranged. I really appreciate your being here. I've heard that you're also an excellent typist and we really need your help."

"Yes, I typed all of my late husband's term papers when we were at university together before the war. He wanted to go to medical school, but got called up in the last days of the war. We got married before he was to report to the front, and though I've never heard anything from the government, I received a strange letter from America telling me that he'd been killed."

Mary O'Daugherty sat bolt upright and then heard the rest of Anka's story. "From America? Where in America?"

"Well, the first was from your state of Louisiana, but then I began to receive other letters, a few from the State of Massachusetts, more from Indiana...then back to Massachusetts. Only one of them told me about my husband's death. The others had no letter in them, just a money order in American dollars made out to me. This has been the only reason that Pappa, Mama, baby Katherine, and myself have been able to survive. The SS had taken most of our animals and seed stock toward the end of the war, and we would have had nothing to eat if this money hadn't been coming from America."

Mary was very pale by now. When Dan had come to Europe over semester break looking for Major Shadow, he had told her the other side of that same story one night after many bottles of wine...complete with the letters from Louisiana, Boston, and South Bend. It was, she thought, a very cruel twist of fate that had brought this child to seek work at her nursing office. She needed to think about this; she needed time to put the whole thing together in her mind. How much should she tell this woman/child? How much should she tell Dan?

Anka Richter...that's why she thought she knew the name, because on that same evening when she and Dan had been drinking, he had told her the story of how he had killed Anka's husband, and the heavy remorse he continued to feel over what he'd done.

CHAPTER FORTY-SEVEN

Mary's Moral Dilemma

Mary needed to think this thing through; she needed to talk with someone, but who? Who could she trust to advise her, to listen to her, and whose judgment and good common sense she could rely on? Brian was her boss and her lover, but she couldn't trust either his judgment or his ability to keep quiet about the whole thing.

Who could she trust? Who could she turn to for advice? Who knew her and Dan Fleming? More importantly, who could give her the advice she needed to deal with the situation? Dan had mentioned a priest friend of his at Notre Dame, a Father Fitzgerald, or something like that...Fitzgibbons or...no...Fitzgibbon; that was it, Father Fitzgibbon, his hall rector...Cavanaugh Hall at Notre Dame...or was it Zahm Hall? Dan had spoken with admiration about this priest, how much he trusted him, how close he felt to him.

"Thank you, Anka, that's all for now.

"Sarah, could you show Anka where she'll be sitting...across from the conference room, the office just across the hall, where we keep the older files. I'd like her to help catch us up while you and I work on the current stuff that comes in.

"Thanks, Sarah, I appreciate it."

"Go with Sarah, Anka. She'll show you where you're going to be working and just what it is that we're trying to do here. If you have any questions I'll try to answer them for you."

"Thank you, Major O'....Thank you, Mary. I'm sure that I'll be very happy working here for you."

"Sarah, could you close the door on your way out, and if anyone other than the colonel calls, could you tell them that I'm in a meeting and left orders not to be disturbed?"

"Yes, Ma'am."

When the door was closed, Mary went scrambling through her purse for the letter with the newspaper clipping that she had shown to Doctor Casey the previous afternoon.

"Ah...I knew it was there."

"Dan Fleming, Zahm Hall, Notre Dame, Indiana," in Dan's distinctive handwriting, was the return address in the upper left corner of the envelope.

Sitting at the typewriter on the stand beside her desk, Mary O'Daugherty began typing on her unit letterhead, addressing the piece of paper to "Rev. Father Fitzgibbon, Rector, University of Notre Dame, Notre Dame Indiana."

"Dear Father Fitzgibbon," the letter started, "We've never met, but I'm a nurse, and a friend of Dan Fleming. I had helped him locate your Father Porcelli, the amnesia victim who was a resident at our hospital. Dan has told me that he holds you in high regard, and how much he values your advice and friendship. So, I'm writing to you today to seek your advice on a matter of extreme importance to Dan and to a woman I've recently come into contact with. Fate has thrust me into the middle of this matter, and I don't know what to do.

"I know that Dan has told you about how he killed Heinrich Richter towards the end of the war when Richter fell into his foxhole in the middle of the night, and how he's been sending money anonymously to Richter's widow and child every month.

"Well, through some bizarre twist of fate or Providence, Anka Richter just walked into my office, assigned to work here by the base personnel office and the hospital commander.

"She briefly told me her story when we met and I was dumbfounded. Of course, I couldn't say anything, but I can see the aching in her heart to learn the fate of her husband. I also know the aching in Dan's heart because he had killed her husband.

"Can you help me, Father? What should I do? I look at this sweet and innocent young mother and widow, and though she doesn't know it, I hold the key to what she wants. But, I know that Dan, because of his tremendous guilt and shame, hasn't revealed himself to her or explained how it is that he comes to send her money every month. While I don't want to betray Dan's confidence, (as Dan may have told you, there's a very strong emotional bond between us), it'll tear me up to watch this child's suffering, knowing that I hold the key to her peace.

"Father, I need your advice. How can I honor the confidence that Dan has placed in me, while every day I watch the suffering of the widow of the man he killed and who he's been supporting?

"Please help me, Father!"

She signed it, "Yours in Christ."

The letter went out in the next day's mail. It would find its way to the Notre Dame campus in a matter of three weeks, and into the hands of Father Fitzgibbon on a Saturday evening, after another Irish victory sparked by Charlie Costanza and Dan Fleming.

The priest read and re-read the letter a number of times. The wisdom of Solomon that the letter's writer was invoking was in short stock, and he was at a loss as to how he should respond. It was a moral dilemma, unprecedented in Fitzgibbon's experience or his scholarship. How do you recommend cutting the baby in half? He needed to pray on this and to meditate, seeking God's help in resolving this conundrum.

"She signed it 'Yours in Christ,'" he kept thinking to himself. "She must figure that I'm an archbishop or something."

CHAPTER FORTY-EIGHT

Father Fitz Makes a Very Big Mistake
and Dan Suffers the Consequences Of It

The problem of this Army nurse in Germany kept returning to him no matter how hard he had tried to concentrate on reading his office or on preparing for his Monday morning class. Betray Fleming and cure the widow, or ignore the widow, and maintain Fleming's good faith ruse? How to characterize the situation from a moral point of view? Does one "good" trump its concomitant "bad"? Which "bad" is worse and which "good" is better? The more he thought of it, the more he was inclined to present the problem to his Monday class in Advanced Problems in Moral Theology. Not only would he benefit and learn from the discourse...this was a very bright, very experienced, and very committed group..., but it may help Mr. Fleming come to some resolution of the problem in his own mind.

"Yes, that's it," he thought to himself. "I'll present the issue to the class on Monday afternoon and be guided by their collective wisdom."

Monday was cold and rainy, a particularly gloomy atmosphere to begin the week on the Notre Dame campus. Father Fitz concluded his opening prayer and then addressed his afternoon class.

"The law of unintended consequences, ladies and gentlemen, is something that we occasionally come across in the course of our lives. It's less of a philosophical problem than it is a concrete problem when it does manifest itself. It's the type of situation that we can speculate about and discuss in class, but one we can never really understand until it confronts us during the course of our lives.

"Let me give you a hypothetical:

"A young soldier called to arms by his country kills another young soldier in combat. The other young soldier was likewise called to arms by his country. Before dying, the one soldier shows his killer a picture of his wife and child, and the surviving soldier, overcome by remorse, takes it upon himself to anonymously support the bereaved widow and child. He discloses his situation to a close woman friend who by happenstance comes into a relationship with the widow of the deceased soldier. The widow is in constant anguish about the fate of her husband and the source of the regular sums of money she receives from the anonymous donor. The close friend of the surviving soldier is inclined to reveal the information she knows, thereby comforting the widow, but betraying the confidence of her friend, the surviving soldier. Her other option is to sustain the confidence she has been given by the surviving soldier, and allow the widow to continue in her anguish and suffering.

"Well, class, does the law of unintended consequences apply here? Surely, there's no harm in comforting a widow, but on the other hand, one should maintain a confidence. Maintaining the confidence will allow the widow's suffering to increase, but alleviating the widow's suffering will entail violating the friend's confidence.

"Well, what say you?

"Mr. Dalrymple, it's good to see you back. I trust you had a productive summer. What do you think?"

"I did, Father, thank you.

"I think that by maintaining the confidence, the friend is allowing, not causing, the widow's grief. There's no unintended consequence because there's been no precipitous act. Disclosing the privileged information is an affirmative act that leads to the unintended consequence of breaking the privilege."

"Thank you, Mr. Dalrymple. Miss Chrysler."

"The poor widow suffering because she doesn't know the fate of her husband should be the primary concern. It would be an affirmative act to disclose the information, but the good to be gained by the disclosure would far outweigh the harm caused by violating the confidence. Maintaining the confidence would only exacerbate the pain and suffering of the widow."

"Saying and doing nothing then, in your view Miss Chrysler, is a positive act?"

"Father, there's a semantic difference here, but it's all word-play. The friend can prevent a far greater harm by acting, and her failure to do so would, to my mind, cause the greater harm."

"Mr. Fleming, you're awfully quiet today."

"I think I'll pass on this one, Father."

"Oh come on, Fleming, you have an opinion on everything," teased Flanagan, his classmate.

"Look, I don't want to deal with this. It's a personal matter. Lay off, Flanagan! I don't want to talk about this."

"Gentlemen, gentlemen, peace please! Mr. Flanagan, what should the holder of the confidence do in your opinion?"

"Well, Father, I agree with Miss Chrysler, the greater harm will occur to the widow…."

"Did you ever think of the pain the release would cause to the other guy, the guy who's carrying all the baggage, the guy who murdered the other soldier, the guy who made the woman a widow?" Dan's voice had been increasing to the point where he was almost screaming, and then he suddenly started sobbing in front of the class.

"That'll be all for today, class. There'll be a test next class on the first three chapters of the Aquinas book."

Dan sat with his head in his hands on the top of the classroom desk as his classmates filed out. His eyes were closed and he continued sobbing softly. The priest came over, sat in the seat next to him, and softly placed his arm on Dan's shoulder.

Bolting upright in his chair, Dan exploded at the other man.

"You had no business telling the class about that! That's my private hell that I shared with you in confidence. How dare you tell them about my pain, my torture!"

"I didn't mean to identify you with the hypothetical."

"You knew it was me you were talking about! You should have known that would set me off!" Dan was now screaming at his priest friend.

"Dan, I didn't mean to cause you pain. I have a problem that I don't know how to resolve. I thought that I'd get the class' opinion to help me respond to the problem."

"Whose problem is this anyway?" asked Dan. Who's this person who holds the confidence that apparently he's afraid of betraying?"

"It's not a "he" Dan; it's a "her." Mary O'Daugherty wrote to me because she knew that we were close. I don't know how it happened, and I'm about to reveal another confidence, but the wife of the soldier you killed is a civilian employee at the hospital in Germany where you found Father Porcelli."

"You can't be serious! This can't be true!"

"I'm afraid it is. Anka Richter, Hans Richter's widow, started working at Mary O'Daugherty's hospital in the record room. Your friend, Mary, needed help in her office to straighten out a backlog of files, so Frau Richter was assigned there. Apparently, Mary and the widow have developed a friendship, and Anka confided in Mary about the pain and torment she's been experiencing not knowing how her husband died, and why some anonymous stranger who has the answer to her pain is sending her a check every month.

"Mary wrote to me asking for advice about what she should do. It tears her up to witness Anka's pain, knowing that she holds the key to eliminating it, yet at the same time she doesn't want to betray the confidence you've placed in her by telling Anka your story."

"Father, I can't do this. I know that you want me to authorize Mary to tell the widow what she knows, but that'd destroy me. I couldn't live with myself. I'm a murderer, Father! I killed an innocent man! You knew that!"

"Wait, what did you tell Mary?"

"I haven't told her anything yet, Dan. I just got her letter a short time ago and I've been wrestling with it. It was stupid of me to raise the issue with the class. I should have known that it would trigger pain in you. I'm sorry that I ever raised it. I should have told you about the letter and asked you how you wanted it handled."

"I wish you'd done that, Father. I can't tell you what I feel like right now. My demons are crowding together in my head, pushing to escape and poison the rest of me. I don't know what to do. I don't want to cause this woman any more pain than I already have, but I can't face her. I can't confront her and say, "Hello Frau Richter. My name's Fleming and I killed your husband, Heinrich, and made your child fatherless. Nice to meet you. Nice weather we've been having, isn't it?

"I can't do that, Father! I can't! I can't!"

"Dan, I've screwed this up enough. I shouldn't tell you what to do or how to handle this. But, I think you should at least authorize Mary O'Daugherty to disclose what she knows to the widow. That will bring her peace, and you won't have to confront her."

"Oh no! No, Father! She won't be content until she faces me, looks into the eyes of her husband's killer, and asks me why. 'Why did you kill the only man I've ever loved, a good and decent man who bore no malice to anyone, a man who would have been a wonderful father to the child that he had never met, and will never get to meet because you murdered him; a man who would have been a wonderful doctor, curing pain and suffering?'

"I can't do that, Father. Don't you see that disclosing what she knows would only be the first step that would eventually lead Anka Richter to confront her husband's murderer?

"I can't let Mary do this, Father! I can't."

As he said this, the normal class bell rang, and other students started walking into the room for the next scheduled class in that space. The two men left separately, each going in opposite directions.

Dan's prowess on the football field started to decline after this incident. There were reports filtering back to the athletic department that Dan had been seen during the week after curfew at some of the bars near campus. On at least one occasion, it was reported that Charlie Costanza went out looking for his roommate and had to drag him back to campus. Dan's grades were slipping too. He started missing classes and, for the first time in his college career, started failing quizzes.

CHAPTER FORTY-NINE

Father Fitz Enlists the Help of Marie LaFleur

It was on a Wednesday evening before the Columbus Day weekend that Father Fitzgibbon placed the call to Boston.

"Hello, Chicago operator, this is the Boston operator. I have your party in Boston on the line."

"Hello, South Bend operator, this is the Chicago operator. We have your party in Boston routed through and on the line."

"Thank you, Chicago. Father, go ahead, your party's on the line."

"Hello, is this Marie LaFleur?"

"Yes, speaking. But you'll have to speak louder...I can barely hear you." "Yes, Miss LaFleur," the priest said in a louder tone, "this is Father Fitzgibbon from Notre Dame. I'm a friend of Dan Fleming."

"Is Dan all right, Father?" Marie's anxious tone revealed how she felt about Dan.

"Yes and no. He's not in any immediate danger, but something happened that has pushed him back into despondency and despair about his experiences during the war. I believe that he's told you about the German soldier he killed in the last days of the war?"

"He did, Father, but what's wrong with him now? What's he doing to himself?"

"It's a long story, but he's started drinking again, missing classes, failing tests. And he's in danger of being thrown off the football team. The only reason he hasn't been thrown off the team and expelled from school is because of the intercession of his roommate with the coach, and my intercession with the Dean of Discipline. But, we can only help him for so long.

"I know that the two of you are very close, and that he's young Daniel's father. I was wondering if you might write or call him to see if he'd listen to what you have to say."

"My God, Father! This is terrible. How did it happen? And of course I'll intervene."

"I'm sorry, Marie...your last transmission broke up. Could you repeat what you just said?"

"What precipitated this, Father? What set Dan off?"

"I'm afraid I caused it. I feel terrible, but I got a letter from a nurse that Dan had known in Germany."

"Mary O'Daugherty?"

"Yes, that's her. Dan told you about her?"

"How he had met her during the war and how he reconnected with her when you sent him to look for Father Porcelli; yes Father, I know about the relationship between Dan and O'Daugherty."

"Well, about a month or so ago I got a letter from Major O'Daugherty telling me that the widow of the German soldier that Dan had killed was working for her in the hospital in Germany as a civilian employee.

"The widow's in agony, not knowing how her husband died, and why some mysterious stranger is sending her checks every month from America, a mysterious stranger who had told her that her husband was dead. She finds it devastating that someone knows what happened to her husband, but won't tell her how he met his death.

"Mary O'Daugherty has compassion for the widow and wants to tell her, but she won't violate Dan's confidence. She wrote to ask me what she should do.

"I didn't know, so stupidly I presented the situation to my class as a hypothetical, hoping to get some insight that may have eluded me. That's what triggered Dan.

"The whole thing's my responsibility and I feel horrible about it. I never should have brought the situation up in front of the class. I've spoken with Dan's roommate and he doesn't know what to do either. More than once he and I have brought Dan home from one of the bars in South Bend after closing, covered in his own vomit, and soaked in his own urine. It's bad, really bad, and I'm the cause of it.

"I'm calling in the desperate hope that you can intervene and bring Dan back to himself...help him escape from the demons that are now running his life."

"Father, I don't know what to say. I don't know if you know this, but Dan and I have been talking about getting married. We both have ghosts and demons from that accursed war, and we both understand what they can do to us. Whenever my demons are in danger of catching up with me, I pick up young Daniel, hold him close to me, and sing some of the French lullabies that my mother sang to me as a child. That's always worked for me by pulling me into the present and out of the horrors of my past.

"This helps me to skip over the bad part of my life...not forget it, because it'll always be there and it's part of who I am today, but I can keep it from overwhelming me....from suffocating me."

"Marie, Dan can't keep his past from overwhelming him. He's desperate for something like you just described. He's stuck in his quagmire of terror from his past and just wallows in its guilt and pain. It's self-destructive, and it'll eventually kill him if something doesn't bring him out of it.

"I know that you love Dan, and he loves you. If anyone can reach him and help him, you can. Please call him, and if you think of anything further that I can do, please call me. Again, I feel terrible because I caused this...."

"You didn't cause it, Father, the insanity of the war caused it, and when we step into our pasts and relive that insanity, it can drive us mad as well.

"We conjure up our own reality and superimpose it on ourselves and on a world that doesn't understand it, that never had to face it. Dan and I, and from what I've heard, yourself, are members of an elite club, a club of madmen who've faced evil and the horrors of war, who've seen the death of innocents, and we're destined never to lose that imprint, that branding on our flesh....on our souls.

"I'll follow up, Father. I'll be in touch with you. Thank you, Father. Good-bye."

The overnight express train to Chicago hummed in rhythm along the tracks as the young woman and child struggled to find sleep, the one because of her fears and distress, the other because he knew that his mother was upset.

Arriving in South Bend at 6:00 A.M. on the connecting train from Chicago, the mother and child had no problem hailing a cab.

"Where to, lady?"

"The Notre Dame campus, please, Cavanaugh Hall."

"They usually don't let us drive on campus, but maybe the security guard at the main gate will let us in because you have luggage and a young child with you.

"You're early for the game. Usually they don't start arriving till Thursday. I don't know if you heard it up in Chicago, but there's some talk in the South Bend Trib that Fleming might not even dress for the game this week.

"I don't know what's going on there, but he went like a house on fire for the first three games, and then didn't even get in last week. There must be something that we don't know about."

"Yes...I'm sure there's something."

"Sorry pal, I can't let you on campus."

The retired South Bend police officer working at the security booth at the main gate was polite, but all business.

"My passenger has a young child and luggage and needs to get to Cavanaugh Hall."

Leaning into the back window of the cab, the officer addressed Marie. "Who are you visiting at Cavanaugh, Ma'am?"

"Father Fitzgibbon, but it's a surprise and he's not expecting me."

"Just a minute, please."

Flipping through the campus directory for his number, the security officer soon had Father Fitzgibbon on the line.

"Yeah, hi Father, this is Mike at the security booth at the main gate. There's a woman here in a cab with a young child to see you...says you're not expecting her."

. . .

"Yeah, I don't know, hang on Father.

"Ma'am, what's your name?"

"Tell him it's Marie LaFleur and young Daniel."

"Marie LaFleur and young Daniel."

. . .

"OK, Father, I'll send them around."

. . .

"Yeah, you're welcome, Father."

Turning to the cabby, the guard handed him a campus pass and said, "Here's a pass. Turn it in when you leave. You know how to get to Cavanaugh?"

The driver nodded and drove through the gate and around by the golf course, the ROTC building, and Sacred Heart Church and the Grotto, finally pulling up at the loading dock behind Cavanaugh Hall.

"How much do I owe you, driver?"

"That'll be $2.50, Ma'am."

Handing the cabby three one-dollar bills, Marie said,

"Thank you, keep the change."

As the cab pulled away, Marie wondered whatever had possessed her to pack young Daniel and leave Brighton for South Bend on such short notice. Next

Monday would be Columbus Day and a school holiday. The nuns at school would be on a retreat Wednesday, Thursday, and Friday of this week before the holiday, so she and Daniel were able to leave Tuesday afternoon after her 1:00 P.M. class.

"Excuse me!" she called out to a passing student. "Can you tell me how to find Father Fitzgibbon?"

"I can, Ma'am. Follow me and I'll take you to his office. Here, let me carry your bags."

Entering the hall, they moved down the long corridor to the rector's suite. "Thank you...thank you for your help."

The knock was not unexpected and instead of a bellowed "Enter!," the priest, dressed in his black cassock, hurried to the door to see the young woman and child standing before him.

Holding out her hand, she said, "Father, I'm Marie LaFleur, and this is young Daniel."

"Well...I...I'm...thank you for...I didn't expect you, but I'm grateful that you're here. Where are you staying?"

"I left somewhat abruptly and never made reservations anywhere."

"I'll set you and your son up with a room in the convent at Saint Mary's....if that's all right with you. I'd have you stay on campus here, but this is an all-male school and I'm afraid it would cause great scandal."

"That's fine, Father, I'm familiar with convent life, and it'd be a welcome experience.

"When can I see Dan?"

"Leave your bags here and we can walk next door to Zahm Hall. Let me call the rector to let him know we're coming."

"Hello, Father O'Conner, this is Father Fitzgibbon next door. I'd like to come over for a visit with Dan Fleming. I have a woman and child with me. Could we use your office, and could you have someone get him down there without telling him why?

"Good, thanks, Tom. We'll be over in about ten minutes."

CHAPTER FIFTY

Dan Fleming Hits Bottom and
Then Skyrockets to the Top Again

Opening the door to his office, Father O'Conner called out to a student who was starting to unlock the door to his room.

"Mr. Lynch, would you do me a favor? Go up to the second floor and ask Dan Fleming to come to my office right away. Tell him it's important."

"Thanks, I appreciate it."

Taking the stairs two at a time, Steve Lynch knocked loudly on the door of room 245.

"Hey Fleming, O'Conner wants to see you in his office right away. He said it's serious."

Slamming the door open, Dan confronted the shocked fellow student, grabbed him by his shirt, and both pushed and carried him across the hall, slamming him against the wall across from his doorway.

"What the fuck are you doing, you asshole!" yelled Dan. "For Christ's sake, it's not 7:30 in the morning yet! Are you fucking crazy! Go away and leave me alone!"

Undaunted by being slammed against the wall, Lynch said,

"Fleming, he's serious! I don't know why he wants you, but it's important; he means business. Come on, let me down before you kill me."

"Tell him to go fuck himself! I'm fed up with his bullshit and this whole fucking place!"

Dan then turned to re-enter his room, when he saw Charlie Costanza's massive hulk standing beside his bed, shoulders squared and ready to confront him.

"Why did you do that?" Charlie's tone of voice made it clear that he meant business.

"It's none of your fucking business! That's why!"

Charlie rushed toward the smaller man, picking him up and slamming him against a wall locker. As blood started flowing from a massive cut in his cheek, Dan went berserk and began pummeling Charlie in the face and throat, knocking the larger man to the ground.

The noise brought half the floor to the room, and as Mike Lynch pushed through the door, half a dozen others followed him to see Dan on top of Charlie, choking his roommate. Collectively, the swarm pulled Dan off the now unconscious Costanza.

Charlie was still breathing, but barely, and the realization of that shocked Dan back to reality.

"Oh, my God! Oh, my God! What have I done! What have I done! Charlie...Charlie!"

"Nice job, football hero, you fucked up again!"

Five of the six students faced Dan, screening him and keeping him away from Charlie. Lynch, who was a trainer, administered to the prostrate form on the floor, and Charlie slowly began to regain consciousness.

By now, Dan was in tears as the phalanx of students began moving him toward the door and shoved him out of his room.

"Charlie...Charlie?"

Dan was slobbering all over himself by now, his hangover long evaporated by the surge of adrenaline.

"Get out of here, asshole. Go see what O'Conner wants. We'll take care of Charlie. Go ahead...screw...you asshole!"

Crumpling against the wall across from his doorway, Dan sat sobbing until Steve Lynch came out of the room.

"Charlie's OK. Why don't you go slap some water on your face and get down to O'Conner's office. We'll take care of things up here."

"Steve...I'm sorry...I'm sorry...I'm..."

"Yeah, yeah, Dan. I know...I know, Dan. You'd better get moving though. We'll take care of things up here. Charlie's gonna be OK. He's gonna be OK. You'd better get down to O'Conner's office, but clean up first."

Going into the second floor bathroom, Dan looked in the mirror at the blood caked all over his face and neck where Charlie had slammed him into the wall locker. He cleaned himself as best he could, using a towel that someone had left in one of the showers.

The cold water stung as he slapped it onto his face. He didn't like the face that looked back at him out of the mirror. It wasn't a successful student-athlete in that mirror. Looking back at him was the gutter drunk that he was fast becoming for the second time in his life. The bleary, bloodshot eyes in the mirror couldn't be his, he thought, they must belong to some zombie, someone long dead, but not yet entirely dead...at least in his own mind. Was it his mind that was thinking this? Was that his image in the mirror? Dan wondered if he were in fact dead or alive, dead or insane.

"I'm not dead, Dan. I'm still alive and living in your brain."

"Come on, Fritzie, go back to your grave and leave me alone. I can't deal with you right now. I killed you and I almost killed my best friend in the world just now. Go away, Heinrich, for Chris' sake, and stay dead. Smitty, you too, stay dead, would you. I love you, but for the love of Christ, would you stop haunting me and stay dead."

"Dan, you fucked the woman I love. Why did you do that, Dan? Why? Why?"

"Smitty, I didn't mean for it to happen...it just did, and we had a child together, Smitty. If I had known, I would have named him after you, but Marie...I mean, Yvette, named him Daniel, Daniel Charles."

"I understand, Dan. I'm going to leave you alone for a little while now, Dan. I'm going back to my grave with my friends who were in that tank crew. They're pretty crispy now, Dan. We all got together in hell, Dan. You'll like it here, Dan. We'll be waiting for you."

"Jesus Christ, Smitty, why don't you stay dead and stop tormenting me? Why are you haunting me? I love her, dammit! You loved Yvette. I'm in love with Marie. She's a different woman now, Smitty. She's not the woman you loved, Smitty...she's a different woman now.

"For Chris' sake, Smitty, leave me alone, will you? Get back to your goddamned grave and stay there. I can't deal with you anymore. I love you, Smitty, but you're driving me fucking nuts."

Opening the door from the bathroom, Dan walked down the hall toward the stairway. Reaching the rector's door, Dan tried to compose himself, not knowing what awaited him inside.

His knock was met with the muted and soft voice of Father O'Conner. "Come in."

The voice was soft, tentative, like the speaker didn't quite know what would happen after the door opened. What did happen would be burned in Dan Fleming's memory for the rest of his life. Lined up before him in front of the rector's desk were Marie and young Daniel in the middle, flanked by Father O'Conner to their right, and Father Fitzgibbon to their left.

"Oh, my God! Oh, my God! Oh, my God! Marie...Daniel...oh, my God..."

"Da-dee, Da-dee!" Daniel bent to pick up his son as he rushed toward him.

"Marie...why are you here...what's happening?"

"Father Fitzgibbon called me, Dan. He told me what you've been doing to yourself, the drinking, the letter from Mary O'Daugherty....the whole thing.

"I thought we had agreed that we'd tell each other when our demons started acting up.

"Dan, I love you. I can't let you do this to yourself....to all of us, Dan; young Daniel and me, as well as yourself. I need you, Dan. Daniel needs you. Dan...You're bleeding! Dan...Dan..."

Marie went to the father of her child and put her arms around him and their young son. She buried her head into his chest so tight that she could hear his heart pounding.

"Father Tom, can we step outside for a minute or two? I think we can find some place we should be right now other than here."

"Yes...ah...yes...right...good idea," Father O'Conner responded to the other priest's suggestion.

Closing the door behind them, Father O'Conner gave his fellow priest a quizzical look.

"So...I'm sure there's quite a story behind this?"

"Tom, if I told you all of it, you'd never believe it. Suffice it to say that I hope this is the end game in Fleming's struggle between good and evil, between hope and despair, between choosing to live or allowing himself to die, slowly by inches.

"This is a universal veteran's struggle that Fleming's going through. You'd have to be a combat vet to understand what just happened in that room, and what's been happening to Dan Fleming over the past month. We all have our demons, Tom, and there's nothing we can do to eliminate them. We learn to live with them....to realize that they come from a world where we once lived...a world that we don't have to keep reliving.

"We don't have to beat our ghosts and demons, Tom. They're part of who we are, of what we've seen and done....a part of what we've become. All we have to do is to learn how to let them sleep peacefully without disturbing us. I have an old friend of mine; we called him "Dead-Eye" when we were in the service. He visits me from time to time, but I've learned not to get all wrapped up in trying to struggle with him. He is who he is. We've both done what we've done, but that's over now. That was then and this is now. I just let him pass through my mind. I don't wrestle with him. I let him see that I'm still here, and then let him pass out of my mind back to his grave. He only stays if I don't let him go....if I trap him and struggle with him. Fleming has to learn how to do that. It's the only way to deal with the ghosts and demons of our past, Tom...the only way."

"I hope you're right, Father. You certainly know more about this stuff than I do. I was too young for the 'Great War'. I was studying in Rome during the most recent conflict and got stuck there for the duration.

"Fleming's implosion is widely known on campus. I'm not sure how this woman and child figure into the whole story, but I hope they can help him."

"The child is Dan's son, and the woman is the child's mother."

"Ooo...kaaay...," said Father O'Conner, as he drew out his letters. "That's probably more information than I need to know."

"It's very complex, Father."

They walked over to the caf and finished a cup of coffee before they returned to the Zahm rector's office.

Marie opened the door to Father Fitzgibbon's soft knock.

"Come in, Father! Come in! I think we've worked things out. I think things will be OK now, Father.

"Father, can I see you outside in the hall for a minute...privately?"

Stepping outside, Father Fitz held the door for Marie. The other priest stayed in his office with Dan and his son.

"Father, I have two favors to ask, two things that taken together will help Dan. First, I want you to marry us this weekend. Also, I know you've got connections with the War Department. Can you get me a free flight to Europe over Christmas vacation...to Germany, and to the hospital where Mary O'Daugherty's stationed?"

"I don't know about your second request. I'll do what I can, but I don't know if I can pull it off.

"About your marriage, there's normally a waiting period in Indiana after you apply for a marriage license and take a blood test for syphilis. But, I know the person at Saint John's Hospital who does the blood tests for the county, a working nun, so if we can get you down to City Hall before noon, I think I'll be able to legally marry you on Sunday. Will you be around that long?"

"I'm supposed to leave early Sunday morning to head up to Chicago and back to Boston. I'll try to change it to leave on Monday, and try to get a substitute to cover my Tuesday class. I'll be around for my one day honeymoon."

"I'll work on the plane, but I may not have an answer for another month or so."

"Father...it's important...no crucial...that Dan doesn't know anything about my trip to Europe."

"I don't understand, but I won't say anything to him about it."

While they were talking, Dan had become transformed, playing with his son and telling Father O'Conner how wonderful it was to be a father.

Father O'Conner was clearly uncomfortable, though Dan, in his delight, didn't notice that. When Marie and the other priest returned to the room, Father O'Conner excused himself, saying that he had an appointment.

After O'Conner had left, Dan turned to Marie and Father Fitz and said, "I know what a disappointment I've been to the two of you. I wish I could do what you want. It'd be a ten-ton load off of my shoulders if I could confront the widow and tell her how it came to be that I killed her husband. But, I can't bring myself to do that now...maybe someday, but not now....maybe not ever.

"I wish I could tell you or Mary to go ahead and tell Anka who I am and what happened, but I can't do that. I'm dragging the chains of that man's death around with me and I know that all I have to do is to drop them and let them go and fall to the earth. I know that intellectually, but for whatever reason, I can't bring myself emotionally or psychologically to do that. I wish I could, but I can't."

Walking slowly past Marie and Father Fitz, Dan said, "Father, I think I should leave now," and seeing the disappointed look in Marie's face, he added, "There's some unfinished business that I have to deal with upstairs. I shouldn't be long. I'd like the two of you to get to know each other. I shouldn't be too long, and I'll be back as soon as I can."

Picking up young Daniel, Dan left the rector's office and took the stairs two at a time, with Daniel in his arms.

"Da-dee bleeding," Daniel said to his father, as Dan carried him up the stairs. "Daddy's OK, Honey...Daddy's gonna be OK."

Reaching the door of his room, Dan hesitated and then knocked. By now the crowd had dissipated, with everyone off to class or back to bed.

"Come in."

Charlie's voice was neither angry nor hurt, just mellow, as if nothing untoward had happened that morning.

"Are you sure you want me back?" Dan asked as he entered the door.

"You know, Roomie, you're tougher than you look. I haven't been whacked like that since the Michigan State game last year."

"Charlie, I'm sorry. You know some of that shit I've been carrying around?"

"Da-dee carry shit, Da-dee carry shit," came the echo in the room, and Charlie broke out laughing. "Yeah, what about it?"

"I'm afraid it's been getting the better of me over the last month or so."

"Tell me something I don't know. I can see that.

"And who's your young friend? Did I hear him call you 'Da-dee,' or was that my head ringing from the concussion you just gave me?"

"Charlie, I'd like you to meet my son, Daniel. "Daniel, this is your Uncle Charlie."

"Uncle Charlie," the child said, looking at the massive, furry hulk standing before him.

"Uncle Charlie big."

"Big Uncle Charlie," Dan retorted, echoing his son, and both he and Charlie started laughing together

"Charlie, I've got a favor to ask you."

"As long as it doesn't end up with you sucker punching me again." "That was no sucker punch; it was a good clean shot."

"You know...I'd kill you in the ring," said Charlie.

"You and what army? If the Germans and the United States Army couldn't manage to kill me, what makes you think you could do it?"

While they were talking, young Daniel had picked up a football that was sitting in a corner.

"That's a football, Daniel."

"Football, Big Uncle Charlie?" Daniel asked, somewhat puzzled by the object that he was cradling into his stomach, trying to keep from dropping it.

"Seriously, Charlie, I'm sorry for the way I've been acting. I want to ask you to forgive me and I do want to ask you a favor."

"Of course, I forgive you....you dummy."

"Da-dee dummy," the echo repeated.

"I've not put up with you this long to give up over one knuckle sandwich. What's the favor? Plenary indulgences are hard to come by, and they don't come cheap either."

"Charlie, Marie's here with Daniel. We want to get married Sunday afternoon in the hall chapel, and I'd like you to be my best man."

"Jeeze, Dan, that's awful sudden, if you ask me. I'd be honored. I can't think of any better offer that I have on Sunday, although I'd have to shave and probably dress up. But, what about your brother Tommie?"

"Charlie, under normal circumstances I'd ask Tommie, but like everything else in my life, these aren't normal circumstances. Normally, I'd ask you to be an usher…but, if you don't mind being the second best man, I'd love to have you as my best man."

"Well, if I'm gonna to be your best man, when do I get to meet the bride?"

"Marie's downstairs with Father Fitz in O'Conner's office. Come down when you get dressed. By the way, do you own a neck-tie other than the one you wear to dinner?"

"I don't think so?"

"I don't either. I'll stop by Gilberts today and pick up a couple of them for us. It wouldn't be fitting to have a wedding without the groom and best man wearing clean neckties."

As he was being carried toward the door in his father's arms, young Daniel turned to Charlie and said, "Bye-bye, Big Uncle Charlie."

Father Fitz had wrangled the blood tests and license in time for the Sunday afternoon ceremony. The groom and best man were standing on the altar with Father Fitz, both looking like they had just gone through a meat grinder. They were waiting for the bride to come down the aisle on the arm of Ed Miller, who had agreed to give her away. Janet Miller was sitting in the front row pew, waiting for her husband to do his duty and join her.

Outside in the hall, unknown to all the participants except Charlie, was the entire Notre Dame football team and most of Zahm Hall.

Dan and Charlie did look pretty beaten up, not from their fracas earlier in the week, but from the game against Michigan State the previous day.

Marie and young Daniel had gotten to see their first game of American football the day before the wedding.

The Irish had been in a scoreless tie with Michigan State for three quarters. Towards the end of the game, though, they were down by a field goal and were being badly outplayed. Dan had spent the entire game on the bench, looking occasionally in the stands to see if he could spot his fiancée and their child. Finally, toward the middle of the fourth period, the starting right halfback twisted his ankle on second down and had to come out of the game. The ball was on the Notre Dame 12 yard line, and it was third down and 13 yards to go to get a first down. It was clear that the Irish were being outplayed by State. They were beaten, worn down, and on the point of collapsing.

"Fleming!" the coach yelled, "go in for Howard. Call a 32 slant and try to get the punter more room to get the ball out of our end zone – now go….go!"

A 32 slant play had the blockers on the right side block in towards the middle, and then the full back would follow Dan into the hole. Dan was a blocking back on this play, and his mission was to clear the linebacker out of the way of the fullback.

"44 in for 42!" Dan yelled to the referee, reporting into the game to replace the injured Howard.

Entering the huddle, Dan could see the worn and beaten looks on the faces of his teammates. They had been hammered both on defense and offense by the bigger State team and were at the point of breaking, of giving up and being routed over the last part of the fourth period.

"32 slant," Dan told the quarterback and the huddle.

"No! No!" The fiery voice of Charlie Costanza exploded into the huddle. "44 dive! Dan, I'll clear that big son-of-a-bitch out of your hole if it kills me.

"Take it out to the 25 for the first down and then go all the way!"

It was as if a lightning bolt had hit the huddle. Charlie had energized the team on the field and each of them was ready to reach down to that place where men go when they are beaten, the place where they know they have to go if they're to survive. And they each knew what they had to do.

The center snapped the ball and the quarterback handed it off to Dan, who momentarily bobbled it, turning completely around to recover it.

On the sideline, the coach was screaming in exasperation, "32 slant, you idiot! What are you doing?"

Turning his back to the line in order to recover the ball, Dan completed his 360 degree turn, only to see the State linebacker lining him up to plant him in the end zone for a two point safety. Then, out of nowhere, the massive figure of Charlie Costanza moved the linebacker out of the hole as if he'd been hit by a locomotive. Charlie drove the State player into and through the center of the MSU defensive line, effectively screening half of their team out of the play, and giving Dan a clear lane down the right side of the field.

Breaking to his right, Dan sailed up field, past the chains, past midfield, with half of the Notre Dame sideline running along behind him.

The roar from the stands reached a crescendo as Dan cut sharply to his left at the Michigan State five yard line, just as he was about to be tackled by the MSU safety, leaving the safety flying through the air toward where he thought Dan would be.

As he cut behind the outstretched legs of the safety and ran over the goal line, Dan knelt on one knee and gently laid the ball on the turf, oblivious to the crowd noise and the roar of his teammates running towards him. Dan simply couldn't breathe. A month of smoking and drinking had left its mark on him. As he caught his breath and turned to stand up, he was shocked to see his entire team pouring in from the three-yard line, not just the team that was on the field, but entire Notre Dame football team from the sidelines. Fans began jumping out of the stands and onto the field, running to pile on the celebration. On the bottom of the pile, Dan lay on his side with his knees up to his chest so he could breathe. It took the referees, the police, and the stadium announcer fifteen minutes to clear the field and line the teams up for the point after.

Spotting his roommate in the melee, Dan ran up to him, "Charlie, they should give you the game ball after that block!"

"Nice run, Roomie. I only opened the door for you."

"No, Charlie, you made the whole thing happen. I thought their safety was going to catch me on the five when I cut back. If I hadn't been drinking and smoking for the last three weeks, I bet I could have outrun the safety too."

"It looked good, Dan. When you cut back, you left him floating, tackling air where he thought you'd be."

Moving to the sideline for the kick-off, Dan was approached by the coach, the one person who had not come up to congratulate him after the touchdown. "Fleming, I want you in as center linebacker in Howard's place when they get the ball. And you'd better be prepared to run a lot of laps at practice on Tuesday and explain to me the difference between a 32 slant and a 44 dive."

"But coach...but coach..."

"No 'but coach' to me! This is a team effort. You do what you're told or you're off the team. Do you understand me?"

"I understand you, coach..."

"Now get out of my sight!

"Nice run...by the way..."

Dan stayed in at linebacker for the rest of the game, and with his fresh legs, made a lot of tackles when his weary teammates were out-muscled or out-positioned by the State offense. State had moved the ball, but when they threw a screen pass on third and two from the Irish five yard line with twenty seconds to go, Dan read the play and stepped between the receiver and the ball, intercepting it to end the game. When the final whistle blew, the scoreboard read: "Home – 7, Visitors – 3".

The next morning, the Chicago Tribune ran two pictures of the touchdown play. One taken from the sidelines showed Charlie Costanza stacking up the State defensive line like so much cordwood. The other, taken from the press box, showed the State safety floating in air as Dan ran into the end zone behind him.

The headline read: "IRISH EKE OUT VICTORY OVER INSPIRED SPARTANS."

Unseen by Dan or Charlie, the paper lay at the end of the bench next to Pattie-Jo, who was Charlie's guest at the wedding.

Ed walked Marie and young Daniel together down the aisle. The ceremony was short, and when Father Fitz pronounced them husband and wife according to the laws of the State of Indiana, the chapel doors opened and the place flooded with well-wishers.

Ed Miller shook Dan's hand. "Congratulations and my best wishes to the two of you." Having said that, Ed reached into his pocket and passed an envelope with a check for one hundred dollars to Dan.

This would be the last time that Dan would see Ed alive.

Father Fitz had arranged for the dining hall to cater a small reception for about two hundred or so of the couple's closest friends; well, actually, they were all friends of the groom.

The married couple – and their son – spent their wedding night in a hotel in South Bend, planning for their future and talking about how they'd deal with their demons if the need ever arose again. Young Daniel wasn't sure what had happened that day and the day before, but he sensed it was important to his parents.

"The sad part of all of this, Dan, is that I'd love to tell everyone I know that we're married, but the nuns would fire me if they ever found out. Only single women, chaste, single women, are fit to teach proper young Catholic girls. I guess I'm chaste, sort of. You were the last man that I was with and look at the beautiful outcome of that liaison. Maybe there's a petition I could file somewhere to become retroactively chaste. When you become a lawyer, would you look into that for me?"

"You know...that was the first time for me. I hated you as much as I lusted for you, and now I love you far more than both of those emotions combined. We're very lucky, Marie. For all that we've been through, we found each other; we're blessed because of that. And you're my sanity; you're the person who can reach into my soul during the depths of my despair and rescue me from myself, from my demons, the ones that I seem to allow free reign over.

"It's funny, Marie, after all that I've been through, I've become a hero playing a schoolboy's game, a diversion for millions of people on a Saturday afternoon when they listen to the game on the radio, and on a Sunday morning when they read about it in the papers.

"The millions of men, women and children who died in the cauldron of that war are all forgotten, but some college sophomore's in all the papers in the country because he ran nearly the length of a football field and no one stopped him. But, you know, Honey, football will help us to a better life. It pains me to be away from you and Daniel, but they'd probably throw me out of here if they 'officially' knew what was going on. Everyone knows we're married, but no one knows it."

Dan took his new wife and child to the station Monday morning. She was wearing the ring he had given her. His was back in the dorm room. He only put it on his hand at night when he was going to sleep, when he was flooded with dreams of Marie and Daniel.

Instead of incinerated German soldiers and a man with a bayonet in his chest, Dan's dreams were now filled with visions of he and Marie watching Daniel grow up, picnicking together in the summer, and coasting in the winter. A glorious life was ahead of them. And when Smitty or Heinrich walked by, Dan said hello, acknowledged their presence, and watched as they gradually drifted out of his mind.

His ghosts didn't own him anymore. There was just one exception though, and he still fought to keep her bottled up in a corner of his mind. His greatest fear was that she'd escape and confront him. "Why did you kill my Heinrich?" she'd ask him, and he knew that question would destroy him. But, Heinrich, Smitty, and the rest of his ghosts just floated in and out, now less and less as he stopped struggling with them and learned how to accept them. They were part of his past; he could accept that fact now and learn how to live with it. That was then, and this was now.

But, she was different…

CHAPTER FIFTY-ONE

Marie Tries to Solve Mary's Dilemma
and Help Ease Her Husband's Suffering

"Frau Richter, my name's Marie Fleming. My husband was a soldier in the United States Army. He killed your husband, Heinrich, in combat during the last days of the war. He's terribly grief stricken about your husband's death and the role he had in it. It's my husband who's been sending you a check every month because he promised your dying husband that he'd look out for you and baby Katherine."

"Wha...What's this you're telling me?"

Anka fell into the nearest chair, not so much in shock as in disbelief that here this stranger arrives, talks with Major O'Daugherty for a few minutes, and then the two of them confront her with this...this story about the greatest loss in her life...a story that makes no sense...a story that's implausible...

"Anka," Major O'Daugherty broke in, "Anka, I know Mrs. Fleming's husband, and I know that what she says is true. When you first started working here, I realized that you were telling me the other side of a story that I already knew. I wanted to tell you what I knew, but felt I couldn't violate the confidence that Marie's husband had placed in me. I wrote to a priest friend of her husband asking for advice. He got in touch with Marie, who decided to come here to tell you herself as one woman who had been scarred by the war to another. Marie lost her whole family to the Nazis in France. She met her husband during the war. They married and have a young son."

"I came, Frau Richter, because the pain of your husband's death is with my own husband daily. He's the person who sends you a check every month, like

311

Major O'Daugherty says, because he's distraught over having killed your husband."

"How…how did this happen?"

"My husband was in a well-camouflaged foxhole in the woods in front of his unit's position. He was posted as a sentry to protect the unit against any attack at night. In the middle of the night, your husband and other members of his unit were moving through the woods, and your husband fell into my husband's foxhole. My husband…I'm sorry to have to tell you this…and I don't know any other way to say it…stabbed your husband with a bayonet. Your husband died in my husband's arms, the two of them praying together; you see, they're both Catholic. Your husband died shortly after that. My husband buried him and has been overcome with remorse ever since. He wakes up nights calling out your husband's name from his sleep. My husband is haunted by what happened that night, and by what he did. He feels tremendous guilt and feels a responsibility to provide for you and Katherine as best he can."

There was silence from the other woman. She sat, slumped in the chair and motionless, crying silent tears to herself for what seemed to the major and the wife of her husband's killer to be an eternity.

Finally, she composed herself, straightened her dress, and stood holding the back of the wooden chair for support.

"Why are you doing this and not your own husband?"

"Simply because this is slowly killing him; eating away at him. It overwhelms him at every stage of his life, no matter what he does to put the war behind him. He carries your husband's death and other ghosts with him. He knows no rest. He's a good man who didn't ask to go into the service. His country called him, and he answered the call, much like your own husband. My husband's a good man who frankly doesn't have the courage to face you and tell you the story that I just recounted. He doesn't know I'm here, and the reason I came was both to try to reduce your own suffering, and in some way maybe to help my husband deal with his own torment.

"I'm carrying the pain of this war much as you, only not as bad."

"Easy for you to say!" Anka snapped at Marie. "You have your husband and child. You'll have a life together. You'll have the chance to grow old together. Your husband robbed me of that chance. I'll never be able to have that comfort in my life. My daughter will never have the comfort of having her father to love her, to help and advise her in life. No, your husband took all of that away from us, and from the world.

"Heinrich wanted to become a doctor to help save peoples' lives, to help people, to heal the sick. He was very much like Jesus and never had a selfish thought in his head. He went into the Wehrmacht because he was drafted. He didn't want to go, but he had to go to protect his country. It was his duty!"

Now her anger had turned to tears.

"Why did he die? Oh God," she screamed, "Why did he die?"

Then she collapsed again into the chair. Mary O'Daugherty approached her and placed her hand on Anka's shoulder. The widow composed herself and rose once again.

"Well, Mrs. Fleming, you've done what you came to do. I hope never to see you or your husband again."

"I'm sorry, Frau Richter; I'm truly sorry, as is my husband. Like your Heinrich, he was only doing what he was called to do. Like your husband, he's a kind, gentle, and sensitive man who got pulled into the madness of war, and I'm afraid it's driving him insane."

"Well, if it's driving him insane, at least you have him. I have no one. Will your husband tell me where Heinrich's body is buried? I will have him taken to our village for a proper burial with his family, and when my time comes, I'll be with him again in death."

"I'm sure my husband would do that, except he doesn't know that I'm here. I'll send you a post office box in the United States for you to reach me, and I'll send mail to you in the care of Major O'Daugherty. Is that workable for both of you?"

"I mean that...I never want to see you or your husband again, but I must deal with you if you're to help me locate Heinrich's burial place. You can contact me through Mary. I think you should go now."

"Again, I apologize for the craziness that has cursed all of us, and you in particular.

"Major, can I see you outside for a minute? Good-bye, Frau Richter."

Once outside of the office, Marie spoke first.

"I know how this poor woman must feel. Carrying all of this around in her head, and then out of nowhere a strange woman arrives and tells her how her husband died. I can feel her hurt and pain; it's an experience I've gone through in my own life more than once during the craziness and horror of war. My own parents were good and decent people who tried to act in the best interest of their country, and who were murdered by the Nazis because of it. I was a nun in a convent before I met Dan. All of the other sisters were murdered by the SS. I was the only one who survived because I was raped by a young German soldier who fell in love with me, as perverted as that may sound. He was killed by a partisan sniper, who then committed suicide when the building he was hiding in was torched by the SS.

"I know the horrors of war, Mary...may I call you Mary?"

"Yes....yes, please do. I feel like I've known you for a long time, Marie. Your husband and I ....before you were married...helped each other deal with those horrors that we'd both experienced. He told me about his friend, Smitty, and what had happened to you after the nuns were all killed, and how he had hated you because his friend had loved you..."

"Mary, it was a different world then, a world of madness, a world of life and death, and nothing much in between; a world where I was with a man, probably many men, who'd be dead within the week. Dan had told me about the time when he first met you, and your experience on the triage ward with men who soon would be dead.

"We've all been through this same hell, Mary, in some ways worse than Anka, but in no way could our losses be as bad as hers. I'm drawn toward this woman because of our shared pain and suffering. Be tender towards her, Mary. I sensed in that room that there was a bond between the two of you, a closeness of two women who'd suffered great pain, and who had found some measure of peace between themselves."

"I've only worked with Anka for a short time", said Mary, "but you're right, there's something between us, something I've never felt towards another person, an openness and honesty about her and her life. I think you coming here and telling her how Heinrich died will help her break out of the trap she's been in since she received Dan's first letter. When she finds her husband's body and returns him home to be buried with his parents, she...."

"Mary, how can I do that? I mean, I don't want Dan to know about my trip here. How can I get her the information she needs to find her husband without Dan finding out about my trip?"

"Have you met Dan's former commanding officer who lives in Indiana?"

"Yes, yes, that's it. Ed Miller should know where Dan killed Heinrich Richter. They were both serving together, and from what Dan has told me, the site's in close proximity to the village."

"Marie, are you staying at the hotel downtown?"

"No, I have no reservations. Father Fitz wasn't able to tell me when I'd be leaving. He gave me 45 minutes notice to get to the airport. They were holding the flight for me when I got there. I had arranged with Dan's mother for her to take young Daniel on short notice. Nothing happens to me in an orderly manner. It was a good thing that I had a bag packed for myself and a diaper bag to take to Dan's mother's house."

"Then you'll stay with me." "No, I can't do that."

"Of course you can. I have plenty of room, and you look exhausted." "I am pretty tired. You're sure I won't be an inconvenience?"

"Not at all"

"Let me give you the key and have a driver take you there. I have some work to do here, and I'd like to be here for Anka to answer the questions I'm sure she'll have."

Picking up the phone, Major O'Daugherty asked her secretary to get a car and driver over to the hospital. When she was finished, she turned to Marie and said, "The motor pool will have a car here within fifteen minutes. Here are the apartment keys. The top one lets you in the building and the bottom one, the silver one, lets you into the apartment. It's on the second floor, just as you get to the landing."

"Mary, did I do the right thing by coming here and telling Anka?"

"Of course, you did. You know, your husband was always talking about how different people create their own reality. Well, you've just changed Anka's reality for the better. You've given her the tools to finally put her past behind her and to create a new life for her and Katherine in the future. She has no excuse now for wallowing in the past. She should be able to look to the future for her and her daughter without the fate of her husband constantly eating at her."

"I wish I could do that for my husband...put Heinrich Richter into his past."

"I haven't told Dan this, but I've been offered a position at Boston General Hospital. I think I'd like to take it and to bring Anka and Katherine with me."

"That concerns me because Dan will be in Boston for the summer, and in fact we've been talking about him transferring to Boston College so we could be together. The problem, though, is that if he loses his football scholarship, he'll have to use the GI Bill to pay for the rest of his college, and we won't have money for him to go to law school.

"But, in any event, if Anka's in Boston, I'm sure that she'll search Dan out to confront him..."

"How can you be sure of that?"

"That's what I would have done if Heinrich Richter had killed Dan instead of the other way around. I'd be afraid that Dan would have a complete breakdown if he ever met Anka. The whole reason I came here was to reveal the cause of her husband's death so I could ease the pressure on her, Dan, and all of us. I don't think it'd be good for her to come to Boston."

"I'm sure that I'll be able to control her. I've been looking at newspaper advertisements for apartments on Beacon Hill. I think if we get one near the hospital, Anka will have no need to go exploring the suburbs...."

"Anka and Katherine are going to move in with you?"

"We've talked about moving to Boston. She's interested in doing that. I've not asked her to move in with me, but it'd be difficult for her to afford rents in Boston on the salary they propose to pay her. I'm trying to get her more money, and may have some small success, but it won't be enough to support her and Katherine in their own apartment."

"Is that appropriate in America....for two unmarried women to be living together? In France, that could suggest an improper relationship between the women."

"Oh, no, no...not at all. It's quite common for unmarried women to live together in America, sharing an apartment to save on the rent. I'm quite attracted to Anka and her daughter, but only as one would be attracted to one's sister and her child. 'Auntie Mary' is what Katherine calls me. She's such a sweet child; no one could help but love her."

As she said this, Mary's face turned crimson.

"Well, I'm concerned that Anka will try to find Dan, and I'm worried about what he'll do...to himself...if that happens."

Soon the driver from the motor pool arrived. Mary walked Marie down to the car and Marie couldn't understand why she opened the front passenger's door and spoke harshly to the driver. "Soldier, be sure you don't flood the carburetor! It's important that Mrs. Fleming get to her destination."

"Yes Ma'am," the driver said submissively, before he slowly pulled away from the hospital and drove to Mary's apartment.

Marie slept the rest of the day and all through the night, waking at 6:00 the next morning, only to find Mary dressed in uniform and making breakfast.

"Ah, you're awake. In the Army, the work day starts at 0:700 or 7:00 AM. How do you like your eggs?"

"Over lightly is the way you say it in America, thank you. Teachers in America get up early too. My first class usually starts about 7:30.

"Mary, we're close to the French border; is there any way for me to get back to the village I left from to go to America? Rene and Anna Bourque took me in when I was pregnant and with no place to go. They were like parents to me, and I'd like to visit them now that I'm so close...if that's possible."

"That shouldn't be a problem. There's an American base just over the border. I could arrange for a driver, as long as it isn't the lout that drove you today."

"I sensed your displeasure with him."

"He's an idiot. To make a long story short, when Dan was here a year ago to identify Father Porcelli, the Corporal who drove you today was supposed to drive us away as soon as Dan had pointed out the priest. He stepped too hard on the accelerator and stalled the car. It was a disaster and resulted in Porcelli having to be restrained and placed in a strait jacket. I can barely trust him to drive you here from the hospital, and I'd never let him take you out into the country."

"You do think you can get me a ride though?"

"No problem. When do you want to go?"

"If we could make it tomorrow, I'd stay overnight and be back in two days to catch my flight back to America."

"Consider it done. I'll have someone pick you up at 0:600. I think you have about a six hour drive. I'll arrange for your driver to stay overnight at the American base there and pick you up the next morning for the trip back here."

"That'd be wonderful, Mary, absolutely wonderful."

"Do you know how to contact the Bourques?"

"No, but once we get to town, I can show the driver how to find their farm house or the mayor's office. I'm so excited just by the prospect of seeing them again. I feared when we said goodbye, that it'd be forever. They won't believe that I'm back here. We've exchanged a few letters, but that's not the same as seeing them in person."

"OK, I'm off to work to give the American taxpayer some return on his investment."

CHAPTER FIFTY-TWO

Anka Confronts Marie

The day flew by for Marie, walking around the small German town, a place where she couldn't have even thought about visiting a couple of years earlier. She was exhausted when she got back to Mary's flat late that afternoon. It was the good kind of exhaustion though, where your lungs have been filled with clean air, and your muscles stretched. She rested on the bed in Mary's room and soon fell asleep. After an hour or two, she woke to hear the lock on Mary's front door turning.

"Mary?" Marie shot up in bed, startled out of her sleep. "Mary, is that you?"

"It's not Mary. It's Anka."

"Frau Richter, what are you doing here?"

There was no answer, but as Marie got out of bed, she saw Anka moving swiftly into the doorway to the bedroom, blocking any exit.

"Why are you here?" Marie asked again. But her question was met by silence from the young German widow; silence and a deep, intent glare, a glare from the eyes of a woman crazed with grief.

"The Bible says, 'an eye for an eye, a tooth for a tooth.'" As she said this, Anka pulled Mary's service issue 45 automatic pistol from under her coat.

Marie, having faced death so often in the past, wasn't panicked by the sight of the crazed woman with the pistol. She thought to herself, "I must keep her talking if I have any chance of ever seeing my son and husband again."

Anka's eyes were glazed over, as if she were in a hypnotic trance.

"Anka, I know how you feel; I know what you're going through and why you want to kill me. You want to do to my husband what he did to you, and you think that by killing me, you'll be avenging Heinrich's death. Anka, if you kill me right now, I won't be able to help you find where Heinrich's buried."

At this, the widow started crying. In her own subconscious, she wanted to kill Marie to avenge Heinrich's death, but when Marie put that into words, she devastated Anka. The widow's whole nature was gentle and compassionate, but she'd been overcome by grief, anger, and her blood lust for revenge. When Marie confronted her, it was as if someone had punctured a balloon with a pin. The air of hate and evil inflating that balloon rushed out, propelled back to the netherworld of human nature from which it had come. The hell that was Anka dissolved into tears as she threw the gun down on the bed and hurled herself into Marie's arms, sobbing uncontrollably.

"I want to kill you! I want to kill you! I want Heinrich back! I don't want to live without him!"

"Anka, Anka." Marie called her name as she cradled the despondent widow, gently pulling her head to her chest.

"Anka, I'm so sorry about this. I'd do everything in my power to bring Heinrich back, not only for you, but for the sanity of the man I love."

Anka pulled away and dove for the gun she'd discarded on the bed. Grabbing it, she turned it on herself, quickly pulling the trigger, only to hear the click of the hammer hitting on the empty cylinder.

In despair, she threw the useless weapon at the dresser by the doorway, breaking its mirror. Standing there, staring into the broken mirror and looking at her own reflection in its jagged glass, Anka collapsed into Marie's arms.

Marie slid the unconscious woman gently to the floor before retrieving the weapon. Marie removed the clip from the pistol's handle and then ejected the round that had failed to chamber. She opened one of the drawers in the bureau and dumped the bullets into it. She then took the gun into the living room and hid it under one of the sofa cushions. Taking the now-empty clip, she hid that in the back of the refrigerator in the kitchen.

Finally going back into Mary's guestroom, she lifted Anka onto the bed.

Shaken by the whole episode, Marie collapsed on the couch in Mary's living room.

Things weren't quiet back in South Bend either. Ed and Janet Miller were continuing to meet with Father Fitz in the hope of saving their marriage.

CHAPTER FIFTY-THREE

When All Else Fails...

"Look...I know...., this is tough for me too."

Ed and Janet were getting ready for their third meeting with Father Fitz. At the end of their last counseling session, he'd asked them to go home and make two lists to discuss the next time they all met. "I want each of you to list all of the reasons that you were attracted to each other, and then list all of the problems that are now interfering with that attraction."

He knew that they'd discuss the lists with each other before returning. They did do that and had reached the Gordian Knot, or rather, the two Gordian Knots that were interfering with their relationship.

"Ed, I can't tell this man that I don't want to be a mother and a wife anymore, that I want freedom, independence, and my own career. I know I can't have that...that my duty is to you and the children, but I can't help feeling the way I do."

"Janet, if we're going to make this thing work, we've both got to be honest and open with him. How can I tell him that I'm drinking too much because I murdered my commanding officer? If I can do that, I think you should tell him how you feel."

"Look, I know we've got to work through these things, individually and together, but we've got to include Father Fitz in that discussion.

"Janet, there's something else I've got to tell you...you and Father Fitz. That story, the one I told Dan Fleming about how I killed Stadholm, isn't entirely true."

"But you killed him in self-defense....you had no choice....he would've killed you."

"No, Janet, that's not how it happened. I...I...murdered Stadholm."

"Ed, what are you telling me?"

"I went to his tent....he was drinking, and we argued about sending the entire platoon into the valley rather than a small squad. He pulled his pistol out, pointed it at me, and said he should execute me for insubordination.

"I stood there.

"He chambered a round. Then, laughing, he placed the pistol on his field desk. He had a demonical look on his face...I see that look every night.

"'Miller...I've not heard that Fleming's dead yet.'

"I didn't know what he was talking about. I'd heard about the confrontation between the two of them over Dan's Silver Star recommendation, and that Stadholm had ordered Dan to lead every patrol from then on. But, I was shocked at what came next. Stadholm looked me in the eyes and said, 'Lieutenant, I want you to kill Fleming. If he isn't dead by this time tomorrow, I'll court martial you for cowardice in the face of the enemy by refusing to lead your platoon into battle. A dead Fleming or a court martial for Miller, your choice, Lieutenant.'

"At that point, I was consumed by an overwhelming hate, very deep, very intense, but very calm. Slowly, deliberately, when Stadholm turned to take another swig of whiskey, I picked his .45 off the desk and, pointing it at his temple, I pulled the trigger.

"There was only a click; the round he'd chambered was a dud. He spun around as I ejected the dud and chambered a new round. We struggled for the gun, but in spite of the adrenaline surge we both felt, he was falling down drunk, and I easily overpowered him and trained the pistol on him.

"He pleaded for his life, trying to barter it for money, promotions...shoot him in the leg so he'd be removed from command...'Don't do it, Ed...Ed, we're different from them....you and me....we're officers. They're scum. Ed, if you want me out of here, shoot me in the foot. I'll say it was an accident while I was cleaning the weapon. Please...please...don't do it, Ed. They're scum...Fleming's scum...we're different.'

"It was easy then, like making a decision on whether to insure a business when it seems to be the right thing to do. It seemed clear to me then that the right thing to do....the only thing to do....was to kill Stadholm."

"Oh Ed," Janet held her husband tightly on her chest and they both cried together. After a time, Ed Miller lifted his head.

"I've never told that story to anyone. The first sergeant only heard the gun discharge, but he hated Stadholm like the rest of the company, so he concocted the suicide story. He said that it was only a matter of time till one of the other company members killed him, and that I'd taken a lot of pressure off of all of them that day by doing it first.

"I've never confessed that, and it tears me up that I intentionally murdered that man. No matter how evil he was, I had no right to kill him."

Ed started crying again.

"It's all right, Ed, it's going to be all right. I understand now, Ed, and it's gonna be all right. You've got to tell Father Fitz. He'll understand and give you absolution."

Getting more in control, Ed said, "I don't know how anyone can forgive what I did, Janet. I think I'm beyond forgiveness."

"Tell him, Ed, that's the only way to get this off your back."

"I can't, Janet."

"Then I'll tell him for you! Get your coat on; we're going to be late."

It was fortunate that the sitter had picked the girls up earlier. Ed sat silently on the passenger side of the car as Janet drove out to campus. He didn't speak till they were standing side by side outside the door to the priest's office. Janet had raised her hand to knock when Ed stopped her.

"Janet...I'll tell him!"

"I can do it if you want."

"No, I have to do it myself...I know that."

"OK, I'm with you...you know that. And I'd marry you again, even with all of the shit you're carrying around...in spite of it. I don't want my freedom, Ed....I want you...I want what we had together...."

Ed's knock was met by the invitation to "come in" from the priest, who was expecting them.

Chapter Fifty-Four

Mary, Anka, and Katherine Move to America

"Well, Brian, I guess this is goodbye. You've been a good friend and a good commanding officer."

"Hopefully not a bad surgeon either, Mary. You know I'm sorry to see you go. I'd do anything to keep you here."

"I have to do this, Brian. Opportunities like this come along once in a lifetime...if you're lucky. I'll be building a medical surgical emergency ward from scratch. It'll be totally up to me how to put it together, how to design it, staff it, and assign specialties.

"For me, this is a chance to revolutionize emergency medical treatment along the lines of the article I wrote in the American Medical Journal last year. We've broken all sorts of new ground in the treatment of wartime casualties, and I hope to take some of what we've learned and apply it in a civilian setting.

"I'm excited to be going. And yes, you know that I'll miss you, but I could never be happy as an Army wife or officer, and you'd never be happy as a civilian. Your career....your whole life is in the Army. Your whole life IS the Army. We had a good time while it lasted, but like all good things, this too has come to an end.

"I hope that when you're stateside, Brian, you can make it up to Boston so we can have a mini-reunion...replay some of our past."

At that, the Colonel's ears perked up and his eyes brightened.

"You can be sure of that, Mary. If I'm within 3,000 miles of the East Coast, I'll be sure to make it up to Boston."

"You are a cad, Brian, but I've loved the time we've had together, and I've learned from you. I'm a better nurse from all we've been through together."

"That too, Mary...I'm glad you're a better nurse...I was hoping you'd say that you were a better lover after meeting me."

"That too, Brian."

Mary stood up from the chair in front of the colonel's desk. He was sitting in the other chair across from her and he rose when she stood up. He grabbed her and pulled her close to him, starting to unbutton her blouse.

"No, Brian! For Christ's sake, leave me alone!" she said, forcefully pushing him back. He almost went over the top of his desk from the strength of her shove.

"Mary, I can't live without you!"

"Well you goddamn well better learn how!"

At that, she turned to leave her commanding officer's office.

"Mary...you've got a cute ass."

"Fuck you, Brian."

She stormed out the door, slamming it behind her.

"Is everything OK, Ma'am?" the young WAC secretary asked, hearing the ruckus and sensing that all was not well between her boss and the former chief of nursing.

"It's OK now, Corporal. Good luck with Colonel Octopus for the rest of your tour here."

"Yes, Ma'am. Thank you, Ma'am; I know what you mean."

Mary grabbed her duffel bag from in front of the secretary's desk and hauled it out of the office, leaving that place for the last time.

"Better lover...huh!" she thought to herself. "If I wasn't on top, it was like making love to a log....better lover...yeah...."

The car from the motor pool was waiting in front of the hospital, and to no great surprise, it was the same driver who seemed to pop up whenever Mary had needed a lift.

"Well, Corporal, it's good to see you again. I would have thought that your tour would be up and that you'd be a civilian by now."

"Oh no, Ma'am. I love the Army, Major, and I re-upped so that I could stay here. I'm a lifer, Ma'am, and I'm going to stay here till I retire or they throw me out."

"That's good, Corporal; you fought the Germans and now you're staying in to fight our old friends the Russians...I admire you."

Missing the sarcasm in her remark, the driver straightened himself in his seat and replied, "Yes, Ma'am! Where to, Ma'am?"

"The airport, Corporal; thank you."

Neither of them spoke on the twenty minute ride. He puffed with pride over this officer's recognition of his obvious patriotism, while she was lost in thought about her relationship with Anka, especially after the episode with Marie Fleming.

Mary had returned to her apartment after work to find Marie asleep on her living room couch, a broken mirror on her dresser, and parts of her issue .45 caliber pistol hidden all over her apartment. Anka was there too, collapsed on Mary's bed amid a pile of shattered glass on the floor.

Marie explained that Anka had intended to kill her to revenge Heinrich Richter's death, but couldn't bring herself to do that. Then she had tried to commit suicide, but the weapon had misfired (probably because Mary hadn't cleaned it or used it for over four years.)

Mary and Marie had carried Anka from Mary's bedroom to the guestroom where Marie had been staying. Marie's suitcase lay packed and open on the floor, ready to be closed in the morning when she was scheduled to drive over the border to visit the Bourques before leaving on her flight back to America.

As they carried her, Mary noticed Anka's thighs. Their creamy white color reminded Mary of a porcelain doll that she had played with as a child. That doll had been her favorite, and she cried and cried when one of her brothers had thrown it up in the air as if it were a ball he was hitting out of his hand with his baseball bat, shattering it into tiny pieces.

Anka had become Mary's new porcelain doll. Anka and Katherine were closer to Mary than any sister and niece could be.

Once, when Anka had confided her grief to her, Mary had pulled the younger woman close to her and held her as she sobbed and sobbed on Mary's chest. Mary remembered her embarrassment as she felt slightly aroused by the feel and scent of the younger woman in her embrace. Not like with Brian, but a deeper, more profound intimacy, an arousal that she knew was wrong for both of them, a feeling that she knew she could never surrender to.

Yet, her attachment to this woman-child and her daughter had remained strong, strong in a platonic sense, an emotional attachment between two women, both of whom were bereft of love and facing a world alone, by themselves. Anka at least had Katherine to love her, and as devastated as she was over the death of her husband, this child was her reason for living. Mary had said that to her over and over when she awoke after that horrible evening.

"Anka, you must never try this again. You have to stay alive for Katherine's sake. She needs you and you can't abandon her! You have to make a new life for her, Anka, for her and for yourself!"

"Mary....Mary....I'm sorry...I'm sorry, I'm so sorry! I tried to kill her so that her husband would feel what I'm feeling; pain from the death of someone you love more than anyone in the world. But, when I couldn't do that, when I couldn't kill Fleming's wife, I tried to kill myself and failed. Then I just collapsed.

"How could I have done this to Katherine? What would have happened to her had I been successful with either one of those attempts?

"Mary, you've got to help me! You've got to help me get out of this place, out of this country. This place reeks with the stench of evil...evil and death!"

Again, Anka had melted into Mary's arms, burying her head between Mary's breasts.

Mary fought her impulse to arousal this time, but the thought of her shattered porcelain doll wouldn't leave her mind. She would not...she could not...allow Anka to become another shattered porcelain doll in her life.

"It's all right, Anka. It'll be all right. I'll get you and Katherine out of here, Anka. I'll get us all out of here."

"We're here, Ma'am."

The Corporal's voice snapped Mary out of her reverie.

"The airport, Major...we're in front of the terminal."

"Oh...Oh, thank you, Corporal. I'm afraid that I was lost in thought."

Taking her duffel out of the tan staff car's trunk, the driver handed it to Mary, stepped back, and saluted her smartly. Mary returned the salute.

"Have a good flight, Major."

Thank you, Corporal. Good luck with your career."

The crowd at the airport was like being at a circus. People were moving in random directions, some running, and most hurrying with a sense of urgency from the awareness that if they didn't hook up with their flight, the plane would likely leave without them. They were almost exclusively male, and most of them were in one uniform or another of the victorious fighting forces from all over the world, and flying to destinations all over the world.

Mary was worried. She had arranged for Anka and Katherine to get passage to America on a military flight. It hadn't been easy, but knowing that Marie had been able to fly as a civilian buoyed her. Mary kept pushing and pleading her way through the bureaucracy till she found a colonel who was familiar with the byzantine Army travel regulations, and who found an exception that allowed relatives of active duty military personnel to fly stand-by if there was space available on a flight.

A word to a friendly former patient, the corporal at the airport who was responsible for scheduling and filling the flights, and two additional seats were "reserved" on the flight that Mary was scheduled to take back to the States, where she was to be mustered out. The seats were reserved as open but not available, but in reality, they were reserved for Katherine and Anka, who could take them as they became available at flight time...at least that was the plan.

Now, though, Mary was getting anxious about how she would find Anka and Katherine in the sea of humanity before her. As she wandered through the crowd looking for them, Mary heard the public address announcer state, "Major Mary O'Daugherty, please report to the Airport Commander's office. Major O'Daugherty, please report to the Airport Commander's office!"

"What could go wrong now?" Mary thought to herself, as she hurried to the installation CO's office.

When she entered the outer office, Mary saw a desolate Anka and her confused daughter sitting on a couch while an Air Force sergeant was speaking to them.

Mary approached the group and said, "Sergeant, I'm Major O'Daugherty. I was just paged by the P/A announcer."

"Yes, Ma'am. These two German nationals here requested that I page you."

"I'm sure that only one of them requested it, Sergeant; the other is a child of three."

"Yes, Ma'am. They both have stand-by tickets, but my manifest sheet shows that the flight's full and there's no space available. The older woman over there said that you could explain something to me that would allow them on the flight, and I tried to tell her that there was nothing I could do because all of the seats were already accounted for. If there's no space available, then there's no space available. I'm sorry, Ma'am, but there's nothing that I can do about their situation. They're "standbys" and the flight's full. There's nothing I can do to get them aboard the aircraft for Boston."

"Sergeant, you should have two reserved seats on your manifest with no names beside them. Those seats are reserved for Frau Richter and her daughter."

"No, Ma'am! They're flying standby. I'm sorry, Ma'am. There's nothing I can do."

"I understand, Corporal...I'm sorry, I understand, Sergeant. I realize they're listed as standbys, but I'm trying to explain that Colonel Croker had arranged to reserve two seats so the flight wouldn't be full and they'd be able to travel with me."

"No, Ma'am, I'm sorry, Ma'am, but those seats are reserved and they're standby. I'm afraid there's no room on the plane for them."

"Sergeant, this is very frustrating for me. You don't have a name or a passenger for either of these seats, so if you don't place them on board, the plane will take off with two empty seats while they're stranded at the airport."

"If it does take off...it does, Ma'am. I don't control that. All I know is what my manifest says, and it lists those seats as reserved. Air Force regulations don't allow me to place a standby passenger into a seat that shows as reserved on the manifest. Those are the regulations, Ma'am."

Mary could see that he was getting angry now and digging in his heels, resorting to the ultimate weapon of an enlisted man in conflict with an officer....the Regulations. She was ready to explode and was fed up with the idiocy of the situation. Realizing that she wouldn't get anywhere dealing with this imbecile, she asked, "Sergeant, who's your next-in-command?"

"Ma'am, I work for Lieutenant Myerson."

"Where can I find Myerson?"

"He's on leave, Ma'am. He won't be back till Tuesday."

Mary thought that she had seen or sensed the start of a smirk on the Sergeant's face at the thought that he would be the highest authority in the situation.

"Who does Myerson report to?"

"Major Ryan. He's in a staff meeting all day."

"Who's above Ryan?"

"Colonel Greene, the airport commander."

"That's his office in there?"

"That's off-limits, Ma'am."

"Maybe to you, Sergeant, but I'm fed up with your intransigence, bordering on insubordination."

At that, Mary moved around the sergeant and started striding towards the closed door.

"Ma'am, don't go in there! It's forbidden! Ma'am..."

Pushing in front of her, the sergeant tried to block her entry to the base commander's office.

"Sergeant, if you don't get out of my way right now, I'll see that you're court-martialed for insubordination and striking a superior officer!"

"I never struck you! That's not true, Ma'am!"

Pushing him aside, Mary entered the base commander's office and walked to his secretary's desk.

Noting the sign, "Colonel James Greene, USAF," on the wall beside the door, Mary approached the secretary and asked, "Is Jim in his office?"

"He is, Ma'am. Who shall I say is calling?"

"Mary O'Daugherty, Major Mary O'Daugherty."

"Is he expecting you, Ma'am?"

"No...no, he isn't, but I'm due to fly out of here within the hour, and I've run into a few difficulties that I thought Jim would be able to help me resolve."

"Ma'am, usually Sergeant Shannon deals with problems that arise with the flight schedules. Have you spoken with him?"

"Yes...yes, I have, but he wasn't able to help me. Lieutenant Myerson's on leave till next week, and though I know how busy he is, I thought that it would only take a minute of Jim's time to resolve the problem."

The secretary had a confused look on her face. On the one hand, she was supposed to screen access to the colonel. On the other hand, this Army major sounded like she could be a close friend of her boss. In the end, she decided that she was in a no-win situation and that it'd be better to interrupt her boss for a stranger than to turn away a good friend of his who was having difficulties.

"Colonel, there's a Major O'Daugherty here to see you..."

...

"No, Sir. I don't know what it's about. She said that she's having some sort of problem and Sergeant Shannon couldn't help her out. Lieutenant Myerson's on leave and Major Ryan's tied up off base all day at a staff meeting..."

...

"Yes, Sir. I know that you don't want to be disturbed. I thought she was a friend of yours...."

...

"Yes, Sir...yes, I will."

Hearing only one side of the conversation, Mary expected to be summarily dismissed, but was both surprised and pleased when the secretary pointed to the inner office door and said, "The colonel will see you now, Ma'am."

Mary's knock on the door was met with almost a pleasant invitation of "come in."

As Mary stepped through the doorway, the secretary thought to herself, "Good job, bitch. You got by me, but I won't fall for that next time."

Saluting the base commander, Mary said, "Good morning, Sir. I'm Major Mary O'Daugherty and I need your help. I'm traveling with two dependents, my sister-in-law and my niece. Since dependents can only travel stand-by, I had arranged to have two seats on my flight reserved so that they wouldn't be filled. Now I'm afraid that the plane will be sent off with the two empty seats while my sister-in-law and my niece sit here till hell freezes over waiting for two empty seats on another flight to Boston.

"Sir, could you tell Sergeant Shannon to allow my niece and sister-in-law to board the flight so that we can all travel to America together?"

"Your sister-in-law....she's married to your brother?"

"That's right, sir."

"Of course...of course...that was a dumb question, wasn't it? Although, I suppose that she could be your husband's sister."

"I'm not married, Sir."

The colonel seemed pleased by this piece of information.

"She's an American?"

"No, Sir. She's a German national with a passport and a visa stamp from the Department of State that allows her to come to America to work."

Mary was extremely grateful to the Boston General Hospital attorney who had pushed through all of the paper work necessary for the Department of State approval to bring Anka and Katherine into the country.

"Sergeant Shannon wouldn't allow them to board the plane and occupy the two reserved seats, is that correct?"

"Yes, Sir."

"Well, the Sergeant's correct. The protocol set out in the regs is that a standby can't bump up into a reserved seat on a flight in the event that the rightful passenger does show up at the last minute.

"Poor Shannon would be in quite a pickle now, wouldn't he, if he gave the seats to your sister-in-law and niece, and then General Danielson and his aide showed up just before takeoff to claim them.

"But, I do see what you mean. You must be on the 09:30 flight to Boston, Otis Air Force Base."

"Yes, Sir, that's right."

Shuffling through a pile of papers on his desk, Colonel Greene removed one of the thin sheets of carbon paper with a copy of a flight manifest attached to it.

"Ah, yes...I have it....here it is. No secret passenger flying under orders. That happens sometimes, Major. Someone on a secret mission will transit through here without his name ever appearing anywhere except on my copy of the plane's flight roster. I'm the only one who knows who he is and I don't ask any questions because my orders come from SHARPE HQ directly.

"I'll help your relatives, Major."

"Private Merriweather, would you have Sergeant Shannon come here as soon as he can? Oh, and would you contact the tower and tell them to hold the 09:30 flight to Boston till it gets clearance from me?

"Thank you."

Shutting off the switch on his intercom, the colonel turned to Mary.

"Shannon was only doing his job, Major. He doesn't interpret regulations, he only follows them. He just knows them and enforces them. That's why they need officers, Mary...if I can call you Mary. You and I are paid to think. We think; we understand the purpose of the regulations, why they were enacted, and when they don't apply to a situation, even when on the face of it, it looks like they do. Poor Shannon, enforcing a regulation against the stated wishes of an officer must cause him a great deal of pain and confusion. He doesn't think outside the four-square box of the regulations, whereas we do. We understand nuance and we exercise discretion where we think it appropriate.

"In my judgment, I think it appropriate to allow your relatives to board that flight, so I'll use my discretion and order Sergeant Shannon to board them."

Before Mary could say anything, there was a knock on the door.

"Come in, Sergeant."

"Sir, you wanted to see me?"

"Major O'Daugherty's two relatives are cleared for the reserved seats on the 09:30 flight to the States. Will you see that they all board the aircraft without delay?"

"Yes, Sir. I'll do that."

"Sergeant. I'd like you to personally escort the three of them to the flight line to be sure that they don't encounter any more delays.

"That's all."

Shannon's face was turning a deeper red as he saluted his commanding officer and turned to leave the office.

"There...you should be OK now, Major. Shannon's a good man....knows and follows the regulations to a 'T,' but doesn't have it upstairs to be an officer. He's a lifer and will retire someday as a Sergeant. It's a shame...really is....

"Anything else I can do for you, Major?"

Responding to his cue, Mary rose from the chair where she had been seated, saluted, and started to turn to walk out the door. Half way through the turn though, she stopped and turned back toward the colonel. Walking coyly over to him, she kissed him softly and gently on his cheek.

"Thank you, Sir. I'll always be indebted to you."

As she was walking toward the door, the base commander stopped her.

"Major...one more thing."

"Sir?"

"You've got a cute ass."

"Thank you, Sir. You know it when you see it. Thank you again."

With that, she slowly edged through the door, where the red-faced Shannon was waiting for her. It took her a second or two to resume her military bearing.

Shannon was holding two suitcases. Anka had two more, and Katherine was wearing a small yellow pack on her back that her grandmother had made for her to take to America.

"Are you ready, Ma'am? I'd get someone to carry your duffel, Ma'am, but the plane's late taking off as it is now. I'm afraid you'll have to carry it yourself, Ma'am."

"That's no problem, Sergeant. Where do we go?"

"This way to the tarmac, Ma'am. Follow me please. Your aircraft's warming up now, ready to approach the flight line as soon as you board."

"Sergeant, I'm sorry to have given you such a rough time, but it's really important for my family to leave Germany with me."

"Yes, Ma'am, I was just following the regulations, Ma'am, and regulations are regulations. But orders are orders, and you heard Colonel Greene order me to place your relatives into the two reserved seats."

"Yes...yes I did hear that, and I do understand, Sergeant."

"This guy is dumb as a stump," Mary thought to herself. "Maybe the colonel was right about him. He was right about one thing anyway...I do have a cute ass."

The pilot of the DC-3 came back to speak to the passengers while the co-pilot remained at the controls.

"We'll take off in about twenty minutes. We got bounced out of our position on the flight line when we were delayed. I hope you all have food for the flight. We'll stop in Ireland to load up on fuel, and then fly across the Atlantic to Gander, Newfoundland to gas up again. Then we'll fly down the coast of Canada, through Maine and New Hampshire, and into Massachusetts, to Otis Air Force Base on Cape Cod.

"For those of you who are interested, I'm scheduled to make the same flight back to Germany next week. It's a lot easier when we don't have to worry about Messerschmitt's or Folke Wolfes diving down on us."

"Captain?"

"Yes, Major."

"How long will the whole flight take?"

"Well, Ma'am, that depends on a lot of things, mainly the weather over the North Atlantic. The meteorologists think we have a good shot at a clean flight with no trouble. I don't know how long we'll be in Ireland or Newfoundland; that depends on how many flights are ahead of us. I think it's safe to say though, that this time tomorrow, you'll be sitting in the sand on Cape Cod."

CHAPTER FIFTY-FIVE

Coming to America, to Boston, to Beacon Hill

The gods were with them, at least the god that Mary was concerned with, and their refueling stops and jump across the Atlantic went off without a hitch. The plane landed at Otis, and after Mary had helped Anka take her and Katherine's belongings off the plane, she went to arrange for them to stay at the women's section of the Bachelor Officers' Quarters. Well, not exactly....

There was no women's section, so the Officer of the Day, who's in charge in the absence of the base commander, ordered the Facilities NCO to stencil signs at the entrance to one wing of the BOQ that read: "WOMEN'S QUARTERS. NO ADMISSION WITHOUT PERMISSION."

Once they were in the BOQ, Anka and her daughter shared a room with two single beds, while Mary had her own room. They all slept for the better part of a day.

For Anka, the whole experience was as if someone from outer space had lifted her and her child out of their world and moved them to another universe. She wondered if she'd ever see her parents again, or their little village. She now owned the Richter farm because Heinrich had no brothers or sisters. His father had left the farm to her, but there was no one there to care for the animals, so she gave them to her parents to use and care for, and she asked her father to keep an eye on her new property on the other side of the valley.

Both of her parents had encouraged her to move, remembering how they had suffered after Germany's defeat in the First World War. Neither of them wanted their daughter and grandchild to relive their privation.

On one hand, Anka wanted to get away from everything that reminded her of Heinrich, but she was also afraid that she'd never see her parents again. And Mary, the woman who had become her benefactor...she felt very close to her, but she was concerned. She sensed that Mary wanted more out of their relationship than Anka could give. Mary seemed attracted to her in a way that made Anka feel uncomfortable. She appreciated all that Mary had done for her, and loved her in a way that women can love each other, without becoming intimately involved.

Anka sensed that Mary was fighting something within herself to keep from loving Anka in another way, a way that would be a mortal sin for two women in that type of relationship. She loved Mary as a sister would love another sister, but she couldn't bring herself to love her beyond that, and she hoped that Mary would understand that. Anka thought that Mary had always felt comfortable with men, and if the rumor going around the hospital was correct, she and the hospital commander were having an affair with each other. But, she was helping Anka and Katherine make a new life. Whatever reservations Anka had about Mary's attraction to her were overcome by gratitude because of all that Mary was doing for her and Katherine.

Anka had always been highly organized, "a very Germanic trait," Mary had joked. She had helped Heinrich with his papers and study materials, and it wasn't long after going to work for Mary at the base hospital that Anka had mastered the obtuse Army record keeping procedures and streamlined the office. This earned the gratitude of Mary's secretary, who took credit for the whole thing, and was likely to be promoted to sergeant as a result of Anka's work. Mary knew, though, who was responsible for the change in her office, and her attraction to this young German widow was only heightened by her sense of organization and self-confidence. To Mary, Anka was at once a waif, the frail widow and mother, as well as the self-reliant survivor who would move mountains to protect her child, as well of the memory of her deceased husband.

Mary, too, sensed that Anka was feeling uncomfortable. Sometimes Anka would look up from her work to find Mary looking at her in a way that made Anka feel uncomfortable. Anka would blink, blush, and look down quickly when this happened. Mary, too, would blush and avert her eyes if Anka looked up too quickly. This had been going on for some time in the office before Mary had decided to leave the Army and take the job at Boston General. And though each woman was aware of it, neither of them had said anything.

Mary's feelings for Anka were always just below the surface of their relationship. Initially this didn't bother Anka, because of the stories of Mary's relationships with men, especially the hospital commander. It had become more of an issue for Anka when Mary told her that she was leaving the Army to take a civilian job at a hospital back in America, and that she'd like to take Anka and Katherine with her. Mary told Anka that she'd like to hire her as her personal assistant at the hospital to help organize the emergency medical department, where Mary would be in charge.

But, for now, the three of them had just crossed the Atlantic Ocean and were spending their first night in America on Cape Cod, a place that Mary had told them was a destination for tourists from all over the country.

The bus ride off the Cape to the Boston bus station was an adventure for Anka. Once deposited next to the Boston Common, Mary hailed a cab to take them to Pickney Street on Beacon Hill. The movers had already set up the furniture that Mary had placed in storage before reporting overseas at the start of the war.

"It would have been cheaper for the War Department to buy me all new furniture than to store this all of those years," she thought, somewhat absent mindedly, as her thoughts wandered back to the pre-war associations the furniture evoked. It was as if the presence of the furniture confirmed that the world was back to normal. Her favorite armchair sat next to a crooked reading lamp. How many hours had she spent there before her plunge into the madness? Joyce, Dickens, Hemingway, all writing about a world, a world she had only known vicariously until she was plunged into the madness of the war. The pain, the hurt, and the suffering they wrote of were now real for her, a part of her world, part of her life experience, not part of some fantasy world conjured up by a writer of fiction.

The words were real for her too. Now she understood; she had experienced the devastation of the human spirit, the despair that grows out of evil, and the fruits of madness run amok. Hers was no longer the world of imaginings; her reality had been altered. The foundation of her life had been irreversibly shaken.

And, now this furniture, it was a vestigial remnant of a life that could no longer be resumed. Having lived in that hiatus from normal human life, a hiatus filled with horror and lived at a base human level where little mattered other than living and dying, with not much else in between. It was a life where she had lived one day to the next in a world of permanent change, a world where the unchanging reality was that everything changed. Every day some would live and some would die; that didn't change. But, every day the various iterations of evil would present themselves in horror under different forms, with different nuances on the changing faces of its victims, in their pain, in their screams, and in the rancid smell of their burned flesh and vision of their shattered bodies.

No, Mary O'Daugherty's life had forever been altered, warped, distorted, and discolored by her trip through hell. She'd never be the same; she never could be the same. Her furniture, immutable as it was, bore witness to and highlighted her own changed reality.

"Mary?" Anka's words interrupted Mary's reunion with the fruits of her previous life.

"Mary, this is such a large apartment, where do you want Katherine and me to stay?"

It was a large three-bedroom apartment, formerly the first floor of a Beacon Hill townhouse that had been divided up into three spacious apartment units.

"Why don't you and Katherine take the large bedroom?"

"We shouldn't do that, Mary. That should be your room."

"No, no, Anka. I think the two of you could use the extra space in the larger room. Katherine could have her own room, but I understand why you want her in with you after what she's gone through. And besides, I've been living in a small apartment or room since I joined the Army. I don't need a lot of space."

"Mary, do you think my parents will be able to come over some time to visit us?"

"That'd be wonderful, Anka. I'm sure that as civilian life resumes, there'll again be a regular ship service between Germany and the United States. Maybe someday there'll even be civilian flights across the Atlantic. I'm sure they'll get here some time, and maybe sometime sooner than we think."

"Leaving my parents will be an adjustment for Katherine. My mother cared for her all day after I started working at the hospital, and I'm sure she'll miss her terribly. That's why I'd like Katherine to be in the same room with me."

"That's fine, Anka, take the large room."

"Mary, what will the future hold for Katherine and me? I don't mean to be selfish, and after all, we are a hardy people...God has been alternately testing and punishing us over at least the past two generations. But, I worry about her, and I worry about us, the three of us. Mary, you worry about Katherine and me; I worry about the three of us. You're like a sister to me. No....no sister would do as much for us as you have. I worry about you, Mary. You've been so strong and without your love and nurture, Katherine and I would have been back in the hills, trying to dig enough potatoes to survive the past winter. Instead, you've opened a new life for us, one where our choices are not between starvation and survival. You've opened us to an incomprehensible world...a world of limitless options...a world that offers a promise to me, but more so to Katherine, a world where she can grow without limit."

"You're tired now, Anka. We're all tired and need sleep. Our minds do funny things when we're tired; they play little tricks on us and wander all over the place. Katherine's future's for another day. Tonight we all need sleep. But, there are limits here too, Anka, especially for a young woman. Most girls grow up to be married, to be housewives and mothers. Some of us become nurses, teachers, or secretaries. Unfortunately, that's the reality of growing up as a woman in America. In that regard, we're similar to the rest of the world. It's a man's world here, as it is in Europe. At least here, men can't beat woman and treat us as if we were their property. But, there's still a long way to go. I've met a few women doctors over my career, but I wouldn't need all of the fingers on my hands to count them.

"But, it's late and we're all so very tired. Poor Katherine's sleeping on the foot of the bed in your room. Let's call it a day, Anka, and see what tomorrow brings."

"Mary...this woman, Marie Fleming, she lives in Boston, doesn't she?"

Mary shot bolt upright. Anka's question had cleared the cobwebs that had been forming in her head.

"Anka, she does live here, and I'd like you to consider meeting her again and forgiving her husband. He doesn't live with her now. He's going to school in another state..."

"Indiana?"

"How did you know that?"

"That's where all the money orders have been coming from over the past year or so."

"How did you know that Marie lives in Boston?"

"That's where the money orders came from before then."

"I hadn't mentioned that to you before we came because I was afraid that you'd change your mind. She doesn't live far from here, Anka, and I'd like you to get to know her. I don't know her well myself, but it would make you whole to forgive her husband, and it would help make him whole if he knew that you forgave him."

"I don't know what to say, Mary. I've never hated anyone like I hate him. I don't know that I had ever hated anyone until him...I don't think I even knew what hate was. But, I don't know that I could ever forgive him."

"Anka...Anka...that hate will eat at you, make you bitter, and ultimately destroy you and poison Katherine. We can't carry hate with us through our lives. We must let it go, Anka."

"Mary, you're right, our minds do play funny tricks on us when we're exhausted. We're both exhausted and need sleep. I'll talk with your Mrs. Fleming because I need to find where my Heinrich's buried so I can arrange for a proper Catholic funeral and burial at home with his parents. I just don't know how or when I'll be able to do that.

"Good night, Mary."

"Good night, Anka."

And so their first day in Boston had ended.

It had been late winter when they had arrived at Otis Air Force Base, and the weather was gray and often nasty, struggling against the impending change in the season. The last vestige of that New England weather gradually faded into early spring, as the piles of white snow shoveled off the sidewalks gradually turned gray, and eventually into piles of dirt and sand, waiting for the cleansing March rains and wind to wash them away, back into the soil.

Mary O'Daugherty, a civilian at last, was consumed with the challenges of teaching an old, long established organization a new way of doing things. Anka worked long hours with her, while Katherine was attended to during the day by an elderly Irish widow who Mary found by placing an ad in the Boston Pilot, the newspaper run by the Catholic Archdiocese of Boston.

CHAPTER FIFTY-SIX

The Easter Rebirth Eludes Dan

In South Bend, Dan was looking forward to the Easter vacation. He was now in his junior year and could see the end of his college career. He was in control of all of his demons but one, and was eager to move on from Notre Dame. Over his Christmas vacation, he had met with the Dean of Suffolk Law School in Boston, and had been assured that a place in the school's evening division would be waiting for him upon his graduation the following year.

In Christianity, Easter is a time of rebirth, a time to make a new start, and Dan was once again hopeful that he'd be able to make a new start by confronting his one remaining demon and removing that burden from his shoulders. Marie had told him that she'd help him; that as a woman and mother, she'd be able to develop a relationship with Heinrich Richter's wife, contact her, and help arrange for the face-to-face meeting. Though she didn't mention that she had already met with Anka in Germany, Marie suggested to her husband that the widow would want to know where her husband's remains were located so that she could retrieve his body and make sure it had a proper burial.

As much as Dan wanted to do this to remove the burden of guilt from his life, he was afraid to let his wife attempt that contact. He had no idea how Marie would be able to contact the widow in Germany; he wasn't even sure that his money orders were getting through to her every month. He couldn't bring himself to confront the widow of the man who he'd killed that night in the woods. The chains he wore around his neck could be broken by one confrontation. He knew that on an intellectual level, but on an emotional level, on a psychological level, and on a spiritual level, his guilt over having killed Heinrich Richter kept him from contacting his victim's widow.

Every month, though...every month...he was forced to confront the Richter's ghost when he went to his bank in South Bend to take out enough spending money for the month ahead. He also withdrew enough money for a twenty-five dollar postal money order that he sent to Germany as faithful as clockwork. He usually did this on the first of the month. About a week prior to that he began to feel a discomfort, a gnawing in the back of his mind that bothered him physically and emotionally. In contrast, he felt a palpable sense of relief after depositing the money order with the post office clerk in an envelope addressed to Mrs. Heinrich Richter. He would be at peace after making this monthly offering to his remaining demon, a peace that lasted for a little over three weeks.

It was probably not a coincidence that Dan played his worst football games on Saturdays just before the end of the month, and his best games on Saturdays just after the start of the month.

Dan was especially in need of Marie's love and support this Easter after the tragedy that had befallen the Miller family. Things had been working out for Ed and Janet. It had been almost a year from their first counseling meeting with Father Fitz. Gradually, Ed had begun seeing their marriage through Janet's eyes, and he'd been more successful, slowly at first, at sharing some of his combat experiences with her, letting her into his soul, opening it layer by layer, deeper and deeper, like peeling an onion. They were at a point in their marriage now where they could communicate at a much more intense level than "What's for supper?" or "How was your day?"

It had been a slow and gradual process to establish communication between them at the deep and intense level a marriage needs in order for it to grow and prosper, and especially a marriage beset by the problems the two of them faced. Ed's revelation that he had murdered Stadholm cut the Gordian Knot that allowed them to begin communicating with each other.

Ed and Janet had been making progress on rebuilding their relationship, when on a dark, rainy Monday in March, Ed stepped off the curb of a street in South Bend to race across and get out of the rain. He was in a hurry, late for an appointment, and trying to beat the traffic that was stopped at the light about twenty feet away.

The driver of the LaSalle Street bus was in a hurry too. The rain had delayed his run, and he was five minutes behind schedule. He knew that some of the people on his route would be standing in the rain and would call the office to complain about his being late. His bus was the first vehicle at the light with a clear city block in front of him, so he was poised to make up some of that lost time once the light turned green. The rubber blades on the windshield wipers were old and cracked because the bus company had a lousy maintenance program; they streaked the glass rather than cleaning it, and the blower on the defroster fogged up the inside of the glass instead of clearing it.

Fate had it that the light changed just as the bus driver simultaneously reached over to wipe the inside of the glass with the cuff of his sleeve and stepped on the throttle. At the same moment, Ed Miller bolted off the curb trying to beat the light, beat the traffic, and get out of the rain. He did none of those.

They said that he had died instantly and "didn't know what had hit him." Dan, in his grief, thought it ironic that after having battled his way across Europe, Ed died at the hands of a South Bend bus driver.

The wake was on a Tuesday night. Father Fitz had called him the day before, in the afternoon, to tell him the news. Dan had a premonition when Father O'Conner had personally come to his room telling him that Father Fitzgibbon was on the phone for him, and that he should take it in the Zahm Hall rector's office. For not the first time in his adult life, Dan broke down crying when Father Fitz told him the news of Ed's death. Struggling to control himself, Dan eventually regained his composure and asked the priest, "Why? Why, Father Fitz? Why now? Why Ed? Why? Why?" The priest, unusually taciturn, answered Dan's question with a three-word question of his own. "An angry god? I don't know, Dan, I just don't know."

The rain hadn't let up as they exited the black limousine in front of Sacred Heart Church. There weren't many cars in the procession, but they all stopped too, and their occupants hurriedly got out and walked up to join the small group behind Ed Miller's casket. Janet had the baby in one arm, and was holding her older daughter's hand with the other. Dan stood on one side of her, and her sister on the other. Janet's mother had died three months earlier, and now Janet and the girls were left alone to face the rest of their lives without their husband and father. Marie stood behind them.

Janet sat in the first seat in the front pew on the right, next to Ed's casket, while holding the baby in her lap, with her daughter and sister sitting beside her. Dan and Marie sat next to them. As Father Fitz began the Mass, the smell of incense wafted out of the sacristy, compounding the gloom of the cold dark day and the damp, dank, dimly lit church.

It came to the point in the funeral Mass, the Mass of the Dead it was called, where Father Fitz would deliver a homily. For most priests, this would be a sermon saying that the deceased was now at peace in the bosom of the Lord and the rest of the congregation should repair their own faults so they'd enjoy a similar fate for eternity upon their own demise. But, Father Fitz took the opportunity to extol Ed's life and struggles, and to address the question on everyone's mind:

"...And so, dear friends, we're left with questions that know no answer. Why Ed? Why now? Is this the fate of a war hero at the hands of an angry god, a god devoid of compassion, who has deigned that this man, this decorated veteran who had survived the torments of hell during the war, should die in this way, at this time? I want to give you an answer, but dear friends, I have no answer. We all know that Ed Miller was a wonderful human being who fought bravely during the war, and who came home to work at providing a future for Janet and the girls. This is a moment that challenges our faith in God, each of us, laymen, religious, as well as those of us who are ordained. Is this the act of an all-loving, compassionate god...to allow...or worse yet...to cause this husband and father to die at a point in their lives when his widow and children most need him?"

At this point, Father Fitz halted in deference to the loud gulping sobs of Janet and the quiet whimpering of her older daughter. Marie, too, for all that she had been through, was filling with tears at the words of Father Fitz, and leaned heavily in the arms of her husband.

"No, Janet," the priest continued, "this can't be the work of an angry god. A priest colleague once raised that same question to me about the madness that he had experienced during the war. Why does our god allow men to die? Why does he allow pain and suffering to exist in this world of his? Why did he take your husband and father from you at the point when you most needed him in your lives?

"The only answer I have, Janet, is that our God didn't cause our pain, our loss, through Ed's death. Our God set up a world that operates by certain rules of logic and order, including laws of probability. Though we'd like him to intervene, he doesn't do so because he recognizes the free will we all have, the free will to create horror and suffering on an untold magnitude as we've all just witnessed, as well as the free will that results in accidents and illness that take the lives of the innocent, like Ed.

"No, Janet, it's not the wrath of an angry god that has stolen Ed from us. Rather, it's a god who has given us the freedom of our human imperfections, and it's no consolation to us that Ed has been taken from us in an accident, the result of that human imperfection.

"The charge we all must take from this is to live our lives in Christ the way Ed lived his, struggling to make sense of the seeming irrationality around him, dutifully working to provide for his family, and to assist those who Providence sent his way, grateful for his blessings, and trying mightily to overcome his demons.

"An angry god? I dare say 'No,' but rather, a god who unfolds creation each day, and who gives us the chance to participate in that act of creation. Each of us who continue to involve ourselves in that creation as every day unfolds before us is both sure in our faith, and saddened by the loss of our friend and brother."

Leaving the pulpit, the priest returned to the altar and began reciting the creed of the Roman Catholic Church in Latin.

Janet gulped in her sorrow and tears. Marie buried her head deeper into Dan's chest, and Dan reflected on the priest's words and tried to recall other words that could comfort him in his own sorrow, confusion and grief...but none came to mind.

EPILOGUE

The ending to this story seems unsatisfactory. It was hoped that Ed and Janet would completely work out their differences, and that Dan, Marie, and young Daniel would get on with their lives. But, life doesn't always happen that way. It's ironic that Ed survived the war in Europe, only to get killed crossing a street in South Bend. But, that's the way life goes sometimes.

This story also contains some vulgarity and violence, especially in the first part of the story, and hopefully this was not objectionable. If you've ever been in the military, you understand that there's not a lot of hyperbole there. In any event, it's the violence and vulgarity that sets the stage for these folks to confront their demons later in life. You can see how these traumatic events affect the characters' perception of reality after they return to a "normal" life and how their own reality differs from the other characters (especially Yvonne Chrysler and John Flanagan) who haven't shared these traumatic experiences.

Father Fitz is an especially enigmatic personality. He's at once the wise counselor who helps the returning vets adjust to civilian life, yet on the other hand, he's unable to help Mary O'Daugherty with her dilemma, and precipitates Dan's melt down by presenting the situation in hypothetical form to his class.

All human beings are both flawed and noble. Every person is capable of the most selfless and generous actions, while at the same time capable of selfish and malicious behavior. There's a struggle in the world between good and evil. Sometimes that same struggle occurs within us. Father Fitz embodied that struggle and gave into the evil side of his nature when he murdered Deadeye.

Mary O'Daugherty's experience in the triage ward is based on a similar incident in real life. The senselessness of watching young men die for no reason shocks any human being to the core.

Mary has her own way of running away from her hurt, and she fights to repress her attraction to Anka, because she knows she shouldn't be attracted to another woman in that way.

Poor Father Porcelli went to war to bring comfort and solace to the troops, but then he realizes that the leadership of the Army is less concerned with the spiritual well-being of its troops than it is with keeping them well-motivated to kill and to die. As is true in real life, some soldiers serving with Dan Fleming ended up thinking of Father Porcelli as "Major-Father," a military man first, and a man of God second. That's what causes some to question the unspoken role of the Chaplain Corps in the grand scheme of things.

Anka represents the ultimate victims of war, the survivors left behind after the death of a loved one, lost in a senseless combat.

Rene and Anna Bourque take in the pregnant Yvette and treat her as their own daughter, an act of graciousness and generosity borne out of the cauldron of hate and suffering they all endured. Beauty, charity, and love do exist, even in the depths of horror, even when the world has gone crazy.

Yvette/Marie, the ultimate survivor, loses her family to the Nazis, and as a young postulate in a religious order, is raped and witnesses the murder of all of the other nuns in her convent. She survives by selling her body, and when she has a liaison with Dan Fleming, she's drawn to his decency and integrity, his hate for her, and his passion for her. The fruit of their encounter opens a whole new world for this woman, where she leaves the ravages of her past and adopts the beauty and joy of motherhood. How many today, in the past, and probably in the future, survive the horror of war and go on to deal with their altered reality?

Dan Fleming, the central figure, is a little bit humble, a little bit arrogant, a little bit crazy, and a little bit wise. Dan survives the combat, but struggles to survive its aftermath. His over-scrupulous conscience nearly strangles him after he kills Anka's husband, Heinrich, in hand to hand combat. Heinrich dies in Dan's arms, and Dan pays monthly conscience money to the dead man's widow as an act of atonement. Dan Fleming is "every man," bounced through a turbulence not of his choosing, and deeply scarred by it.

So where do the survivors go after this? How will Ed's widow, Janet, bring up their two daughters? What happens to Anka and Katherine? How do Marie and Dan bring up their son, Daniel, and what happens to Dalrymple? What happens to Father Fitz? How do these characters deal with their lives after surviving the horrors of war? How do they define reality over the rest of their lives and deal with the day-to-day problems all people face?

It is hoped that this book provides each reader an incentive to look at one's own life, and to be sensitive to how that might differ from the lives of the people you encounter over the course of the years. It is also hoped that if you have a friend or relative who's a combat vet, you know a little more about how they think, and about how their own reality differs from yours. And finally, if you are a combat veteran, thank you for your service, and may you learn to live comfortably with the adjusted reality of your civilian life.

www.ingramcontent.com/pod-product-compliance
Lightning Source LLC
Chambersburg PA
CBHW071043250626
47159CB00002B/348